Betsy,

To novel views of your adopted people and peoples everywhere beauty fertilizes far more than the chicken and the egg.

Scott Lee

ADAGIA

ADAGIA

Symphonic Variations on a Term for Life

Scott Lee Hartstein

Copyright © 2010 by Scott Lee Hartstein.

Library of Congress Control Number:		2010902167
ISBN:	Hardcover	978-1-4500-4727-2
	Softcover	978-1-4500-4726-5
	Ebook	978-1-4500-4728-9

All rights reserved. No part of this book may be reproduced or transmitted in any form or by any means, electronic or mechanical, including photocopying, recording, or by any information storage and retrieval system, without permission in writing from the copyright owner.

This is a work of fiction. Names, characters, places and incidents either are the product of the author's imagination or are used fictitiously, and any resemblance to any actual persons, living or dead, events, or locales is entirely coincidental.

This book was printed in the United States of America.

To order additional copies of this book, contact:
Xlibris Corporation
1-888-795-4274
www.Xlibris.com
Orders@Xlibris.com
74773

Contents

To those who dream of leading another life . . .

The concept of an introduction is not innocent or ahistorical. It forms, as Derrida suggests, a tympanum, a resonant membrane, between the inside and outside of its text and audience and so negotiates the terms of the articulate to be. Like the mysterious line at the merman's waist, the preface forms the image of the juncture of the chimera that is reading: it melds and blocks the incompatible worlds it conjoins and ostracizes, a crucifixion neither fish nor fowl. The preface must be yet another misrepresentation of that it presents in advance. It shows the book to come as other than itself and so becomes a thing beside itself. The preface is the between which forms both the barrier and the channel for the hoped for future reconciliation it delays and supplants, a virgule between the harmonies and impossibilities it virtualizes.

A self-conscious preface, like this one, does not foreclose its paradox for the explicit it shows cannot compass the possibilities that open it to the others that form its absent flanks, "the reader" and "the work." However, such a reflective version may better serve both as it eschews the default expectations such forewords might otherwise satisfy. The praise the typical preface heaps in advance presents not just a preview but the critical frame and taxonomic field thought most beneficial: it supplies not just a judgment but, implicitly or explicitly, the structure of valuation most advantageous. It tries, in short, to produce the reader in advance of the reading, but this usual modality reflects already a concept of artistic process that is here already misplaced.

Hartstein's writing does not submit to normative aesthetic categories and indeed resists them and thus demands a preface that itself undoes its typical function. The regular preface submits to the notions of unity dominant since Aristotle and the more flexible but no less predestined notions of Kant's third Critique. In the latter, judgment itself is itself a transitional form: "a mediating link between understanding and reason" and the usual preface attempts to articulate this judgment prematurely. However, this disposition constitutes a model of art as associated with a law that is universal, extant, and binding. All these prejudices, Hartstein's work disallows, as its presentation plays against such formalism much as jazz plays against the very forms it entertains.

This novel is a process that, from microcosms of the semantic and syntactic to macrocosm of the plot, plays with its materials. To call it "fractal" might be evocative but misleading since such would suggest a mathematical predictability, a formulaic basis of variation. Though the work is, as fractals are, self-similar across scales, these are iterations without pure predictability and such as have an anticipated indeterminacy that allows for not just an endless complexity of participation but also an endlessness of interpretation. This openness is profound and improvisational.

The work entertains its own possibility and so feeds on what it has already suggested and what is to come not as a trajectory of necessity but as a living variation for which the reader bears a responsibility. This call upon us is not for judgment but for commensurate invention. To dine at such a cornucopia is more than demanding for it offers not one unified feast, however large, but a table set again by each last course endlessly anew.

This multiplicity and verve, makes each reading a series that departs from its last guess. It is, as Blanchot says of Proust, a "complete incomplete work." Finish and form, unity and judgment, are not the ends to be desired but the beginnings of the subsequent pleasures. While the normal novel is rarely novel, this is nothing but. To again cite Blanchot, "the work is the expectation of the work," and this preface is nothing other than a fragment of that expectancy.

Daniel Fineman©

Allegro ma non troppo

Marcel's mother experienced him moving inside her for the first time one bright winter day in southwestern France. This poignant moment took place at home, early in 1958, without any high-sounding word or idiomatic token of manifold realities. It began weaving its pleasing way into her every thought and feeling, independent of any dream she might start nursing in order to make or remake the world in an old double-breasted image. It appeared as if the other's naked beginning, first discernable movement, were the original sign of a double life carried on in what might amount to an underlying dialogue with any would-be interlocutor designating her as a woman. She felt the future child cradled within her long before any other presage of gestation. Her expectations for life were shifting almost portentously as surely as the future child himself. She found her thoughts of him curiously following her body, *parlando*, as if she were more of an organic whole whose speech was suggestive of some vast and intricate code unraveling in cosseted song. She had aged as gracefully and free of religion as language combined with rarified music as soundly as the most ancient winds whose clement push launches a craft. She was that old and he that young.

"Not so quick," she thought to herself, crossing the line wherein meaning doubles back upon itself in time, thus signifying one thing to some and something distinctly different from the first to others. Here, old-world knowledge, read literally, had turned out to be moving, becoming counsel—none too smart and wise for slowing elders (governed by a New World disorder)—in order that we may all be advised to take more time with what really matters, heightening thereby more than figuratively a sense of lower and slower tempi. One attuned to both the past and present could henceforth hear the same expression interpreted, with a grave accent placed on the less-experienced individual—often the younger of the two—set out, hell-bent on hastening the future's advent, trying, as one may, to arrive at the vital core of a thing or essence in a brief space of time. This dangerously modern attempt to act and react without allowing a proper place for archaic language to recall our sound and soundless origins (*quick*, for example, having once meant both *pregnant* and *alive*), shorts, short-changes, and short-circuits, the former who may thus view with long-term capital interest, youth-bound energy, sensitivity, dexterity, understanding, learning, and yes, even rapidity, as if in the blink of an eye, the preponderance of truth and untruth in most human matters, if not the quick of all matter. Where and when one may more or less gently exhort another by saying "not so fast," "not so sharp" remains not so far-off below this verbal bas-relief of the same quickening mark and remark.

It is imperative, believed this curious thought's protagonist, going forward with artful vigilance, a keen edge, a vital advantage, a distinct vigor, an attractive style, a key signature of voiceless truth raised above the proper pitch, be given to this particularly fine, singularly acute point.

Marcel's mother was heavy, meaning gravid with faith arising out of mature hope for him. Her charity was not distant from the light of day, for it too was to be lifted up and out of her flesh and bones—no more, no less. She had already been duty-bound to this up-and-coming relationship, minding its very commencement as temperature, humors, blood, water, and dispositions mined—in short, mind—the body.

She had assigned some definition with alacrity to his name long before his person would emerge. The name cribbed her eager sense of a full life and a replete, almost-gorged expression of one's dreams. She too had been marked by a ponderous fate accompanying her name, realizing that if she was known to most as Cassandre outside her home, within her were wrapped the madre-perl gifts of many a prophet's identity. The name flattered her properness and propriety, with minimal doubt, bemusing her wildest fancy, entranced aspirations, and enthralled hopes like a *cortigiano* whose courteous ways leave even a daring courtesan wanting more.

She wished to pass on the evenhanded lessons she had learned in the past about the science of predicting the future as if she were going to manifest the conclusive inlay of some knowledge set with marquetry into the *tabula rasa* of a young mind. Her expansive source of thought, perception, feeling, will, memory, and imagination—her brain, in conjunction with her swelling body—labored about a future man whom, she hoped, would never engage, on even a single occasion, in an overt struggle with his fellow man. Life struck her as too precious to destroy, no matter the cheerless circumstance. Any disagreement should lead to a truce or parley of peace's full range of instruments. Therefore, she thought categorically, creating a new life with her husband carried, with the amatory act of love, the ulterior action of chasing out, once and for all, the demons, the *djinns* as Victor Hugo called them. These little monsters, together with their pernicious motive, had long inhabited her mind as if nightmares were being amortized over the years in mortmain. The result often produced an effect of intoxication vis-à-vis those many presumed angels circulating within and without her person.

Cassandre thought much and often of untold creative energies and dramatic grit in the modest though stylish comfort of her residence. They varnished her inscrutable, changeable life like the essence of Venetian terebinth, or dragon's blood, which display luster and brilliance in Her Majesty of Majesties—the violin. She wished for their graduated genius and cast of mind to husband the heart of any significant creation entering her life, to weave harmony into the deepest folds and cockles of daily existence, as if, following the trajectory of the violin, dancing sounds of rhythm and melody gave way to a more generalized courtship with what is still—eternally derived from—life. Inventive forces have come into being like a kind of prolix dream and that they positively distort, condense, and displace reality through a florid language and amicable name all their own.

First dreamily, then resolutely, yes, clearly she garnered strength from the most illustrious of all classically romantic composers who ferried attentive souls, beyond their woe, to the sustaining, prolific shores of substantial love. She mused quietly to herself anent another form of ineffable gestation that way. She felt he carried on a musical tradition like a mother of the genes and aspirations of significant ancestors. She imagined he tortured himself, very nearly "beyond belief," as it is not too uncommonly said. Yet through it all, through all the ups and downs, the doubts, the untrammeled estuaries of flooded thought, the unequaled distrust, the seemingly uncompromising skepticism, the loathsome brooding, the ghoulish insentience, the broiling betrayals, the preening emotion, the cerebral confusion, the haunting succubus, the panicked breaches, the disquieting turpitude, the unsettling sadness, the bewildering lethargy, the harsh reality of raw anguish, the gnawing haste of stark tedium, the irksome task upon task unmastered, the self-conscious, simpering looks, the psychological or social misreadings, the rhapsody of tempestuous misgivings embedded in dead-end undertakings, the refusals to grow and take part in the details of history, the implacable indifference, the ostensibly wasteful delays, the numerous mental miscarriages, the trebled slinking, the endless nights sans sleep, the fulsome distrust, the abounding jouncing of a restless soul, the "*allegro molto* of a racing mind," and the immense silences surrounding a grief-stricken, heavy, broken heart, he appeared to never waver in his faith in himself, in the truth he represented to his truest self. Or if in fact he did flinch, vacillating, and this veritably, it could be observed by rigorous standards; for thousands of days on end, leading up to his forty-fourth year when he finally let his first major work breathe, he released it in order that his writing might vibrate along seemingly tympanic lines of unprecedented orchestral emotion. He was more than knee-deep in truth, miming with transparency its most comely simulacra. It was solely in view of a dreamy hesitation, a quixotic delusion, that he escaped the seemly fetters, indeed, the self-imposed bondage incumbent upon one who adopts a musical ancestry. His Pascalian wager was to bet that a future exists full stock, like none other, when it is fully remembered and thus honored, not unlike royalty which inherits, at the very least, from its title, an entire society in advance. One could hear something of the chaos inherent in a work of art as it simmers and exposes beauty, according to a sense-bound poet, "through the veil of order."

The scrupulous rigor inherent in this impractical lover of romance, Cassandre thought, haunted every fact and fiction of his ever-churning life no less than it elevated the serious-minded creator beyond a full range of Viennese masters' times. It appeared as a necessary evil, or ill that, so she was led to believe, for arriving at *le mot juste*, a symphonic sound had to be infused unfrantically in the chambers of her heart, the byways of the mind, and even to the bone of all the shattered hopes. Suffering led to a salutary reaction, a distinct and almost normative cadence redoubling his good sense at that succession of points when he finally reversed fate to express himself, to engage in art and recreate a world as if he were the Demosthenes of sound who would speak without failing the common will transcending the eternal good. When all is said and done, with or without ill-favored *longueurs*, the inimitable Reinhardt had instilled in each protomodern movement while penning for chamber musicians, puissant symphonies or voices, beyond the backdrop of fundamental noise and frenzied stress or disquieting distress, something indispensable—married to the improbable—in the apparent, pulsing conversation of a profound absence.

Beyond self-reliance, what served to nourish the cause célèbre for romantic expressions of the unstinting self? In some substantial measure, such artistic exploration showed that the jolting artist knew, as well as any, what the great English poet expressed in the warmth of passion's viscous inkshed: "The road of excess leads to the palace of wisdom." Simply put, Cassandre's place housed splendid forms of sagacity, if only a harmonious sense of life's renewing, recyclable, ever-renamed spirit. Hers was a space propitious for artistic expression—and bewitching pencraft—just as her sense of time was auspicious for musical development, *in extenso*, as if it could preserve a dream. This preservation and reserved self-preservation kept any representation conveyed properly from unwanted interruption like the *ton filé* and brio of eighteenth-century violin virtuosos whose names vigorously strike a chord, to this day, as clearly suggestive of lucidity as their art—Leclair and Chevalier de Saint-Georges. The future mother's every displacement, just as her very being at rest, would earmark movement of all kinds for a central role in bringing definition, if not meaning, pausation even—like that exhalation whose repose follows the beat of a heartening inhalation—*to life.*

The baby-faced Cassandre was moved by peacefulness and calm. Both afforded her a cozy sensation of being complete, not scattered by modernity or the passing of risqué fashion in a multipolar world. She extracted a like sense of accreted freedom from quarrels by listening to the calibrated "meditation" from Massenet's *Thaïs.* The often short, though sensuously ample, luxuriously gratifying, even lavish phrasing echoed a human voice liberating itself from any external hostility. As surely and gradually as land adds itself to the shore of a body of water by alluvial deposits, the composer deposed—far from any solemn, public, godforsaken oath—many an act of writing that testifies to breathing individuals imitating the heavens' winds more generally. With this stroke of striking genius making a single man's mark on all of humanity, this unorthodox deposition removed from power—stripping the strongest stars of their stripes—thereby taking in one-and-the-same stride, "taking out" meaningless sound by replacing nonsense with significant airs that fill even the most incidental voids. With little more than a full compliment of strings, any stridulous strife, any strident striving to accelerate a *stringendo,* tightened the musician's grasp of just how badly people need more and more instruments for unleashing their stress, indeed, their heavy accent put on words amounting to nothing.

And one such hallowed voice, set out with composure to account for everything and everyone, sounded as the ringing, stirring repercussion, the after-effect of an engaging conscience like either a *staccato*—or *spiccato* turning into a *détaché*—of, among others, Vieuxtemps. It seemed to evoke and actuate no less than the archaic reverberation of mystic poesy, indenturing language hither and thither, not unlike the imaginative English composer nominated to renown by his parents, bound to be known, entirely without pseudonym and classically, as Will Child. Music—the anticipated mother felt with expatiating acuity—glorifies joy, heightens elation, dampens sorrow, thunderclaps passion, clarifies tone, titrates our concentration around a purpose, doubles beauty as a grace note, rectifies wrongs, and relieves grief by intensifying life's most essential experiences in forms far more full than people who polish off their hunger by consuming chocolate.

Call it the dream of Marcel's first cooing or the amorous talk surrounding the child she shared *de haut en bas* with Marc, his father, whose inner and social life could barely be differentiated, even splitting hairs, from hers; whatever it was, Cassandre disdained enmity, love's antagonistic opposite, in all its shows of force. Any somber aggression she felt coming from the outside world countered her beliefs—to the core—in herself, and only served to strengthen her common resolve with Marc. Both believed that "in union there is strength," a conjugal vision wherein phenomena seemed to originate for the two as if either one were a natural messenger of desire. Both promised themselves to be like nature herself—discreet parents whose tenor would first multiply, then divide and dispense in equal portions, parceling out righteous skills, solace, and knowledge with an even hand. At any time, either could be accused of loving to distraction. The holy band ringing their fingers was bound to bind them to a medley of sterling symbols, all of which would play out in such a manner as to further circumscribe, mark a boundary, and galvanize the singular union of their body and spirit with *savoir faire*. Their virtuoso determinedness and discernable perspicuity in fulfilling the promise of their nakedly virtuous engagement to one another never ceased to search for viable, single-minded solutions to counter life's problems as the librettist never appeared bereft of counterpoint for the soul extraordinaire.

As relates to this subject and its landmark experience, however, Cassandre never found herself either vociferous or even vocal. She never expressed herself with hauteur. Words, she believed, laminate things and prolong feelings about this or that as art, which planes, grazes, or scrapes reality's surface. And with respect to related subjects, her silence, multilingual in origin, no more reversed the inner stream of her thoughts to the point of others hearing their ebb and flow pronounced, in reality, than a Swiss Guard abandons his post before the nearly sanctimonious preserve of an everlasting, albeit ostensibly, ceremonious vigil in our day and age just outside the imposing organ of the Holy See.

Cassandre and Marc were implanting within Marcel's nature all the potential profundities and layers, notwithstanding any infinitesimally small or vast surface, of their culture. They would view their miracle of procreation with the most farsighted partiality. Giving Marcel the dearest name known to them, and this, *bien entendu*, of course, in their French tongue, redoubled both the mother's and father's sense of serenity and commonly felt subjective pleasure. Naming him thus would tie the young person to both a family, thanks to a language and, at the same time, the trebled kin of creative energies bound in unparalleled literature. Through the prism of astutely subjective vision, they would achieve their uppermost objective—punctual and universal truths, beauty, and, come what might, enduring goods—for goodness' sake.

Cassandre was not insouciant or peremptorily self-assured, mindful that she had become at this point of her offspring and environs. All the while, she realized to what extent she was appearing as a whole being—one distended with her full potential and another human inside her. Would her child inherit her girlish good looks in equal proportion to the inner life, providing her with as much hope as escape, from which she would be increasingly set free?

Cassandre's good-natured vision of life included everything conceivable under the sun, including the great philosopher Bergotte's commentary on vision itself: "The eye sees only what the mind is prepared to comprehend." She and her husband already found themselves preparing the young mind of their progeny—he, they envisioned, who would seize upon the entire universe as his playground and, at once, workstation. In this way, he would come to understand and renew the greatest of novelists who writes: "The real voyage of discovery consists not in seeking new landscapes but in having new eyes." Or he could romance and thereby meditate the most all-encompassing of dramatists, conceiving of productive relationships *Measure for Measure*:

> As those that feed grow full; as blossoming-time,
> That from the seedness the bare fallow brings
> To teeming foison; even so her plenteous womb
> Expresseth his full tilth and husbandry.
>
> 'Tis very pregnant
> The jewel that we find, we stoop and take't,
> Because we see it; but what we do not see
> We tread upon, and never think of it.

"To each his own" might seem like a motto of habit and independence of oneself from others. Yet the body, if not the mind's eye, is born no less than it goes on, cradled from its inception, in and out, to and fro, which is to say clinging to constant movement. Oneness is, like uniqueness, the future progenitors thought together, fleeting nonetheless. It may force us to trespass on truth though one may do so without poaching beauty. It may well be a myth, one in which people tend to believe, one causing internal truths to swell like an external pressure system makes the skies and seas billow. The mystery of an extended idea of some original unity stretches individuals' conceptions of themselves as they attempt to navigate and make sense of an aqueous humor disposed, for the duration of life, to look out for the development of days and nights inside their mother. Perhaps through an understanding of dreams and linguistic play are we able to better fathom what constitutes the full amount, extent, or duration of what we once were before becoming what we are today. An individual's past could surge forth from the interplay of an elaborate narrative just as stories or a play could arise out of history's womb. Like a tale, allegory, or even cogent slogan, assembling all the component parts of a world at once factual and fictitious, wholeness may forever evade humans once they have parted ways from the uterine valise.

This pair of formerly excellent French students had long hitched their brimming wagon to a type of incredulous belief in the power and the glory that derives strength, even luster, from onomastics—that study of names, which seemed to them like a determinate inflorescence in the botanical world, where entire fates flower beyond explanation for having had as their axis of growth the settling presence of enriched nourishment, combining the light of day with the unfathomable, boundless night. This form of deep-seated credence in the art of names conjugated their confident hope in voices, such as those of Reinhardt's choral poem—"There Is a Rose in Flower"—for therein they heard and understood an exact language unfurling petal upon noteworthy petal. It allowed the cultivated lovers of beauty's garden to photosynthesize all that which shines brightly or no. Planted firmly in verdant love, they found themselves adazzle with beaming and glistening smiles, even into the night sky fallen pitch black as if billions of radiant eyes had lost their vision and life.

Theirs was an austerely pessimistic optimism, coupling antiquity's cynical introversion with modernity's extroverted gaze. What they craved would eventually feed them if their longing was quenched in time. Given their familiar context, founding a person upon the placid tradition of a name did not exclude any future hybridization of the family member with some hinterland of the mind or that of the most obscure society itself; but it certainly did not include such occurrences either, and for good cause, as Marcel's parents saw it, this in view of the possible variations, which stem from the formation of a new proper noun. Like any meaning comprised in neologisms or portmanteau words, whose open-ended nature assembles a constellation of letters around some sound that attempts to capture the fullness of a past—or some future—it was felt the very choice of "Marcel" would predetermine a selective, related memory. This would be one relative to none—in fact, none other than itself at its foundation. It would be a question here of one relating, indeed relaying, a double lineage—like a significant acronym wherein the signifier and signified unite both form and content—as distinctively clear as it would become, among others, clearly distinguished among any habitué of letters. *Nomen est omen* (a name is a sign). A Marcel by any other name might not spell, the couple imagined, inspired by repartee with immortals, as sweet an enterprise!

"Art begins, in a word," Cassandre remarked amorously to Marc, "where life comes and goes nameless, for some time at least." Her intuition often led her intellection, positioning her mind to follow the full body of her senses.

"Does the proverbial Shakespearian rub consist and persist, like any for that matter," wondered the spouse upon digesting her formula as he himself ciphered in his bloc-notes, "in the will to inscribe one's own name with something akin to a quill upon the palimpsest of a time whose passage records, still, as if on the surface of an extensive common corpus, each movement, civilized or other, extending both in and beyond the deepest conquest of space?" If so, Marc observed within himself, Marcel would forever be reminded of his literal heritage as a measure of the figurative and literary one, the living and dying—especially the dead—proof anticipating him. He would thus grow into a man of his age and, at once, not unlike his biological father, a man for all space and time.

This well-versed, writerly geniture would be true inasmuch as the entire material, like the wholly physical nature of this highly visible reference to a most memorable disyllable of sound, where not the quasi-totality of the person and the personage's being on either side of that, might recall an invisible world, just as a symbol is said to unite, to associate and bring its points to bear on two disparate halves.

The throbbing name may serve as a gene for a certain vivacious character like a color that as light may express something bright. All names may end up fixing character around the most constant aspect of a person, place, or thing. To be born as "Soledad" in the Spanish-speaking world, let alone outside that sphere, conditions the being inhabited by her "solitude" to embrace it as a *fait accompli*. From the outset, she is strikingly similar to the solitary person herself, least, alone, since so close to many like her. The very determination of a name—like the future, the will if you will, translated into a certain character, one indicated by a common noun—derives the significance of its defining moments from the place of an empty otherness. Herein, an *ennui* could be said to occupy a person's life, that of the mind or other. To bestow the name of *Jesus* or *Caesar*, each a proper noun with unique implications for the whole of the sacred and profane worlds, alters the perspective of the person according to the predeterminant "patrilineage" of his character denoted in each of these names. In the former case, one might regard, Marc thought, like the individualist philosopher, the son of man from the point of view of the oppressed, the persecuted. In the latter, one could refer, not without good conscience, to the take of the persecutors. The professor drew from this duality the affirming conclusion that whatever men have felt like dying for is perhaps in equal measure worth settling and living for.

Both Cassandre and Marc liked holding hands as they strolled along the banks of a small creek babbling beside the happily populated hamlet in which they dwelled. It was there she once delighted, in coquettish jest, by gauding him with playful indiscretion: "I love your secret scent," she unobtrusively divulged, making him exude sweet-smelling silence from his blushing cheeks and upper lip. More than judicious talking, they preferred attending to the sounds of nature with their ears—ears no less alerted—whenever they were briefly exiled from their home to the more human wavelengths within the confines of larger villages, towns, and cities. Similarly, they saw their bodies as fragments or figments of their imagination, creations like the one taking place within Cassandre beginning with the fleshing out of a conception—as true as art commencing well before any pigments color reality. They found and founded life—and what precedes living color in black and white and all in between—in making love.

From time to time, they cherished deep embraces followed by long, lingering kissing of one another. One sensed, on the tip of their tongue, a shared literary ambition tarried leisurely enough, though not aimlessly, a delay filled with youthful languor and lighthearted sensuality. Affectionate caesuras such as these breathed new life and respite, for a time, into their words as if their provenance had come from a queue of authors. These loving pauses reinforced the good, meaningful sense and natural speech rhythms that buffered them from rampant econometrics otherwise employed in daily commerce and the warring marketplace.

If both moved behind, at a distance, and in the same direction as the lessons of history, it was not without follow-through. Neither ever attempted to undercut the possibility of ethical judgment. The couple quietly espoused, within reasonable limits, that truth and absolute value—in art and music, for example—may be known with relative certainty. They would come and go after their son with the full weight of the past checked in view of an indefinite, if not vibrant, period of time yet to be. The one was learning from the other, her husband, and vice versa, how to extract the knowable from the knowledgeable like perfume drawn from a wide and essentially long-standing array of truly fragrant flowers. They completed and complemented one another as they found themselves improving, to be sure, learning to read anything or anyone against the grain and between the lines, separating the nourishing wheat from the chaff of reeking lies and pernicious fiction. Duly inquisitive—and because the curiosity derived from pedantries moved them, in the extreme, to pursue the highest degree of possible understanding in words, ideas, ideals, and things, to follow the course of the most exacting literary and social science—they took ample care in rendering unto the future Marcel what was Marcel's.

They sought to assist the prospective man—now awash in vital fluids—in advance in order that he may come to inscribe himself in a schizophrenic, part-secular, part-religious domain that was the globe as they saw it. While Marc liked to believe Sephardic music had endured in excess of hundreds years only to prove the culture of the Iberian Jews made more love than war, he was no more credulous with respect to the innocence of either the new religion, namely, the economy, or the neo-new one for that matter—children—as those promiscuously unearthing their almighty dollar from their execrable billfolds would promote it, consciously or otherwise. Together with Cassandre, Marcel's progenitors lent credence to the words Stendhal wrote, knowing that if the child were to look to another for sustenance, for inheritance of the mind and spirit, it may as well be to the greatest authors of French society: "One can acquire everything in solitude, outside of character" (*De l'Amour, On Love*). In the eyes and ears of his parents, "Marcel" bore the distinct advantage of a noble, reticent character, character acquired as early as the name was pronounced in great writing.

Marcel would thus have a natural place, one which could not be suppressed without expressly changing the name, in the history of French literature. In time, believed his creators, he would come to read Castex and Surer like his father in high school or earlier. The young mind would dance with words and, in turn, valuable books, as if he were growing up, in small part, cum the thirteenth century's "Royal Estampie" (*La tierce estampie roial*) afoot in his life—life about to acquire flight of fancy feathers. Later on, he would evolve grandly into a disciple of Balzac, Flaubert, and above all, creatures like Mme Bovary herself. He would turn into one who frequents the *philosophes* of the real, mingles with the chatoyant imaginary, and devours books beneath his bedside lamp. His name would remind him of a really rich surface covering true, protected depth like the terrifically evocative title of an old yet most relevant compendium of printed matter. Alternatively, the name would act as an intimate, handy memory triggering sensational familiarity with a whole world of words and ideas like the presence of an effective book filled with special meaning on the nightstand where it is readily available versus a work fetched with less expediency from the library or study.

In reading, he would swallow the whole of individual quests, conquests, and requests, the ones upon the others. He would persevere to preserve the most virtuous of traditions great artists have wisely and skillfully laid bare for the future—the truest present of all! The young mind and soul would learn to participate in his very own "Marcelification," licensing a pure conscience to monitor reality. He could come to concur with the artist Marcello in *La bohème* who sings out—ringing romantic truth—with a brief albeit reflexive phrasing: "My brush paints on its own!"

Marcel would personify his better half even before having full knowledge of her or him, solely, on appropriate occasions, surrendering, or desisting from the most valuable parts of himself, for a song. He would evolve into someone jaunty, well-bred, and dapper without affect, like a reader whose imagination grows by virtue of any writer who creates a place for a literary prosthesis to append the mind with fancy and flight. The very air coursing through his lungs would set a bright, reedy tone of reality on its billowing way like a harmonium whose bellows echo beauty's oxygenated atmosphere. Perhaps he would even come, at one point, to a courtship imbibed with delicious music, virginal tones whose aesthetic sequence acts to intensify the full range of human emotions for the listener, as the march of coherent sound alone had done in the early stages of his mother and father's union, even before Cassandre had adopted—a couple of years earlier when they had first made their eternal vows of common fidelity in the bond of marriage—Marc's last name.

Cassandre did not fully know whether Marcel's future accomplishments and relationships might come about by virtue of her having played *La mer* while the human creation lingered in her womb. Or perhaps, his sense of perpetual wonderment might arise from an incarnation akin to *fine champagne*'s distillation before it ferments around the epigastrium. He would be made to receive and correlate the impressions shepherded to him by various forms of art as the sensorium regulates the corresponding senses. In any case, she was convinced he would need an inner reference, an intuitive compass that would dignify and orient his presence on earth as sure as his locomotive powers and faculties would need the most common "skin, hair, fat, flesh, veins, arteries, ligaments, nerves, cartilages, bones, marrow, brains, glands, genitals, humors, and articulations."

She believed, now no less than any other time, in the words of *The Little Prince*: "L'essentiel est invisible pour les yeux" (What's essential is invisible to the eye"). She wished, more than any person discovering this very world of quintessential discovery—or so it seemed to her—that her princely progeny, her noblest of inventions, would grace a self here and there, above and after all. What is necessary and sufficient had already been enough for her, very nearly as if she had lived with grace at Port Royal; and so she would begin by placing her son on the same path, once razed, which is, to say, absconded like deities themselves. If she were to give herself to her dream with Marc—without the trifling or tedium of a frivolous narration or some falsified plot—it was to be raising Marcel while giving him his natural innocence in advance and never borrowing on the principal, even less, if possible, on the principle. Their bond invested this dream, like a stock one can reasonably bank on to perform better than others, thanks to the sustainable growth of a brand name.

For the basic, essential, elemental quality of a man remains to preserve at once his self and the beauty of life descended, in the eyes or this couple, from the artful conjunction of the most highly eminent past with a glorious future. It is one, in a copulative word, in sum, which serves as a common promise of their conjugation in an eternal present given to, by and by, his name.

In granting him his personal moniker, his most eminent namesake, for life, Marcel's mother was, in her mind, authorizing the fullest possible independence for an individual. Much of her authority in his life really stopped exactly where it started, in designating his name. It functioned in a similar fashion to poetic license. The circle of life would thus come to spiral, to ring itself around an existence as Marcel would become himself *in toto.*

She had understood that the steep slope of introspection arises from long-suffering once out of the womb, not to speak of the mysterious enshrinement within the body's cocoon-like envelope predating that; and thus, if there was to be a "turning back," it should indeed be to unite at once the mind and spirit, *l'esprit*, with both times and places the body will have been once outside what in Provençal was known as the *coco*, the eggshell. These experiences where we are exposed to endure pain, injury, or death are precisely those that teach us most about ourselves in particular and life in general. Lessons from parents or teachers thus appear relatively harmless since they are often based in an anticipation of negative suffering. Their wisdom anesthetizes us from the rigors and travails of unpleasant, even hurtful, awakenings. Learning precisely how to carry on despite hardships enlivens our existence, opens our hearts to others, and affirms we may be wholly more than ourselves. Integrity derives its social standing from this sense of different states united within a complete person. Our actions taken together with the critique of their ethical ramifications and efficacies do not elude us as readily as truth and various values, either absolute or relative.

On the one hand, to be unaware of the family story condemns any of its constituents to repeat no more or any less than the selfsame narrative in its multifarious forms. On the other hand, freedom itself liberates the newly formed flesh and blood from that point at which its conception follows all the laws of the universe, the physical being first and foremost among them. Mother and child gravitate to one another "until death do them part." There is, to some extent, a naturally occurring filial relationship of the reader vis-à-vis the real substance of great literature. We are influenced by and associated with places, causes, races, or schools of thought encased in books, like the son who grows beyond the body, by virtue of a literary prosthesis, which attaches itself to an imagination whose potentialities and lineage increase for as much.

Marcel would himself perhaps come to know his father before him for the latter's presence of mind, for his omnipresence of spirit, or for that absence of body, in the end, which appeared to have given a resounding consent to a form of life that takes offense to the cult of the individual. The individual, beyond any particular worship or ritual of a single being, seems grounded in a perpetual give-and-take. He or she alone literally comprehends both the denotation and the connotation, if any, laid bare in his or her name. One may understand this to comprise a certain responsibility to the outer and inner self as well as to those present at those monumental moments of his or her creation.

Yes, to respond to his tall order truly was to be, for Marcel, a libation of the gods in the most literal of senses. For the future author of his own destiny contained—within the shell, the protection, to be sure, the emblematic shield of his name—from a time anterior to day one, like the acorn the whole oak, in truth, one might say, the entire phloem of those woods rooting earth and air, long before any civilized world, encapsulating the very seed of a canvas which would itself appear as much as water to a god where one might exist, water from universally clouded depths whose fluid revelation, whose discovery *per se* is precisely due to a type of ancient, if not obscurely magnetic, divining rod.

Naturally, Marc and Cassandre lived in the country—France—most well-known for her nearly blinding display of landscapes, art, philosophy, science, literature, language, cuisine, capital, intellectuals, wine, democracy, Catholicism, soaring, elegantly laced stone houses of prayer and stained glass (churches and cathedrals), perfumes, cosmetics, salons, villages, coastlines, and—as Hopkins writes—"inscapes" or museums of all kinds. The French of their generation were not foreign to themselves or strangers to saloons, for example, following the lead of their ethnology, anthropology, archeology, sociology, and psychology, all knowing of the *esprit* of refinement and mathematics, perhaps due to the fact they traveled the world, exploring others from indigenous perspectives, from the point of departure of another tongue. They were as attached to culture's charge as the spindle fiber is, during mitosis, affixed to the region of the chromosome designated by the heavily laden centromere.

Taste determined most categories everywhere here, in brief, just as taste reigned at the time of France's farthest-reaching kings. It continued to play a preeminent role in the style of those who sought, simply put, to preserve it, like Marcel's parents—M. and Mme de Beaurecueil as they were known collectively to the villagers of their native Eus-sous-Soleil, which passes for the sunniest town in France, perched on all 360 degrees of an otherwise unassuming hill. It seemed self-evident to acknowledge taste's overarching presence in their home, their marvelous habitat situated in the southwestern part of the land called *Roussillon*, "The Crackling Earth." The distinction of life's flavors may have had its origins in their kitchen or cuisine as with a preponderance of the French lovers they held sacred; but the same mouths that perceived culinary delights daily expressed themselves well beyond the taste of good food. The packaging and processing of sustaining words or deeds did woefully little to season or spice up their lives. Led to avoid the preternatural caricature of bad taste, French people, in selecting their relationships to the material world, collectively and individually turned away from price points, overemphasized health considerations, frozen food, TV dinners, convenience, efficacy, expediency, and false prophecy. They banked on art, literature, clever journalism, and music to sense, in moderation, anything they consumed, thereby prolonging and deepening their physical and mental pleasure jointly.

Even if no praetorian guard stood watch outside their property and although no Napoleonic imperial soldier protected the valuable lives of its inhabitants, and furthermore, despite the absence of the elite foreign legion to serve them in case of dire need, a patrician harmony filled the air of their home, a harmony together with all the silence whose architecture modeled the totality of Cassandre's most prophetic works. Neither she nor her husband could be easily wounded since their susceptibilities strengthened them. No wonder volumes of La Pléiade lay quietly beside carefully selected records, themselves arranged at opposite end from the bureau, enclosed beyond a baize door, where papers bore the mark of erasure from the *maître de maison*, he who acted, on his own right, outside the home, as *maître de conférence* at the local university. On one site, as the other, Marc loved to heed the analects of beauty's calling, recalling with *élan* and slight *rubato*—to the happy few who heard him speak, those occasionally listening on tenterhooks—the appeal of a Schubert lied: "Where time escapes me today, someday I will escape time."

It would appear that he had hoped the composer's lyrics might, at some point, not unlike digressions that infuse a story or history with renewed breath and deferred purpose, transport the totality of his own creation—according to the course he set out for himself, for his couple, for his pupils, what was no less true for Marcel himself, when he might come of age, perhaps in writing, perhaps in some other medium—to another place like that which the neighboring mountainous terrain represented for Pascal when he declared, "Truth this side of the Pyrénées, error beyond." Marcel, a *magnifico,* would serve and act as more than an anecdotal exception to one such rule or ruler like the Sun King. In no way would his word resemble that dark entry of a page others bandy and chaffer, higgling and haggling like a venomous snake with its doomed prey.

Marc was a gentle man averse to platitudes. He was most prone to taut life's lessons. He preferred cool, even gently warm breezes to the gales of any thunderously forceful outburst. The seventeenth century referred to one such as him as an *honnête homme*, implying, for hundreds of years of schoolchildren who have attended Comédie-Française, an honest type whom it is difficult, as Molière astutely observed with bon ton, to make laugh. The calm interior of his abode enchanted visitors no less than a music box enthralls the eyes and ears of a child. Marc acted, or rather did not act in the artificial sense anathema to Rousseau, like an ambassador for Claudel himself, the poet who believed that *l'Oeil écoute*, "The eye listens." He was a diplomat of the mind, as well trained in this or that type of détente as in the *Sturm und Drang* of the soul. He read the *état d'âme* of people, from the Greeks to the Latins, and beyond, piercing the mystery of any contemplation with the ethereal azure of oceanic eyes as alert as fish penetrating the high seas in search of ever-present, abundant food, enduring lessons swarmed in his reading of the universe, as if to defend those within earshot from the possible sting of ignorance. Mild-mannered and refined, he confected, together with his wife, an inner life for himself, family, and friends, at the limit, where intimacy in/formed art, and art, intimacy. The painting of a porcelain elephant, adjoined by a book lying on a tablecloth next to a paper cutter and flowery vase *au petit feu*, all captured, in this work hanging over volumes of poetry in the salon, the spirit of the Dutch masters without entreating modern fantasy to any form of betrayal. Active life appeared to withdraw here more often than not, leaving the man to little more than his undiluted study, if only to contemplation itself. The episodic, anfractuous nature of profound silence could be plumbed here as if the absence of communication buffeted great writing, art, and music only to leave conversations in these parts to their bare essentials.

Listening, to Marc and Cassandre, was like the embodiment of reading—*animato*—in the air, to such an extent that, it could be said, a smooth talker is first a smooth reader.

Beyond physics properly speaking, various forms of expression related to the more physical realm, sports, for example, coincide with art in the mind of the attentive listener and reader. In golf, one often attests to players "reading the greens"; in what amounts to collective play, the offense "reads the defense"; in face-to-face, human intercourse, our physiognomies pass under the scope of people "reading people." These terms issue the authority of a reader, just as they delineate the crafty position of the player, or actor, in everyday drama, one who perceives the intricate and elaborate complexities of human interaction. Much as a writer sends forth characters to decipher the greater world or, in a sense, to poll the "unreadable," even unpredictable, realms of phenomena unknown to a probing intelligence, people everywhere seek to interpret any true meaning in the nature of someone, or something, through close scrutiny and perception, on many levels of experience, taken in at once.

As sure as the body alone with another may reproduce, the mind or spirit may produce a well-to-do imagination, truth, appurtenance, or reality, especially when coming from the arcs-boutants buttressing the heart. Only do the depths—like the Virgilian instructions of time, combined with Einstein's forceful perception of space-time, expanded by Hubble's deeply penetrating view on the extensive subject, perhaps not unlike the ephemeral itself—believed Marc and Cassandre, live on, surviving (in) the final analysis. Only does what is consistent or, at least, substantial and elemental, however unpredictable—like students of the French eighteenth century, known to those responsible for guiding them as *éléments* midst a labyrinthine universe—last.

It is in volumes made up of inscribed pages fastened along one end and enshrined between covers that we sound out realities foreign or similar to our own. Unlike conversation—which is ill-suited for pauses, gaps, condensation, thoroughness, and extensive elaboration—books afford us the sincerity of a prolonged gaze, the range of a truly definitive notion, the adequate expression of counter—or afterthoughts, the forum for a community of like minds, and the liberty to come or go at any stage of a subject's development. Thanks to reading alone are we able to supply ourselves with the means, knowledge, or opportunity to undertake new investigations, projects, and rapprochements of others. Words may serve to summon pleasant cadences that, in turn, make melodies refine one's vocabulary like sugar stemming from cane raised with the intent to sweeten and fatten our love of life. Artists, like Marc, garden words, raking sense and the senses, plowing meaning to seed it, in double-digging, with the unifying, all-consuming significance of a French-intensive style. It is in textual form, which authors of chant enunciate, like those who underscore one of Reinhardt's abounding sacred works—announcing to future mothers everywhere, well beyond the limitations of their most overflowing language, where sound outlives any sense of even the replete word, as if a joyful musical vocabulary were lifting song out of a momentous mystery fraught with the unknowing darkness of life's pregnant silence and into the lily-white, succinctly profuse message of Gabriel—"The Angel's Greeting."

Cassandre's becalmed voice—often low, soft, and cheerful—greeted Marc's ears like the most welcoming of friends whose salutation only sweetened a mutual respect. "Good day, dear," she nearly seemed to whisper to him in semitones, her cheeks colored by a natural blush and eyes lit up by renewed anticipation, as they rose together each new morning. Not too high-pitched then, its moderate tenor often flowed from a mezzo-timbre that purified the air like crème de la crème sanctifying the aesthetic backdrop of a palette. To listen to her was, for her dear husband, to attest to Telemann's inspiration for *La Musette* earlier and no less than the poetic beauty of Puccini's Musetta. There was nothing base or defiled about the character of her voice, as her personality, beginning with the sound flowering from her parted, full lips. Thus, exercising her vocal chords, she could gently sing life's praises in various degrees of midrange thought as well as any reflection in the more concentrated high-end.

Already forever and a day had the pair, who were beginning to parent Marcel, come to imagine a good life for their creation, projecting to follow him and his own invention wherever he may lead in the maze of bound tomes, letters, spirit, bodies, or others. They were utterly receptive to any signal he might send forth, like astronomers looking to perceive even the most infinitesimal sign of life from distant spheres or readers consulting the relic and reliquary of close-knit dreams tidily laid down for the ages in colorized literature. They secretly hoped, not unlike a conductor before an ensemble, to mold the sound or silence emanating from the member of the family they were now orchestrating, in order that brut noise could be made to be mellifluous and eloquently validated throughout time. Marcel would be trained as an ever more perspicacious listener and reader. He would come to forge the line departing from naïveté and arriving at the discretion of a generalized *raffiné* as well as informed viewpoints.

Marcel's future incubated like the seasons with each passing day in the womb. To conceive, he might later think like his father before him, means more than a simple physical act of love as is commonly equated with the term.

For this child, forefathered and guardianed, it could be said, by a love life in correspondence with the whole of French literature, conception was invested with both literal and literary, even pleasingly argotic genes. This heritage extended his imaginary and make-believe worlds, to be certain, to the Middle Ages and first troubadours; but it also garnered a bounty from times long past, times contributing to each letter and every nuance in the spirit of a language, which so made up his personal story.

Both Marc and Cassandre read the likes of Ronsard and Hugo enough to fill their every human strain with the dearest content known to humanity. Since form mattered to them, forming a new life acted to substantiate no less than what concerned their every waking thought and feeling. Marc was careful to scrutinize each *pensée*, each sentiment—austere or other—beginning with the first one of the day, in such a way that he would come to apply the simple principle of observation to the first days of his baby, in order, that is, to take first steps first. If he and his wife might end in immeasurable suffering, it could be attributable to a principle whose credo embraced all of life with no shortcuts. Steadily, as sure as Cassandre's belly was becoming distended, the life of the child too would mount in grandeur—in every sense of the word.

The moral dignity of human form, here superimposed upon the body, came to derive increased strength and definition from the ethical realm of those who conceived it. And Marc and Cassandre had no difficulty ascribing their poetic way of living to great authors whose insuperable imagination and intelligence, whose gentility and wisdom, whose natural civility and culture, had provided the blueprint *for life*. They wanted their boy to associate himself with the finest representative of their own literary antecedents, as careful, in the choice of the representative they were designating under the guise of the day's leading figure, as entire countries are about their choice of a president or chief justice. If the time of emperors had revolved, we still have access to it through the looking glass of a certain character whose *forte* was the remembrance of such times as those interesting all men and women, universally uniting the one with the other. Poetry would translate the multitudes in the typical as if it were truer than history. Nevertheless, through the portal of history, which may be a mere, however elaborate, story contained within books, we may handily regain the poeticized treasures, indeed, the boundless and bountiful instructions for a future life, of lost time. Music too has something no less profound to say, of course, with respect to space and time.

"Whatever you should want to be," Marcel's mother would confide in him while he remained, gesticulating in her womb, as she lay philosophically upon the bed, "we will support you." Upon hearing this discreet bit of confidence, Marc added, as if he were still elaborating his thoughts in writing, "Remember in any case, to be an author is no less worthy than becoming an artist or composer, and Marcel might well become, at very least, the first among equals, given the reputation which will have preceded him." Both assumed that the head start they were giving to Marcel de Beaurecueil's signature might indeed inflect his direction. Both understood that in order to cultivate valuable memories and to recapture a proper sense of fleeting time, the greatest liberty possible would be most desirable. They esteemed they were actively placing any natural predisposition for the world of the humanities, *beaux-arts* or *belles-lettres*, within a situation rooted in the deepest, most irony conscious of literatures, the art of a body wherein the literal remains married to the figurative for the better part, indeed, the whole of life's worst parts. He would live up to the letter, in their eyes, to his name, making of its letters an aggregate, whose composition forms an ensemble like a body of musical literature. For as much, he would be no less a man of character—the specific instrument whose quality would feature the very alphabet of his ethical and aesthetic distinction, together with each note composing the personal integrity of his social personage.

"There will be something particularly noble about him, a little extra sparkle," divined Cassandre, who marshaled all of the past to serve as the basis for an art more or less practiced by every expectant mother, namely, foretelling the future. Her art had the advantage of being coupled with an artistic hypothesis, a broad supposition not unlike what the ancient Greeks understood a theory to be: The child prodigy would have as many aligned characters guiding him as need be—like *scholia* upon a well-schooled, Latinate text—in order that he might come to the proper way, the truth, and the light in pursuing his quest for the gospel according to him himself, as she would see him, Saint Marcel. He alone would choose those individuals or associations coming to figure in the ranks of his history or biography as in his stories or autobiography were he ever to pen such a work. He alone would internalize a tradition based on taste—atavistic taste—transcending the ages, which, over the course of a lifetime, only enhances the flavor of all that is elegant, indeed eloquent, in life as in death. Yes, he alone would be charged to render a past its due just as he alone would bear the responsibility to signal to those following him, first his parents, then others, just how to position oneself vis-à-vis the past in absolute terms. And music, long before he will have acquired his brand of eloquence, would act as Darwin noted it animated human ancestors who "endeavored to charm each other with musical notes and rhythm."

Three seasons in the womb would not leave him indifferent to his task. For it was there he was gaining the foundation for his relationship with his mother. His visceral attachment to the nurturing she would provide had, as its commencement, the innermost *chambre* next to her heart. With Cassandre, the age-old riddle to know which came first—the chicken or the egg—was resolved from the moment she and Marc conceived of a variant to the conundrum that gave rise to their offspring: The idea of Marcel preceded any fertilization; and it was this notion that would make his life all the more fecund from the point of view of a world, and history, of ideas. She fully knew the little effects of love that art and its conception distend or extend.

Thus, it can be said, his link to his mother was, for Marcel, becoming more and more cerebral from day one, from the beginning—that is, when his parents first united. So the bridges, the connections he was developing *in vivo,* were in short at once corporal and mental, but nonetheless spirited and not in small measure unlike the rocking motion within the belly of the womanly mammal transporting him by virtue of the vintage tradition into whose sheltering berth his parents were docking a rare craft, as they christened him with the appellation Marcel.

Cassandre enjoyed daydreaming about Marcel's own dreams while he was not yet removed from the placenta deep within her. It was as if it were her way of being parturient before parturition. "What are you discovering about yourself?" she would think, at times out loud, though in altered form so that Marc could hear her, asking, "What are you learning from all this?" She wondered singly whether the two sides of Marcel's brain might be developing along the lines of two riverbanks, two worlds, one patrician, one plebeian, very nearly two universes—one steeped in fact and the other in fiction—two genders. She let it float in her mind, then to her husband, ideas of twins or doubles of all kinds. Thoughts of synonyms caused her to consider the other one hears in homonyms too. She looked within, as was often her inclination, and she found a doubleness or duplicity to her attention. She noticed herself focusing on two subjects at once, as if both tragedy and comedy were simultaneously possible within the same person, one matriculated in a larger group, one upon whom all rights and privileges to artful breathing could be conferred by the sign of a redoubled imagination—a truth certified by any diploma testifying to a comprehensive examination of the life of a mind and soul.

Marcel's future mother was then led to conceive of the novelist or dramaturge as a traveler, an enterprising agent of change who necessarily develops a second text beneath the apparent surface of the first, a theater within the theater, a love or passion *mise en abyme.* She found herself reminded of an old attaché case—carrying professor—to cite but one often speaking about "others"—who passed through l'Ecole des Chartes, a slightly narcissine and nonchalant man named René de Broglie. This tall, lanky, bemused student of the ages had first echoed these thoughts, mapping out the ontological role played by various figures of doubles in Shakespeare's *oeuvre.* He was a modern master of history, always allowing his students to learn, to become educated without a doubt, so to speak, on their own terms and time. Young, largely Parisian intellectuals were marked by the greatest possible latitude and longitude of thought and discipline, in combination with mimeographed copies of his key course outlines. Neither they nor the professor tampered with truth.

Such scrupulous word-for-word study directed Cassandre to muse over the international success of the French expression *un mot à double entente* (double entendre), at which point she paused at length to cherish a profound coincidence contained in one of these words itself: *Entendre* means both "to hear" and "to understand" in French. It is therefore a double word, one whose components each carry—for those who adore music—the means to a natural end, whose particularly heavy significance leaves one bloated with possibilities in the long term. As one is unable to hear, short of listening, so too are both the long and short of it misunderstood if one does not properly hear what sound is, or may be, even if improperly, "saying." In turn, she came close to imagining her son overhearing her husband under his breath when the latter would declare, from space-time to space-time—*entendu*! "In what way are his ears recording the message, indeed the massage of our love?" she tenderly asked Marc.

Neither was convinced that pregnancy implied the privileged arena of biology while the child was in the womb; neither felt literature had little to proffer in other words. "If literature is," replied the professor who knew the proper dose of enthusiasm versus reality, "only as good as what you give to it, then it flows and follows, that so too is an infant-to-be, in equal measure, just that which you give to him or her." Literature, described differently, in no way vanished from the lives of Marc and Cassandre while a miracle of biology was occurring, *au contraire*.

It is literature, scientific or other, which—if it does not bear explanation—supplements the natural with an understanding, an *entente* of the language and codes nature employs. Any prescriptions that determine our nature, Marc believed together with Cassandre, remain subject to human interpretation, any genes, for example, subject to the morphology of those very same units within a chromosome. If psychosomatic manifestations—no less than somatopsychic ones—both affect one's world view, their origin may be in the language of the womb, more precisely in the perspective this secret, veiled chamber brings *to life*.

Marcel's mantle of language and perspective were becoming structured there, but how? Was he asleep or waking? Could he anticipate the chirp of a bird, the taste of milk, the scent of a flower, the sight of a hydrangea, the jiggling of his own body, the feeling of his first loss, the vision of an *auteur*? The de Beaurecueils thought of how imagination would first occur within him and to what object or *objet d'art* it might attach itself. They wondered about his imaginative powers that would serve to guide him, turning his judgment away from the feckless, the inauspicious, the inauthentic. They sought to explain to themselves where such creative energies have a locus according to biologists and to what experts find them to be connected.

Cassandre had a knack for stripping away layers of unnecessary queries, but some did nevertheless remain. She could not help but believe that imagination might have had a rudimentary place—however fundamental, in Marcel's preexistence—insofar as he may have even imagined his body in motion and a thought or two arising out of this movement. "But what might that zigzagging intellection have been?" Cassandre conjectured that it might be something along the "ciliary," somewhat supercilious lines of "Eggi'm eggaleggive eggand greggowegging!"

Further advancing where myth adjoins mystery, if not mystification, his future mother imagined Marcel already wanting to be the master, the keeper of his word. For Marcel's parents, keeping one's word reflected one's own grace and salvation. To do honor unto another meant first to esteem, dignify, even revere the self. It translated into constantly redefining the nature of one's word by synchronizing the dose of any verbal input with qualitative changes in our experience vis-à-vis the fluid, albeit, at times, inert reality of symbols communicating sound and meaning

To show interest in the world is first to show interest in one's own way of life, without a doubt, in one's way of viewing, regarding and respecting life. Thus, they believed, the tendency they saw around them for successive generations to be filled with self-aggrandizement and self-promotion emptied the self of a basic humility necessary for sticking to a word with which others could live for keeping a word worth preserving. They saw how advertising co-opted poetry, frightfully coercing and perverting her, in such a way as to ravage and pillage the most sensuous or beauty-laden lines, leaving art's virtues just as soon as those, in time past, who scorched and burned the earth only to viciously think of a one-time profit. They felt their bodies—first among unequal parts their ears—excoriated, abraded, and chafed by the high and low pitch of pecuniary matters, as if their skin were worn all over, like the ebb of sands in the invading tide while their nerves were incessantly torn like ships wrenched or snapped from their moorings in a relentless headwind. Cassandre and Marc had once found themselves inside the church of *Saint-Sulpice*, before Delacroix's version of "The Merchants Being Chased from the Temple"; and this single viewing of ingenues by an artful genius was enough for them to wish forevermore that chronic advertising would be diagnosed as a societal menace or deafening pandemic, a monoglot Alastor and money-grabbing clientele hunted down and banished from everyone's voyeuristic eyes, only to leave a healthy germ or trace of the painter's sense of color and culture in its stead.

If commercial-free days could be found at the foundation of entire lands such as those of good old Nova Scotia, so too could they be established there where tone-deaf business people falsely lead others through a personification of folly and conceit without misgivings. Would-be adepts of antiquated freedom, lazy rotations of the sun and nature—the supreme artist whose works build upon disillusionment—allow themselves to be lured up the garden path, where poor souls are religiously taken for a ride, their leg systematically pulled and their free will mutilated, maimed, or handicapped by a nemesis. In a round-the-clock society organized around the profit principle, able-minded people are, in so many ways, dismembered, crippled, and disenabled by overwhelmingly abusive, cherry-picking, untimely profiteering, and bosh at every turn and street corner. The French say(s) it matter-of-factly: "Les gens (se) font marcher."

Just how we see the world may be profoundly enhanced by observations of the role minutiae play in our lives, as if the veracity of a simple still life were capable of giving us more perspective—through its depiction of a single loaf of bread, the serrated peal of a lemon or some antique crystal—than grand, historical, historic even, biblical, or illusionist tableaux. The well-defined shaped mass—as if freshly baked for our visual, thus intellectual, or disabused spiritual sustenance—refers us to our most immediate daily needs in such a way so as to refashion and reorient what we take for granted in the light of some magic. We may be invited to partake in letting it furtively knead our recollection of the homey smell that staple of a delicious comfort—first to our nose, then entire well-being—the one we associate with bread rising out of the continuous, even, arid glow of the oven's warmth. Indeed, it could represent our entire mind, hardening with the images derived from the steady exposure of our memory to all the times baking may have brought a rustic wholesomeness to any of the animal functions of smell or hearing, sight, touch, and taste. Such a phenomenon provides more than an olfactory grain of pleasure for our intuitive or acquired perception of space and time, like a visit to the shoreline furnishes our mind with an entirely new perspective anent our life and lives on the mainland.

A familiar object may envelop our every fiber like none other. The time-honored living legacy of something as slight yet almost enigmatic as yeast may provoke or act as a starter to the well-bred imagination, which evolves along its own lines, culling memories, reveries, and impressions—raising out of the cindering senses long forgotten, buried splendors for the perception of space-time—more than even the collective magnificence displayed along a picturesque development of coastline up and down the Levant.

In a similar vein, we may find more revealing an untimely cough, a social gaffe, a slip of the tongue, unexpected laughter, or a nervous twitch; and this might be more illustrative of our long-standing and deep experience in the world than our adherence to any overarching theory or discourse. As sublime as it may be to go out, handsomely dressed for a night at the opera, where we might hear "The Entrance of the Gods into Valhalla" of *Das Rheingold*, or "Siegfried's Idyll," we may arrive at more profound knowledge of ourselves through less subtle or smaller magnitudes of grandiose staging, where art and life commingle. Truly dramatic resolution thus arises out of entirely unexpected, unsuspecting arenas of life experience.

Like a full, enriched vocabulary, expression, or word, a sensation becomes a condition for intense interest from the moment we are free and able to perceive the spectacle memory that cultivates over time. A corporeal memory, which far exceeds the logic or incoherence of our mind, may be incited by some raw, at least tangentially familiar, frothing reality like the one evoked for our senses by the taste of a leavening agent that serves to ferment notions of space and time, no less than a leitmotiv of music *per se* swells, in due course, from the depths of Wagner's monumental operas. Things may be apt to perform the function of an artistic arrangement, moreover, based on a wide array of wholly natural settings all around us. From the moment we are trained—as devotees of music and art in full view, to listen to our bodies and, subsequently, to the world turning over in our minds as we attune our perceptions to a form of perspicacity blended with titrated complexity—we may uncover the full scope of the human enterprise, indeed the unique experiment of being particularly concentrated around all that is known and unknown. Yes, we may thus sense ourselves just as the artist hears various songs in the exhilarating harmonics of nature, singularly and substantially *alive*.

We may ultimately find ourselves, as well as Wordsworth, "Learning from Nature":

> One impulse from a vernal wood
> May teach you more of man
> Of moral evil and of good,
> Than all the sages can.

A true soul barters exclusively with necessity and the essence of desire.

Mr. Homais, a risk-taking, chapped-face, miscreated account executive in an advertising firm based in the Paris suburb of Choisy-le-Roi, lived, during a few months of the year, near the de Beaurecueils in a *pied-à-terre* and represented, if not that undomesticated quackery of the huckster's soul by night, then that tendency to sell or sell out by day. He was a rumbling *bête noire*, a miscreant full of *idées fixes* and *reçues*, a semiconscious sot lodged part-time in a somber *garçonnière*. The largest group of those who bought the shabby combination of his redundantly jejune words, saccharine smile, tomfoolery, childish images, impairing blight, uppish tone, *reductio ad absurdum*, and bottom line were in the United States since, simply put, it is there that more buying of whatever is sold per capita takes place than in any other land on the planet.

For Mr. Homais, advertising provided a livelihood from the movement within relations, which constitutes putting one's best foot forward in order that others might see how far one might step without overreaching, like an able gull or perambulating pigeon attempting to scavenge some salvageable food from among nearby humans whose close proximity eventually scares them to rapid flight from their covetous pecking. Nagging self-promotion, gibberish and swindling, in other words, seen by the execrating businessman who rips the society asunder, countermanding civility, presented neither any drawback nor even less any waste of time. Using jingles, chicanery, sleight of hand, bait-and-switch tactics, hocus-pocus, and mumbo jumbo to promote the advantage of his product, business, or bonanza in order to increase sales did not cost him much either: The one-line byline or brief commendatory publicity notice requires little depth outside of its catchiness, often expressed in tones ranging from bass or vulgar to popularly falsetto. It was an ongoing, pestering, spurious force unlike the more episodic push of a mother giving birth or the hair-raising pull of an eagerly awaited feuilleton whose fictional installment satisfies the curiosity of a faithful reader.

By leaving too little to chance and free will in trying to collect money for services, the devout upstart resembled more and more individuals who would become one with the bad fortune of a self-styled nuisance—literally causing damage, destruction, annoyance, inconvenience, and generalized vexation. His was an opportunistic situational morality, which ruled the day. His brand of morals cauterized the senses of those gullible individuals duped into swallowing his processed characterization of talent and self-interested spiel. In nothing did Mr. Homais doubt the God moneying his trust insofar as he was always wagering something, economically of course, like a blind man addictively betting he would always be able to picture fully a painting by knowing its title alone.

Advertising's intrinsic distortion stretches beyond too much of the natural or inherent good of the goods in question. The trick of Mr. Homais's professional rigmarole could be seen as he would sententiously yank and jerk from others what he wanted—yes, for himself first—and this, by various means of manipulative rambling through different media, incoherent pulling, that is, by any and all "attractive" means or premeditated pranks. His was not the province of postmeditated maintenance and little-confused ameliorations of life.

"Sophie did not have her watch properly adjusted," he once railed censoriously to his colleague Ségalaine upon seeing a print ad for Patek Philippe, which fell in the domain of his purview. "I see," she replied, half blasé, half objurgatorily, in turn, only to propitiate her boss *illico*; "that model should know better than to sell our product without the hour set at ten past ten." "Yes, the hands should look like the extension of Venus's arms, what others might take to be her legs!" inveighed the fulminating Mr. Homais, clearly demonstrating how one can, all at once, apply serious study of the unconscious to the most fanciful of pop or popular subjects and be as consistent as a hobgoblin in making a bewitching fetish in and out of a disarming brassiere.

While the de Beaurecueils were not overly or overtly privy to the inner confines of the blustering business world, they were no foreigners, in a sense, to the greater world at large. They could only imagine such a confidential conversation between their neighbor, Mr. Homais, and his associate. Yet, so it seemed, their conjecture proved itself, for the most, astoundingly accurate, just as their reasons for arriving at any conclusions about his entire profession proved, without a doubt, foolproof.

If, to many, it might appear desirable to lead Mr. Homais's professional life, given the exaggerated remuneration, which came about as a result of an ethical vacuum and selfish aspiration, Cassandre amply preferred her life as a librarian and specialist of rare documents. Marc too would, so he told Cassandre when they first began dating in *hypo-câgne*, always prefer a mind that inquires for the sake of inquiring to one which inquires for the asking so to speak, one seeking something from another exclusively for one's own purpose, one, in other words, expecting some added value or exchange in return. They both believed, in merging their thought with a good humanist's, that it was a human's obligation to uplift the life of others, to make daily encounters and things more pleasant, rather than painful, by any measure. Together, they cared little for the dismal attachments of material riches, the coefficients or brut products of multiplication, the unwanted adjuncts of an antisocial void, and the nonessential attributes of things made holier than thou.

The notion he had often heard in America of "giving back" appeared to both of them quite suspect, almost wrathful insofar as it coyly masks or subverts raging, furiously "competitive nature" at every turn in the road paved by an allegedly free-market culture of capitalism. The would-be principle driven by profit, as much as by individuals propelling themselves into the future, is accompanied by things running every which way amok. Anteing up to reality seemed to be increasing, according to Marc and Cassandre, as if individuals were no less than their representatives playing cards, all decked out for business like a joker assuming all of the values and none at the same time. More and more, professionals appeared to bluff themselves all the while as they gambled with their own lives or that of others. This out-of-control, though heavily invested, partisan frenzy—no less than society's falsifying subterfuge and torpedoed truth, its impoverished underbelly—became all the more self-evident to the de Beaurecueils as they found themselves frankly "expecting" Marcel; for they did not wish to subject him to any more, or any less, than a liberal understanding of the world and the universe beyond like a prebeliever introduced to some, or all, of any faith. Truth is—like beauty and goodness, they believed—more of a sure thing, a good bet. Their act of conception was a demonstration of spontaneous generosity, an effusive act not uncommon to selfless parents everywhere. Giving themselves to one another, and thereby, in effect, to any other, tenanted their existence with all the basic building blocks of more than fortifying protein as if the poor were nourished with some cheese-laced quiche. Unlike most individuals who impose themselves in the paltry name of money or so-called charitable giving, however, Marcel's parents would consciously attempt to efface themselves to every extent and at every moment possible.

Just how then would the child of such disinterested rearing make a way, take away at once, for himself if he would end up seeking to understand both *entendre* and *comprendre* rather than to stand for this or that? In his parents' incandescent eyes, the latter usually carried with it the promotion of the self or a group with a common identity before the unselfish types the de Beaurecueils so adored and recalled from those authors who reflected on time's inception. No murderous projection animated the plot they were planning to carve out—excavating in his honor, little by little and, painstakingly, more than fossilized memories of artistic passion.

The two had dated for quite a time, reading widely and deeply together all the while. They gauged and wagered the whole weight of space-time—the preoccupation and occupation—of culture and any veritable beauty of art acting upon the unborn child without any intended archaisms. They learned, fixing a certain mastery in the mind and memory, to encircle the logic of Dante's literary trepan, his *Divine Comedy*, by thinking both clockwise and counterclockwise, by imagining the past through an idea of what future its rendition implied, thus departing from the present at times in a similar manner to those who leave on a safari equipped with binoculars and water enough to witness the abundant legacy earth has mothered to this diverse day and age.

Marc had witnessed, as a young professor, students elsewhere on a neighboring university's grounds discussing their future as medical doctors. He had remarked to Cassandre then, what was only more enlightening now, namely, just how the students conceived of altruism in France. Society's motif of helping humanity, so loosely employed in the United States, held different sway in the more methodical and less accidental hexagon. The recompense or remittance for work done on the body suggested to him that the French lived, relatively speaking, within their means. In France, dreams and daydreams were first shared and communicable within enthused reason. This tended to add measurable meaning to European lives as subjects in school come to have the magical power of an incantation for students who live within themselves—as the subject's subject, "buying into," as is said in America, the lessons of a significant teacher. Marc guided his disciples in delineating a poetic line of thought, interpreting all the permissible artistry within those guidelines and developing the most of themselves. Conversely, to believe a person's word without meaning is tantamount to giving heed to immoderate noise; meaning, that afflatus of the spirit, like sense or import generally, derives its content from a circumscribed music. The inner significance of something is its silence navigated like a vessel trolling for the high seas' hidden catch, buoyed by the wind-wrapped pursuit of a quiet life far from the clamorous bustle and rumors of some yonder shore.

In France, the mind, *l'esprit*, was treated on equal footing with the *corps* as canapés serve as counterweight to dessert in a well-conceived meal. *Mens sana in corpore sano* (healthy in body, healthy in mind) suggests, in the Latin sense of the term, an equality, which, according to the student of philosophy or sociology, if preserved, maintains a natural balance between the human organism and the universe. Indeed, Cassandre and Marc reveled in exchanging tennis shots every now and again, all in the name of a lifelong courtship with manifold forms of game playing, all of which served to promote a sane lifestyle, one with love at both ends.

Said another way, in the land where Mr. Homais was busy brazenly endorsing his own products, like other lupine characters who would eventually fall upon their comeuppance in the same so-called space, an identity *du terroir*, a relationship to cultural norms, and traditions goes on, only effaced, removed from itself. A watch means one thing to a Frenchman—whose time on earth appears almost plainly indicated as if decorated with the volume and cherubic stature of a Renaissance frieze—quite another to those living outside Gallic borders, let alone across the seas. Hence, the huge sums medical doctors reaped per hour or per diem in America, as compared to the tightly controlled amounts awarded to those exerting their profession in the homeland of the words, notion, and more benevolent deeds of *laissez-faire* and *laissez-aller*.

No more liberating than a death sentence in the end was an economy based on a promotion of the self first of all, one in which the leaders would increasingly gain their stature at the expense and at the loss of the other, leading to a medical system, which could conceivably deprive tens of millions of its citizens any coverage. There exists a system of checks and balances that assumes social security to be like the existence of one's neighbor whom, one hopes and trusts, will more than likely live in good health, in both body and mind. Yes, social security could prove to be like the self or spirit itself, a *fait accompli*, where not in a perpetual state of becoming, thanks to a common, expressed understanding of being and nothingness. It could, when properly conceived, make it both easy and simple for people everywhere sharing in its common bounty to keep their word and revel in any silence interspersed with life's momentous promise.

It was true that worldly affairs appeared more litigious as seen from an overseas vantage point at the time of the de Beaurecueils; and thus, it was nonetheless true that Marcel's parents did not want him any other than aware of the fullest possible meaning and significance of his word or words. "What better way to have him *stick to his word*," asked Cassandre of her bona fide husband, "than to have him bear the name of the greatest *honnête homme* of our time?"

As generally, Cassandre pushed further ahead with her thought: "Would the odds not tithe in his favor were the worth of his name tied to the value of his word and vice versa?"

"But it will be difficult," warned Marc, "to make a living on words alone, like someone trying to eat with nothing but bare utensils." Indeed, Marc spoke the idiom of curious people and students like the pianist Reinhardt who wrote for the violin even though he may have been daunted by the diction of his day, by language's evolution. Like him who single-handedly adjusted the sonata form inherited from Haydn, Mozart, then Beethoven, nothing signaled an end to Marc's involvement with young people confronted with past ages: The challenge of artful persuasion served to make transparent what for less-tasteful speakers and writers appeared as opaque. Their growing spasms would learn to multiply, modulation upon modulation, according to the hand of time.

A *life* then could be translated into a *living* from day one, if imagined, if conceived so, and provided a will to live or act it out just as many things may be made to give an impression of freshness, if not sweetness itself, by simply being stored in a *bonbonnière*. Before Rousseau's *Social Contract* came a contract of the author's person with himself, a kind of understanding and positioning of himself in relation to others, one which penultimately sought less the place whence a pair of shoes might come than those privileged sites of an imagination, which classes, orders, clarifies, encases, inventories forms, dreams, writes, and dreams some more. And thus, before the personal documented agreement, this side of the betrothal we keep with and for ourselves arise notions of contracts themselves. Some choice nations wish to bind their citizenry to an ever more frequent, ever more intense fight, a "struggle for life" despite others, at their expense even. There is a viable alternative from that point when a land nourishes notions of selflessness, which include a fortified self and equitable mouth, when a solid ground cultivates acts of generosity, authentic charity, and genuine kindness, when a territory yields to others what others naturally, individually, and collectively yield to it, like milk submitting its ingredients to the process of manufacturing butter, *crème fraîche* and cheese.

If a majority of French people viewed contracts as a legal binding, approximately the same amount believed their basis rooted in economics. To ensure action in a domain was to tie the signatories to an exchange of money in some form or another.

Yet Marc saw the nature of these writings whose limits are enforceable by law as founded in notions of the self and the collective that preceded an economy; and therefore, he thought, this unique framework might extend far beyond any affairs directly related to the currency common to all. This form of social psychology girded a kind of composure that remained with the man, in both word and deed, deep within Marc then at all times. His ambition was not to take the offensive, trying to change the world through power or money, but rather to seek change through culture. It is culture that changes us as individuals, he believed. It is thus culture we may and, at times, must defend in order for collective change to take place. The preservation of memory comes at that priceless price.

He lent his thoughts to one of his special friends—the president of the Earth Development Bank—Mr. Franklin Smith. At odds with the president of the United States's wicked bonhomie, erratic pugilism, and laying down of the law, paradoxically, this alternative American figurehead believed—perhaps not long before yet certainly long after any other—that one must always give more, if in possession of more, to neighbors far and wide, as if to provide them, in perpetuity, with a fountain of soup, an invigorating geyser of hope.

While Mr. Smith viewed this principle as healthy for nations—the rich looking out for the poor, thereby inciting a balance of resources on a global scale—Marc saw as true the same phenomenon on an individual basis. The optimal way to riches, whatever form they might take, passed necessarily through an intelligent understanding of and compassion for others. Both Mr. Smith and Marc had learned this at their respective university, which explains why the former named his three children after preeminent American schools—Harvey for Harvard, Stan for Stanford, and Wellesley for his girl. Mr. Smith himself, when in his precocious teens, had chosen to attend Stanford since, from his youngest days, he had discerned a superior faculty and type of uncommonly equaled peerage, there where the acronym of the university press formed the impressively abbreviated SUP.

Of the three young Smiths, it was the garrulous Harvey, the eldest, who found himself on leave in Paris from his liberal arts college on the west coast of the United States. He was "spending" this, his junior year abroad, at the Sorbonne. It would also prove to be the occasion for him to be introduced by Marc to Schumann's *Kinderszenen* ("Scenes from Childhood") that musical tableau of the space-time when we are all richest, namely, during the unencumbered freedom of our youth, then when our mouths spout the damnedest things during a stage when impulse control leaves us uninhibited and all is possible. The young master would view the younger American with youth's generous qualities in mind: languishing emotions, boundless feelings, available dispositions, exuberant affections, blind attachments, freedom from wisdom's constraints, indefatigable curiosity, and fundamental questions, to name just a few.

The real enrichment of one's person comes at a price, to be sure, and that is not scorching and burning the field of visible dreams of others, not acting indifferently to their impoverishment, not exploiting them in the process of their most basic nutrition. Mr. Smith had learned this too in school, where he found enduring lessons that balanced the adornments of learning with a foundation of definite shape and volume like as many Ionic columns supporting mythic scenes—at the core of civilization—carved into ancient Greek pediments and entablatures. These amounted to moments of metered truth manifest, framed and raised high for some time akin to the cornice of eternity.

As if to better understand the nature of barbarians worldwide, one must find the foreigner in oneself, in one self, one attached to the alien, the stranger, the language from above and below. Normal is to accept one's beguiling weirdness, one's predisposition for disease, as if it were someone else inhabiting the self, extremes and all. It is to come to grips with one's own bodily odors and thereby accepting of others'. Normal assumes all the potentialities of the human experience, including intermarriage; it is not conforming to a reality based on consensus like a gnarled apple that cannot renounce the consumer in search of perfection, the individual who finds idiosyncrasies of this nature to spoil the whole lot of reality. The bank officer held out high hopes his son would learn these vital lessons of cosmic reason, this insightful expression of self-revealing thought in words or things—this form of the old-world Logos emanating from victorious mouths—while studying, on the move, outside his native land.

Like Mr. Smith with his family and employees, Marc, who bolstered each individual's expressiveness, enthusiastically encouraged his wife and students. Little surprise then when he would ready himself to position any intervention vis-à-vis his child with a design to patiently prod Marcel to explore, imagine, and develop along original lines, never losing sight of what various artistic traditions had bequeathed to the future.

Mr. Smith was obliged to research what were to become known decades later as win-win situations. Altruism, as he knew it, arose out a sense of duty. He loved to think about the word for *duty* in French—*un devoir*—since the word was kept alive daily in assignments young pupils fulfilled for their schoolmasters and mistresses.

Every Frenchman was raised, *élevé*, with a sense of duty toward his fellow man. He was dispassionate and indifferent, impassible even, selfless like the consummate comrade in view of the greater whole.

This did not exclude the Frenchman's entering into relations with women of "his" society, relations not lacking in passion, compassion, and at times, self-directed interest of many kinds. Indeed, Mr. Smith found relations in France much the way Marc taught his students to see them, altogether variable, that is depending on whether men were entering into contact with, on the one hand, men or, on the other, women. Neither needed an economic argument at the foundation in order to act both personally and socially in responsible fashion.

It could be envisioned that more than a generation removed from Mr. Smith's presidency at the Earth Bank, the leader of the United States would be forced to acknowledge that, more than ever, it would make sense to invest in the poorer nations, in the more deprived individuals of the planet (like parents turning life over and, with it, either inscribed or unwritten pages of wisdom to kids). This holds true so long as it is a given that borders would become more fungible and osmotic than ever with respect to crime, terror, violence, drugs, disease, migrations, transportation, and communication. Whole nations, it could then be argued, might find themselves realigning their outdated ways of thinking and acting. Entire currencies would fluctuate, monies no less than markets, goods, and services. Assimilation of different cultures into the mainstream would put its imprint on the fabric of great democracies worldwide.

Of course, like every politician and unlike the true statesman of old, the American president would only *act* as a leader. In fact, he would merely be reacting to pressure from either advisors or constituents, not acting out a vision, a new perspective one could first imagine, then try to implement, with some propitious design and order or any amelioration for those around oneself, in mind. Music and perhaps art generally are the very basis of a language that could be deployed to allay fears and calm the sense of vulnerability people feel across the globe.

Marc and Cassandre did not wish to see their child become an actor but rather a visionary of his own word. Were he to prophesy in any way, the act of doing so should first begin with his own reality, with his own self, one radiating out from there. They wanted him, to be sure, familiar with the facts of life in every sense of the word, even if said "facts" may never exist in isolation. Utmost in their minds was the fact that he might be conversant with the truth of which the facts will always remain but a subset. They wanted him to act out of passionate or, alternatively, dispassionate compassion.

"To arrive at the truth, do you recall what Degas said of painting?" asked Marc of his wife.

Cassandre responded, "One does not paint with words."

Her attentive husband added, "It took me imitating the masters twenty-two years before I acquired a sense of taste in my own eyes." And thus, Marc set out upon a balmy reverie covering the entire surface of things like an aromatic ointment applied to the skin. His daydreaming confounded Degas and Manet, a confusion that took, as the emblem of its canvas, a simple tableau of some *Asperges*, viewed in unison with the literary rendition of a profound remembrance.

The artist acts, in truth, to portray his own nature within the confines of his own culture. He remains like the unborn Marcel, outside the realm in which a person increasingly learns how to act in order to turn out to be one whose purpose is the commission of a profit or return for oneself above all. He triumphs, in creating something of beauty, over death, hatred, inaction, ignorance, and prejudice. No less could as well be said—in point and counterpoint of fact—of music's realm (like any wellspring of profoundly living, vibrant, encircled, circulating beauty).

Marc witnessed a tendency within the delivery of the news, first in print, then, years later, on the television, to act like the subject upon which the reports were modeled. Less and less was it informed by a tradition like the one responsible for Degas's *beau ideal* as he expressed it at his life's end in saying that "only after years of study and copying the masters could one be suited to reasonably paint a radish from life." Nature is lost and unredeemed when it is ignored by a whole culture, one armed with too little cognizance of earth's truest bounty and dream-filled crop. The politicians act and so, in turn, do the newscasters, following the reporters. If stunned by this or that act of violence, the astonishment plays second fiddle, as Marc saw it, to the principal speaker's acting dazed and bewildered. Increasingly, the theater of life would tap the theater itself in order to preserve some semblance of a normal flux of life. Violence and death in presumably civilized societies could occur in the most unseemly manner, and yet, if the main players were trained no less as actors than as demagogues versed in the art of persuasion, the scene or stage, in other words, the circumstances within society itself, go on, unmarred by villainy or vice.

While the French were all able to see, at one point, for example, the horror of a murderous day in an isolated German school and while the world was able to read accounts of the sad event, no one seemed interested in what was taking place at the heart of European politics: both the chancellor and the president of the German Bundestag were thrust into a new era of portraying the country's shocked grief in words, an act for which they appeared far less trained than their American counterparts. *Could they not have chosen silence over representing the violence?* asked Cassandre within her mind. *What good brings the idolatrous act of lowering the flag to half-staff in these cases, as in any case using an oriflamme to express one's feelings?* she thought. *It is silence*, she figured, *which allows our words to go beyond things and to surpass further linguistic expression. This is where silence unites with music to render a fuller form of life.*

So long as Marcel would live, Cassandre hoped, like Marc in equal measure, he would idolize nothing, save that literature in particular and art in general—music included, of course—in which he would find, indeed *found*, a center of the universe, a peace equidistant from the circumference of hatred, a seminal freedom from hostilities together with its margins. This would be a literature of self-reflection, a score mixed with a careful consideration of the way things and people work or play. It would be texts written by the keenest minds and uniquely tender souls. Sagas would fuel poetry, epics would found novels, essays would give rise to serials or pamphlets. Even journalism would be reinvented by attention given to form and meaning, both cornerstones of truth and the contents of civilization.

Children should no more be idolized than a flag. The newly formed Zionists should no more worship Zion than Christians the pope, the acclaimed and proclaimed vicar of Jesus Christ. Citizens should no more regard with blind adulation their president than an actor the stage. The rapacious Mr. Homais should no more stupidly admire the body than people should look to medicine for a cure-all.

Moderation tempers all things. One should heed the Shakespearean calling to love moderately, even moderating moderation itself, thereby abating extremes, as a friar recommends to the young Romeo and Juliet; for in such action alone, and not without it, do we find joyful, if not potentially less happy, excesses of life. It was with the most innocent of loves and lovers in mind that Cassandre imagined her very young boy sharing his own earliest thoughts on mild limits, nonviolent restraint, tenderness, and the rosiest of affections, as if the youngest voice adjoins the oldest in expressing true profundity: "When someone loves you, the way they say your name is different. You just know that your name is safe and sound in their mouths and on the tip of their tongue."

What's more—silence—taken together with veritable eloquence, that elegance of words that define things and ideas as seen from all sides and with their full aspect, Marc and Cassandre believed, modulates or fashions every mode of true moderation. This is where the Golden Rule of treating others as you wish to be treated has a silver lining for the self: musical karma nourishes the soul, *moderato*.

Literature might prove to be, once again, for Marcel, like the body acting as the foyer of all worthy silence, if not sounds, handed down from generation to generation. It would house and conjugate truth's multitudinous forms more variously than an *ostinato*, that repeated musical figure, rhythmic pattern, or motive, most often occurring in the foundation of sound—the bass. As sure as he would be handed over to the mother of half his genes upon his first experience seeing the light of day, literature would cradle his dreams and kindle his glowing spirit. This is why his parents invested his genes with generations of intelligence and wisdom about the nature of life and art. They endowed him with a name whose summation could flesh out nothing less than the poetry of living creations, if not one's being in a fullness expressed by none other than a silent partner.

In the final analysis, Marc and Cassandre had thought long and diligently about the nature of what was literally and figuratively "becoming" as they had reflected on the culture of what was to be more truly attractive. Their common mind-set had led them to agree on the authors of their predilection as it did on the destinations of their travels and the name of their future son. A boy, they believed, who might come to understand humanity in its specificity, just as in its totality, would likely be one, just as all of us who pass through the humanities, to varying degrees, in some form or another. He would then pay tribute to his understanding as he might see fit. This does not necessarily mean his contribution would seek, *a priori*, any reward or obolus. On the contrary, Mr. de Broglie had instructed his students just that, recalled the de Beaurecueils, in writing: "The purest adventurers, indeed, only the true explorers acceded to the least defiled path, if not discovery, free from adulterants, leaving mapmaking for the days and even eras following their full-strength quests and conquests."

Recalling her old professor's wisdom, Cassandre mused to Marc, "We should refrain entirely from giving our human creation a name."

"Let him be free," laughed Marc ironically, "to assume the name which any individual he shall encounter might lend him, for even a name is not necessarily a gift which gives forever."

To follow the logic of his parents, Marcel might then come to explore precisely what was in the name, surname, namesake, or even nickname of all the great artists and thinkers. Marcel was to be no less than his name; and on that vast body of thought, where both the guide and guided find themselves holding the helm, transported by a mix of what is known and unknown, not unlike the voyageurs of the high seas or highest heavens before them, he would be the one to found himself and the fortune of his own personal, or individual, sanctuary. This was to be his temple, as sure as those leading from his eyes to his ears, as steadying as those leading from the Hebrews to the Greeks. His name would connect him to the world as people relayed themselves, in the first days of the telephone, to one another, beginning their conversation with the words *Allô, j'écoute*.

Here, in a word, would he come to take refuge in and solace from creation's most wondrous worlds and the exquisite conceptions of entire constellations, both on earth and beyond. Here, indeed, would he come to take in everything and give to those who themselves would come to give of themselves the just return on their mental, physical and, spiritual investment. Here would he come to take the godly elements known to humanity and inflect their elasticity in the forms corresponding to person, number, tense, mood, and voice, making them decline and climb once more against all the most sapient odds according to the climes of a divine imagination, which suggests the one animating Johann Christian Bach's cosmopolitan Grand Overture or, among others, Beethoven's multiple overtures to *Fidelio* (which begins with Marcellina interrupting her work to relent in saying, "Well, go on, I'm listening," followed by the injunction of a solemn declaration, "Unless you take me as I am / I shall simply close my ears"). Here would the intrepid Marcel give meaning and significance to his—not unlike any other—name. Here, in sum, would he discover the vast movement that rests or, as in musical shape, remains moving though not too agitated, passing from gene to gene and generation to generation, in the sap of sublime silence.

Adagio—Scherzando Assai

It is a supreme paradox that a professor of literature and a librarian should mate and prefer to life an art form that takes as its point of departure an absence of verbal language. But then again, the French, taken as a whole, have always fueled their existence with paradox even if this may appear to others as contradiction. To take the *contre-pied*, the opposite, of a stance marks the earliest training of the subtle mind here. Inhabitants of France thrive "beneath the canvas" of existence, as if everyone were a character in an international drama. It is therefore no wonder that life in the womb interests these people as much as any other, if not more. The imagination has time to slowly, methodically form its contours, its objects, its cells, and the necessary fluids for regeneration. The soul takes shape out of this darkness that is at once systematically arranged and whimsical. It is precipitated and crystallized by a rate of change occurring over a long, tirelessly protracted period of time, *lento*, like a stalactite ceaselessly dripping in the proper temperature and mineral-rich water until it forms a column with the bedrock beneath a cavernous arch.

Marcel had now taken hold, within his mother, for several months. It was springtime or, as Cassandre conceived of it, *primavera*. Even if his parents were wrong about the gender of the future infant, they were prepared to name her Marcellina, Marcela, or Marcy, even Martine or the Mediterranean couple's seaside favorite—Marina—where she might turn out as one of the *beau sexe*. Strangely, these girls' names reminded Marc of a musician he had once heard at the university, a violinist by the name of Célimène Bonnemaison. She played while well into her pregnancy, and he found, in her performance, that the music did not suffer as much as her back. The bow of the violin seemed to feverishly stroke, and thereby stoke, his nerves. This could largely be traced to a technique of bowing and fingering, which adjusted for the added weight as if, by slightly arching the back, she were adding more essential color and a bubbling *sautillé* to the notes. Marc recalled going backstage that night with an American collector of Stradivari, a jovial and memorable friend of his named Bill Woodward, who offered Célimène the chance to play with one of Paganini's bows that he had just received from London.

He then fell away from the reverie of that night and turned to Cassandre, asking her if she would like to hear one of the Rasoumovsky quartets Célimène had played that night as if there were nothing of greater spiritual, ethical, or intellectual nobility and worth. It was instantaneous that Marcel's future mother agreed to the music; for, in her too, it brought back the experience of hearing another potential bearer of children play with utter abandon, dissert in harmony with melodies all but bereaving, as if existed only the past defined by Beethoven's op. 59, no. 1. Cassandre's preference was for the interpretation made and recorded by Il Quartetto Italiano.

There too, as Bill found present in the wealthy cello of the Hollywood String Quartet, or, better, in the infallible and supremely sensitized memory of the Smetana Quartet, Cassandre felt as fluidly as the bird feels the wind, the presence of a female influence upon the great works of European civilization. Her rich taste defined itself not by any militant views about women's presence in music at a time when professional musicians were overwhelmingly male, but rather by an absence of indiscretion, a sense of difference, and unequalled parts whose whole Marc fully shared. Cassandre simply liked the touch of a woman, not to speak of Italy, in the sound of music. And this did not keep her from fully appreciating, indeed loving, Marc, who remained faithful to the same Vienna whose orchestras proved as virile in his day as they did at the time of those great composers who passed along her streets and in her palace halls or gardens.

The music began, and Marcel seemed to move once again, in tune with the quartet's tone. Did the fetus have a life of its own? Some remote possibility exists that Marcel was perceiving sound or simply treating his mother as an impresario for the day he would make his *entrée* onto the world's gurney and stage. There was little doubt of the play within his body, for each movement of his muscles demanded at once composure and the coming together of new muscles on the part of his mother. An envelope of love felt as though she were stuffed with a burgeoning letter whose form and content left desiring affection, craving the reality touch alone could reach and longing for pitiless sympathy. This awareness of her body left Cassandre and Marc to rework Salieri's famous dictum in their mind as if it were the stage for a Parisian opera, deftly afoot in obliging dance: *Prima il ballet, poi la musica* (First the ballet, then music)!

It appeared to this couple, in other words, that language indeed followed music as a guerdon follows some good work, but that dance preceded all other art forms given the evolution of all types of movement. Marcel was choreographing existence for the couple insofar as his motion, taken as corporeal, if not spiritual commotion, formed the object of their reflection and the subject of much of their intimate conversations. Marcel was positioning himself among other life forms, from the least developed single-cell bacterium to the more advanced in structures we find making up humans. Yes, composition, makeup, make-believe, and that sense of wonderment indigenous to the human species—all would follow the development of Marcel's life like the reader who followed the nature of characters in *Bildungsroman*.

If Cassandre and Marc wished for Marcel to grow inside, it could be envisioned that Marcel himself wanted no less than to grow "outside." For the moment, he belonged to Cassandre, heart and body. His mind was, not unlike the soul, however, another, graying matter. "This tissue forming all around me constitutes the fabric of my life," he soon seemed to realize.

"Cell upon cell, I am layered, in this dark cell, in the confines of this translucent aggregation of cells, like *crème anglaise* with blackberries (*aux mûres*) in a *mille-feuilles*.

"I see nothing but soft, obscure walls here.

"I am free from being accused of immaturity. Everywhere, I am following Mom's own maturation. I know this because the fluids are, beginning with water, traveling in and around me like the seas washing over schools of fish.

"I hear liquids sweeping and swooshing by me as a nurse hurrying a patient to be cleansed. Sounds of a heart's throbbing appear as a thud, thump, and tick of the metronome for life's constant, timely beat. It seems to keep pace with the fastest of metabolisms like a hummingbird, alighting upon flower after flower, visually twittering just the other side of dusk. The roaring of blood resembles some ancient, forever-lost noise, which forms the backdrop of a lifelong constellation of sonic marvels.

"A feeling of warmth overcomes my every change in position from one point to another as though every movement were processing a sequence whose development was composing a specific musical course. Comfort, affection, tenderness, and love—all surround me like calves around a female deer. I am an animal, feeling even my mother's craving for more food. Each sound and feeling thoroughly feeds me. From the creation of each organ and system within me to their neophyte functioning, I am growing, attached to this 'foreign' body, which envelops me. It speaks the same yet a slightly, lightly different tongue than I. Its complexity baffles, awes, marvelously calls on me to begin making someone of myself, again and again, to no less than a singular end.

"Words have no meaning here, save the significance of sound itself. What passes for 'Ubucatoba' here could as well be called the king and queen of feelings, or love, elsewhere. If I hear my name, the one others have designated to be mine, I am at first indifferent in the face and on the surface of it. My ears help me to recognize myself in other ways. They transform all this commotion into a type of symphony, serenade, divertimento, or divertissement. Or perhaps they resemble more of a variation on the theme of growth, a development. I don't rightly know.

"They tell me I am swimming. They let me grasp, to the degree I am able, that I am floating, bathing, immersed in becoming myself. I have no doubt, no reason to doubt, who I am since the sound appears as an echo of my greater self. I am without interruption on my way somewhere. I am a pale reflection of the Red Balloon, either leading or following a silent adventure of the artful spirit ascending, front and center, to civilization's illuminating backdrop.

"I am suffused in the tides of increase, from a simple to a complex form. I have no healing to do since any injury to my organism restores itself, making me whole and sound. I am sinless, anxiety-free, constituted with all of nature's most perfected laws and amendment-free. Perfecting my constitution means caring for my good health and well-being once and for all.

"Nature seems to foresee imperfections and thus the need to make amends. It is reasonable and plausible to try enclosing all constitutions in some kind of framework, given there are more of those beings out there who exhibit imperfections than I, who am here perfecting myself.

"Nature is a perfection of imperfections, a purification of impurities, a transmogrification of nothingness turning into even the most minute living development of a system of systems, no less than a symphony that fantasizes silence where and when organic ensembles of instruments realize their full potentialities, all at once and as one. The body knows this better than any. Writers may have the first and last word, speakers the lasting sound of music, but the body comes first, this side of truth. If beauty is by its side, it is because it comes before beauty, in the design and order of protoplasm.

"I am a prototype of myself here. I am a microcosm of someone whose time alone on earth will be told in view of a macrocosm to which I will correspond in varying degrees, namely, in my future self. I'm curious to know how much of me outside of here will remember and take into account all that I feel, hear, and smell at present. Since I don't really seem to use taste here, perhaps I may safely conclude it develops along the lines and contours of art. For 'taste' is—as a category—less of a general, one-time construct *per se*, but rather a perpetual, ostensibly acquired refinement (not as much of organs as of organisms), functioning within the realm of an aesthetic. It is found and enhanced there, beyond the strict minimum of these parts, wherein a whole life takes sustenance from an ever-growing inner life 'outside' the body. Taste becomes more of a 'second-degree' sense. Adults ingest entire milieus and contexts, wrapped up in the taste of this or that quality or quantity of food, for example. It appears as though taste is acquired to guard both body and soul against malignancies such as poison or vice. My guess is that all creatures like me, at this point, 'taste' more of the same as others. Whereas they might perceive, through the remaining senses, a world of difference—beginning with hearing no less than feeling—in the earliest days and nights in here.

"I say this, seemingly, since I am not the prototype of any other here even if others may wish for me to assume the role of another. To vary, I own up to all my actions here since there is nothing artificial, nothing adopted in how I am verily acting here. I am clearly me in all this obscurity, or at least so I feel. I am foreign to nobody here—all having passed through these parts—last of all to myself, this 'me' others may later make speak in alien ways and means

"My body is exploring its potentialities. It's developing as a nation, which would someday remember its whole population as it acts, moves, and decides its own fate. I am whole like entire peoples who dream of finding themselves once they have distanced themselves too far from this place.

"It may come to pass, I imagine. I will have to reconstitute myself in the image I have of myself here in order to remember who I am, in order to be myself once outside of here. I may be asked to represent the best of not just myself, a person, but also a people, or many peoples. To be a representative of any other body, I will have to remember the perfection and perfecting of my own body here. I have to preserve the whole genetic code I am developing, the one I am extending to more than a simple or complex language from generations past.

"The code is to language what the body is to the person. This is a defining moment in my life. In my greater life, the totality of the code, combined with language, will act to condition what I present and represent to others, so I imagine.

"As soon as I betray my code, my way of speaking and viewing the world—my *term for life*—imperfections burgeon, begetting a need for healing. Failure sets in, together with the possibility of ill health. The unexpected enters like a boat into an unknown cove. Here, I get to be what I have to be—wholly myself.

"I am all tension, entirely without pretension. I am denuded of unnatural exaggerations, unless the code conditions some surprise scientists have a hard time predicting.

"I am mildly, sweetly comforted here, as should everyone be, by another's nourishing watch."

What is the artist made of that lesser humans are not? Marcel appeared tucked away in darkness, where science might say he could be found bereft of even rudimentary vestiges of imagination to bear with him a clue that might help answer life's greatest questions. Perhaps he could envision things, expressions of love, the rigor of an aesthetic, long before acceding to the universe. If so, it is possible his intuition could be marked by the moving manifestation of a particular combination of genes. Or it could be his genius would come entirely from a relationship to society, which his parents would help foster from the earliest days. Just what would be his relationship to an artist's entertainment, to art's unique quality that inspires learning, remained to be seen. Perhaps the composition of art arises from the point of view at which a unique vision arrives after having come from another, be that so-called other a person, place, or thing.

It struck Marc as no coincidence that gnomic poetry flourished at the dawn of the modern world. The pithy aphorisms expressed by the seventeenth century, taken with the fundamental principles they brought to bear on their surroundings, showed themselves to be the fruit of divine perspective and maximum intelligence. An eminently evocative name summed up this poetry to Marc's mind. Thus, he thought, "Marcel" would be born into a tradition made less of otherworldly creatures—who, acting as angels, according to Pascal, act like stupid animals—and more of humanists or men and women of letters. And this conception would extend itself from within the womb, without a doubt, to any expression of a person's name, however long, given the nature of that lineage of which he or she will have been composed.

His parents hoped he would end up being a character consociating with his own life or work. They wished for him to have character or *caractère* as La Bruyère understood the term. One such social force struck them as immutable, natural, and all too likely to return galloping if ever stilled. The question of Marcel's first "retreat" from the world and continence begged a response from Goethe's *Tasso* in Marc's mind: "Talent develops itself in retirement; character forms itself in the tumult of the world." Marcel's movement would never tire even if he would find himself, in the literal sense of the word, "retiring" in the womb, as if an integral part of his future were no less than the *passé*.

Both Marc and Cassandre would come to know, from one of his more gifted students, what Jewish mystics instructed followers as to the unity of life, precisely that the divine congeals reality from an invisible perspective. They would further come to understand that the chosen people revered the intangible. In the estimation—understand "esteem"—of Jews worldwide, only "Adonai" (the eternal, ever-being), as a word, is, was, and will be tangible. The French word "Dieu" or the English "God" were not discernable by the touch, in a word, palpable, given they derived their significance from a source external to the sacred Hebrew. But given the nature of this metaphysical geometry of sorts, Jews were not themselves converted into triangles. Only "Adonai," or what they call our God, *Eh-lo-hey-nu*, could assume such a form, as any other moreover. Since the Hebrew believers remained only too human, umbrageous even, they could still have a view of such appraisable, surmised, corporeal—though nearly indivisible—matters from outside the use, indeed, exterior to the system of symbols in other words. The fervor Jews feel for wordless, fundamentally inexplicable, and magical music no doubt has a seat in the pews whose congregation turns, once and for all, toward an absolute reverence of imperceptibility's limit—a unifying silence.

Jews surely believed things as much along the lines of great artists as they did along those of great diplomats: one must lend particular scrutiny to a man's silence and gestures, his movements, often over and above what he says, since a quasi-blind principle of uncertainty governs and ensures the most certain human beings among us. Something about the comity of this sturdy verity prompted a wish for a lemon *soufflé* in Cassandre at this point, causing her to fantasize wistfully about lightly beaten egg yolks.

Principles were made by man and therefore exist to be upheld as much as conveniently let down on occasion. They guide characters no less than the invisible. And their author guides others through an art of laying them out in writing, painting, making music, dance, or other physical manifestations such as constructing buildings and monuments. If all of Judaism could be summed up as the preservation of a single book, however sacred, even two or three significant tomes, and this not without the requisite poetry and music surrounding readings of the text, it is because, unlike Christianity where the word is considered having been made flesh, the word itself is the only tangible effect (manifested in the Torah, Midrash, and Talmud), of all that is made of a divine cause.

This basically ethical and physical composition doubles the full weight of history, culture, and art on the Jew as a potent form of ontogeny with which each of us—first unborn, then alive—must more or less reckon. On the one hand, while a person may believe in this or that God, such faith is totally bereft of any proof derived from the senses. On the other hand, faith in others—in people, speaking simply—passes necessarily through various discernable manifestations of phenomena. It appears true that truth may be sensed as sound—just as beauty with art, just as virtue with music, just as silence with refrained serenity—by a human being. For all these human forms may provide the basis for a thoroughly meaningful life and a perfected heart, where gods alone once acted as both master and servant to that dominion. Once sensitized to the art of letters, to the word and promise of language or literature, a child's guarantor of goodness and light could prove to be, from the inception, the most truthful as well as the brightest antecedent of his or her name. In this, the most prescient of precedents, Marcel would be no exception. His universe would come to be born from his sense of things gathered, thanks to a razor-sharp remembrance—beyond partitions common to the mind, body, spirit, and soul—in this world.

Marc and Cassandre made what figured to them as an honest living based on ethical, even more than moral, life. Philosophy, science, and art informed their research in the domain of books. They lived in an age that valued thought over words' traditional agency. Marc's efficacy saw to a restoration and scaffolding of phonemes as well as morphemes, however. His primary gift was to give the simple pleasure of reading to his students. Cassandre ensured the place of books in the lives of truth's disciples by taking stock in the library and preserving a sense of order on or around the shelves.

Marc relied on books—reading and writing—to disperse and dispel the hoard of banalities, abstractions, family trivialities, and commonplace realities cluttering his mind. They filter the everyday cru, retaining only the richest bouquet of musts and lees. In books, the reader and writer felt he could pass unnoticed or at least, as he was, without the worldly trappings of manifold roles.

While Marc understood religions in both absolute and comparative terms, he read texts as vast surfaces animated by characters, mythical or other, coupled with action. In some settings, decor or descriptive phrases took precedence over psychological insights in his eyes. In others, development of a thrilling plot captured the attention of the reader who traverses various moral tensions or dilemmas, on the surface at least, until some type of crescendo and resolution occurs. In most every Hamlet of the world, he believed science has usurped nature's power, replacing divine fatality with the story of a conscience whose liberty gives rise to the pursuit of freedom from tyranny's injustice. Poisoned by the tense totality of a hero's destiny, a Renaissance prince of Denmark seems to have announced the twentieth-century poet's summary verse: "Discipline, you bleed!"

Both the librarian and professor had their doubts about the ability of a school to teach writing since they held the belief, albeit unspoken, that writing was nurtured by the style one brings to bear on existence. "We live poetically," Cassandre liked to say to those who could not quite seize the reason, the fundamental, driving worldview behind the fact that they lived within their means. They made do with daily existence by walking to the bakery together, whistling coffee in various cafés, staying current with the affairs of friends, incorporating the framed contents of museums into their lives, learning foreign languages without recoil, and bicycling throughout both their region and Europe.

They saw themselves as anything but bookish. This allowed them to perceive which character in this or that artsy novel was as mythomaniac as the variety of storytelling they read in the works, the words, the world of yet another of Marc's former students, Etienne Montalban. It is one thing to produce mythopoetics *en connaissance de cause* in full knowledge; it is quite another to be religiously tied up like a *legato* or *legere*, "ligated" to the story beginning with one's existence.

Etienne wrote, once he had left Marc's tutelage, a work of fiction titled *Inside/Outside* in which, ultimately, there was never made to appear any outside world since the main character was all spirit or mind. Etienne had given him the name of Dr. Rémy Villedieu and the role of a professor of theology. Le Figaro's review cast him as an absentminded professor whose brilliance had inherited the infamous *je ne sais quoi* of the French academy's patrimony. Marc preferred to view his character as present-minded, only elsewhere. The distinction lay in an opening to the world that Marc could never quite communicate to his student, one which made ever more room for both what is without (as opposed to within) and nature surrounding any absence.

Yes, he sensed the mounting role played by analysis and spiritualism of various sorts from the end of the nineteenth century to the present. He noticed the concurrent recession of the sacred realm. He believed, for example, canonizations and "heroizations" would increasingly occur in more timely fashion—when and where the miracle of fiction joins the fiction of miracles—given people participate less fully in the sacred world, thus leaving them bereaving for anything resembling a religious way of life, a habit whose flock and frock bear the signs of some sanctity. Marc anticipated that more and more standing ovations would overtake both concert halls and opera houses alike, leaving the astute admirer to an obstructed view of the stage, that secular pulpit rendered invisible from the point of view—no less satisfying—attended to and appreciated at the seat of bewildering art. An accelerating secularization of things and ideas makes some crave a whole host of realities other than those swallowed in more or less communing with the profane world. An everyday man would soon enough be made to extinguish his banal role of putting out fires in favor of some burning radiance of the Savior.

Nevertheless, Marc believed in the fundamental, evocative power of the ineffable, the invisible, unspoken, and unspeaking natural world all around. This is why he taught language and literature like a first-time "ligion," a process like a *legato*, linking a general education to furthering itself, not one of indoctrination or religious training. In the first instance, he did not seek to "tie up again" a world already past or elsewhere in relation to the myths of religious faith. He scorned the often reactionary needs of organized religions. The ties of religion bind without restraint; they secure false freedoms and girdle the soul. Marc rather wished to begin by having a reader "tie up," make links with one's own past. The next step, once fully accomplished, would be to align one's experience with the present and past in correspondence to a more mythological past. It is central to a modern life to know what role parables, allegories, fables, parody, and satire play in relation to our past, present, and thus, future.

Marc's sense of what's "outside" differed from that adoring Adonai, insofar as the unifying principle did not necessarily have to be one of a principle, even less a single author. His sauntering system need not be applied or even conceived systematically. Were it to articulate itself, his method would be the first to recognize the unique singularity bespeaking a veritable absence of some regular or step-by-step manner of procedure, to acknowledge moreover every absence of knowledge within. His inner life, not to be confused with domestic habits, proved anything but routine.

Hence, Marc's conviction, together with Cassandre's, that the value of a true composition and an authentic work of art could remain priceless. Perhaps memory, more than anything else, would show itself more systematic than the rest, insofar as remembrance breeds with the keystone, the philosopher's stone and touchstones of the soul. Marcel would thus be looking back and mindful of reminiscence itself, not to speak of artistic mementos, at once the culmination of a tradition "put together" in remembering, and the purest expression of its genesis.

"The more my cells develop memory, the more efficient will my systems be. How does my heart remember to beat? Something engages the trigger of neurotransmitters and synapses, which act together to keep my organism in balance with a developing equilibrium. My life span seems codified and etched into a genome. It astonishes the neutral observer that some see these would-be questions scientifically, and others religiously, as if their conceived 'God' were the author of a divine plan. It could be properly religious or simply ethical, for one to fully reckon with another's point of view, however limited that may be. In some measure, a believer's conception of the eternal differs and resembles that of my parents, who wish to see me as eternity's scribe.

"Certain time spans click on, activating the countless manifestations of my genes. My mother's own organism acts to instigate this process of activating gene expression, as if natural and cultural influences were present in her body. After all, there are stimuli and responses I receive from her body. It is as if I am in a 'wet' dry dock, being made into a ship. And Mom is my captain modulating ballast, thereby creating stability in my body and future character. Soon enough, I will be launched from this fair slip where divinity docks inside a not so slender, man-made space."

Beginning in April, Eus slowly warmed under manifold shades of Mediterranean sunlight. Both the country outside—replete with vineyards dating from the time of the Caesars, cultivating grapevines bordered by lanes of plane trees—and, naturally, the inside of the de Beaurecueils' ataractic home, moved from a period of hibernation to germination. No dream, no less than Cassandre's body lain dormant, like partners dancing a *salterello* in sextuple time. Life seemed to leisurely pick up pace as the cusps and foils of foliation's tracery appeared on the branches adjacent to the porch. Plush wisteria draped over a dainty trellis provided the thrice-lauded backdrop for microcosmic bees busying themselves in combing the sugary bunches of light blue segments of nature as if they were Parisians industrializing *l'Ile-de-France* with the macrocosmic ambition of leaving the most gratifying of cultural artifacts and architecture—thereby sweetening daily customs—to posterity's buzz and afterlife. Bright-colored poppies peopled the earth around the Spanish-style walls whereupon twisting and turning woodbine climbed toward the open air. Clusters of white and yellow asphodel covered the more distant parts of the lawn, just as classical legend had overlaid the Elysian fields with this unidentified, pre-Indo-European flower. Sweet-smelling, autogamous stamens pollinated images of other forms, themselves fertilized with fresh emotion, particularly in the foreground of the front and back yards. Birds, echoing music's mime and avian badinage, made the mornings sing in their fanciful flight and perched repose.

Cassandre called Mme Salazar to clean the home, to make her residence into something of an *auberge*—an inn-like refuge even more inviting to her couple, family, and friends—as was the custom once a year. Dust was removed, lifting a particulate matter's clouding of time, from all the nooks and crannies, including the few paintings and pair of *ancien régime*, scarlet suede armchairs they had purchased with their first professional wages. Mme Salazar polished the heavy bird's eye maple commode from Brittany, where the Quimper faience was displayed for an appreciative eye, one that loves both the *grand* and *petit-feu* in these translucent ceramic matters. She restored the shine to the wooden floors, then freeing from dirt door handles, tiles, cupboards, lamps, chairs, and tables alike. The kitchen's newly shining copper pots and pans—lining the shelf next to a flagon, a pewter pitcher, a tankard, jugs, and an earthenware bowl—transmitted a small-scale twinkle to the ductile soul's windows as if they were conducting the same heat as a Chardin interior, all seemingly resistant to any corrosion of wiry, coiled, recoiling time.

Minou, the powdery cat, found a farinaceous mate near the pool of the neighbor's home where their gurgling purr docked by the shallow end, lapping up the water like bloated boats bobbing up and down rhythmically. Friends called a bit more on the telephone then in person to see how winter was treating the mistress of the house. All the while, as anyone could tell, there was no room for idle chatter, chattiness, or inane chitchat in the de Beaurecueil entourage and home life. Birds chirp, frequently shrieking and even squawking, unlike humans who alone are—as if bound to another greater than oneself, outside as inside—uplifted less by wings, more thanks to a solo song or gliding *portamento*. If there ever were a place for any type of that voided conversational variety, it was for handcrafted small talk *par excellence*.

Over the course of the next few days, Marc occupied himself by putting the finishing touches on a lecture he was to give in Montpellier, a formal talk expounding the theme of "Reading and Writing . . . the Empty Novel."

He pondered the possibility of an extended work without plot other than unfolding life, an all too sparse description of space-time developing like a seemingly amorphous symphony dedicated to rendering the sauntering sound of an amoeba's meandering life span. Perhaps these classic components of the traditional novel, he thought, manipulate the reader self-righteously, harping on the senses, especially on feelings or a dull, doltish, pigeonholing imagination. A steady infusion of poetry in writing, as in life, allows for unlimited free-form and organic intrigue to take shape. Characters may thus come and go freely. Said, tried and true art makes of reading and writing a profoundly open-ended arrangement for one and all implicated in the scripted experience, whether any individual or character might be real or fictitious.

The choices of music the couple made moved from the more full-bodied romantics to the more baroque, then on to early classicism. The deft play, alternating between major and minor keys in Reinhardt's work gave way to Tartini, his student Marcello—that "Prince of Music" whose "poetic and harmonious inspiration" made more than a name for himself—Veracini, Nardini, Manfredi, and Cambini. A Mahler's *Adagietto* deferred to a *Concerto Grosso* by Archangelo Corelli, in addition to a concerto for four violins by Vivaldi, Uccellini's Romanesca and a "Symphonia" by Glück's master—Sammartini. Dvořàk reverentially escorted a cello concerto, quintets, and sextets of Boccherini before all these prodigious talents were made to bow before the grandest father, with respect to the muse, following Bach—Haydn.

Each day, by splendid weather, the shutters were opened onto the garden as the promoter or inventor of the quartet and modern symphony played on the hi-fi (an English word which devotees of the gramophone and phonograph have appreciated like none other, a word whose provenance was Anglo-Saxon, as if it signified the prelude to an entire language of long-lasting seduction. The pleasure the audiophile took from this tidbit of foreign lexicon provoked no less a sensation of buoyancy than any of the overtures to *Fidelio* acted as the ever-present aperture, the sign of enduring faith, which preceded the opera of one of Papa Haydn's students and friends. In the notion of fidelity, and its inverse inscribed in the word's relief, the admirer of classicism and the mother of indispensable inventions recollected, huddling around other words, words which lured a requisite sense of humor into communing with the author who wrote of Franz-Joseph's music that it often sounded "like a pretty girl sitting on a lap, with another indifferent girl in the heart").

The philosopher was not alone in his research on faith at this time; Marc too worked, in good faith, on the subject. He held fast to the word deriving its meaning from studied conviction. His sincerity had examined past perfidy, which manifested itself in both those around him, like the coercive Mr. Homais and entire nations provoking the need for a *cordon sanitaire*, countries potentially hostile or ideologically dangerous led by disingenuous men and colonial or imperial nerve. But Marc had no illusion about the nature of language and words. He knew what Pascal and Saint-Exupéry had understood before him about faith, namely, that it lies in the domain of the heart, not reason, and could therefore be made to say anything, circumstances permitting.

To be in a situation, as Sartre, the former *Normalien*, put it, such was the condition determining the nature of faith. Is faith possible or real, and if so, to what extent? Absolute confidence in a being outside oneself, call it god or any other, held little or no sway with the conscientious professor of literature, just as the student of Normale Sup. Either one, to varying degrees, had seen betrayal, fabulous creations and reason denied in the name of faith. Demagogues drank of the neighboring vine at the same time as they intoxicated their subjects in order to manipulate them in some fashionable way. Thinkers of a less-than-inferior ilk witnessed, over time, imbeciles acting as beastly, brutal savages, poisoning other people—to be sure, entire peoples—with a deadly concoction of arrogance, stubbornness, intransigence, deception, lacking education, shortcome knowledge, callowness, and wanton posturing. They represented not only their infertile selves but also most—and worst of all—callous individuals mixed up with political or institutionalized power.

Equipped with a wise sense of humor, Marc could crackle inside as he chuckled nervously at such pathetic silliness. Once he seemed to crunch, crump, and crumple when confronted with the crude hot air of those can-do solutionists whose crinkled faces almost creak behind their sweet, crusading, unconscious smiles—those facades of bitter justice invariably dissolving into no less than a mouthful of thin air like the sweet tooth whose calculating bite crushes to smithereens the kind of hard candy flavored, as a crutch of physical pleasure, by the elderly. At space-times such as these, the professor was all too capable of muting ludicrousness, most especially by lavishing sardonic rumination upon none other than himself.

Nearly emptied of doubt, Marc remembered the deception of a young student from Poland who attended his course on poetry. She went on from the university to École Normale Supérieure where and when she became, by virtue of scholastic cross-pollination, best of friends with a likely prime minister of France, the prince of Machiavelli's Paris, whose authoritative future was not simply academic. And yet, albeit of good faith, indeed, tender herself, and due to a complicated course of events, the fair-skinned Ariana Kaplanski fell out of favor with the most gifted of likeably Jesuitical students she frequented at the École (said normal and superior) of more than just Sartre.

Marc recollected, sometimes in dilatory fashion. One day, Ariana's rabbi invited her—so she said—to attend a performance of Bach's B Minor Mass in a small but stately church, honoring Saint Anne, near the heart of Cracow. The proper noun itself of this town reminded Marc of the suffix *cracy* signifying *government*. And this insight heightened the pleasure of listening ponderously to Ariana's story, just the opposite of a disagreeable *diminuendo*. What's more, Marc remembered Ariana having confided her predilection for a single book she considered more than any other relevant to an exalted life—the dictionary. To her pleasant way of thinking, words determine knowledge well beyond what names and physiognomies do for personalities. It was this young language student who once proffered, with an almost-lilting brogue whose accent was, at this point and on this particular subject, for the ear—the heart—of the trained interlocutor, reminiscent of a Scot speaking in a foreign tongue: "A word is not a word until it means something to you. Until a word bears with it some meaning or significance other than sound, it is, at one end, but noise or, at the other, music." Marc sensed the methodical young person from a distant, self-studied land—in many ways akin to an agreeably attuned stranger, one in touch with investigating natural phenomena—was capable of talking or conceptualizing, at least sounding like, a scientist interested in defining moments without procrastination.

According to Ariana then, when the rabbi, an elderly gentleman of ninety years with a denudate head, heard the first bars of Bach's masterpiece through an ear trumpet, his body was set in motion, tingling as if he were a living being or elfin creation three, nearly four, generations younger. He nearly seemed to be on the verge of salivating as if his soul were adhering to the envelopment of a sole, variable, mucilaginous sound. He had grown up listening to this ensemble of compendious sensations, and he found them exalting like none other, Messiah included. As a result, his memory seemed to have control of his muscles' movement more than any socialized training geared to control impulses of various orders.

If in his frailty one could make out some obsequiousness, it merely submitted the attentive, obedient subject to the emission of a higher power or ambient voltage. It was as if an all-encompassing verb was conjugated before the altar of meaning, amplifying the rabbi's belief in truth, beauty, goodness, and unity. He appeared to experience this issuance of music's pinnacles, notwithstanding its valleys plainly lower, as fundamentalists who stake palpable claims on some inexplicable interaction with their God. The difference between the two, however—the play—purified Ariana's thought: What the Jewish teacher really meant by his body language, nearly independent of himself, as with his body of teachings, was the same as certain others who most assuredly believe in something like the possibility of a faith. His amounted to a credo of no less than uncertainty, doubt, ambiguity, chance, coincidence, intangibles, serendipity, timing, and spacing.

In simple terms, the rabbi was animated by tunes, tones, and assorted curios—which are to the *bric-a-brac* of the mind, what *tchotchkes* are to the antique store of a Jewish way of life. He would be the first to confess, cantillating, if he could never perceive the eternal, his calling referred to as God, he could nevertheless intuit and fully sense divinity—to the point such matters may ever be fathomable—in the most highly artistic traces of mindful hearts and spiritual souls set in various times. While he perceived Bach with a vibrant sense of *déjà vu*, one could deduce no less of the *presque-vu* in the more eternal *jamais-vu*. It appeared as if a demigod had spoken akin to the chief of a music-based, aboriginal, autochthonous tribe in a faith-filled idiom intelligible to the careening masses.

Musical profundity, color, diatonic variation, harmonizing of various melodic lines, even something of the precursor to dramatic contrasts that defined classicism to a degree, all came together in Bach's *magnum opus*. Fugal phrasings and themes were delivered here in biblical proportions. Ariana liked to think that the rabbi's stout preference for the baroque lay not only in a sense of order it lent the observant man of faith but also in a sense whose crescendo was not reached toward the end of the work, but rather little by little, here and there, throughout the grand masterpiece. Flourishes abounded in the mass as they teemed in her conversations with this spiritual leader of Jews. Both men congregated around daring and inventing new forms of study coupled with experimentation. For having followed Marc's propos closely, Ariana challenged the rabbi after the concert by inquiring as to why, if a Lutheran could create such beauty in the name of Catholicism, why then would he himself not consider attempting to prove the efficacy of something similarly untried, in word and in deed, examining the validity of an epistemological hypothesis good enough for the former—converting? The rabbi's response proved as swift as decisive—he retorted half ill-temperedly, half sardonically, and wholeheartedly—"I prefer, rather than passing through the secretary, going directly to the boss!"

He later explained that humans do not need another to atone for their own sins. Living with oneself is one's own responsibility, one's own account of the world we inhabit. To be truthful, he added, to paint a fuller picture of a human idea, "I am not even sure religions do well to teach redemption based on notions of sin." Children, entirely innocent in every other respect, surely understand sin as something they have inherited like prejudice.

Marc's interpretation of this drew its strength from a wisdom he had nourished as he would find himself listening to students, witnessing the action of men as measured against the promise they hold out for others. Marc had studied the same philosophers as Cassandre's professors at l'Ecole des Chartes and had arrived at similar conclusions to those they transmitted to his wife: no one, apart from oneself, should be trusted in the end. Hypocrisy literally means to be below the crisis. Marc and Cassandre viewed the world with this grain of marine salt in mind. Each of us is, as Pascal writes, nothing but a speck of sand in a vast universe that likely has an inconceivable circumference.

Ariana was thus well trained in the ways of those who believed in a history rather in an ever-evolving story of godliness more than in a reverence for piety itself. She had once found the definition of hypocrisy as "the homage vice renders to virtue" in her favorite dictionary whose editors she felt compelled to write since they had misappropriated the author of this maxim, attributing it to Voltaire when she knew pertinently La Rochefoucauld had written it first. As much as she loved their work, both on defining words and filling out proper nouns, even they, erudite and amiable, sought to justify their error in a short reply.

Marc learned as much from listening to his students' stories as he did from other disciples of Dante and Balzac: Nothing was absolute as sure as nothing is absolute; of this, both de Beaurecueils were certain. Not even our self or being is perfect, unadulterated, and complete. At the limit, what a European author wrote seemed to define the inherent nature of and propensity for hypocrisy: "I have nothing in common with myself." Of this, they would even be made to speak when the heady provocateur Harvey would come to visit this region, these parts he would first see as so foreign to his own native ways.

Everything moves, however minutely, as sure as static itself manifests the frequency of a vibration. Witness, in times of crisis, science, if not its leading proponents, resorting to principles to decipher and rationalize the universe. Science is not simply observation inaugurating absolutes; it is theory combined with facts and thus subject to be revealed as much in human reason as in human error. It is sufficient, since so frequent, to note that economists approach this no differently than scientists set back during similar cataclysms. The aforementioned men of numbers surrounding, and surrounded by politicians, most often painfully evoke, again and again, moral principles as if they had disappeared until the fateful or inexplicable day defining the crisis. In any land promoting the lure of unlimited opportunity, there where the bawdry and tawdry often lie side by side, vastly disproportionate wealth takes hold, ushering in, by strong-arming, a plethora of moralities and, in asymmetrical, converse proportion, a dearth of ethics. It is in the stasis of real, inviolable principles that art's dynamism makes manifest the beauty of design, order, and even profound disorder. Marc believed we should look to literary scientists, great authors, and artists as true leaders, leaders who could rightfully displace politicians' exaggerated discourse insofar as thinking stylists of reality rule their lives according to principles and aesthetics any human being may follow, beginning with the tiniest among us.

Man hardly knows the limits of his creation even if exist some fortune, indeed a chance, for those who do know them for and in themselves, to create works or goods that beautify existence like none other on earth.

"It is quiet in here. It makes me think and allows me to reflect or meditate. *Maman's* is a timely vigilance. Hers is a *piqué* stitch in the fabric of my existence as tolerant and patient as the most refined of seamstresses. She sees to my every need, and this without even looking: the organism, if not the imagination, listens and keeps watch in the dark! She oversees all things, beneficently. I see why they call her Mother Nature (*La Nature*).

"With her here, I can take all the time in the world, within reason. The reproductive system has a logic I must follow. The womb has its reasons the esprit, perhaps unlike the mind, will never know. A certain time frame is imposed for my stay here like form inside of which classicism suckled. To begin with here, as in the very nature of life itself, my sojourn in these parts is not open-ended.

"The end—emerging to live a good and natural and loving and full life—explains all the varied systems my body and mind have the means to develop here. The means justify the end and vice versa. The meaning of life will issue as I come to understand the adaptability of these various systems of organic thought in relation to a greater nature: I wonder what I will be able to *digest* in life, for example. I await the culture and agriculture I will be in a position to metabolize. To some extent, I will be able to filter noise so as to perceive sound as I do here midst the roaring, spluttering, and hissing.

"Reason is what gives me this conscience. It is what permits me to know I will live and die. It is what differentiates me from other forms of life like the cow, which only ruminates."

Marcel moved again, painstakingly, on his own, just as Cassandre was beginning her siesta. Strange as it may sound, she was now doing everything in her grasp to encourage this form of independence. As he had everything needed within her, she was bent on supplementing that exigency with nothing more than what she felt he required. She also considered deeply and without exaggeration what he could possibly want. This did not mean initiating some false regime fashion would have her undertake. Her life already included music, healthy food, balanced thought, and dreams akin to those found besprent over centuries of unmatched literature. In view of this equilibrium, it is perhaps not too surprising that she never vomited during the early pregnancy even if she would come to urinate with greater frequency and less regularity. Her mind and body were regulated by her esprit, poised in a state that lay, besprinkled here and there with the soothing waters of quietude, betwixt extremes of any kind.

She would add any number of dimensions to Marcel's life once he would appear, outside. She would oversee without overlooking what he would truly *need* in order to fully assume his destiny. She and Marc appeared to want urgently to exaggerate the importance of literature and reading, to offer the vital illusions of art and music in order for him to gain full access to the society of his choice.

To reply to such self-imposed imperatives, they did not believe in overextending themselves in any domain. Paradoxically, coaching Marcel to be a writer would be, in a sense, furthest from their minds, as if it would overtly, indeed, overly bewray their ambition, thus appearing too muscular an approach in the hearts and minds of the future tutors.

As Cassandre dozed, she thought of how antiquated the French public education appeared and yet how efficient it was for achieving its ends through humane means at every turn. Overstatement, inflation, self-aggrandizement, and apostrophes of all sorts were discouraged as a matter of course. Humility, on the other hand, mixed with self-awareness and knowing one's limits, led French schoolchildren to accomplishments, big and small. Industry encouraged the very nature from which this approach to life arose and flowered by developing on a human scale. A product's dimension was, for example, no more to begin with "king size," only to increase from there, than people shopped at "super"-*marchés*. What was later termed *ultra*, *mega*, *hyper*, and the like derived from and conjugated America—perhaps, as its citizens advertise, "land of the brave," most assuredly home of the skyscraper—not France of the de Beaurecueils' days. By virtue of art and poetic fiat, fiduciary zealots of industrial econometrics, economic anarchy, jingoistic foreign policy, and savvier-than-thou marketing could be held, on balance, in check. Perhaps the pilgrims to the ways and means of retail therapy could be guided as visitors humanized by the awe seen in and around a unique City of Lights, one whose pretension to reach the heavens limits our overall view from its mansard to no more, or less, than seven nearly identical stories, stories whose veritable variability and fluctuation lie uniformly beneath the modest skyline, in a word—to be precise—within.

The bedroom she shared with Marc was barely large enough for a queen-size bed and a modest chest of drawers. It appeared denuded of any ornament save the simplest of Catalan style. The crown moldings—embellishing in strip form the very surface of simplicity—were in a dark wood, perhaps mahogany, as were the frames of a few photos from their prenuptial days that hung on the wall adjacent to the nondescript window. A gold bedspread lay over the mattress. Cassandre covered herself that day with an alpaca blanket that a friend, whom she had known since the age of three, Isabelle Duplessis, had given her. She felt a special fondness for the blanket, with its expected touch of pastel pink and powder blue, its light yellow, chartreuse, turquoise, mauve, and *soupçon* of navy, all the while envisioning the day when she could use it to cover her newborn while taking him on walks in an old-fashioned stroller. To judge from just how it draped and dropped over the carriage, it seemed to smell of mother's milk.

As she lay there serenely, Cassandre listened to the wind rustle the English-garden hedge just outside the shutters, with a wisp of birds here and a fleeting wish for integrated happiness there. She felt the urge to be at once as calm as possible in order to sense her developing child and as though a hike up the nearby Canigou would fortify her already poised morale. She could see, from where she was lying, the peak of the mountain in the distance. It conjured memories of the most recent winter when the snow atop the hill caused her thoughts to turn to the entire chain of Les Pyrénées and the many times she had traversed them to enter Spain at various points. She found herself at peace with the image before her, as if she were admiring la Montagne Sainte-Victoire painted by Desforges. This was one of the earliest recollections she had of great art; and, as with all such matters, aging only acted to enhance, maintain, and improve the pleasure of those reveries touching upon subjects that had become as many sacred guarantors for her imagination just as a pince-nez ameliorates vision. The promise of the future may amount to a declaration of coming excellence, success anticipated if enhanced, by loyalty and devotion to a beautiful past.

Mr. de Beaurecueil too had works of art of whose high-water mark he was particularly fond even if he rarely spoke of them. Existence was supplemented, to his way of thinking, by the Reinhardt's violin concerto. And while he had his favorite, personalized interpretations of this particular romantic's repertoire—those most sonorously individualized and purely musical of Thibaud, Heifetz, Rabinof, Kreisler, Szigeti, Suk, Oistrach, Schneider, a mature Milstein, a self-assured Stern, a polished Szeryng, and in some more pronounced ways, Francescati's human warmth and accented fire among them—he distinguished the sensory stimulation of the Mediterranean artist (who interpreted a work through multiple representations of the same object, say la Montagne Sainte-Victoire), and a given composer (who needed the likes of Tost, Clement, David, Joachim, Ysaïe, or those who followed in order to represent his craft). Unlike the drafter of music, a painter like Monet represents his own perception *ad libitum*, together with that of any potential witness to his art, and this, without any interpretation or reading and elaboration of another interposed, in the free desire he portrays in his various *Notre Dame de Rouen* or *Haystacks*. Music requires a third party, "drafting" behind the original creator's *obbligato*, if the audience is to seize on the fullness of a form's intent or spirit what should not be left out. Art, by contrast, reveals itself immediately once painted, sculpted, or designed and engineered by architects. The latter, like a dancer who has internalized the music at the source of his or her movement, displays a form more self-contained in a sense while the former touches upon the very nature of later concerti, which literally means "to vie against the ensemble," one, then another, against all, not unlike Marcel at this point, expressing the miracle of a genetic code—scripted entirely in relation to the various organs of his mother. A kind of aggressiveness was thus endemic to the concerto, particularly the romantic one, or so found it the reader of texts as there would prove to be a bold and enterprising form of hostility in the newborn seeking everything necessary for his own form of expressing himself, yes, his typical way of living before the extended period of learning about getting along with others, which molds and casts life.

The knowledge of these varying art forms, ingested by an audience in light of the self that created them, comforted Cassandre at present; for she had come to learning her husband's view the day he made note of it to Ariana so that his student might come to know the nature of indigenous aggression, discordant rabble-rousers who litter the globe with rubbish and rubble or slatternly selfishness versus that which is cultivated, rightly, or errantly. For this, he would delineate the nature of true aggression by citing Giraudoux's words, stating, "The first casualty of war is truth." He would pose the same brutally honest, sere, and sincere question as Freud, together with Einstein, as a type of *poste restante* left, in perpetuity, in the name of any local or global inhabitant of this world—"Why War?"

As for peacetime soundness, endemic to positively aggressive playing is an absence of falsehood. Passivity neighbors this verisimilar truth.

Cassandre basked then in the warming presence of a silence augmented by the breeze and tempered, late-afternoon, lemon-butter light. Soon, she would rise to cook what would amount to a moveable feast, a *sacrum convivium.* Following the *amuse-bouche*, which represents the benefit of being ingested without a sign of any bite mark, she planned on serving the *escalibade* she had begun to marinate three days before, together with pan-seared veal in a bouillon reduction and red potato puree streaked with celery. An *escarole* and lambs' lettuce (*mâche*) salad with bits of pancetta, garlic-sautéed croutons, and pine nuts would follow. This *plat principal* and greens from the garden would lead to an assortment of cheeses—including a mild Cantal, some Époisse, and a Morbier—her sister had brought from *le Jura*. The whole meal would begin, once the finger food would have tickled her guest's appetites, with a small portion of a *Coque*, that savory Catalan tart Mr. Aragon made so well just down the road. This would amount to little expenditure of her energies since the meal's composition figured among the simpler ones, especially given that Marc was, as he said, *plus fromage que* dessert (more inclined to cheese than dessert) and thus more favorable to ending his repast with a fresh apricot or berries from the woods. So in light of the fact she was not yet *entre la poire et le fromage* (literally "between the pear and the cheese") at the meal's end, not even thus far in the kitchen, Cassandre profited from a few more minutes of peace and quiet. Only when she would rise would Marc too extend his legs to the hi-fi and turn on the Haydn violin concerto he had been contemplating.

Ariana was coming for dinner, and Marc found himself arranging a few thoughts with respect to the great classical composer's comments pertaining to the five Mozart concerti for violin. The master was overheard having uttered some cavalier bruit that he would have no more to teach his pupil and peer; therefore, he himself would abandon that particular genre, leaving any perception of a din for music's grandest protégé and prodigal son to hush *summa cum laude*.

Marc generously found in Ariana's French language spontaneous flourishes, polite ornamentation of oozing thought, ideas that interwove themselves like a trill around what is called in his Gallic tongue the violin's arc and soul. He wished to communicate this to his student with a strict minimum of words and no feigned wisdom or clamor whatsoever; in light of this purpose, the incomparable Viennese master, or perhaps a few of his antecedents, liberated the necessary terrain for both the generation immediately following him and those to come up and down from the centuries. He was a singular founding father, though not without significant musical ancestry, at the genesis of any grand subsequent "creation" in such a way, Marc believed. The appreciative ear could exploit what amounted to an unleashed, indeed unleashing beauty, in the best of senses. He felt both taste and reason would sense the luminous delights animating "Happy Slaves" like Juan Arriaga who, similar to many with the explosive constraint of spellbinding compositional bonds, graced the earth all too briefly, mastered, if not bettered, solely by death. Thought, as the astute listener saw it, presents basic freedoms as commitment to music does for the ear. Both good reason and the tasteful museum of melody ease, relieve, and soothe one's conscience.

It followed then that no one should either interrupt a work written as a play of sounds or a man in his train of thought, thought manifested by either silence or verbal equation. The question, "What are you thinking?" to Marcel's future father—as to those who came within the earshot of his speech or the reach of his writing on the subject in the final analysis—amounted to nothing more than an indiscretion, an intrusion, a misleading semblance of the greater question of solitude.

And Marc did not figure alone in this belief; Cassandre followed admirably most every nuance of the fundamental principle by which she herself currently enjoyed her rest and isolation (what is the same word as *insulation* in more than just French), *l'isolement* from the world, Marcel not far behind, or up ahead.

Nor were the de Beaurecueils isolated or desolate as a couple. They enjoyed the good graces of several ménages whose education resembled theirs. Although they counted a limited number of intimate friends among their inner circle, those among them tended to be teachers or professors and artists. Indeed, their immediate neighbors to the north, M. and Mme Pinlou, often shared an *apéritif* on the terrace overlooking the de Beaurecueils' pool when the weather was more clement and the days less temperamentally long.

Robert Pinlou specialized in eighteenth-century literature at the university, and Marc occasioned lengthy discussions dealing with the full deck of

Rousseau, Chateaubriand, and Goethe. Professor Pinlou's research touched more directly on the scabrous Crébillon fils and provocatively salacious yet proper Montesquieu. He was not unlike Marc whom he never found lacking either deep or broad insight in even the most narrow of fields related to the Enlightenment. His interest in literature *per se* did in no way surpass Marc's; but then again, on the other hand, it did not include the philosophical, more particularly phenomenological, inquiries of the latter, or was his devotion to music as all-encompassing as that which played such a deep-seated part in the de Beaurecueils' home and *Weltanschauung*.

On the contrary, Mr. Pinlou, who, every now and then, could catch furious fire from a white-hot temper, took keenly to questions of "consensus reality" and politics. He catered to scrutinizing adversity in literature, having myriad successes in writing with special focus on characters whose adversaries enhanced their most distinguished features by the simple fact of overcoming obstacles of different orders. At the root of his preoccupations and the confident expertise he shared somewhat more passively with Marc figured a profound concern for the future of literature, which seemed too often oriented to arrive, both from and at either one of two perspectives—reality or history. The social satire, combined with the style of *les Lettres persanes*, for example, brought Robert to the conclusion that modern writing and commentary carries with it shortcomings in the domain of eloquence and taste since the reference for any reflection is viewed overly directly. Flaubert should have rightly been counted, in his eyes, as one of the last defenders, with the *style indirect libre*, of a reality-based art that succeeds in escaping a certain solidification or ossification through art and by way of the memory that fashions it. This seemed as sure to Robert as Emma Bovary's dreams structure every word of a great author within the novel that bears her name.

Art facilitates participation in reality as the tree-lined *traverses* surrounding Eus joined particular homes to the world beyond. Artistic virtualities and actualities move with the wind like a sedating hush, and when moving into a headwind, art's potentialities provide relief from stentorian airs, whether they originate in someone's garish, loud, and insistent culture like that of the fatuous, uppity Mr. Homais or in nature herself.

"I am whole here, as a good character in some novel or unfolding book. While I depend on someone else for survival, I am able to make believe I live alone here. My ties to the outside world bear the mark of a strict minimum of needs.

"I don't know the difference between good or bad, god or evil devils. Ethical systems remain unknown, foreign to me. I am eager to explore and discover them, like everything else. As sure as my extremities will disclose themselves, beginning to take in the world following the revelation of my mouth with the nipple, I will soon commence to embrace all things, this side of my limits.

"A look of cleverness is already within me, one that turns to a look of cheaters and tricksters alike, depending on their acts.

"I could as easily grasp action consistent with art as with life in general, and this according to those circumstances in which I will find myself immersed. Place me in a home which values *x*; I will come to know and perhaps subscribe to *x*. The same is true of *y*. This is the greater context, the subtext of what is meant by learning one's ABCs. Numbers can be counted, in this sense, with little difference.

"Lend me the good fortune of landing in a home where art is served like the *plat du jour*, and I will be sustained, in truth, by beauty promoting the development of life's most vital lessons.

"Let me first appear, then live, or develop in a culture as elegantly poised as that of the French, and my chances for supplying with necessities or prolonging a valuable life will be increased by the multitudes surrounding me with a similar sense of refined truth and beauty.

"If I have specifically spoken French here, it is just by chance and great good fortune!"

Ariana was due to show up shortly. Marc went into the bedroom to kiss Cassandre on the forehead and ask her if he could invite the Pinlous for a drink with his student since Ariana held out the fervent hope of becoming a teacher. Cassandre shivered as he touched her. She agreed with far more than her beautifully bulging body the idea was worthy, and so Marc telephoned the neighbors at once from his bureau. Robert answered and agreed without hesitation, especially since, he added, "the evening promises to be altogether mild and pleasant." Marc asked Cassandre to know whether he might have time to listen to a Beethoven sonata since he was interested in how the exuberant English Jew Yehudi Menuhin followed the lines for the violin of another great virtuoso, Rudolphe Kreutzer. She replied, "Yes, of course!"; she would listen, axiomatically, from a distance, to what emotions were sewn with beautified elegance, if not graceful eloquence, by the articulate, interweaving piano and violin that bears the connoisseur's name.

Within less than an hour then, Cassandre found herself putting the finishing touches on the salad as both Ariana and the Pinlous knocked on the door at the same time. Curiously, the "Entrance of the Guests," from the opera *Tannhäuser*, was now playing solemnly in the background, thus ferrying to the fore voices singing as if their lives were clinging to a last breath of air, voices shuttling the troubadours to the bars of a mythic though modern poetry. There was little need to introduce further those Marc saw as visiting dignitaries, keys still dangling in their hands. Their acquaintance had already been made outside. The master of the house simply added, for the enticing consumption of the young student, that Mr. Pinlou taught a subject already quite dear to her heart, indeed, her entire being.

Upon hearing this, Ariana's face, whose high cheeks, Slavic, aquiline nose, and rounded chin that seemed born in a medieval Eastern-European Madonna, radiated with understandable pleasure. While she found a number of questions rising spontaneously to the surface of her attention, she politely withheld all of them until such time as they were sitting in the living room.

This did not keep her from asking whether she could help Cassandre in the kitchen. "Everything is prepared," Mme de Beaurecueil replied. "Let's sit and talk. Marc," she added, finding herself in the act of prompting her husband, "what might you offer us to drink?"

"What do you desire?" Marc bade the enjoined, using a formula he had once heard posed by a stewardess on board one of the initial Air France flights to Morocco. Ariana opted for the same as the hostess, an aged Banyuls port. This hint of good taste married a thought which had just occurred to Marc: the host would spontaneously lavish some of the couple's finest fruit of the vine on their scholarly guests like the great medieval tapestry in the Musée de Cluny gives forth unstinting delight for those devoted to their *seul désir* (sole desire).

For the moment, Ariana treasured the bejeweled experience of sharing this smoky Mediterranean wine with the de Beaurecueils since it was Marc who first introduced her to the sculpture of Maillol. As she sat attentively next to Robert and Catherine Pinlou, whose penchant for cooked wine was only exceeded by that of a good Paddy whisky on the rocks, she admired the painting of the elephant, book, and letter opener that hung next to the hi-fi. She recalled the distinction Marc had made in class between Maillol's sculpture where women appeared as robust creatures with large mature hips and adolescent breasts and the artist's painting where the same subject figured in much thinner form. She seized the occasion to venture a question about this: "Mr. de Beaurecueil, did Renoir not fully understand the two media as Maillol's work elaborates this difference?"

Marc saw the development of art of this nature, from beyond Rubens to the present, as culminating with the neoclassicism of the Catalan-turned-Parisian. But the interlocution begged no less than one other response, and that pertained to the different roles women present to both themselves and artists.

Ariana appeared fascinated by this idea that the same subject, say women, in the hands and eyes, indeed the attentive ear of a creator, could be handled or molded diversely. And the fact that this creation could impact the women formed by the experience, by uniting them with the artist, where not art in and of itself, captivated the young student's attention to no end. Because of her solid grounding in Polish culture, combined with a hesitant politeness, Ariana found herself wanting to refer to paintings of less representational, more abstract figures of women like those Marc had brought up in a class on Ernst or Tanguy, his *spécialité*; but instead of vetting her stimulated curiosity higgledy-piggledy, she contented herself with a minor voice in the conversation, read a major wish to pursue further study of the distinctions Marc was accustomed to making—not any old how. She fell upon the piercing intuition, at this point, that learning in particular and questioning in general are similar to religion in that they reveal just how impossible knowing with certainty is. Doubt in these matters is not dubious, she thought.

In the meantime, Robert could not help but ask himself whether Marc's pupil had the makings of a teacher, an artist, or both. So after accepting an invitation to stay for dinner and as they moved to the dining room table, he asked her.

She appeared stunned by the suggestion, for never had she imagined that it was within her power to create a work of art. "Does it not require talent to create?"

Cassandre suddenly felt compelled to announce the creation that lie within her as if to point up and out that the very notion of what constituted creation was a question for each of us to pose anew.

Once everyone had congratulated the expectant mother with heartfelt joy and hearty restraint, given how early still it was in the pregnancy, Marc deferred to those mystics who believe that each of our existences acts to begin the world again, as if we are all enceinte—with meaning and meaningfulness's progeny—by our very nature of simply being. Life's studious host also played two short pieces, one by Saint-Colombe, the other by Marin Marais, to illustrate how an abiding student may come to assimilate not just the whistling artistry of a true master but also—indeed "The Bells of Sainte-Geneviève," so conducive, with their driving appeal—to learning.

Talent for the master was not central; what was necessary for creating a work of art could be acquired. What was ineluctable—yes, indispensable as Rilke noted to the young poet—was a desire so strong that one could not imagine living without creating, a feeling that should rightly accelerate with time in its proper place. Of course, this represented, for the man or woman of letters, indelible writing. Marc further reminded Ariana of Goethe's comment on talent, which arises from holding the world at bay and being removed from the world. He sensed that she might confuse her grades in school with an indication of artistic temperament or ability, desire even.

In making this last point clear to her, Robert chimed in by recalling the likes of Shakespeare or Molière whose education, training, and art came as much by traveling with their troupes, of from being backstage, as any other.

Cassandre served radishes with butter from Normandy and Breton salt. To compensate for the additional guests, she prepared a small savory omelet with *chanterelles*, which whet her husband's appetite for the song of the E string, oyster mushrooms, and *fines herbes* she had purchased that morning from a local farmer in the marketplace at the base of the hill. This served as an alternative to the *Coque* for those who preferred a dish literally *fait maison*. Marc poured a red Marqués de Cáceres Rioja, always attentive to the coolness it must have in order for the fruit to be most fully aromatic. Like the French, generally speaking, he naturally appreciated all about this meal without reading or computing. His senses guided the value and esteem he assigned the combined offering he and his wife were making. Elevated to a kind of sensitive celebration were the nose, eye, ear, and touch of the tongue. All the senses made everyone involved most appreciative of Cassandre's care, love, and domesticated science around—in addition to beyond—the home.

Marc then let stream yet more of this otherworldly rendering of reality, this divine thing made manifest by the audiophile who appeared, this one time, quite out of character; for music, to which no one would fully attend, would serve as a time-honored harbinger adding value to pleasure—an enjoyable sensation already trumpeted by more than Wagner—as it did in baroque times to enhance each party around a banquet or dining experience. In a well-established culture of food, art mediates the relationships people maintain with respect to all that is consumed. There would be no superfluous force-feeding of any form of culture, no room for unseating nature's arousing, ever-raising place in the setting of enjoyment around this eminently French table.

Marc had conceived of this evening's entertainment in pondering the classical concerto, its creator and disciples, a short-time past. He had long wished to dine surrounded by sound like that experienced around the table of Boccherini's patrons who alimented themselves with the musical ambassador's octet (*notturno*). He did not wish to drink from that particular wellspring of fluency just yet for as much. This would be the first instance Cassandre would ever have witnessed her spouse pairing his most prized delicacies—whose composers flawlessly infused music's heyday with their fruitful, capacious, and timeless vintage—together with the roomy hospitality bringing good wine and all that which accompanies intoxication of the body. Marc had already discreetly begun this musical coupling, which promised to elevate his wife's culinary and conversational offering to a quasi-religious experience to be sure. This art liquidated thorny subjects, *aporias* and thoughts leading to a dead end.

To the duo of teacher and student, the host now led with the "Overture to Alexander's Feast." This was followed by a tender and generous bit of chamber music written by the man whom no less than Bach traveled hundreds of kilometers to hear—Buxtehude.

The conversation flowed together with a just resemblance to the inspiration composing mortals in light of an immortal fire like a brightly burning *symphonia concertante* spreading heat from person to warming person and course to course. The engulfed and engulfing participants included a discussion of a subject Ariana had heard brought up in another course at the university, that of professor Habamini who often spoke of "genetic memory." She was fascinated that the professor's suggestion might include a memory so deep it could never be expunged or accessed, much like Pascal had written of predispositions. Under such conditions, Marcel could already be programmed in the womb to speak and write the most eloquent possible French in particular, or simply some, indeed, any language in general.

Cassandre listened attentively, as was always the case for the wife of music's doyen, but found she was herself a bit distracted by the food, which, even though she herself had cooked, held out excessive appeal in view of her redoubled appetite. Evidently, the 1945 Puligny-Montrachet Marc was now pouring only served to tantalize her indulgence in the repast, especially with the veal, like the discovery of one rare bone that shows up to entice the curiosity of an archeologist, setting the student of the earth and dust out on further digging, whereby he or she may satiate a hunger for the future's bounty, one collected by unburying some heretofore unfound past in yet other vestiges of life.

Of course, the piece now flowing from the speakers augmented the crisp grace and earthy, mineral elegance of the wine. Marc had chosen a work designed for the ancestors of such a spellbinding meal, Heinrich Beiber's Suite *Mensa Sonora* (Sonorous Table). The splendid combination proved to be a sumptuous entrée for the same composer's "Table Music," served up with generous portions just before Johann Hermann Schein's *Banchetto Musicale no. 2: Padouana in D* (Musical Banquet). Marc had opted to withhold and pass over both Mozart's wind divertimenti—composed for the express consumption around the archbishop of Salzburg's private table—and his *Haffner Serenade*, voraciously written for a festive banquet, as well as Michel Delalande's "Symphony for the Royal Supper," preferring not to hearken the most regal and proportioned of dining experiences at this time.

Cassandre could not but imagine that the steely professor of philosophy to whom Ariana referred had hit upon a depth of one's conscience, which science alone could not fully sound out, ultrasound, or elaborate. She wondered whether Marcel did not already possess a memory of literature. He most likely already embodied certain characters. He might choose to be representative of others, others endowed just the same with a memory that might be conditioned by factors no more intelligible than archetypal. He could eventually come to layer sound on a canvas of silence like this settling music, this sediment in her gut, transforming all around her as if a Vermeer was laying down vision's most minute reconstitution of daily incidents and life.

Since she did not know the answer to her mental query, she did not venture to talk of it at the table. In such cases of doubt, she preferred the simplicity of asking Marc his view in the salon, on a long drive, or at breakfast. Few things interested him and her more than the nature of memory. They had already witnessed in their lives, in the life of their minds, just how lessons they had scrupulously assimilated, from teachers and friends in their youth, had been integrated into their way of thinking, as if they were now second nature. This familiarity with intelligent ways of proceeding in life stemmed from a memory of essentials, first and foremost. Listening to ample quantities and carefully selected qualities of music created—in the view of both these amateur musicologists—a place akin to a fertile garden in which the memory of events, ideas, words, and relationships of all kinds could take hold and grow into a veritable culture of human nature and the mind-sets of beings everywhere. Together, they were a superintendent to memory's hidden undertakings, to memories' involuntary superiority with respect to free will or idle wishes, just as Jean-Joseph Cassnea de Mondonville presided over Louis XV's charge to exercise grand restraint in amusing courtly muses and courtesans alike.

Cassandre felt, at that moment, as though even the blood nourishing Marcel bathed his memory in such a way as to energize and activate all his creative juices, however much in latent form, even before what would amount to some sort of byproduct of his art or life could be perceived by those around him. Of more than one thing she was certain—Marcel's memory would not be unlike any child's, as tied to his mother's existence, that is, as the umbilical cord growing around him, as sure as his lifeline was currently smiling upon vinous laughter. Perhaps he would even remember, once informed by his mother, that she nourished her spirit—without ignoring her body or the Middle Age's sense of wine's virtues—by partaking in some of the 1929 Château Pétrus Pomerol Marc served. He had inherited this softest of all red viticulture from his father. It accompanied the delectable cheese course and the concerto for three violins, from *Tafelmusik* by Telemann, now playing around the table's discursive ensemble. Would the French child not learn instinctually that food, wine, and song mean wholly different things from one nation to the other? What might signify pleasure for one could be guilt, obesity, and sin for the next. Cassandre believed in the end, without any formulae or codification, that all the earmarks of soothing words and deeds, good food too, acted like melodies, if not life's fermentation, in the kind of rhapsodic continuo with which she viewed this pregnancy to be underscored.

The dinner ended with a *digestif*, burning everybody's tongue and throat, a little like seared poetry as the grandfather clock struck, with its pristine tinny trademark sound, twice a dozen times. A couple of works from the same period would bring to a close the participants' highly selective pleasure—first a celebratory cantata, again by Buxtehude, then *The Triumph of Time and Truth* by the "master of masters, Handel, who so admired the other. Ariana was to return to a family, the Vaubans, whose generosity had opened their doors to this foreign student during her year abroad. Before leaving, she asked Mr. Pinlou whether she could attend his course on hermeneutics and "The Century of Lights."

"Of course," he responded. The professor was delighted at the prospect of such an eager, winsome, and keenly obliging student in his midst. He let her know he would do anything within his reach to encourage her in the endeavors surrounding long-lived French literature she had already so courageously begun.

To that end, Robert differed little from Marc. Both would follow her as she would follow them.

In fact, what distinguished Marc in her view, beyond all the other teachers she had ever encountered, revolved around this notion of following. In listening to others as in reading texts, Marc's purpose was not principally to lead the way for young adherents, even less to point with certitude to the rectitude of his own interpretation; on the contrary, his main focus, not unlike the sum of his principles, always rested with the student's interest.

Marc's purpose centered around preserving, for those who followed him, a sense of accrued wonderment systemic to the individuals who gave themselves to a formation, a training in the art of formulation, in French literature. To the secular realm of art in general, his figured as the ethical equivalent of the moral imperative held out by Jews whose mission amounted, *in toto*, to preserving the Torah, *L'dor vador*, from generation to generation, for eternity.

Little wonder in one sense, grand wonderment in another, that Ariana would never forget this musical moment to which she had been brought with such lavish abundance and aesthetic riches, this fleeting grasp of beauty Marc had orchestrated for her visit this evening, all summarized by the very last selection—"Dido's Lament" by Purcell. For his part, her master had used a studied theme, one that combined a musical epoque, a sonorous *épopée* composed by something of a virtuoso generation, together with more immediately digestible fare. In preparing for his student's arrival, he easily uncovered the powerful lyricism of links between all these masterpieces, as if the Haydn violin concerto he had contemplated served as a land from which differing viticultural delectables could be uncorked and appreciated, beyond the body, in the soul of a familiar, poetic *terroir*.

The young listener, for her part, would never neglect, or leave behind unintentionally, the curiously romantic love her teacher displayed throughout this soiree, with an especially time-piercing sign of devotion at the end. His full-bodied, affectionate concern showed itself steeped here in sensational emotion but also in the design and order which marked baroque and classical compositions and which took shape and sustenance from a devotion to all for which life is worth living, namely, preserving, if not a sense of an Aphrodite, then the muse herself. Marc had saved for the finish what would add polish to all the rest, the parting words, tragically expressed by a dying princess: "Remember me . . . remember me . . . but ah, forget my fate . . ."

Marc considered widely what exactly should be remembered forever, just as he thought of how we should use our time on earth. He realized the extensive beauty of the Jewish adventure and how its condensed version could be found in the Torah. This pillar of civilization was not to be confused with a document like the American constitution, or that of the state of Massachusetts, which served less as a set of guidelines, delivered with equal care for both ethical and aesthetic form and function, than as a constellation of supposedly inviolable laws to be enforced by people for people. The professor was able to deduce this based on a conversation over the telephone—about both education and America's founding—he had the day before with Harvey Smith, who was planning a trip to see his father's friend described by an all-knowing man as "a paragon of literature."

While one could speak of the rule of law, in order to impose order on what would otherwise be randomness and disorder among all the kingdoms, animal, or plant known to humankind, one is obliged to recognize, in matters unrelated to the *polis*, that no such rule exists, *a priori*, in the domain of art. Some great art—like the works of the composers Johann Vanhal, Jan VanHals (same person, different name), Jan Vorisek, Stephen or Etienne Nau, Giovanni Vitali, François-Joseph Gossec, Friedrich Kuhlau, or Biber, and their suite—come and go without imposing themselves as essential to an enduring legacy, and this, even if highly appreciated in their day. They take on the form and aura of alternate tuning among imposing names as if they were employing *scordatura* to express phenomena or unique sonic characteristics off the beaten path. Perhaps they lacked a certain fame that may have served as capital for the inheritance of space-time. Celebrity and quirks of personality may just be required, even unjustifiably, to promote one's proper place in time.

Like the most genuinely, skillfully cultivated, harvested, and composed wine, these composers aged well. There came a point, however, a turning when they no longer retained their optimal level of those ripened ovaries and accessories of a seed-bearing plant containing a wide variety of forms—fleshy fruit, in other words—that acted as their point of departure and primary material or subject to flesh out. They blended into space-time. Their arrival to this day, like their good fortune, took a turn, morphing less into vinegar than into the spirits of some underappreciated, ambrosial yesteryear of fermented, intoxicating silence.

Principles of art are not so much discovered as they are explored as if nothing existed or exists preliminarily. At each turn, the true artist's universe is in both a culmination of the old taken with the revelation of a new world.

And with the death of an artist, as with that of any commoner, borrowing the words of Ariana's rabbi, "so too does a whole world die."

The preamble to one's artistic constitution then, Cassandre believed with Marc, occurs, in fact, before, properly speaking, one's existence takes place.

In this way, Marcel's preface to life was being written with each passing, loving day and night, a fact of fiction to which his progenitors were eminently attentive. His name would preamplify, in short, a literary existence, according to his parents' physical calculations. Much like an instrument sensitive to sound in general, and voices in particular, he might receive signals only to augment the importance of their resonance in subsequent stages. Where the thinker hypothesizes, the artist comes to expatiate and dilate truthful beauty.

Nothing, in the de Beaurecueils' minds, Marcel was receiving or had received with the punctual, physical conception, strictly speaking, privileged a discourse of biology alone. They believed in a balance of artistic justice almost as ferociously, if not more, as in social or legal justice.

"Poetic license begets poetic justice," Marc's professor, M. Castex, was once rumored to have whispered in his ear. Marc came to understand that *begets* is a word cohabited by *bigots* and thus also by the very notion of prejudice, which proves the true or untrue nature of his subject, namely, man is not capable of pure judgment, whether based on man-made principles, principles discovered in operating within the world or universe, or other. He should therefore be encouraged to take himself as his own subject in a lifelong pursuit of clarifying his vision of himself. One may make as much of light's varying aspects in the master cinquecento portraits of Titian or, as space-time progressed, Philippe de Champaigne, the authoritative self-portraits of Rembrandt or Chardin, the line of Ingres or color of Delacroix, and the interiors of Vermeer or Maes.

If laws indeed exist, laws of physics, light, or a more popular understanding of the term, one has the right to choose among them in order to best suit one's own temperament and style, in a word, the pronouncement of one's own subject about the world.

"At times, I enunciate with the same effect, yes, with the same affect of language as seraphim, cherubim, thrones, dominations or dominions, virtues, powers, principalities, archangels, and angels—divine silence."

Questions of the message and the messenger abound in French literature. To articulate words artistically is to make things, phenomena, or ideas "sing," as if one were fully aware that the word *pronounced* contains *pronoun* within it (a composite of *nuntius*, meaning "message or messenger," and *pro*, meaning "in place of" or "before"). It would very nearly appear that, as if by homophonic contagion, by sound alone in other words, a pronoun resembles a pronouncement insofar as both replace something, in the one case a noun and in the other a message.

Marc liked to take all the time necessary to ponder questions such as these in addition to others more *outré*, and he found himself more acutely curious about them at this point in his life. After all, Marc's future son's preexistence preceded the proper noun *Marcel* as did the pronoun *he*. Syntagmatically speaking, that is, *he* existed like a nominal group, before any pronouncement on *his* part. The messenger seemed to arrive prior to the message that, in this case, Marcel might transmit, beginning with his first cooing or crying. As silence precedes sound, so too does sound advance sense, and this not unlike meaning, which comes before significance.

The substance of Marc's thought, as the substantive simply put, bordered on a type of nominalism that took abstract terms, universal laws, and concepts as devoid of objective reference. Existence is, so it would seem, either empty at the core or full of nothing but names like a quatrefoil whose lobes trace the balance and counterbalance of a central void at the heart of all matters, both light and dark. Living is another matter altogether. And so it could be that Marc could nod off thinking, like memories that fade when conducted by tacit approbation and an economy of both scales and means.

The unlimited implications of a name explain why Marc took that of his future child, Cassandre by his side, to signify a destiny that encompasses that form of reality not necessarily based in the kind of realism represented by the likes of Balzac, Zola, and those who followed them. His would sum up a fate tied, bound to a life as perilous as any that will have been known in literature. His would be the Christian name of a creator, or author, whose clear and intricate worldview made things come alive with words.

It makes one think of the tradition among Ashkenazi Jews whereby no newborn was given the name of a living person, not only so as not to rob that person of life's fullness but also to point to the fact of just how precarious leading a full life can be for certain types. In the same vein, no professor or doctoral student was permitted to write, in the days Marc passed through the academy, on the subject of a living author. One had to wait until his *corps* would become a *corpse* in order to consider his work an objective *corpus*.

The messenger has to pass, to come, stated simply, and go, in order that a clear, full message might be considered as such. His birth marks the beginning as his death seals an end, hermetically or otherwise. Remains the test of time to know whether his message will endure or fade away never to be rehabilitated.

How one such test works is of general interest. Those who administer, judge, and record it impact current and future generations. Time, however, as ever-flowing space, supersedes the test itself. Civilization may not always be advanced without fail by those who themselves prove perdurable against all odds.

Entirely valuable *opera*—works, in other words—find themselves abandoned for no good reason, *chef d'oeuvres* warranting conservation no less than the most preeminent among those retained for eternity. Silence and sound yield, in view of human life forms, to the art of meaningful expressions of passion and love. The messenger may fade before the message, like Hermes who lived on—yes, gloriously raising himself (more than bundled up and communing with the silky accent of the elegant French Hermès)—in his name. We are thus free to consider a name as electrifying and magnetic as those early cables, those "live wires," appearing to harness the power of lightning (echoing the potential of lightening both the living and non-living), thanks to which Morse communicated the first signs of his elaborate code.

That which is retained forever arises in either human or ideal form. On the one hand, either people revere the various forms of God, gods, animals, plants, and the presence or absence of underlying unity in the universe or, on the other hand, some mysterious nature reveals the ample exquisiteness of human forms. No doubt what passed as classical took as a starting-point form, blending with it ideas or content, whereas that which came later, romanticism, gave ideas their suitable form. The legendary or mythical material that manifests these truths can be comprised of the flesh, mind, spirit, or a Pleiad of others, folding ideas into things such as stone, wood, oils, metals, and various natural forms of content born from the earth's combination of basic elements. As a name therefore announces new life, could a text not serve as a pretext in a similar vein?

Although it was understood from before his conception, Marc and Cassandre hoped Marcel would become as cultured as his namesake in the sense that he would live as one with his truest nature—nature both internal and external to himself—as he would seek to essay defining that being in the world. "Does creation come from without, from an absence, not to speak of a *Deus absconditus*, or from a presence within?" Cassandre asked Marc the next day, fortified by self-reliance and the brushed azure cashmere of her chemise, reminding her husband of his favorite camisole, that sleeveless underbodice suggestively referred to as a short *négligé*.

The reader of texts distinguished between human creations, first of man himself, then that which man creates, whether another man in his image or another image—a different form of man, that is. He had come hither from a time and place that remains off-limits to reason alone, as if even the scantily dressed were covered with enough light and levity to obscure the fine particles of the tenuous *propos* of any order. Perhaps it is more true than false that through imagination we may gain greater knowledge about precisely what life holds out for us between upright faculties and matching bookends.

Although her husband had never spoken of his belief in a biological or paleontological theory, as one furnishing clues to man's origins, insofar as it describes him as the result of complex bacteriological development, Cassandre now learned that, in his eyes, all ideal forms sprung from one such point of departure, like as many oceans flowing from the baptismal combination of hydrogen's pairing with air.

This notion, however rudimentary, however deeply encoded in the most basic building block of matter, seemed likely whether as yet identified by name or not. If ontogeny recapitulates phylogeny, so too perhaps does ontology. In reverse, nonetheless, Marc conjectured out loud, "Phylogeny recapitulates superior ontogeny." So too does goodness breed goodness, and excellence the love of its likeness.

Nothing seemed more beautiful to both de Beaurecueils than the perspective of creating a creator, a liberator of literature, one followed by the entire species as a model by which to live and evolve, for he would necessarily reflect on the past as Aristotle and Hegel before him. Perhaps even entire "movements" or schools of thought would rise up and out of his personal, individual creation.

They imagined he would father more children—if not directly, then indirectly—through the inscription or encryption of his ideas, style, form, and mellifluous eloquence in no less grandiose a fashion than that of a double violin concerto of Johann Sebastian Bach, that demigod whose adoration of life was at the antipodes of romanticism.

Marc was convinced of the role played most notably by Wilhelm Friedemann, Karl Philipp Emmanuel, Johann Christoph Friedrich, and Johann Christian Bach, among the other offspring (and eight generations of Bach musicians), in establishing their father, in the strong and sensitive sense of the word, as pivotal to the history and art of music. The most highly prolific Telemann in Leipzig, like Heinichen in Dresden, did not have the benefit of this reinforced human and musical presence in his life, much as Boccherini found himself more distant from the Vienna of Haydn, Mozart, and Beethoven, off serving the Bourbon crown here, the Hapsburg's there, remaining therefore less a presence than a lamentable, albeit glorious, absence on the musical stage. A critical mass of interest inflects, said in other terms, the mass, which is preserved above all others.

Each lover of music realized that he and she, in creating their child, found themselves excluding certain forms, just as the felicitous imposition of great musicians had eliminated the happy presence of noteworthy others. The future parents could no longer be carefree, penniless, or irresponsible, full stop.

Neither could never more be unmoved by an infant's grinning and bearing of beauty's mounting stages of life. They could no more exclude youthful marvels than include in this perspective any close-mindedness, repression, or authoritarianism from either side of the public spectrum. Their wish circumscribed the affirmation of patterns good enough to embrace life's multiplicity, diversity, and inherent differences, what can often figure as a melee between confusion and discovery. Together with the major composers, artists, and writers, they would not undermine the minor, or little ones, any more than minorities serve themselves by undercutting others. All things not being equal, however, the scope of their otherwise egalitarian love, would reflect ardor in a relationship to itself at once reflexive, symmetric, and transitive. Given their more-than-singular interest in the stuff of which exclusively inclusive dreams are made, the multitudes would be invited indirectly to the table as a realistic measure of their capabilities, quantity, or effect on others perhaps less popular though no less human.

Marc and Cassandre thus came to view their creation as privileging a fictional world taken with all the nonfiction elements comprised within it. For they saw characters not unlike the way in which geneticists viewed the elaboration of developmental theory, indeed entire existences at times, based on the fundamental characteristics of two chromosomes—X and Y. The lone exception on which the de Beaurecueils reserved judgment revolved around theories of science or literature as human creations since any related notions are no less subject to inherent falsification than to an external form of the same. Men were the creators of so-called truth, just as they were of lies, legends, myths, and works of fiction, all of which pretend to bear some grain of truth, generally speaking.

Specific men's work is worthy of preservation more than others', to the extent the former will have understood relations in the world like those of relativity set forth by the Einsteinian revolution. Therein, the person doing the measuring must be taken positively into account in the measurement of any matter or phenomena before anything is thus understood. People—their kindliness, search for beauty, and truth—figure at the heart of the universal grid, which shapes gravitations. Shakespeare's kings knew, in many cases, they were as likely to find themselves as regal as asinine—no more or less so than torn tragedians who could view themselves as inspired clowns. The rub—like the stuff that dreams are made of—is hidden in the subjective intercourse we have with ourselves and the nature we perceive. Every great rule of culture or civilization follows a specific subject that arrives at a law or laws for the species or universe as a whole.

The Sun King knew no less in establishing himself as an "absolute monarch" on the basis of both divine right and a tragic flaw inherent to man, mythical or other. In one sense, his gaze, obsessed with, rather possessed by ancient Greece, coupled with a perspicacious view of his own supreme role in the world, fathered modern classicism in France. If he single-handedly turned reverence away from the altar and toward his place overlooking the nave at the court of Versailles, it was not accomplished without the slight of hand indigenous to litterateurs in particular and art in general. He was, in keeping the world at bay, literally and figuratively remembering himself at every turn. Every memory, like each *mémoire* of the time, should first have praised the ultimate landlord—His Majesty, the king. Every bit of the past's glorious fabric should serve to blanket the legacy of the future, covering it uniformly with the most becoming *raison d'être*.

To this day, *mémoires* are written in the bastion of French culture, in or out of the *Académie française's* purview, to consolidate and synthesize the legitimacy of the present rule of truth in view of an aging past. The longest single regime in France's history was characterized, indeed founded, by wordsmiths, architects, musicians, artists, sculptors, tapestry makers, manufacturers of faience, craftsmen and women whose craft more than once surpassed their craftiness—walking, if not running as they did, the full gamut, on occasion, undoing worlds of visions all the while, making them as they found themselves remaking both their various tones and themselves with a full spectrum of colors (wherein the infrared parts may well have been grasped by the mind, in theory, even if they may have appeared to the point of being reached far less easily by the naked eye in practice)—illusionists, in a word, who promoted as much the glory of a man who deemed himself at once sun and son of all others as that of their own forms of art or that of inspiring works around them. Art, long before and long after politics, inherited or other, elevates a person. Art enlightens more than presumptuous kings; artistic endeavors alone enhance the light of day for even the humblest of human beings.

The willful act of imposing a fictional nature on oneself and, in turn, on one's subjects, however formal, created the flourishing of a golden age for the entire civilization, wherever French was or would be spoken. In much the same way, Marc and Cassandre had hoped the amalgam of an illusive reality with the world of fiction would be most illustriously seized, and rendered, by an individual who would come to learn how to lend himself a hand in building a life as a novel or, at least, plainly something new and strikingly different.

In the end, as in the beginning then, to watch a creature grow, one wrestling—in body, mind, and spirited words, as in terms of silence at intervals—with that measure of his own nature corresponding with nature herself, this formed the basis of life for Eus-sous-Soleil's more reclusive inhabitants.

"I am alone here, happily remembering my favorite subject is an upside-down 'we,' me! Through me, stabilized by the nutrients of a life-sustaining cord, passes a world of transformations. I am the common denominator to myself in and out of this world. I am irreducible to nothing outside of myself. In order to perceive accurately, I must first be in touch with myself. All flows from this pivotal position of me with myself, coupled with others in an artful dance of truth with illusion. The greater is the obstacle to my becoming myself, the greater the transparency on this subject. This is how others, foreign or familiar as mother here, may serve to reinforce just who I am at times such as these."

Solitude would play a large part in Marcel's life as his parents imagined it. They believed, as Rousseau had declared, "Man is born free, and everywhere he is in chains." This social contract made Cassandre dream of Beethoven's fourth piano concerto in which the soloist breaks with classicism for the first time in history, according to Marc, by exposing the theme before the orchestra members begin their *tutti*. The professor understood that the Third Symphony, the *Eroica*, would come to echo at length Beethoven's discovery of a new elasticity in the framework of a classical ideal.

Marc's counterpart could not refrain from imagining her organs as instruments for the developing play inside of her body. As she assigned a place and purpose to each within her, she took solace from a thought, indeed, her reading of Rimbaud's *Voyelles* (vowels): (*U*). "Peace of grazing lands studded with animals, peace of wrinkles / That alchemy imprints on studious brows." She now looked upon the heartbeats within her deepest cavity as regulated by a rhythmic systole and diastole like a continuo. The lungs appeared to expand and contract with currents of air like the violins aspiring to sing for masters and mistresses alike. The spleen cropped up as if tempered by the tenor of humors like the cellos. The liver provided a sensation of being regulated by the cleansing of woodwinds. And the brain gave the illusion of being united—yes, electrified by the conductor's baton!

This conception of her inner body struck her as consonant with a harmonious conversion, a change whose nature Marcel was coming to share, remaking this unity in a specific image of transformational experiences themselves, one type of which remains just how humans feed over the course of their life. Marcel would come to grow out of his mother's body and into a place of self-fulfillment, self-realization, and self-actualization—first by all that is physical, followed by the intellectual, social, then spiritual—should he so choose. In at least one respect, he would not prove to be unlike a honeybee first developing in larval form, only to undergo a metamorphosis, a variety of rebirth, whereby it may bristle in the hive and carry on industriously, from flower to flower, before returning to cajole sweet nectar—transforming this ambrosial product by a metabolism, beginning with its proboscis and ending with the fragrant likes of immortality, somewhere, combing the outer world (further removed from mother's centering influence), it makes itself at home in a given setting—beyond its posterior segment.

Once again, she saw her child as available to play before actually beginning to play as though he bore the message of music in spawning silence, in her various movements, voluntary or involuntary, before the veritable message was born in a sound world. The instruments of the orchestra further struck her as representatives of nature, as if he would use them, as soloist, as a sounding board to both define himself, lend his ideas a form, as the venerable romantics or anti-classicists had done, and thereby define a greater nature as he saw it. He could go on to write a part for himself as soloist or a simple member of the ensemble, conductor included. With this in mind, reality's protagonist would not necessarily discover himself least alone in experiencing solitude.

In sharing her fantasy with Marc, Cassandre learned that Ariana had once shed light on a Hebrew etymology that reinforces the notion one must live alone, to be sure, yet, at the same time, affirm *life*. The word *cha'yim*, she divulged at the time, on a long drive to see some medieval ruins in the countryside surrounding Eus, means "lives," as if to suggest that *life* is by its very nature plural. One's wholeness is thus derived from another, just as if we are *alive*, by definition, solely when, like Marcel, we find ourselves bathing in another's presence. A life takes on meaning and significance from the point of departure of other lives. The professor might make note of another member of society: "The hive is quite literally *alive* with little more to show than the buzz and physical gratification of the bees which build and reside in it!"

Existence—that is, ultimately, as in the beginning—gives rise to meaning when *people* are engaged in relationships. Marcel was thus, at this point, more than a fetus; he was already playing several roles, including that of a future child, boy, potential writer, dancer, and living entity, in sum, within the larger *tableau vivant* of life. Therefore, it could be said, even the sound of words may be transformed by the different meaning one discerns in them, depending on whether an individual is alone or with others, whether someone is, in other words, living or not.

"To use the noun in its singular form, *cha'ya*," Ariana added as she adjusted her chignon, recalling the lesson her Chiron-like rabbi had communicated to her, "refers not to a person but rather to the life of a beast or insect." The community of man, his culture, like the community of nations, should thus be considered immediate, without the need for mediation or media to be sensed. The soloist needs the orchestra as in concerti where the converse may be equally true in order to affirm what the first romantics perceived, namely, the solemn declaration, the giving assent of a solitude bathing, like Marcel could be observed at present, in a greater social *corps*. This larger corpus appears to be the context in which he finds himself flowing no less than the blood, air, water, and other fluids like corpuscles whose free movement collectively sustain all of life.

Were the soloist giving a recital alone, to a forest of trees, the question might thus be, from the perspective of the Hebrew language, "Is he or she *alive*?" It was Marc's clairvoyant interpretation that, of course, the answer is yes, he or she may well be heard and alive since the soloist communes with the composer, who is no more dead at that point than the parchment on which the score was laid down. Similarly, this logic could be extrapolated to determine whether Marcel was already *alive* given his corporeal and mental relationship with his clear-eyed mother.

If it is true that "hell is other people," then it seemed equally plausible to maintain that one could seek salvation, a type of heaven, with or without Sartre, in others, by positing their existence as both necessary and sufficient for one's being in the world. Since we create our own paradise and utopia, not to mention certified hell, the totality of our situations, generally speaking, it seemed true that Cassandre was almost hell-bent on making Marcel's universe, heaven and all, a space where life's greatest art would find itself vouchsafed for eternity.

This notion of relationships led Ariana, on the same occasion with Marc, to recount the ancient story of the Persian ruler, Darius. For her who had a quasi-natural penchant of consulting history's lessons, this parable illustrated how one can—and should—view others acting in society, subsuming baser inclinations.

When told by Haman, his prime minister, that the Jews were a bad people, Darius saw that it was the highly ranked government official, and not the innocents, who wished to arrive at wealth without a cost. He thus bestowed clothes, gold, and good fortune on the more common Mordecai, much to the chagrin, "in point of fact," to the shame of his scoundrel minister.

Ariana sensed, in telling this to Marc, that he was pleased to giggle at the idea that Mordecai found himself in concert *with* the ruler of the land as much as playing *against* him. The poetry of the story made of its character a *chargé d'affaires* for the muse. Realizing one's place in society came, in her eyes, with a sense of irony or humor that acted to defend oneself against any invasion from the outside world or those inhabiting it. Ariana concluded that in the interval between sunrise and sunset—a day of driving during which Marc played Furtwangler's rendition of the Reinhardt *Ein deutsches Requiem* to underscore how—life should be affirmed in the face of death. ("For all flesh is as grass, and all the glory of man as the flower of grass. The grass withereth and the flower thereof falleth away. Be patient therefore . . . the husbandman waiteth for the precious fruit of the earth, and hath long patience for it, until he receive the early and latter rain.") The man at the helm of her thoughts accentuated this without sentimentality by making a reflection about the beauty of life conceived by Judaism in general, stating her religion, unlike any other system of thought, taken "without humor, desiccating sufferance and music is like an orange without juice."

Through these few concentrated dimensions, Jews carried on in a world that made of them a chorus of Hebrew slaves, time after time, in a diasporic form of collective solitude. They thus appeared perhaps a shade unlike, say, American Negro slaves who seemed to survive by the dictum, "If the heart hurts, sing and tell a story," rather than, first, "If the heart hurts, laugh and sing"; for individuals can be, especially in the pain of tracking pleasure, very much *alive*!

What the French call *the struggle for life* appears foremost a strenuous undertaking to discern different meanings, varying purposes even, at the limit, among sounds and silence. Cassandre knew how to auscultate her own body and soul. In doing so, she could not help but wonder what sensations Marcel was hearing articulated inside of her. One might find there swells of fluids as constant as the waves upon the shore, as rhythmic as water lapping the seaworthy hull of crafts awaiting adventure's launch from nature's alcove serving as an unforgettable marina. Something syncopated could be present, keeping the beat of a systole and diastole in harmony with its own flowing movements. Whatever precedes a yawn could be forming some perceptible noise. The future mother felt herself both aroused and puzzled by the idea of whence comes a cry before it is declaimed.

This led her to conceive of her body as a concert hall whose acoustics carried with them an effect of being as soundproof as the nearby nave within the abbey of *Saint-Michel-de-Cuxa*. She let herself follow thoughts that compared her tissue to the rose-colored marble of Les Pyrénées, which was used to augment nature's place in town. Eus would serve as matron to her son. The sunniest place in France would supervise his private and public, in a word, musical life.

While some found life meaningful in "binding back," as those of Christian faith had done, beginning around the eleventh century on this site, living *religiously* in other terms, Cassandre did not wish to go so far as to treat the child with religious fervor. True, she was recapitulating her life in a profound way by conceiving, together with Marc, another. By this, however, she did not wish to displace the importance of other sound relations in her life as early as in her relationship to herself. She would continue to love music, art, literature, and Marc. She would not cease admiring architecture and ideas of all kinds. She would not falter in loving love and its likeness wherever it was to be lost or found. Yes, she would love Marcel, she believed, unconditionally, all the while reserving her reverence for godliness, divinity, or that which warranted its place as such. Michelangelo, for example, as she saw things, occupied a place in her pantheon of those worthy of the most inspired, faithful care. Even though Marcel would be raised as her child, he would have to earn his place in her life outside that associated with the role of mother.

This lack of complacency or forced complicity on her part, would, summed up, make Marcel live up to his name as if he were obliged by one of his two natural parents to realize the full potential of an extensive background in which he possessed cultural parents, perhaps even many. Some models would be chosen, *a fortiori*, elected for him like those aligned in the great tradition of French litterateurs beginning with the Troubadours, extending through the entirety of Renaissance writers or artists to the neoclassics and on to a certain modernity opened by the likes, indeed, the loves of Rousseau, Chateaubriand, Balzac, and Baudelaire. They would ensure he might rarely, if ever, miss his mark in rendering an artistic life to the world. For these models, these prime examples of those one should imitate, lent to the letter the fullest possible weight of the spirit, mindful as they were of both form and content. The whole of a culture instilled these "immortals" lessons in the everyday study of those they continue to raise, their *élèves* and faithful readers.

Children in France were, without a doubt, elevated first before finding themselves in the womb, in the very act of marriage that carried within the term the notion of children and thereby family. Subsequent to that, first in vivo, followed by the world beyond, they were raised perpetually as much in this conception of the child by the progenitors as by society itself. Marcel's models would be found in the home, schoolbooks, and manuals used to convey centuries of intelligence and wisdom, beauty and truth, those texts common to all French children each of whom had a stake in the patrimony and matrimony.

But he would also be free to search for his own exemplars, just as Marc and Cassandre before him had come to adopt—while salivating from hunger and thirst for beautiful truths—a select few philosophers, poets, dramaturges, artists, and musicians, from antiquity to the present. He could fill his time with study, reading the contents of works related to all seven continents and the solar system should he choose. He would not need to select his ideas or draw them out based on popular "consensus reality," for his preoccupations might touch on domains foreign to the masses, alien to his times. Perhaps he would become interested in a dying civilization or an aristocratic way of thinking, a rare aesthetic, philology, the combo of culinary finds paired with the enthralling aroma and bouquet of various fine vintages or an orphaned instrument like the *arpeggioni*. Or it is possible that he alone would come to experience the blossoming song of the violin in Beethoven's Spring Sonata as though the budding melody expressed nature, renewing herself along the lines of the fictional Vinteuil Sonata, *piano* (whose tune has so charmed listeners and readers everywhere civilization breathes, seriously flitting about, performing acrobatic maneuvers, and this, thanks to the homemade *main-d'oeuvre* that genius stitches in the purest airs, the *chef-d'oeuvres* of space-time—thickened by a rarified intensity of metaphors and metonymy going beyond the present, if one such dimension even exists—outside, that is, the past and future).

In any case, he would be poised to discover the Western canon before him to the extent that it is an arm whose body works only by that measure of one's mind that exercises itself in handling, above all, in making sense of the extremities surrounding a mysterious universe. The basis for an inquiring spirit of the Occident is herein made at once more sensible, more beautiful, suggesting either design and order or chaos at the cause by some admixture of sound and silence, perhaps underscoring utter meaninglessness—total emptiness out of which a creature's or any child's whole conception takes shape and direction, like cargo taking to the hold of a transporting vessel—at the foundation of all creation, for all space-time.

"I am not avoiding speech or noise, yet I am silent. I am not still, yet moving here is akin to a muted excrescence. I am like those unvoiced declarations of love a couple expresses to one another. To the extent the form of my existence remains hidden, I embody secrets.

"The slate of my pronouncements is *tabula rasa*. I am fit to be tied to any and everything, to any and everyone. If I appear tight-lipped, it is not so much a reluctance to speak as the sign of an inability to know how to speak in others' presence. It's an uninformed, semistimulated reticence, combined with a fear of drowning, which keep me from uttering any recognizable words. My secret code reserves itself for a latter day when I will take on the air of those around me, thereby lending my sounds the form of others more informed in the ways of words, whatever the language.

"I have been made as a brut investment by partners I currently perceive as silent. They may have made a decision to invest in someone and/or something new, but for the moment, they have left the management of their 'package deal' to this body surrounding me like a fortress. If ever I exit this place, perhaps those involved in making me what I am today will begin to make other decisions on my behalf. It will be intriguing to witness with which form of life they begin—a gesture, word, smell, taste, or touch.

"If and when they begin with language, it will be curious to learn what word it will be. Since I may turn out to be cleansed by my mother's fluids, perhaps a proper noun is not such a bad idea for breaking the silence between us. Or perhaps something even more basic would first emerge, like the urgency emerging in a cry!

"I will need more than silent partners if I am to appreciate the bigeminal, analogical fullness of some silences. It is possible I will be otherwise able to decipher the language of art, music, and literature. Apart from adopting a language common to artists, a person may extend the forms of dance, the basic choreography of life's earliest movements began here.

"I am definitely involved in an evolutionary dance, beginning with a couple, their gametes, and my becoming myself here, for the moment, *sans* the sound of less than sanguine music."

Marc thus figured as a living paradox, using words and eloquent persuasion, he referred, without failing, to an essential silence at the root, even before the dawn, of civil society. He would do everything in his power to preserve music with its unique form of rendering that quintessence. This would mean fully developing the child's potential to first listen, even play, then speak. Before the letter, as the French expression goes, Marcel was already a writer, an explorer, a man of uplifting sorts, a humanist in the largest sense; for in the womb he was forming, in advance of himself, a silence whose seed had penetrated another, equally fertile shell of silence. If creation, like creativity, followed procreation as sure as pronouns took their lead from nouns, one could speak or write of a universal grammar, something like the water of words, structuring all things, people, and places.

Marc had once discussed the origins of space and time with Professor Habamini, only to exert a phenomenological view whereby access to the most distant realms passed necessarily through a construct of the self who was making the observation. And Marc's self often shimmered with sweeping recollections shimmying into the crevasses of space-time, which punctuated his being and dotted his mind.

He took it as a given that the big bang theory should have on the launching pad of its central metaphor a significant sound. He conjectured that if man never did actually "bang" females at the outset of civilization but rather made primitive or primate, more likely than not, primal love with her, then the metaphor arising out of the universe's primordial, sensitive silence might more closely touch and communicate with the sounds he shared with Cassandre. Silence will have preceded any noise as sure as the former underlies any sound theory to explain life's origins, for in a nearly inert quiet alone is fashioned any proper perspective or meditation of life.

Both in making love with her, and in making clearer any experience she might have with the new creature in her no-less-than-celestial body, a soft-spoken realm was privileged. It was out of Cassandre's luxurious lap that Marc had derived all the sybaritic wishes he pampered, all the sensuous voluptuousness he equated with a spring day, all the epicurean aesthetics, which enhanced his feelings for the innumerable acts of love he shared with her own sense of physical delights. These multiple senses she cultivated in and around their bed laid down the foundation for his most highly abstract conceptions of words, things, others, and the like.

Based on the laws of attraction he experienced, Marc deduced a world of truth, postulating that before the explosive ejaculation at the foundation of the universe, in other words, there may have been a host of nothingness, of soundlessness, of "beinglessness," of "directionlessness" even, of timelessness at the limit, which spread itself out indefinitely, indeed, infinitely like a vast dark womb, only to subsequently play host to all types of bodies and life, even inert nonliving matter. Light could thus be seen less as the vector of an *éclat*, the result of something like waves and particles bursting brightly, than as the sign of a creation whose backdrop and foreground are united insofar as they are composed of a void, a silence, a darkness like the one in which Marcel was finding and founding himself at present. Absent these less violent conditions, it is possible the universe, as we know it, may not have formed.

Marc, in contemplating this subject, laughed inside himself, not without a sense of tacit irony, when he recalled what a musician at the court of Louis XIV once said, "Sephardic music has endured hundreds of years, proving that the Jews have made more love than war." He had heard that somewhere before, as if it was beckoning to his mind with the allure of a refrain. He could not but wish to speak with yet another famous Jewish violinist whose view on more physical matters related to tender silence, to a love of oneself or one's work, of one's word or worldly formula and war. The man in question, Einstein, constituted a take on universal creation, force, and destruction like none other. In lieu of such a conversation, he contented himself in part by reconfiguring a formula Sartre had used with reference to another great mathematician and artist, Paul Valéry, thinking Albert Einstein is a petit bourgeois, but not all petit bourgeois are Albert Einstein.

Short of the pleasure another formula might bring, Marc charmed his zest for life in undertaking occasional outings with Ariana. For in this Eastern European Jew, he knew he was addressing a person who had never been in a fight in her life. She repressed nothing, save language. She appeared all the closer to the truth of all living organisms for as much. This absence of aggression explained for him not just the remarkable *douceur* of her personality, of her generalized gusto in the wake of adversity but also shed light on profound oppositions such as those he might find reaching out to and from any theory of origins.

The pink and purple hydrangeas blossomed as the bees swarmed around the flaming mauve bougainvillea, which covered the stucco wall beside the front porch of the de Beaurecueils' residence. Here, life burgeoned, beauty sprouted, and revitalization vivified a multitude of forms. Marc liked to smoke an unfiltered cigarette in an Andalusian leather chair just outside the door beneath the shade. This porous pleasure let suspended matters circulate freely in his mind. It was spring break at the university, a time for vacation and distance from everyday habits. He and Cassandre had decided however to remain at home and take a series of day trips to Figueras and Barcelona in Spain. They would also see the guileless and unaffected Harvey one of these days.

As Marc sat ingesting the spirit of a hardy Gaulloise, he contemplated the works of Malraux. While this highly cultured man's entire *oeuvre* interested the professor of literature, from *Le Musée imaginaire* to *Les Conquérants*, *La Voie royale* captivated Marc's stately attention as an analyst of texts befitting of a sovereign reader holding his hand out to the way in which humanity's multifaceted word moves us along a path reflecting our manifold states. For this man, whose ministrations elevated culture, action prolonged the dream of literature even if the agent of change remained, by and large, mediated by silence.

Marc's reverie pertained to culture in general. Such a rigorous distraction led him, at this moment, to a reflection of civilizations since he had not yet grown accustomed to opposing east and west in narrow terms. His thoughts passed from the Asian Royal Path to the Apian Way. No sooner had he experienced a brief recollection of various Caesars, coining formula upon formula that surged like imperial legions within him, did he stop for a moment to ponder the expression common to both Jews and Christians who, independently of one another, revere "the lord of hosts." He did not know what to make of the original Hebrew, whose translation for *hosts* figured as *legions*, whereas the Latin derived its significance from a notion of hospitality, hospices, hospitals, hostels, and the like. While he had always found curious that romance languages had never ceased to treat the host or *hostie*, the body of Christ, as a guest, rather than the one extending the invitation to others, he did not fully comprehend how the sacrificial victim had come to play a reversed role in tongues unfamiliar with those born outside the walls of the she-wolf's realm, namely, mother Rome! Perhaps *agape* was the good and right key to open the door of one world of lesser evils, and this, on the backdrop of bad and wrong war that closes off and fortifies a different, foreign fief, feud, or fee against the other's immaterial estate and state of well-being. In parallel terms, to an ample extent, new literature would amount to the testament of great religions, merely borrowing and reinterpreting old dictums, poetry, and stories. In any case, Marc took as the recompense for his thought a reminder of the *Requiem*'s text: "How amiable are Thy tabernacles, O Lord of hosts!"

This reference to a sacred tent disengaged a dream that had traversed Marc's mind the night before. He recalled it in some detail, including a name—the Goretsky Madonna—he had attributed to it during his slumber. A search was taking place in China, in a diamond store teeming with merchants and customers. There was an immediate respect afforded the one whose quest was to locate a tableau whose title he knew in advance. The sole requirement for finding the object sought was to present himself and enunciate the purpose of his presence. He was taken behind the store after identifying some specific diamonds in the main storefront. The garret of a barn lay behind the boutique. It was as though a vast manger, similar to the one sheltering the Holy Family, were framing everything. The painting in question was wrapped in a box with various pieces of hay, cloth, and papier-mâché.

There were actually two paintings, both in need of identification. One represented the Madonna, a Caucasian child, the other something completely different. While both belonged to the researcher, he was told he would have to choose the one that was rightly his. He let them know, however, the choice was false—both were his property. Both were as much his as language itself.

A child, about two years of age, with tufted brown hair and a mischievous personality, played high above in the barn. She let the man know that a specific painting was "the one" and that its worth had far surpassed twenty-five, what he interpreted to mean twenty-five million francs.

An impression of space, astronomical figures, soared up in the mind of the one who knew he simply wanted the painting, nothing more.

The man's effort to preserve a thing of beauty, to first seek it out, then recover it, distorted its value. It flowed that condensation occurred as did crystallization into a single, tightly woven form, followed by a displacement into a crate within the barn.

Marc found it clever the subject of his quest had relocated the whole of this object in a garret, a Chinese manger, in the most unsuspecting of places, as if a sacred Western violin had circulated beyond the borders of those whose ears were most accustomed to revering it.

He thought of it as a *Madonne* even though only a child, "in point of fact" a girl, of about nine months was represented within the frame.

The name was given, seemingly based on the main figure, which was, in actuality, missing. This enabled and empowered the child by establishing her heritage as a sacred family member.

It was interesting to Marc that, given an artist's task—to create a thing of beauty—the infant was not of the Savior's gender. It made him recall the significance of a work titled *The Metamorphosis of the Gods*. The symbolic order, like the name of this painting itself, was as feminine as eternity in his eyes. Goretsky, however, referred to a man, one tied to a name and language, or system of metaphor and metonym. The feminine name, together with the female child, both appeared to prefigure a niche in which greater creativity, within the symbolic order of language, could be borne.

Marc was thus attesting to a transformation within himself. Like his wife, more than a seeker similar to Ariana, he was turning into an enlightened amateur who gathers around memory, a collector of philosophic bits and pieces, a human who is together, uniting himself in the warming bonfire of thoughtful remembrances. Like various characters, the two encountered along the way, different moods and modes of transport assembled (in) their lives. Art came together with books like music with dance, hand in hand. Their interest in truth and beauty, unity and goodness was only matched by their disinterest for any diversiform diversion of the same.

Once Marc had scrambled to piece together some of his unconscious, following the glint of his dream, he realized that his waking thoughts were also capable of reversing course and quickly moving, from the tents and times of religion's dawn, north to the "Burghers of Callais" as sculpted by Rodin. They seemed to illustrate how the residents of an entire French town held the keys, on the one hand, to their own sacrifice and, on the other, to war waged by intruders. Since Marc was not necessarily a serial thinker, he fixed his attention on that which the artist valued seemingly above all. The hands of the burghers made him, therefore, recall those sculpted by Michelangelo for any number of subjects. True, Praxiteles preferred small heads; but these two sculptors had a penchant for robust workers' hands, hands laboring night and day to fulfill the assignment of a commission, like a *boulanger* endlessly kneading bread to supply the mouths of an entire village day after baking day.

Inhaling a sizeable amount of smoke, Marc turned the whole of his attention to the journey he and Cassandre had undertaken to Florence and Siena two years beforehand. The *maître-penseur* had little doubt in his mind that Rome represented one of less than a handful of zeniths for Western civilization at the time the modern calendar had been inaugurated. For the observer of any field, culture had reached an acme around the quasi-celestial body of the Son of Man and the body of works around his space-time. But if this acme would take its observer far from earth, others would arrive to add a human perspective to the rule of either religious or imperial terrain.

An apogee, an apex was reached in Marc and Cassandre's eyes, by the heights achieved within the literature and art of Tuscany. *The Divine Comedy*, not unlike *Decameron*, appeared side by side with the likes of far more than a most solemn list of art's most illustrious marquee names: Ducio de Buonensegna, Cimabue, Giotto, Martini, Masaccio, Piero della Francesca, Uccello, Pico della Mirandola, Fra Angelico, Bramante, Donatello, Cellini, Sassetta, the brothers Lippi, Gaddi, Rossellino, da Vinci, Raphaellino, Brunelleschi, Ghiberti, Alberti, Poliziano, Vasari, Michelozzo, and of course, Michelangelo. There were as many great signatories of that eminently artistic period as there figured representations of humanity's fleshy cursive on the wall of the Sistine Chapel. What is, in some ways, more, countless other *cognoscente*—and *literati*-filled palaces and places of faith alike with their works.

Up until approximately 1400, the ecclesiastical calendar had defined the *hora* as an hour in four parts of ten minutes designed for prayer, a period of time that subsequently became a unit of sixty minutes, each of which was made up of sixty seconds. The world was becoming, at once, more secular and quickened by a new pace of life. As had taken place in Athens around 400 BC, exceptionally intelligent creators united and swarmed like bees midst the flowers of civilization decorating Florence's environs.

Neoplatonism, a doctrine whereby philosophy and religion went hand in hand, animated those days, in large part dominated by Lorenzo di Medeci. The active and contemplative life joined as sisters around the fire of Quattrocento ardor. They positioned themselves to behold praise in the various forms of art and literature, scientific or other.

Marc recalled a part of a sonnet written by Lorenzo, that philosopher-poet who ruled over the Florence of his day, indeed, all of history's bouquet whose colorful aroma flirts with any story flowering from even the days leading up to any birth or revitalization of the dead. The Renaissance man's study included both the straightedged and curves balanced by measured lines whose architecture took words as a basis for the foundation of even the most silent of the arts. Any such enlightened and enlightening vocabulary and any related edifying idiom and language underlined the ostensible fact that an entire collection of works arose, like the most brilliant of days, out of that unparalleled area, words, and works taking their shape from an embryo of solitude mixed with a landscape:

> I' mi trovai un di tutto soletto
> In un bel prato per pigliar diletto.
>
> *[One day I found myself all alone in a lovely meadow to take my pleasure.]*

The *aficionado* of language, literature, and travel found that this verse could have been transcribed as well by one of the newly wedded Brownings who vacationed there centuries afterward, *affetuoso!*

This *Souvenir de Florence*, as Tchaikovsky referred to his recollecting post-Athenian civilization's highest point, accompanied by the contraction and expansion of musical color combined with rhythm, prompted Marc to imagine Cassandre's womb as the field beneath the surface of Marcel's dreams. One memory incited another, this time of Giovanni Kapsberger's *Aria di Fiorenza*, a period piece written in the harder, steely sound of the theorbo or *chitarrone*. A true *souvenir* embodies the reverie that *comes under* the guise of an object of contemplation. Memory as such constitutes, in sum, "a thing of beauty."

Marc and Cassandre had not collected anything from their trip to Italy, save, in a sense, the memory of ochers and earth tones, combined with the reminiscence of olfactory sensations they would forever harvest from encountering small *piazzas* or *places* imbibed with the unmistakably homey odor of garlic, onions, and sizzling olive oil. Little more than the view of the Italian landscapes and countryside gratified their most carnal and sexual appetites like a mother's breast satisfies a nursing infant, creating a warm center of personal and social gravity. This sense of sharing a sensuous well-being indulged their most physical fantasies, yes, making love *per se* the initiation of an ever-urging, once-emerging end.

Lastly, they stored in their minds and hearts all the evocative stimuli, not least among their sensational experience, stemming from sounds of a language whose music of consonants so regularly interpolated with vowels, positioned it—Italian—naturally, for a mount, a display on the stage, like as many mountains upon the earth. In the end, this tongue, *bien entendue*, was to be read and heard in the same manner and style to which it had been first accustomed, elaborated as it was by none other than the operatic ancestors of modern airs, those following Monteverdi and his innovative times. In all, beauty was pronounced—expressed in art's most consummate form and elocution—by the palette of instruments that create an atmosphere and mood, a shape and architecture faithful to antiquity and modernity at once.

In a similar sense, Marc devised, Marcel was experiencing the world as one staged, period after period, from an immaterial perspective. The principal matter concerning his development just now, whether intellectual or physical, relayed the more social art of growing into a belief in the skillful and ingenious articulation of life. *Je crois* in French, that uniquely full pleonasm one can manipulate, in stretching it to the extreme limits of language usage, to suit the sense of one's wishes, signifies at once "I believe" and "I am growing" (*Je croîs*), a mere accent, and rare use in the first person, notwithstanding. By thus identifying the object of one's belief, one grows, it could be said, simultaneously—equal, that is—to one's own sense of measure or measurements.

Marc believed that a rhythm of what matters, intercalated with the inessential, was currently affecting any contractions or expansions occurring within Cassandre. He further believed that one could predetermine the measure of the material world in relation to the immaterial in one's life. One need only keep either object of one's focus at a distance, through observation or memory, as did great composers and inventors of the most significant stripes. He saw the transmission of his intelligence far less through the prism of biology, that branch of science increasingly overrun by genetic theory, than through a more epistemological lens, a kind of camera obscura of knowledge itself. It was as if scotopia was enabling him to see things through night-adaptive vision, reading the farthest stretches of the universe in the dimmest light, much as he imagined his future child could possibly do in and out of utter darkness.

One inscribes oneself in a text, indeed, in the Book of Life, according to one's context for living, *for life*. Father a child with civilization's crowning achievements in mind and he or she will, independent of what gene theory might predict, more likely than not, embody both the material and the immaterial lessons of those pursued artifacts of accomplished glory.

Cassandre herself found she was predicting as much alongside Marc. Yet another proof came to her in realizing that she was herself not just any other "Cassandre" as the French would have it, one, as is popularly said, to whom misfortune arrives as if by the ordeal of some calamitous predestiny. She had been given the attributes of this very proper noun by unknowing parents, parents unaware of the negative connotation in French, progenitors who nonetheless believed their daughter would reap a grain of aristocratic resonance, in her various golden ages, with the cradle of her name. Her sense of property and law derived its significance from this primary bit of language. As a result, Cassandre departed from the negative to accentuate the positive "englobed" in the proper name that had become entirely hers. She understood herself, and thereby every world of difference, beginning with that most important of utterances, that first among words, the premier intelligible utterance—one's name.

She moved as Marcel was moving, not unlike the way grass grows, giving life to those other creatures around and taking light from the sun, moon, and stars, not to speak of artists. And she did this because all is ephemeral, as sure as "all flows" to use Heraclitus's formula, *panta rei*, even more so than "all is vanity," to read from the source of Ecclesiastes.

Cassandre did not find herself condemned, in other words, to lead a life of disaster; on the contrary, she turned an understanding of history around as if to rewrite things, places, and people, to refashion, indeed, reorganize her own person, as she saw fit. The authoritative reference in her name predetermined a connotation, not some denotation of her personality or of any object contained therein, even less the subject of her diction. She was evolved and evolving just as her future son inside her. She found herself navigating the tides of new waters with civilization's stars as her guide. Her current involution was thus as much grammatical, even mathematical, insofar as she was raising herself to another power, as it could be argued, to reason historically.

While it was historic for her in that Marcel would become and be, perhaps in that order, the first creation evolving directly from out of her body, she recognized that others most often referred to such matters as external to their own evolution. In all that touched her life, as with the state of her inner stimuli—now at once mental, physical, and social—she sought to be ever vigilant about her involvement, about her participation, for this very new power she henceforth embodied, carried with it the most mysterious of intricacies. As Marcel was heading outward little by little, his mother never ceased to strive inward, reaching for an understanding of all that is and all that is not, in word and deed.

Marcel would inherit, to be sure, a world steeped in the noblest attributes of civil society. The will of Cassandre and Marc to both overcome adversity and seek goodness, beauty, and truth, would act as a legacy to Marcel even before their death. Any *idées reçues*, any inner world marred by erroneous, tainted thought would never be permitted to take shelter in the de Beaurecueils' abode. This loving couple harbored phenomena as pure as a nascent being, as becoming as being itself. Their will was indeed filled with the sagacity of the magi, of the least—as if it germinated out of the most—magical ages. Their own struggles now appeared to have been passing—like their own faculties and facilities, in exquisite unison with those of the schools where they worked—through the crucible of time.

"I measure time by the growth of an appendage, the formation of an organ, the expansion of a brain, the unfolding like a theme of the body's rhythmic and harmonic variations.

"Time for me engenders a gradual disclosure of who I am, who I might become, what I feel, smell, touch, taste, and hear. With it, combined with the stages developing in me, thoughts of time are generated.

"I contract with time to come into my own here, for time is the benefactor of goodness and goods. Time itself does not know maturity even if it acts as the agent for development from the earliest to the most advanced stages of life. Due to time's constancy, I will be able to measure the passage from simpler to more complex stages of my individual maturation. I will live up to the future to the extent this perpetual growth remains part and parcel of my past.

"With time, I will even 'develop' illnesses in a secondary expression of life—degeneration. I will be alone in seeing myself as 'becoming' at this point, for such is the epithet others ascribe to youth as they find themselves developing their lives. I will be the result of my childlike self combined with a transformed being, one conscious that life and good health encounter defining moments such as those malignant means extending to a final end."

Marcel would be born in less than half a year. Long before his birth, his "naissance," Cassandre's "connaissance," her knowledge of the world was evolving along the lines of the human, slightly willowy works within her. Her thoughts found themselves literally "born with" the creature growing inside of her, just as the leaves are literally borne with the wind. She was substantiated, justified, and connected by this development like a receiver capturing the fullness of its sound from being grounded. Her role as mother no longer belonged exclusively to the realm of the imaginary. She was now integrally related, like bedrock beneath the home's foundation, to a life's creator! She felt touched by the awesome hand, whose index finger reaches into the air love that extends to another creature, thanks to procreation.

When Cassandre slept, she found herself curiously assuming a modified version of the fetal position in which she pictured Marcel himself, lodging inside her. She wished to share in the epic challenge of depicting a child's impression of the world. She felt that her extreme awareness of and sensitivity to Marcel's imminent birth foreshadowed the preeminent crisis of some divine comedy for the would-be double born. This critical insight led her to ponder whether one's sleeping position indicated other positions of one's person in society. It is possible that the fetal position, for example, lends itself to certain personality types. She had some knowledge that others slept in various postures and positions, but her sense of being able to deduce certain traits that could be identified with specific arrangements of bodily parts struck her as inconclusive. Her natural reservation in society may have had something to do with a kind of recess, pose, or pause that one could attribute to the posture assumed during fetation. She reviewed the permutations of what to make of a type who sleeps on his or her back. Perhaps that typifies an assertive nature or, on the contrary, an open-mindedness. She did not have the answers to many hypothetical imperatives, but this did not occult her imagination from wondering what positions Marcel was passively and actively assuming within her.

"Be that as it may." Just how we occupy our place, even our station or standing in life, Cassandre believed, goes or speaks to the core of our temperament and personality. This could be very easily expressed not only in our approach to the active life, to work, most assuredly, but also to a certain passive life one finds in both sleepers and the unconscious. In the case of both of these latter kinds, a delicate reading of silence could be invoked, breathing aside, in order to arrive at any substantially viable interpretation of reality. Perhaps, in the end, music offers the best reading (with its variable moods and modes, with the inspiration of a verisimilar silence) of our various postures, introverted and extroverted, intimate or social. Music is captivating to the extent that it fascinates by the special enchantment of various movements, thereby charming beauty, enrapturing goodness, and quietly exhorting truth *to life*.

The evolving meaning of life, replete with its bounty of questions, was changing, in reality, the nature of things for this mature woman. She remained nevertheless resolute in a belief she had long held with Marc, namely, that questions pertaining to the meaning of life and existence were the proper domain of theology and philosophy. While this couple believed, in the first instance, life itself could not be said to be signifying anything specific, in the second instance, holding fast to a second stance even, they would always affirm that aspects of life such as forms of art, words, ideas, and interpersonal communication were indeed meaningful.

A source of delightful moving beauty and truth lies in finding the most meaningful expression, the fullest form, in rendering one's world to the earth and all its inhabitants collectively—even to all, that is—hopefully with complete correspondence. Rendering one's word to a work could be portrayed as no small consequence, perhaps no less a cause, either.

To speak the truth, Marcel already embodied one of the richest names in French literary history, thanks to his father and mother. Ideally, he would come to the scope and amplitude of his rapturous name by passing through the character of the one who understood better than any other his role in the world. His would be the discovery of a personage who lives for himself and others as both a character and contemplative scribe of society. To know oneself, *se connaître* would pass, as Mounier wrote of personalism, necessarily through the other Marcel, Marcel who would found himself most fully by exploring the character that shared his name and personality, he who apportioned for himself at least some measure of his story and history. He would end by having more in common with others than himself, like the elaborate phrasing of the queen of instruments expressing the likeness, the sameness of others in Maurer's "Concerto for Four Violins," a work Marc considered too foreign to the ears of such repeatedly delicate matters.

Cassandre's Marcel would have the occasion to read Pascal at a young age and come to opine, together with the author possessing a nearly matchless *esprit de géometrie et de finesse* that *le coeur a ses raisons que l'esprit ne connaît pas* (the heart has its reasons the mind does not know). In realizing this Pascalian maxim, this *sentence*, Marcel would be working out—yes, exercising his central powers of self-actualization. For in as much as one must be mindful of a tradition in order to surpass it, what is truly new only shows up in art that moves an observer like anyone respecting the supreme rule(s) of that said art, with a combination of heart and soul tied to the most profound knowledge of the past.

Knowledge of oneself thus acts as the passive or active portal through which an individual passes to accede to the world. Harvey certainly experienced this in his first half a year in Paris as the de Beaurecueils would soon see. Cassandre too was moving through an accrued understanding, a fuller knowledge of a multitude of life's forms. So too would Marcel be brought into the world to bear with him a full range of acts and action—some external, others internal—all of which would make their mark in his forms of self-expression. He would closely follow the life, experienced together with the contour and structure, the style of his namesake. His existence would perhaps mime another's literary destiny, struggling and triumphing over it even.

Marcel alone would be left to respond to his fate. This would never come without a framework, however, so long as Marc and Cassandre were alive, which granted solitude and contemplation ample space-time in order to reach out, make, fabricate, or compose the fabric of a text about society or any other subject for that matter.

This extreme distance, vis-à-vis others, would allow the author's reflection to blossom, often in unexpected ways, branching out into realms of the mind previously unexplored in any other literature. He might find himself confronted with someone whom he knew in childhood, having forgotten her name. Slowly, events could lead him from name to name, association to association in order to unveil the very word that designates and distinguishes her from any other, without some external agent lending this follower of cues even the smallest of clues. It might be her clothes as they could be seen draped loosely around her shoulders, the hair spray atop her coiffured air, the nose refashioned by cosmetic surgery, the surreptitious smile, or a simple lapse of time in her presence. Perhaps it all came down to a mix of the sustaining air and her totality, taken together as a fragrance or flavor of some essential sustenance. Yes, any or all of this could have contributed to evoking the name "Sosthène" for which he might have been searching, only to find it maintained by its original livelihood in a peculiar aspect of her speech coming to a verbal head, a head whose vitality justified any search for what had been nearly left hidden behind.

It fascinated him whence might come the last name. He could search less passively, trying various names on for size, knowing none was correct. The mind might come up blank, but not without other thoughts intervening—the creamy color of her contemporary jacket, the man she is with, the serendipity of finding her here or there, the discovery of her presence once again entering his life, now for a third time following prolonged periods of absence, and so on. It could be no less than hours later, after conversing briefly with her, that a thought of food might pop into his head, one united by her family name—Raymond!

He sought to determine what link there might have been between these two bits of intellection. It seemed as though none existed outside of his taste at that moment, for something at once more common and commonplace, something that might whet his appetite for physical needs as he might have come to discover here—only this could apparently have united, notwithstanding some particular language, the two. Nevertheless, the name Raymond itself did not seem, on the surface, to arise out of what is most popular, if perhaps most pervasive among men, namely, their need for food and the act associated, in the days and nights of old, with procreation. Perhaps this particular woman's rather disjointed, curious nature or the simple fact that she would have figured as an unlikely mother might have made it so that she would have, in effect, lost, at least for a time, her name. Furthermore, where and when it might come time to consider her for an act of love untied to child-rearing, as was becoming increasingly the case within mid-twentieth century French society, the banality of her name would appear on the surface of his tongue without affect. Surfacing was some vague and enticing notion that an entire body was being served up to another, without the indubitable interference caused by words bringing human beings *to life*.

"I am wordless here. Just how I should make sense of this world is an open, not muted question. Humans may find inherent meaning in natural sounds. This constant and inconstant movement—this personal evolution derived from an overarching evolutionary thrust—makes me think. My body reads nature's cues without language as humans conceive of these matters. I'm unsure what word I would use in lieu of neurotransmitters to indicate messages sent and received within me. This transmission model may be wholly inaccurate for the full range of intellection occurring in my esprit. There seems to be a preponderance of unselected material that never turns out to be quantified, or qualified, since the model of sending and receiving assumes something of an *a priori* intelligibility. I am talking about or from the unconscious when I refer to this state within me preceding language, language with its coherence and rules, naturally occurring or other. I would like to ponder the chamber music version of these seemingly silent messages sound. I am searching for some music of the incoherent, inchoate, irrelevant, unformed, unleashed, undisciplined, wild, feral, babbling, colorful, imperfect, unharnessed, unyoked, unknown—all taken in and given expression at once.

"If so, it would not sound like a big bang to my mind. My origins would lie in a wholly different sound, perhaps something more akin to water gliding over various surfaces, inducing life to grow and, eventually, be counted or counted upon."

The imagination can prove to be as mysterious as the mind of an unborn child. How we approach, how we cause ourselves to come near, or how we access such matters could resemble our view of films, indeed, our views on many projected subjects. The mind exhibits cinematic effects. The cause might forever remain unknown when it comes to a juxtaposition of fantastic consequences. Two or more associations may collide in a space of the mind that is without follow-through, given that no center of reason is controlling them. They might be stored, in the one case, based on a scent and, in the other, on an idea rooted in sight. Great art, like great literature, fleshes out in several *plans*, several grounds—fore, middle, and aft, for example—the various contributing effects of a single, singular cause.

In the case of Christianity, the cause interwove the notion of a mission that, to this day, consists in bearing the cross across the globe. The proper version of the story was conversion. The proper story would become history from a single prophet to a multifarious church built upon a play on the word, *petrus*, or Peter, a singular form of rock, combined with an illustrious proper noun, made flesh. Of course, the narration could begin and end in writing just as it could take form in art, music, or cinema.

Images bring with them, in any case, particular advantages that words do not play out like a source of heat shuttling relief to a body and soul on a cold day. Perhaps they more precisely approach the form of language present in a Marcel as he was in his current state. In some respects, images are like music insofar as they remain suspended in a silent backdrop. They access regions of the brain, mind, and spirit that touch upon fantasy life. They suggest imagery most often without ambiguity. They take an imagination and give it back to the conceptualizing mind, to the extent that they plumb its depths. They are like the many authors coming before Marcel and the many flowers before them; they figure as the raw data, some unconscious, some not, which one can mine to sift through the world and arrive at hearing, understanding, and listening to an entire universe.

While some images are immediate, others require a type of fabulous mediation in order for them to make sound sense like a small infant whose basic needs are often very clear, whereas others need a mother or father's interpretation to be intelligible. These latter types of images may be as fabricated as a book, as interwoven as the threads of a bedcover, as dependent on language as a page was on his feudal master. Some of them might be considered typical of a person at a particular space-time, others archetypical and still more utterly inexplicable by any theorist or practitioner, such as Marcel might become. They could lend themselves to humans either interested or disinterested in systemizing thought, to those either engorged with or lacking, for absence of a better word, a conceptual framework.

Becoming oneself entails, for the would-be author, probing the depths of all images and words, whatever their provenance and province of the mind or heart. To be, becoming oneself to oneself and therefore simultaneously an object and subject in the eyes of others—that is a question.

It is this second attribute, that made it easy for Marcel to be appreciated at present deep within Cassandre. This did not obscure however the work he would be obliged, by himself, to undertake in order to accomplish the first part of the equation—to become accepting of his own existence as worthy—in his own eyes. For this, he had a long way to go.

A Renaissance man is one who realizes that his own birth has taken space-time as the rebirth of another great being, if not other beings, who will have literally or figuratively preceded his existence and life, life that he does not simply try to prolong. Et ignotas animum dimittit in artes (quoted from Ovid's *Metamorphoses*, in "The Portrait of an Artist as a Young Man"). [And he applies his mind to unknown arts.] He is the scion of things and times past, an heir to an artistic lineage as well as the unknown. Since form is emptiness and emptiness form, the seasoned young man understands the essence of this chiasmus, as if its derivation comes from a world once removed, a place where what is moved arises out of the simultaneity of this nothingness forming and informing—yes, reforming all the while—any type of existence. He studies the beginnings of humankind to decipher the humanist content stemming from classic or classy, even ancient forms. He supplements the world of antiquity with the mark of his own stylish existence. He creates a berth in which he might maneuver, coupling above all with his own being. For some, this might be in the form of a book or creative undertaking; for others, it lies in their teaching.

For yet others, like Marc, it might be in a combination of the means for learning about the imaginary and real worlds, taken together with that fabulous craft he was creating with Cassandre in the name of the one they would christen Marcel.

The light cast upon Marcel at this point was quite literally claire-obscure. It clearly brightened Cassandre's abdomen in view of the sunshine streaming through the open shutters while Marcel remained in obscurity, shielded from too much brilliance by layers of epidermis and enveloping adipose tissue. This led his mother to theorize that it was possible a baby's normal or natural development might be derived from necessary and sufficient amounts of sunshine much like was required for the expansion of plants. Cassandre's mood was dictated by rhythms of the sun, moon, and stars, thereby influencing the fetal rhythms of growth as well. The seasons act like a melody, mellifluously inflecting moods of the unborn, moving them from premelancholy to a kind of elation in a dancing mélange of generalized darkness and swarthy *complexion*. Indeed, in the constituent temperament or four humors of the body, as medieval physiology called those layers of existence to which moderns may add their version or makeup, Cassandre did not so much perceive everything from outside the safe haven of the fetus as from within.

In pondering great mysteries, she paused for a moment and remembered a bit of poetry she had once learned as a child from a little-known English author. A piece came to mind, which played on the word *light* since in little did she feel herself to be either *légère* or *lumière* these days:

> Day and night
> All is light
> Where none fear:
> All is clear!
> Densely wait
> For Time's weight
> To matter
> And flatter
> Night and days
> Where light plays!

Suddenly, thoughts of the *Frères Lumière* came to the silver gray screen of her mind as she marveled at a prime example of how a name, with time, may inflect entire destinies. These brothers fathered cinema to the extent they felicitously mined the lights, indeed a stepchild of lightning, one of nature's most awesome forces, encoded in their own less-than-obscure name.

No sooner had she posed the faint question to herself, then to Marc, did she begin to rack her brain for the name of the author to her little poem. While it might appear unimportant, insignificant, or dull even to most, for Cassandre, it meant navigating distinctly upstream from her daily mind-set in the hidden waters of her formative years to find, at the source, all those teachers who had contributed to her existence up until this day. She recalled the distinguished Mr. de Torcheville who taught her those first words of English initially learned by sixth graders at that time: *This is a fish!* This deictic term never failed to evoke giggles midst one and all in France, this English phrase, which refers to a submerged creature wrapped in scales whose origins date from the leagues and fathoms in any number of seas. Then there was the incomparable Mme de Maintenant who never failed to lend a morganatic hand in studying the Latin authors and the emperors or nobility of which they wrote. This led to an evocation of her French teacher from twelfth grade, Mr. Bonnefoy, who always knew she would have the highest grade in passing the *baccalauréat*. Suddenly, as if thunder and lightning had struck her, raining down upon her came the name of Goodwin as that of the hand that laid down the poem whose main part she had recited out loud.

Therefore, she was led to grasp that English *per se* is a Christian language. Therein the word "good," not unlike the judicious usage of *bon/ne* in French, figures at the stressed core of all those courses of human endeavor taking as their point of departure a Christic beginning of goodwill, good faith, or goodness in and of itself. The very notion of *agape* embodied Mr. Bonnefoy in her rarely somber eyes. This appeared so even though she felt confident his faith lay more in fellow men as opposed to what would be termed, what might have been designated as some faintly, or otherwise saintly, "divine creation." Before any, he was the one who prompted her to read the great work by Ernest Renan, professor at the Collège de France, *The Life of Jesus*. She harbored little doubt that Mr. Bonnefoy sought to revitalize an account of Jesus's humanity. This seemed apparent insofar as the language teacher found himself placing his personal trust in a work depicting the life of a man, however singular he might have been, might be or might become, precisely *quo hominem*, acting within the framework of other men—that is, within the realm of verifiable history.

In Mr. Bonnefoy's class, the studious Cassandre had seen the light on this subject, so to speak; and it was not necessarily the *way* and the *truth* as the Gospel would have the disciples' disciples believe. It was this man with the seed of a scholar who introduced her to the bonus of life, namely, the good news of the literary arts and work within the world of books.

One thing was clear—if ever there was some truth to be reified and deified, to be sure, it would be most valuable were it the most highly immaterial. However, it would not necessarily arise as gloriously from the light as from darkness. She bore no illusions for the future Marcel having registered many lessons of the past. One's path to personal freedom and good welfare takes circuitous routes, ways, and means, those often demarcated as much by silence and the absence of light as by sounds gestating in the uterine obscurity of day and night. Surely, generations had turned that obscurity into a fertile terrain, here where Marcel would have but one mother to see him through the thick and thin of it. What is known precisely within the limits of its imperfection may reflect a void in the end; but this does not necessarily mean the emptiness is in itself insignificant or signifying as Macbeth said nothing, as a vacuum or the absence of all presence.

Due to the fact that Cassandre was born to a Spanish mother, she too spoke fluent Spanish so that daydreaming would give rise in her to considerations of such expressions as *dar la luz* (to render the light, to give birth). She was not long away from giving Marcel his first glimpse of light if indeed the body that enveloped him at present was impenetrable to even the slightest ray. She felt herself gravitating to the image of a stalactite dripping to full growth in the darkened vaults of a cave; her body's flux was at its most fluid. Cassandre could not keep herself from thinking how narrow appeared the seemingly umbilical ties between clarity and distinction of many varieties. By such abounding bonds, she understood those distinctions upon which all is founded out of nothingness. She wondered how Marc taught his students to make distinctions, both in textual analysis and practical applications of literature to life.

"What is it to distinguish and be distinguished?" she asked her husband who had already received the grade of commander of *La Légion d'honneur*, among other honors. Marc's response, far from immediate, led him to bring up Ariana—in the conversation, that is. His pupil exemplified for him what it was when an individual learns how to pursue more actively, making distinctions of all kinds. It was in her nature, he believed, to be spontaneous and quite social. Given this, he sensed she did not understand how the Vaubans, who lived nearby in Collioure, with a summer home at Espardenya-sur-Tet, a family whose father taught law at the same university as Marc, how neither the de Beaurecueils nor the other professor's couple sought out any meeting among them with Ariana so obviously bridging the two. She had simply never encountered the principle of separation, of division that multiplies independence in France and beyond.

A freethinker is one who is detached, largely unattached to the words of others and worldly affairs. Not unlike a judge—or more precisely a justice—as distinctions are made in the American system of law, the inquiring spirit demands that the *esprit* beg an independence of thought. This esprit is not necessarily tied to some sort of divine providence as a Calvinist would have us think and believe.

Clarity is born, even that of the kind expressed in romantic musical form, less of that which is moved than that which is removed, casting its light upon a described universe or any situation within it. One manner in which Marc taught this was to take his students on a promenade about the campus, asking them to jot down observations about anything and everything they encountered. Upon returning to the classroom then, he would ask students to class their observations in groups they themselves would create. If some saw the abundance of trees and absence of flowers—like the Wagnerian poet hears sounds of the violin, viola, and cellos in forest murmurs, or airs of clarinets, oboes, and flutes in bird's chatter—others noticed the nuances in the ambling gait of passersby in a real-life drama whose resolution comes with the clearness of lucidity. From this experience, what is the same word for both *experience* and *experiment* in French, he would suggest a few groupings, perhaps three at most, in order to demonstrate how they perceived the world around them. At this point, they would undertake to perform the same act vis-à-vis a poem or short text, repeating the exercise of observing all kinds of phenomena. They would first do this, only to put order in their observations later, once removed from the first round when they were collecting raw data of sorts. Out of the disorder—like as many rocks in a quarry about to be made into some sort of construction—out of the chaos, came order.

The young people were well on their way to adopting one of the primary methods of literary science. Their silent study and the art of arranging further acted to exert a kind of confection, an exhortation, in sum, to a type of perfection or a finish that included language's polish.

Ariana, even though naturally inclined to see similarities, excelled at finding differences, thus making distinctions. Marc encouraged her to the point of imagining the life she was currently leading with the Vaubans. He was able to compare their daily train to what she conceived of as the life he and Cassandre were advancing, yes, conducting.

He could further project the life she would come to lead as a distinguished teacher in her own right and writing. He understood that an understanding rabbi had taught her that the Torah or Talmud was not just the law as the Midrash represented the literary representations. Taken together, they presented a way of life, not unlike what the Gospel according to Marc, or others, had affirmed about the words or *parole* made flesh in Jesus's mouth. Both shared the same air and analogous spirit.

Books in general, and sound words in particular, like the power of muses, liberate a person from both himself or herself and society. The most sacred of volumes amount indeed to a path of veracity and true, authentic instruction.

In this sense, Marc went after an ambition of combining the art and science of not only Ariana's three principal instructors—the rabbi, Mr. Vauban, and himself—but also the greatest representatives of all literature. This benevolent direction, shared by the Vaubans, would steer her to rightfully separate all things and words before binding them back as is said of such lofty matters in the form for which she might wish.

It is believed that one in a thousand genes of a chromosome separate humans from one another, a fact that may lead many to conclude how wildly alike humans are. Marc, however, could not avoid the fact of vast differences among humankind. Some of those individuals the students would observe on the campus might be gifted in sports while others could be talented in music. Still, others might be better suited to provide *explications de texts*, textual analysis, to future generations while others would do better to confine their insights or illuminations to a more fictional page and perspective. Despite the appearance of temperament's influence here, a simple statistical fact determined these varying outcomes as well. There were only so many positions of different sorts in society, only a limited amount of wealth and individuals profiting by it. Poverty of intelligence, just as poverty of the material kind, would both exist as long as humans lived in societies since great wealth requires a narrow apprenticeship, a way of being in the world akin to the naked child pulled from obscurity only to learn how to clothe and feed himself physically, intellectually, socially, or other.

Assigning weight to these variable influences made Marc believe within his heart of hearts that if predetermination exists, it could be as much literary as scientifically encoded in origin. He used as a reference the balanced literary erudition and style of Claude Bernard, the savant example of Poincaré, the multiple and nearly monstrous applications of life Rabelais lent his intelligence, the all-encompassing lights of Delacroix. These distinguished men shared a common culture rooted in their mother tongue, that linguistic basis for their worldly confection and eloquent artifacts. They also excelled at punctuating disorder and silence like a traffic light that determines, or frames, random vehicular movement.

By saving artful wisdom from oblivion, Marc's clairvoyance elucidated a type of quasi-pure world for Ariana and the others who listened to him. This process of purification, undergone by his students, resembled a kind of clarification where light heating gently removes those parts and particles, which need not be considered distinguished in the final product, much as butter may be clarified. Their sanity and rationality would arise out of darkness, just as Marcel's own sparkle would first shine. Marc's particular brilliance took hold deep within himself, within the context of a struggle one has in living, not in making a living, *distinguo*. Life was worth living because of a credit one lends oneself first and foremost—*crédit*, that eminently French word derived from *credere* (to believe). He never ceased in his wish to perceive himself and his beliefs, coupled with or uncoupled from, his thoughts, in any given situation. This formed the foundation of the economy in which he found himself, an economy based on credit, belief, confidence, good—and thus, alas, poorly positioned, hence bad—faith. In brief, Marc proved, time and again, to be eminently believable inasmuch as his worldview assumed the shape of a lucid appeal.

"I believe nothing or no one *a priori* here. I trust others just as little. I come to love myself first as I extend outward.

"I'm investigating this place as the beneficiary of a will examines a safe-deposit box containing the keys, which unlock life's mysteries and treasures for the living, well beyond their years.

"What's inside a gene combines with another to serve in my formation. The education I will receive will act as a pedigree consistent with my physical, mental, and social composition. Mother's body may not *grosso modo* readjust as much as it simply adjusts one prolonged time to my development inside her, with the result it may be as natural for her to adapt to me once outside. Once I leave here, all my senses will hopefully remain intact with this same sense of wholeness, this sense I am unencumbered by others. My code and way of thinking will presumably find harmony with other ways of viewing things. If so, it will be at home in any particular place most deeply, and I will need to seek out equivalencies, analogies, and asymptotes elsewhere as many do in schools. At the limit, I may barely even recognize or know anyone else.

"For any body coming after this *corps* will be defined in my life by the intimate knowledge of this corporal, indeed visceral, sensation I find surging all around at present."

To perceive oneself perceiving the world—this was a fundamental tenet illuminating Marc's philosophy. The observation is only as good as the observer. This seemed to him as Aristotelian as it was capitalist in a system where freedom and fairness defined the foundation. This was one of the first lessons that he offered Harvey when the young man finally arrived on the last weekend of spring break. It was in the Perpignan train station, which Dali took to be the "spiritual center of the world," that Marc spoke in these terms with the young American.

Marc first listened intently to Harvey's anecdotal stories of the Sorbonne and a class he was taking on the politics of literature, a bit distracted by his persistent manner of running fingers through the waves of his chestnut-colored hair, repeating apostrophically as if he were turning away from his usual audience *ad infinitum*. "I mean, it's amazing over here! It is insane how smart everyone is! I love it! I can't get enough!"

This was the occasion, following what the student of no less enthusiastic wordsmiths was saying, for the person he imagined was listening intently to let him know what the *Maître de conférence* believed intensely. Contrary to Jefferson, Marc maintained that in dependence germs the seeds of virtue. He sensed America suffered greatly as did the world in which her power figured as the guiding light from that point where her independence was declared from more than just the crown of England, however, in the same gesture, from the crown or crest of international treaties and law everywhere or every time. Unilateralism was a danger whose risk was already run, commencing with the earliest days of a people idealizing independence above the cherished humanity that is born from the bonds of personal and social dependence. By adhering too closely to Jefferson's repugnance vis-à-vis the tyranny of dependence, the New World ran the risk, and thereby, to a notable degree, the course of divorcing itself from the family of nations.

A nation built on the excesses of independence may well have arisen out of an absence of history. Conversely and perhaps asymmetrically, the nations of Europe were perhaps destined to interdependence given a long and substantial past. The American Declaration of Independence has, to some extent, guaranteed a false liberty.

If Marc assented magisterially to the idea the founding fathers represented another watershed moment in the development of civilization's collective intelligence, he nonetheless believed French classics, united transtemporally through the open-ended totality of their documents and instructions, mothered and fathered a more cohesive, instinctive, fundamentally liberating, youth-centered, reproducible, and universal family. The French are simply one among equals, namely, humans everywhere. On this subject, Harvey's impatient questions and sense of mystery, his mystification, persisted. He knowingly larded his speech with intellectual insecurities and punctuated prose. In repositioning himself abroad, the young American might soon enough come to understand more than a lone leader has plundered—by ignoring the cardinal virtues of time's presents, to be sure, by brazenly dismissing the focused values of the arts—civil society's human and inherent riches. Many an unenlightened embarrassment have squandered real power for good, cavalierly opposed rewarding change, sullied forcibly the law, installed haughtiness, or arrogance where humility, imbibed with visionary wisdom, once ruled and curtly given Democracy a bad name.

Opposing creative forces are assembled in calling, on the one hand, a land America after a real explorer and, on the other, a human being Marcel after both a truly literary conquistador and his own protagonist. Given all the emotional upheaval explored in *Remembrance of Things Past*, one could extend the American metaphor and speak of the "United States of Marcel" insofar as all human sentiments, feelings, and thoughts appear covered in this autobiographical endeavor leading to the *discovery* of the protagonist. For when all was said and done, he was the one who showed himself, his true colors incited by foraging extensively in his repetitive "motifs of memory," as well as in his own unconscious self and the very nature of human makeup or constructs, the realization he has not only a unified identity, but a name.

While in a sense, Marc conjectured, America remains a land of explorers, perhaps due to the emblematic value of the name America, it exerts its independence from a point where the fifty states exist coindependently with a primary dependence on one another. While Marcel would come to, as Marc and Cassandre conceived him, embody a literary inheritance according to a human dimension, America would come to found its destiny on worlds far exceeding the realm explored by its founder. If Marcel would seek independence of any kind—intellectual, literary, or other—it would be in the context of a weighty past, not an undiscovered frontier, be it the western part of the United States or outer space itself. This act of exploring appeared to come, for the Americans, to coexist with the kind of discoveries that one can only make while living, searching, and researching among other human beings.

Thus, even the more naive Harvey came to agree that a fundamental hubris appears in the name Americans chose for themselves, as if to suggest that they should be permitted to remain free and independent of anything that would require them to uncover what is already there *a priori* in a given sphere. Each state is bound by a dependence on the greater whole of the United States; yet the totality of states founds itself on forever furthering the exploration, indeed the exertion, of its independence. In the one case, an entire country is formed based on the unity gained from a common wealth of independence; in the other, in a land—France—whose name derives from an entire people, a future man is formed based on the factors unifying an existence dependent on its time and place. What is really in one name is a wish for eternal supremacy through utter independence while in the other, more in line with the very nature of an ethnonym, we witness humans, beginning with the mother and father, who wish for the coexistence of a glorious past with a present tied to the future of varying humanities and science.

Rather than seek to imitate masters—as is the European tradition, Marcel likewise coming here to imitate his literary "grandfather" and namesake—Americans look to independence to define their identity, a freedom on which most everyone wants to stake a name for himself or herself. One can witness them everywhere exerting themselves in the likeness of independence;

it is common to see Americans undertaking even the simplest of activities by themselves when Europeans would only partake in the same situation as part of a group. Whether it be sunning in the park, going to the movies, or eating in a restaurant, Americans find themselves, in their culture and beyond, very often alone as they affirm just who they are with liberty and independence as their "home" base. Many post as a defining trait of their person that they are "fiercely independent." The image they project, the one they wish to attain and be, is the one united by a common desire for independence, whatever the price, however violent the means to that supposedly ideal end.

On the contrary, the image Marc and Cassandre found themselves wishing upon their future human relative, if only that of a humanist, was a future man born into both a family and a community of nations. Marcel's future would be tied, inextricably fitting into the world without end, to both a specific and general past, neither of which he could ignore if he was to find any modicum of independence.

Once home from the train station, Harvey turned to Marc, querying him in a manner that appeared as his first essay in the style of a freethinking Frenchman, "Can it be said Americans have fully understood or underscored the importance of 'Native Americans' in their current society? For we have 'illegally' massacred more than the Hurons. That was but the shameful precursor of other bellicose actions the United States of America would undertake. Incredibly, in the name of democracy, we have unduly ignored international law and consensus all the while." Marc took some faint pleasure in hearing this young American question his country from afar in this slightly oratorical way, one not without articulate political turns in the echo of more succinct phrasing. He suddenly entertained a panoramic impression that the young man was finding himself in the "teachable moment," so much so Harvey could heartily receive Dvořák's responses in the form of either "The Symphony for The New World" or, with an unusually touching, admirably woven, folksy charm—wherein Indians appear languidly dancing to the mi-plaintive, mi-playful singing of native birds—"The American Quartet." Beyond any other, it is infinitely interesting, fruitful and edifying, Marc believed, to build one's worldview on the fabric, the mortar and pestle of a man Reinhardt termed someone "filled with bottomless melodies."

The ideal Marc and Cassandre were embracing, by naming their future son "Marcel" (in lieu of the name "America," or any other, for example), differed from the choice of names for the "United States of America" insofar as Marcel's personality would follow that of a person, himself a subset of a people. The ideal, under whose banner he would lead himself, was that of humanity's totality, not just its political aspirations, whether democratic or other. Marcel was not destined to remain a conception, an idea, an ideal, or other, but rather a man—yes, a certain, at times even uncertain, human being schooled in the ways and means of humanity. His attachment to the world, even if rooted in detachment, would always be tied to other people. He would not be encouraged to go in search of anything, including his remembrances of this or that, without a sense of codependency. He would not be led to believe independence could come without an elevated disincentive or high cost. This would give rise to a way of thinking, indeed potentially, to a literature of attachment and detachment at once.

To be "free" is a lure America holds out, first to the world, then to its citizenry, in order for people to assign value to their liberty.

Over a simple lunch outside, "In Nature's Realm," Marcel's parents revealed to their American guest that they would take exception with this notion of "free-dom" or "free-ness," by recalling the lessons of the very *philosophes* from whom such ideas were interpolated. Their projected goal was to extend themselves to some gratuitous detachment called independence and freedom. One could reasonably conjecture that it is possible, the original thinkers of democracy, following the Greeks, were more inclined to favor some sort of weighted detachment and deliberate freedoms that carried with them both old and new forms of responsibility.

If Marcel were to be born free, everywhere he would wish for others to be no less unbound or unconstrained. Hence, his birth would bear with it a perpetual Renaissance in the nature of his passion—age-old compassion that is never arrested before arriving at the truth and beauty of any given matter. While he might become capable of envisioning himself as first among equals, he would be no less able to find himself, as the Baudelaire "At One in the Morning," as "the last of men." To this extent, his veracity would arise more out of Judeo-Christian sensibilities and this as opposed to Roman law.

And for Marcel's parents, "transcending" the law, be it democratic or other, transformed legitimate beings. Such transcendence does not legitimate "breaking" the law in order to supplant any "foreign" authority. Indeed, rather than a "breaking" point, there is something akin to healing, a kind of justifiable amendment to law-abiding peoples everywhere.

Paradoxically, this transcendence begins with immanence—the whole is inside the whole, just as Marcel lies within his mother bearing the dream of a subject who would come to understand that the full extent of his life, liberty, and pursuit of happiness, is contained in the nature of his being. At the outset, the new frontier, so cherished by a land founded in the name of an explorer, is unthinkable. Only through the byways of discovery, uncovering what is already there, in other words, might a person, or a people, arrive at legitimate transcendence, not the reverse. Marcel would thus symbolize the name of a great discoverer, not in the first instance at least, principally that of an explorer, though investigate systematically, examine, and study extensively he would.

One's choice of words, one's personal or other declarations of independence, is never incidental, just as Mr. Bonnefoy had instructed Cassandre and her comrades. In guiding Ariana and Harvey, for example, the literary master never forgot the one would be thinking independently in both Polish and French, the other in English and a different configuration of the same French. Marc thus realized they nonetheless blended these tongues, whose union they would have to court before consuming any marriage of their mutual dependence on others or foreignness itself.

Only in being cognizant of just how to tie one's destiny to another can one be, or become, worthy of a couple whose word is given, whose promise is rendered and kept, with an added symbolic ring to it. In pursuing a monograph study of Homer while in Europe, Harvey was drawing closer, paradoxically, to the epic nature of the human adventure at home.

While science may tend to a universalism, mixing languages, either in depth or on the surface, constitutes a play within their ultimate expression, effectively amounting to a "particularism." It is a question of what forms a worldview, one not dissimilar to the mix arising out of Hebrew texts with other tongues surrounding Judaism. Sartre's secular meditation on the anti-Semite could thus be argued, or simply posited, no less as a sacred prayer if viewed from the outside by a Jew since it is founded on germane and specific intimate knowledge of an individual, unique experience. This is one acting as an instrument, at once lively, and deadly if necessary, akin to an internalized bow, from which the arc of the existential philosopher's reflection, the arrows of his thought strike more or less accurately their mark.

Language, adduced by the writer's pen, determines the validity of a statement, the potency of a suggestion, the reality of a world depicted. One should thus train oneself, as Marc believed, following philosophy to a high degree, in the art of understanding and expressing oneself from the perspective of a language indigenous to others. This essential part of the human equation could be transacted no less than Cassandre found she herself drawing toward, coming together with Marcel. Through sharing not only a common morphology but also an uncommon lexicon, we may easily find ourselves drawn into caring for others.

Harvey was indeed left with the wowed impression, intense and new, that Marc knew from where the student was approaching all the Smith family friend had made available to his reach. The professor seemed to anticipate the young man's every move and declamatory thought. Through the night and into the next day, up until the time Harvey would depart, the youthful traveler developed a great affection for his father's confidant and advisor. The highlight of the trip was a drive to see nothing more than the archway of a former Romanesque door, still standing by its romantic self, in nothing but barren countryside near Saint-Amand. This visit to the ruins of an overarching solitude was then coupled with an informal tour of a rare artifact of remaining medieval majesty, a fortified hamlet—Castelnou—tucked away on a small hill, in the back lands of this region, without a soul in sight beyond its walls, *extramuros*. Harvey later told Marc he would like to honeymoon in this otherworldly setting, one he had discovered with such austere, intimate, isolated, nearly unceremonious, though solemn, pleasure.

Unexpected to himself, Marc was a little sad to see the young man leave that night from the same station where he had arrived just a short time ago. Harvey, for his part, felt a great honor to have taken part in such a rich inner life of someone who had been, up until this weekend, but a soaring reputation among his father's many accomplished acquaintances. He would give the professor the highest marks for everything from his manner of thinking to his solitary, though in many respects engaging, way of life. He would take back to his studies, his own family, and his country eventually, a new willingness to learn both who he was and what he was capable of becoming, in word and deed, in full. Even though the young man conceived of himself as becoming alienated from his own culture, fretting in the wings behind the scenes of his native English, he was not vexed or troubled, to say the least, by a master of the French language.

Like Marcel, the growing child overturns his or her future, recoils, and prefigures the day he or she will make erratic leaps.

"To death with latent states! I have yet to oscillate between latent moods, predating even that most pervasive spell, which will most often lend definition to my being.

"I am all humor and humors, tempered by a baseline temperament, that varies according to either motion, in or around me, and Mother's emotion.

"A latent mood which will dispel all latent states forms at the outset of art, language, music, and the times. It may come to govern me to be mostly social, antisocial or asocial. Time will tell. Genes and generations together, eventually, with degeneration, will be telling.

"The first ballads could signify the adornment of a species, which was carrying out the purpose of passing a maximum of genes on to the next generation. The muse tickles a human's ability to communicate through language. Goosebumps arise as the body's response to the stimulus of some heightened force of nature. The underlying logic of beautiful places confers a sense of honor, dignity, or reward upon me as though, in witnessing its architecture, I were receiving a garland topped with the titillating, tingling sensation of my first arousing laughter.

"My first sounds may well address a musical center, regulating the signals I will emit, according to some shared emotion between Mother and me. Perhaps even before that day, there seems to be a kind of musical cortex that furnishes each of my movements with rhythm, making my muscles dance long before I actually undertake any walking. In other words, rudimentary music may well be more natural to humans than any cultural manifestations. Music appears to me to be nature's grand offering to anyone who wishes to tend, till, and refine the forms, indeed, what's often more, the content of culture."

It was approaching her final trimester that Cassandre realized, having felt his heart leap from time to time, Marcel's posture already poised him to turn round and round the world of those around him. True, she hoped he would not be an impostor like so many of those in the public purview, especially bureaucrats, technocrats, and politicos who could stir applause for more than a few seconds about a glass of water. She did not despair that he might become a poser even though a great one as Baudelaire. And no less true did she envision a life where Marcel would be free of positions, which would carry with them, *a fortiori*, a mind-set incompatible with suppleness and subtlety.

She was beginning to see her future child as one, it is true, largely and deeply dependent upon his mother's organism for sustenance, yet nevertheless one inclined to independence. From each day forward, her goal would be to make him as independent as the ideal state had always imagined itself in France and beyond. By knowing and carrying the day, through a scrupulous understanding, a willful comprehension of each hour and age, an individual can surmount nearly any situation in which one's person is attached to another. The individual may act as if to follow another, and this by leading a life centered about an internalized vision. Life may offer itself the occasion to go on, compassed by a dial that facilitates seeing through any mass, be it information based, material, or other.

If Marc admired the seemingly political choral works of the great German composer Reinhardt even though this meticulous Bavarian artist counted himself as the least political of musicians, these tidal waves of sound issued from a ferocious sense of independence—entirely laced with dependence. The professor had pinpointed this delicate balance in a realm, he figured, that must have been anterior to any generalized conscience of the vocal *tutti* or ensemble of voices amassed in the maestro's *oeuvre*. If an aria arises out of solitude, so too could it be said, Marc believed, a historically based *Triomphelied* could ascend and celebrate a grand military victory, from the wellspring of a verisimilar seclusion or place of withdrawn active life, even one with a special abhorrence of noisome war in general. In music, as in no other art form, do we find life's dangers somewhat ambiguously supplanted by rapt senses and a mind able to forget any scrofulous peril while celebrating the remembrance of times past and present.

Beethoven's dedication to the *idea* of Napoleon, in the *Eroica* symphony, more than acting as the sign of a devotion to the other *per se*, proves that an artist takes his own independence to be more than simply the means of any valuable expression. One such means also means to signify the end in itself, generally speaking, providing others would not have been obfuscated, decidedly and decisively rendered insignificant. The first great romantic exhibited the contours of a mountainous ego, one which he never ceased interrogating and mining for the essential elements of art faithful to a past in equal proportion to the future. For this ingenious composer and Reinhardt, no less a genius for having rearranged old material in ways never seen or heard beforehand, as for the many masters who followed them, the romantic fervor remained, in a profound sense, dependent upon and balanced by classical poise.

The academic painter David represented, himself knowing how to unite both the sacred and the profane *par excellence*, this particularly French conception of a democratic ideal via the coronation scene of the same emperor at the moment he discourteously crowned himself, with an imperial slight of hand, in full papal view. Thereby, as *caput*, society's principal subject marked himself as a type of ruler whose descent dates from the classic story of the most overarching of French kings, he who had the pews turned to face His Majesty's balcony, rather than the central altar of God, in the royal church at Versailles. The separation of church and state, resulting from this form of hubris, effectively delegates to the one, as to the other, at any moment in time, the possibility of tyranny's wrath. The artist may either reject or embrace, categorically, this form of totalitarianism based on the principle of a separation from both the nation and what could be termed "God's kingdom." Hence, it must be indicated, Reinhardt's numerous sacred and choral works sprung forth to "tune" eternity, in the name of a commanding art, no less than Bach's.

In a world increasingly lured by the legerdemain of the almighty dollar, centuries following the *louis d'or*, *florin*, or *obol*, it was not difficult to discern a faith in the credit-based economy. Said faith replaced confidence in both the church and the state. By any measure, people seemed increasingly preoccupied about their occupation at this time. This was apparent, not so much given the content of their work, but rather based on the revenue, its tangible result in financial and economic terms.

It struck Marc, at times a withering skeptic, as curious that more families did not name their children *dollar* or *peso* so as to grant the child a head start, an advantageous position, in achieving the ultimate end of their struggle *for life*.

If Marc and Cassandre so appreciated Reinhardt's authoritative and commodious music, it no doubt flowed from the headway the great artist made against the tide, which seemed to be increasingly sweeping the globe, a tide uprooting all sense of life's gentle rhythms and submerging all *adagios* in a sea of haste. It was as if this lone composer had stemmed the assault on tempo by a movement's main enemy, namely, time accelerating in the hands of senseless individuals, indeed an entire culture, in and often out of control. He conformed to a due measure of things, ideas, and feelings combining sound wisdom with old-fashioned grandeur, not unlike many formidable conductors who followed him. His *andantes*, as one example, remained stately, not quickened by modernity's rashness. His last works, impromptus for solo piano, showed a full range of color and harmonics. Even if deriving their thrust from a kind of darkness makes it difficult for the listener to speculate as to the logic of its creation, some sort of embryonic art was appearing in the growing presence of a logic and contemplative tone all its own, mostly centered around dark matter. They seemed to be so giving as to be taking the temperature of a keyboard oozing with all incorporated but the surrealist sangfroid of a solitude bathing in 98.6 degrees, where a meditation's lifeline finds its healthiest equilibrium.

After all was said and done, Reinhardt presented the last truly great romantic voice to the world. And he was born just as he died, no less cut off from his first love, no less independent of the very Romance languages he had synthesized with the whole of a uniquely Western and particularly moving musical tradition.

Marc listened attentively to Reinhardt's music and found him to be as eminent a music maker as he was a musician and vice versa. He uncovered in this German's *lieder*, a voice he took as both therapeutic, to use the *parlance* of psychoanalysis, and enhanced by any measure—by any standard, that is—that which does not require a flag to mark its authority.

In whatever case, if therapy there was to be, it was not just of the soothing variety so often felt by those who suffer. Rather, more obliquely, if not saliently, it could amount to the process of a cure or healing for those who dare come from one specific milieu, only to remain ensconced in themselves and in like-minded manners. The sheer beauty of the varied tempi of his tunes, speeding up here and slowing down there, dramatic slowing often redoubled by the languishing of a nostalgia only heard in the Old World, yes, this gift Reinhardt had of allowing his phrases to breathe extended to the inhalation, indeed the renewed inspiration, of an attentive listener.

Marc believed it useful to look out to, up to, and out again precisely *for others*. Inner depth comes at that price. Reinhardt had set his gaze contemplatively upon Hungary whose gypsies provided the melodies for some of his most lively and engaging creations. He bore witness to the most wondrous echoes of ancient Greece.

Similarly, Cassandre served as the penultimate reality for having fully integrated the lessons of Cervantes in such a way as to permit all of Marc's illusions their full and proper expression. And Ariana or Harvey had already begun the most solemn of undertakings by apprenticing in the ways of the other in what Camus had come to embody in the work titled *The Stranger*. As travelers, they would embark on decentered stories whose different characters would seem ferried along from port to port while the boat was picking up more and more individuals over time, none necessarily communicating with the others on board. Nothing would obligatorily occur with a reason, hint of intrigue or plot. Moral dilemmas would not necessarily define epiphenomena, masking and masquerading as true causes of social, psychological, or physical phenomena.

Yes, Marc had convinced himself—a man in no way uxorious—in turn his wife, then his students, that the great French models of ethnology and anthropology, archeology even, were not only worth following as closely and patiently as possible. He viewed these predecessors, these processors of the past of the past, not unlike the laudable Germans', but necessary, if one were to rise out of and above, the ever-denser mass of examples who merely see, hear, or sense themselves in others. He did not necessarily believe in difference for the sake of affirming it *per se* either, and this no more than did he understand a similarity to indicate its own opposite. Marc sought neither similarity nor difference *a priori*, as if some philosophical categories might argue for such inquiry at every turn; but rather, he departed without fail from the same basic principle of his own person interrogating the world of others, wherever they may be found. More often than not, he was able to arrive at conclusive evidence with an eye and ear out, a sense of presence, one even where and when given an absence of data or broad empirical, make that, quantifiable bases for understanding any number, indeed, any quality of phenomena.

From there, he, not unlike an adept reader, might affirm what is the same or variable, then again, maybe not. Thus, he often encountered whole slopes hiding mountains of truth that he could either take or leave, literally or figuratively; for truth may be one affair while beauty may lie in the realm of another. And on many a day, Marc de Beaurecueil could be found surveying the realm of a kind of quasi-polygamous beauty more than any other. In this, did he remain ever faithful to Reinhardt, like a child to the hand feeding its beginning, its overture to the universe, as defined by more than math, physics and time, indeed, a certain material or physical life itself, *da capo*. In the end, he had confidence in art and music to falter rarely before the alter-self.

Musicians and artists, after all, cultivate memory. They make it nearly tangible. They believe some of our most insistent instruction reveals itself in our last error. We have the chance, as humans, to learn and comprehend precisely how to learn or correct ourselves. Memory becomes like the child itself, growing more enriched by each passing day. It enhances life in large measure by virtue of the noble absence encased within its presence. It is memory that transforms itself into the object of an ageless lesson in which students everywhere apprentice with their teachers. Any instruction related to remembering should not overlook the place occupied by the mind's oubliette—forgetfulness—for, with this trapdoor acting as a given in all of us, we are taken by the self-same logic, whether coming or going from the dungeon of reason.

Memory oft served Marc as the quiet sounding board for ontological study and contemplation of all things or souvenirs of space-time. The scale, form, and process of the romantic composer, arriving in Beethoven's hand at the outset, for example, offers a schemata for rendering intelligibility to the world or matters large and small. Even a single word, when filled with the naive candor of remembrance, serves as a present all wrapped up for anyone willing to renew himself or herself by both untying and tying up, once again, the knot of meaning.

Inasmuch as one might find oneself present before another, a being perhaps even radically different from the self in question, one may also render oneself before others through memory alone. This bears creative gifts for the person who attributes to the other the quality of an axis around, which turns an entire constellation of tenderness and ardor.

In recalling his colleague Marthe Albertini, who taught Native American Studies at the same university, Marc never ceased to associate her with a Navajo expression she once shared with him, having heard it in the mouth of a young Italian actor, Marcello Mastroianni, reflecting, "Memory is everywhere, everything, for even what one forgets is thrown to the wind." While Marc understood this insight variously according to his mood, he found it too as a term leading to the conclusion that one need undertake any new endeavor, like a newborn in a position of *point mort* or neutral.

It is memory that allows living creatures to remember themselves as *living* through the defiance or challenge of death and dying of the self in a space-time moved by an external agent. It is as though memory itself disseminates to one's organs what it collects from the Navajo "pollen path." It is there that beauty has come beforehand, as it will come after, there where it lies like truth both above and below, and to either side. It is through telescopic recollection of a microcosm that the macrocosm, outside of memory's realm, coincides, like the very parts of the magnifying instrument, when assembled, articulating a whole greater than the sum of its parts. With this vision of things in mind, it was more instructive, indeed more phenomenal, to take Reinhardt's musical achievements as a whole, which far surpassed the particular influence of even Haydn, Mozart, or Beethoven to name but one trio of inventors conducive to life, no mere mortals, whose uniquely patented music dialogues with the other, from time to innovative time. The last great modern composer sublimated and thus romanced the genial puzzle of classical memory.

"My volition is seemingly superseded by an involuntary system here. I am forming 'without' ceasing everywhere within me. I cannot stunt any particular growth any more than Santa Claus is hardly able to arrive without presents, with but a consoling word, in a home expecting his brand of magic.

"This place allows me to express all of myself, particularly any aspect which relates to my body. I thirst for normal growth. I hunger for strength. My code anticipates the fact that some growth may occur on the body, therefore potentially revealing the other side of life—what is deadly or degenerative in origin. I may have already said such a thing. If so, it's merely that repetition is the work of death."

Cassandre had already discovered entire surfaces of her person changed by the presence of Marcel within her, surfaces which masked many of her happiest faces. She realized her place in the world took hold beyond simple concerns of health, wealth, childbearing, and fun in a realm inhabited by a grand accord between her couple and future progeny. She was more than beside herself as she reminisced within herself about events, such as the first day she learned of her pregnancy from Dr. Rotrou, the ascot-wearing village physician who was mostly concerned with her diet in those days. She was taken by the languorous hours of physical rapture the night of her child's conception, the unforgettable moment when Marc called out, whispering eye to eye, "You are the ear of my art like the rhythm of my heart! The balance of your lifeblood revitalizes the equilibrium I hear from the start!"

Stirred she was, even by the first feelings of a sudden nausea, which she coupled with its Sartrian conception, what turned out to let the idea germinate deep within her scholastic recollection of the philosophic, nonetheless physical notion, that an essential emptiness may lie at the heart of both existence and being despite her partner's deepest attachment. The seeming assurances derived from her thought appeared as true to her as a new creation filling her belly.

She was moved to ponder the significance of chapter 13 in the Gospel according to *Marc*. This passage represented a world denied its life. It contains the narration of a human realm where even the ethical criteria men and women use to augment natural selection appear obliterated. She associated this form of flooding on earth, with paradise lost, in such a way that prompted her to not only bear in mind what follows the paradise of time regained, but what touches upon no less than a host of myths which refer to renewal. The one succeeding the most renowned ark in Jewish lore, for instance, continued floating on the scene of literature, to her way of thinking, following the arc of a flood.

From there, her thoughts lingered around Ariana's world. For Marc's disciple seemed to embody the principle of her faith whereby one is instructed to overcome the animal instincts of alimentation, lust, and dominance by acts of compassion. Cassandre then realized what Leviticus decrees when the text commands, "Love thy neighbor as thy self," that this sacred writing acts as more than a mere conceptualization to be obeyed. Hillel was not alone in decreeing, using the potential of the negative, that "one should not do unto others what is hateful to oneself." Love of another is a structural, architectural necessity; our homes are warmed when they are furnished with humanity as a house of meditation, contemplation, and reverence for all people.

This robust Jeremiahian social imperative must be integrated by a person; it should be used with integrity, like a prophecy completing any worthy action. The figure who loves his or her enemy as himself or herself is ultimately the one acting, at once, as the most conciliatory and compassionate of all if one is to judge King Marc acting in the life of Tristan and Isolde. The true hero is one who gives his life for another without consideration for his own physical existence and then some. He lives by a clear notion of life's sanctity. He is one with another in a realm metaphysical truth alone may illuminate. If this legendary couple, whose story circulated at the time of the first troubadours, really existed, it no doubt "precursed" the positive fate and suffering of kindly acts between two people, heroic or other. In a profound sense then, a mother rises to the stature of a heroine in her quotidian duties and taxing chores. This may be all the more true if the child assumes a great social role, positively impacting others by virtue of significant lessons learned and applied, beyond his or her own personal successes.

Ariana's brand of noneuphemistic niceties, vis-à-vis Marc and Cassandre, seemed to arise out of a tradition of planters who had moved beyond a life of hunters such that living had been transformed into a culture, a cultivating or seeding of all life forms. Since the seed centered all for those who planted it properly or those who simply underwent its random fertility thanks to the pollen path, disseminating the ripened ovule (containing an embryo capable of germination and further fecundity), thus universalized a particular truth about it, namely, through death life draws near.

Cassandre viewed this sacrifice that led to what is livable, joyous even, on occasion as a dissolution leading to a buoyant solution or brisk birth, which could in turn guide a series of resolutions or coming, emerging into being. Marc liked to bring up a fourth dimension, she knew, in order to point out that all was not flat, but rather sharp or acute at times.

In the womb's silence could she hear, understand, *entendre*, or at least comprehend, how to overcome her instincts, her conflicting desires, her innate fears. She could acknowledge here that its medium facilitated a union with Marc free of the ecclesiastical despotism that shackled the young lovers immortalized by the chromatics of a Wagnerian chorus. In silence, nurtured by Marcel's presence deep within her, she could move beyond a world of Eros, Cupid, or Karma, one of the physiological or psychological, just as she could outdistance the world of agape or the love of her neighbor. By virtue of the ineffable realm of the wordless, Cassandre could reconfigure her love to fulfill her relationship with both Marc and Marcel, not unlike what one of the first great romantics, Isolde, had done with her love.

This is not to say that all silence connotes darkness any more than all absence of light signals silence. For in much of that which Cassandre could not see within her, an essential mystery perpetually baffled her in nearly the same measure that it inspired her to clarity of thought and feeling. Due to an overwhelming abundance of silence and obscurity both around and within her, she found herself increasingly taking matters into her own hands. Her experience with Marcel had already made her believe the mystery of a human creation is not unlike poetry in that it need be penetrated or wholly inflected like human experience in general. Life is best lived, in a word, when there exist a fire and passion, a dearth of monotony, in truth, a yearning for poetry.

Only if life, together with lives, animates people open to useful dependence and made ever more independent at the same time can a creation accede to radiance to the kind of glory often associated with the "son of man." If it was the everlasting urge to procreate that was making her rounder and rounder, like a circle spiraling upon its own form within the dimensions of space-time, it was an entirely other dimension, call it a wish Marcel would reach out to eternity, which kept Cassandre's mere breathing inspired. She viewed that formidable place within her, where her creation incubated in divine, sublime nature more than simply some growth in a fertile organ beneath the surface.

Marc too viewed Cassandre's womb as a cocoon, a tomb even, Marcel's beginning as an end. He saw Cassandre in those days as a goddess not unlike those who had inhabited the pantheon of fertility. With some immeasurable good luck, Marcel would follow all her instruction from alpha to omega. To some degree, he would no doubt become an autodidact. Perchance something other than appearance would lead him to self-confidence and a natty look in the face of reality. As a man of letters, he would perhaps seize the rhythms of numbers or the cycles of space-time abided by the seasons, moon, and sun. He would see the west and the east as one, just as the image of the Madonna follows that of Isis upon a throne, which acts as a seat for humankind wherefrom he may shed the animal within him and adopt the *esprit de corps* of humanity. He would feel a sense of renewal upon entering any of the great French cathedrals of *Notre Dame* even if he might never have had his name sanctified during the Catholic faith's ritual confirmation. Both of his parents were in seamless accord; the child would likely, even more, lovingly come to explain that the birth of a universal principle takes, as its axis in space-time, the passage of the planet's most profound darkness during the winter solstice to what the German poet calls "more light!"

Marc believed, moreover, Marcel would come to an understanding of Leda and the swan as a story of man's spirit rising out of animality. He viewed the Greek myth of the underworld, where Persephone reigned, as a similar narrative path of life's natural course.

One could uncover another layer of a similar story in the form of Proserpina who represented the same "subhuman" ways in Roman mythology. Likewise, the cult of the virgin signified this passage to the spirit as Marc, together with a host of other readers, interpreted words and things.

And yet Marc's thought nuanced this *pensée*. His pondering finessed it by adding the dimension of the mind to that of the spirit. The former appeared to him much like that which the early Hebrews had lent to the spirit of the Egyptian goddesses. They appeared most in balance in classical times when the two interacted, much in the vein he engaged Cassandre and vice versa. Through this interplay midst the male and female parts of existence, they could arrive at an illumination of the origins of being. They could come to the fullest possible understanding of life's earliest stages.

Together, these two individuals conceived of their couple in the image of the gods. They therefore put all things into movement along the same arc of space-time as the first nomads—those first wanderers, humanity's initial travelers—who originally personified the gods as goddesses, followed by Yahweh and Zeus. It was this most delicate relationship to one another that provided them with a clear sense of all life forms.

Cassandre's body, now with Marcel indubitably on board, identified with the nave of the universe. By projecting outward to her couple and inward to her future son, Cassandre lay beyond all babbling, potentially faltering opposites. Therein, she held out, or withheld as needed, a world in which the gods appeared as her children, so extensive seemed the omnipotence and omniscience of her sensitivities. After all, little was separating her from the dependent creature inside her body. She felt as though, at last, her own being was in no way subservient to nature. She seemed to have been herself, anything but separated from the dwelling place of her most instinctual and immediate allegiance to anybody but Marcel, thoroughly unlike distant colonies or satellite nations, themselves dependent on a form of jurisprudence foreign to their intrinsic ways of life.

A mother is no less than the fertile ground that yields life as she remains forever somewhere, nourishing and protecting the living much like the magic surrounding earth's bounty. She is the link, the intelligence, between phenomena and their source. Hence, her being goes on, made divine around the circle of life, at the center of words and things by religions across the globe. Her roundness prefigures the symbol of the circle that reminds humans of the earthbound core from where they come and back to where they go. Her godliness manifests an elemental energy that is inflected within us, making her a vehicle, a system of variable energies. As a being of being, she touches upon nothingness and fullness at the same time. Little wonder she should exhibit Christic qualities of radiance during her pregnancy, just as if she were fiancéed to an aura of sempiternal happiness.

While Cassandre viewed Marcel's interior life within her innards as immanent, Marc puzzled together the pieces of transcendence, believing that through this dimension alone could one approach the child. Only philosophically did it appear possible to draw near the essence of childhood without making a religion out of it. Metaphysics would enlighten the reader the young creature would become as relates to a manifestation of the immutable sperm and egg. Furthermore, beyond all conscience, all right and wrong, like all true and false, would come into clear focus.

Marcel represented being itself, *per se*, the One, the unique that is, at once, true and in touch with all that is original. No sooner had he died to the copulative recombination of his genes, not unlike the act at the root of any animal species, had Marcel been offered the occasion to be born onto humanity. His name would be like those of the gods, a mark for eternity.

This is why Marc imagined the future inward, not so much into outer space. What occurs at the subatomic level of a creature determines the totality of its future in such a way that it is incumbent upon the human creation to research these interactions following the path of a search, or quest, centered by being and existence.

Marc and Cassandre's role as teachers of Marcel would make use of their understanding of knowledge's transmission by priests and rituals. They would give the child clues to spirituality and mindfulness. As sure as Yahweh was said to have breathed life into earth, so too would Marc have implanted precious little other within the most fertile terrain he would know. In turn, Cassandre would incarnate the female principle of regenerating, having gone, so to speak, from a neutral body within her to what she conceived of as a male arriving as her firstborn.

He who begat his offspring did so, in the case of Marc and Marcel, in the image and name of a spirit and mind as well as body. A vital force or animating principle of transformation, of perpetual movement, an eminently true "concept," defined Marcel's existence from his earliest hours. If Christ was born of a virgin, it would not prove dissimilar for Cassandre's "wunderkind," insofar as he too would be a symbol of this constant, if not inconstant, play of forms and the change resulting from their nature, function, or conditions. His process of becoming gradually more sophisticated, and in a significantly different form of himself, would mime a greater planetary evolution, sometimes in steady progression, other times in fits and starts.

Out of the matter that is a human's protoplasm, a spirit is born much like compassion arising out of the affairs of the heart. Marc was capable of imagining his wife as *Gaia*, so much did she seem down to earth and up to unearth all truths in her most fertile days. This was his form of recreation, one that is relatively strictly concealed within the confines of the imagining mind. This was no less one of his major expressions of love, an embodiment of his deepest attachments conveyed admirably along the poetic lines of Beethoven's G major *Romance*. In the exquisite capturing of Romance in this form, one whose arousing "shackles," indeed bonds, Schumann, Dvořàk and others—including, once again in F major, the master of Bonn himself—would echo, the writer of music exalts the voice of the beloved no less than he consciously investigates the reaches of human ties, all the while extolling the poetry of sacrifice.

Where others might take the procreative act of love and multiply it in simple, though not always easy, acts of sex, Marc flourished by virtue of a music that kept pace with his heartbeat. He never ceased to be at one with himself and his female partner, even, perhaps especially, when distended by the blossoming novelty of life. In the one individual with whom he lived, Marc was able to reconfigure the whole of all individuals past and present, thanks to an overarching sense of composition and the orchestration of domesticity.

This led him to single out Cassandre as the object of his devotion, much as Beethoven had looked to Cherubini for inspiration in his symphonic writing or to Händel more generally. In turn, Cassandre would single out Marcel as her cherub, that loving god of the individual. She would be at one with him, atoning or not. She would pass, with Marcel inside her, from a state of simple being to a mode of consciousness relative to another's presence within her. From there, it would be on to full rapture along the continuum that proceeds from a gradual awakening of the mind and spirit to one's ultimate sleep, moving on to a definitive participation in a sensible and sensitive awareness of life.

Just as in seemingly equal measure for her mate, it was a memory of Marc's words and voice that sustained Cassandre's deepest and most fanciful reveries. She knew that, like all of the Western ways taken as a whole, it is principally faith in one's own experience that lends meaning to life, values, and others. Marcel had become her Holy Grail, some mysterious, even mythological, matter and spirit inextricably mixed, which set in motion her sense of the future represented as a quest of love. He presented the possibility of her realizing the fullest potential of her consciousness about the world and universe. She was exerting her volition, not without obeying nature's course. This creative incubation came directly out of life, not from the conditions of some social or economic milieus.

Cassandre's sacrifice seemed to rid herself and her couple of the moral imperatives of "thou shalt." She perfectly encircled her own center of gravity. At the core of this center, or heart never hardened by other's verbal stone throwing, loomed a stillness she liked to consider as eternity. This reality appeared to be anchored well beyond all the movement now burgeoning inside her womb and those adjacent organs currently adjusting to her body's dramatic flux. She sought to gravitate around a quintessence of all that is essential and simple. This, in turn, led her to envision herself pruning those branches of her life that did not matter as much as others with respect to her child and husband.

Cassandre's ideas were born of an elite worldview, to be sure. The expanse of her mind and spirit grew with each passing day and night. Psychological insight complimented her understanding of physical matters occurring all around. She was coming to realize fully that a woman might act as a vase for nature or life itself, much as a man may act as one for society. Paradoxically, the more she made sense of what was growing inside of her, the more she found herself outside herself, and as one who enjoys the view!

This pleasure, steeped in the memory of lessons Marc had communicated to her, following her own training with fine schoolmasters, augmented her awareness, vigilance, and sensibilities of what moved her most—the transitory itself. If she had always been big on hunting down truth and searching for beauty, goodness, or unity of purpose, it was this aspect of research, enhanced and completed through memory, which fulfilled her most. This renewed sense of things led her to remember a lesson of Mr. Habamini's about religious confirmations. He professed their purpose is to signal the onset of adulthood by the timely bestowing of a name upon a child.

Through just what byways would Marcel explore his name remained a subject of the de Bearecueils' fancy. They aspired to a form of hope that would leave their child to see nobility in the name of commoners and ignobility, at times, in that of those presumably augmented with particles or effete titles. Cassandre wondered, with a schoolgirl air, what attachment he would have to his own less than decadent, self-absorbed name or to others' for that matter. She hoped he would see it as the lot of an artistic *tombola*. It was after all within reason he could be attracted to explore places like La Chartreuse de la Bigoudainie, beginning with the potent suggestion of a tradition tied to a place within the name.

Furthermore, she held out for a balance, laced between how, on the one hand, Marc and, on the other hand, she would come to teach the young, hopefully prolific boy, how to hunt for knowledge and wisdom.

This awesome series of thoughts, steeped in wonderment, transported Cassandre to the caves of Lascaux and a trip she had taken sometime before with Marc. A sense of darkness overwhelmed her. She could not but believe the spirit can be instructed, elevated beyond nature, much like that of those primitive artists who depicted the hunt upon the most obscure walls of painting known to humanity. She mused to herself that perhaps Marcel's work would one day be classed as *monument historique* for all its transcendence vis-à-vis the ritual of artistic encryption. Perhaps his would be an *oeuvre* whose invisible parts would support the visible in such a way as to most fully illuminate all sensory aspects of life, as so many works of music titled "The Hunt" had conducted inhabitants of Europe's eighteenth century in their search for the trumpeted beauty of a mental and social game. In being born to animal flesh, Marcel would paradoxically set out on the loving path of dying to the self-same flesh, only to be born again as an *esprit*—and compassionate heart of hearts—within his *corps*. For this type of incorporation, this embodiment of art's most serene calling, this quietest of a muse's incarnations, he would need other animals like other humans, much as the tree's branches depend on the trunk. Conversely, if he were a pure individual, what does not exist in reality, he could carry on anonymously.

"The name designated for me appears most palatable. Humans are capable of much worse. I like the way it smells. It reminds me of the scent of Mother's smile—fleshy, wistful, and lithe, *giocoso*. It connotes effortless grace, jocose wit, and urbanity. It would touch me to learn of its past. A fragrant body of knowledge grows up all around the name I am assuming here. Aromas of entire orchards and bouquets of vast fields color each of the letters like as many expressions of pleasure in vowels sung by a virtuoso soprano. An eminently feminine perfume enrobes what will soon be mine as if to be among the first of gifts consistent with Mother's lovely flesh and blood.

"I find the appellation awaiting me appealing, to say the least."

Humility and modesty, even if making their way in high society, remained the cornerstones of those qualities Marc and Cassandre would teach Marcel. Marc's belief in such matters redoubled in conviction the day Ariana and he visited the *Palais des Rois de Majorque*. It was in the courtyard, where an exhibit on *Roussillon's* belfry and carillons, one showcasing the delicate weave of metallurgy used by the church to adorn its bell towers that Ariana spoke to her teacher about two doctors of Jewish law.

Their expertise threaded, she propounded, both the theory and practice of life with an enduring strand of love. "Near the time of the temple's destruction," she said, "Shammai and Hillel were most active in interpreting the Talmud, the text of Jewish laws. And of the two, the one who came to the world from the other's perspective in general, the one who first studied what appeared foreign to the self, in religious matters as in any other, linguistic included, yes, he who grasped life variously assumed the greatest legacy. He ended up, right side up, not unlike a bird viewing all the land in one fell swoop, or a musician integrating an entire solo piece before setting out to play, never missing a note, never quite wrong in the sense of being off. Being 'on' was the key opening onto to more matters of genuine interest, as a matter of summarizing all matters touching on fictionalized fact or factual-based fiction, loves of artistic wisdom often scattered throughout eternity here and there whether in fleeing or fleeting the ever-illusive beauty of *truth*. When all was said and done, one of reality's ancient and enduring investigators figured as he who had arrived at an essentially humble, self-effaced understanding of the world. It was thus Hillel whose disciples flourished to the extent of the fact they came to outnumber Shammai's followers. Ultimately, the former's faith based itself, erected itself, on studious extroversion and introspection combined. The true scholar's confidence in others arrives at a point whence it may or may not have come, and thereby remains, in a word, sound."

This unfailing form of faith champions a basic good, which is to say basically, a unified and beautiful reality.

Marc marveled at the young foreigner's ability to seize the significance of her French experience, here, in a palace designed to honor the Spanish rulers of old, one traced by a craft the church never ceased to embrace. What she said rang eminently true this day. She miraculously converted Marc's affection for her into admiration, just at the moment, before this monument to the rule of law when she shed a tear in view of sunset as the last light of day cast its charged shadow upon the ramparts of the fortified enclosure. He knew she had the walls of Jerusalem in mind even though she evidently did not feel compelled to designate the true and lasting object of her reflection.

This intimate, discreet thought reminded Marc of a text titled *Le prestige de l'âge*, a contemporary novel written by a minor author he cherished. In large measure, the two main characters, one from *Lutèce*, the other from Rome, both represented in themselves and as symbols *per se*, the infinite prominence or influential status associated with the two principal *cités* at the dynamic basis of Europe's foundation. The characters, Marie and Pietro, heaped subtle praise upon one another. They, of course, became quite accomplished in this way, in their quest to be at one with themselves as well as with one another within the intramural confines of their native towns. Through praise, moreover, this extolling of one another steeped in the comprehension and encirclement of ethical comportments, they applied themselves to commend understanding of all kinds.

Marc suddenly felt Marcel radiating from within Cassandre. The one was lending prestige to the other, a power of enhancement oddly similar to that of the subtext inscribed in the pantheon as represented within the context of both the greater Rome and Paris. He already seemed to envelop all the masterworks of great men long past as if his life would lead to the transfixing realization that solely the search to recover what had gone before would regenerate life worthy of the death-defying term *out of this world*. His cloister would be an eternal womb in which depth would exist without end. Breadth too would be here, bound by the miracle of analogy and beauty thriving at one and the same time. To the extent he would contemplate the Great Comforter, his sense of space-time would interlace his understanding of his mother with the very nature of one's life, absent, if it is possible to bear the impossible in mind, all culture. Upon himself and the tangential reference of another at play within his name, he would build his *chez moi* and *chez soi*, his "at homeness" or sense of oneness. Within the domain of his inner world, he would act at once as high priest, king, and first disciple.

It may well be true that it will always have been possible to seize the reality of the day by a detachment vis-à-vis light's most obscure opposite, this divine mix of darkness and the unknown embodied in those earthly creatures furthest distant from us in both time and inner or outer space.

And the very warp of literature, like the arc of music or art's illusion, seems to remain our best chance of understanding the complex science of this or that "lensing effect" through which our vision joins other expanses of the curves reality represents.

The essential absence governing the present would not falsify the memory of things in this world as often is the case of those who, say, in a sport, change the rules of the game in order to record a different memory for the current generations of spectators. In fact, these latter agents of change often act to obliterate the past as if to suggest it should be relegated to the archives of our attention. Marcel's gift would equal his present insofar as both would come from being *délié et relié à la fois*, deliciously detached and religiously tied to both himself and the world all at once like a bow at times atop the intestinal fortitude of the strings.

While others would appear modest, as Cromwell's distant successor observed, since "they have reason to be modest," Marcel would follow Marc and Cassandre's type of ease, simplicity, and humanity insofar as he would seize others as categorically never fundamentally absent, never untied from the absolute unity of a relationship. The key that would fortify and allow one to pass through the walls of his soul could be read in Leviticus as well as any other text, which takes as its point of departure its very point of arrival, namely, once again, loving one's neighbor as oneself.

In sharing this train of thought with Ariana, Marc found himself too little surprised when she concluded, making use and light of an important Hebrew word, "The recompense for a *mitzvah*, a good deed, is the *mitzvah* itself."

Indeed, upon hearing his student speak in these terms, he felt a Mallarméan sensation akin to some reward in the end, some return for an investment in turning out and into the direction of another what the poet, not insensitive to the barrenness of even half a solitude, derives from that "nearly vibratory sense of sound." From the Symbolist maker of verse to the Impressionist artist who crafts painting based on sensation, Marc removed nothing out of the full silence they depicted. He was acting within a framework where one feels as invulnerable as did Augustin Desforges at the close of his creative life. This great painter sought to make good on, and enliven, the muted world. Whether it was a question of a still life with fruit, following the viands or the setting of tables by Dutch masters, Marc's present mind set in motion ideas, which continuously brought him back to Marcel's *mouvance*, his mobility, or sphere of influence, within Cassandre. The tenure of his limitless prestige would likely last, perhaps well beyond nine months and a day.

As the acorn is reputed to contain the seeds of not only the giant oak but also all of civilization, Roman, Parisian, or other, so too did the fetus inside comprise all the potential dimensions and branches of man's culture. Marcel was as moving in space-time as he was in motion for the emotional spheres of those whose sensibilities turned into the sounds of his silent presence. There he was, already authoring dreams where sensitivities hoisted the anchor of what really matters. He nearly seemed to be prematurely singing Gershwin's "Summertime . . . and the livin' is easy!" He appeared to remind his parents of an essential absence at the heart of every grand presence, of something or someone removed from oneself, in such a way as to suggest as much who one is in reality as who or what one is not. Only by being disengaged, at some, if not every stage in a relationship, does an engagement, paradoxically, last.

Absence keeps the pulse of a presence vibrant. It affords us the necessary luxury of memorials wherein we devote our personal pledges to a greater life. The heart of Cassandre and Marc would grow fonder for one another once Marcel would appear as more of an external, independent, and organic presence. Surely, through both the figurative and literal references coursing through his name, Marcel would not find himself absent from a long line of artists' past. His seemed as bound to a fate as the English word for "Jews" could be found, not without the same irony with which one finds "gold," as a matter of fact, in the proper noun "Goldenberg," with significant links to the substance in the common noun "jewels." In any case, given that, beyond the word, it sets the precious stage for music as the altar for religion, "silence" is golden.

This rich inheritance of the name allowed Marcel's parents to understand what Ariana had explained to them actually figured at the core of Hebrew names. Names—in this language whose books begin where Western texts end—are defined by the dense action or presence of verbal roots. Like Jacob, already as a name, implies the character of the boy and subsequent man who would turn out as a deceiver, or like the Midrash implies interpretation by the mere presence of a constellation of specific letters composing the word that signifies the great text of biblical interpretation, Marcel would become, in other words, at the very least, a physical presence, which would implicitly serve to recall a transcendent past. By this, therefore, the potent or potential author would remember the absent, perpetually becoming future.

It seemed as if all art worthy of the name was sleeping with him as early as his first day or night of conception, only to be available to the gentlest of both dreams and wakes. If a careful vigil watched over him in the sepulcher that was Cassandre's body at this time, it would be no less an immortalizing vigilance that would care for him once outside, where his movements would be accompanied by the emergent music of his first cries and utterances. Consistent with his initial sounds, wordplay, and subsequent attempts at formulating meaningful speech, Marc's hope was to wheedle or coax, deploying erudite guile around the young boy, as he would near the age of two in order for him to begin fiddling with a violin. They would go to music stores, look at pictures, hold one purchased for the occasion in the home, anything to lure the *débutante's* interest in creating a box step with this god or "musesend," this unexpected boon and stroke of luck in hand. Cassandre assented entirely to this ambition, fully knowing just what it would mean to Marc were their son to play "second fiddle" to none other than himself—a great virtuoso of this, the sweetest instrument, the heart and soul of an orchestra, almost the genuinely wordless soprano.

Beyond what left them both speechless, Cassandre and Marc had set out to foster the novel from the beginning; however, strangely, neither partook in the redaction of a fictional work of their own. This intrigued both Ariana and the Vaubans with whom she discussed the curiosity of this phenomenon. She was struck that a person could be so enveloped by a particular kind of work without ever having any intention to undertake it himself or herself. The role of the critic and literary historian always seemed ancillary to her since poets and litterateurs garnered the principle renown, of course, where they withstood the test of space-time.

Ariana interpreted Marc's abiding interest in her as one steeped in good feelings, sentiments neither spurious nor scurrilous. She trusted his supervening opinion, this following her own, which she was in the early stages of developing. Nonetheless, she found herself bereft of a full sense of what an immortal writer had sketched as the opposite of her belief in positive, authentic feelings when he showed himself to subscribe to the mischievous thought, "One does not necessarily make good literature with good sentiments." What's more, she saw that Marc in particular acted, with his measured word, as a person pregnant with the totality of good verse and grand fiction, so greatly did his mind and heart embrace all that had gone before him. He had explained to her in confidence, some time before, that he did not pursue a literary career out of a modesty of sorts, not for a lack of proper material. To some degree, one need forcibly contrast goodness with its opposite and use context—in writing—in order to elevate a mind's or spirit's experience to art.

What Ariana learned from Marc corresponded with her previous experience in France's finest academic halls. What her mentor divulged did not clash with a similar abstention she observed in her best friend at the École Normale. There then did she learn that Frédérique Dupin would not, for all her astonishing abilities in matters literary and sociological, pursue a work of fiction in itself. These were not necessarily careerists, like so many others, who found fortune talking about literature and grammar, language and culture. They were individuals of letters, humanists who had chosen careers in the arts and science of literature, given the path provided independence of thought and, to some degree, freedom from financial preoccupation. They were content with becoming *fonctionnaires*, employees of the state, who professed within their treasured domain in return for a relatively fixed, though commensurate, financial situation. This choice naturally led to another advantage—a lifestyle compatible with the indefinite tenure of raising a family and publishing what could amount to a plethora of scholarly books.

Ariana gleaned from the seeds of this difference that the life of an artist carries with it the moods of a variable temperament, fluctuations derived from a type of constant, saturnine "tenebrousness" or gloom, whose obscurity always begs illumination. It appeared to her the critic's concern was more or less fastened to time; whereas the authors she most admired gravitated around an essential liberation of themselves, if not others, from the fetters of history through the story of a search leading them to the timelessness of something eternal. This story could be, as well done as any other, a simple recovery of memories displaced by the happenings of space-time. And this form of the everlasting, to which Ariana so assiduously adhered, could be found turning and returning beyond all revolutions of the heart or other. All devolved to love in this scenario.

She tended to view the model of a critic as a theoretician like Hegel; whereas the writer appeared more as a practitioner like Goethe. She believed that, in large measure, Frédérique identified with the great thinkers such as Marx, Durkheim, Dumézil, and the fictional Bergotte as opposed to the great poets of the same time, the muse's scribes whose names endure without number. Where one speculated about universal truths, the other was made to amplify the same.

In a similar manner of how Mr. Dumézil benevolently watched over all the *caciques*, those who scored highest on each of the *aggrégation* exams designed to form future professors and researchers in France, both Frédérique and Marc looked after Ariana's literary ambition. They were the ones least insensitive, in sum, to all that remained unsaid—like as much obscurity—in the light of her personal expressions. Indeed, independently of one another, both cited the passage of a work for her by Desforges's unmatched literary contemporary, Blaise St.-Dieu, where the author makes a novelist's grandmother refer to her subject, himself a budding writer of fiction, as "one who speaks better than a book." Under their tutelage, she would come to make *catleya*, even *catalpa*, with the world of letters, those flowering providers, one and all, which furnish an eternal, abiding love with no less than its own excrescence, thus regenerating a sense of marvelous beauty. She would find that words embody no less than the potential and power to create the character of a person. By simply evoking "scruples," an author sets a scrupulous tone for at least part of a work. Like words of which it is composed, literature holds out perfumed clusters of wondrous insight and style, which nurturing care alone causes to grow and, indeed, blossom, no less than both common and rare petals of the orchid family.

Marc's preoccupation with Ariana was not dissimilar to the fear he already harbored for Marcel, namely, that he did not wish for either to become professional wordsmiths. His contention was that professionals often became obliged to speak or write whereas *amateurs*, by the very definition of their likes and loves, shared their art without external compulsion. The internal world is spared a fundamental violence that occurs in turning out from that point where one is free to express oneself most fully without consideration of institutional codes or constraints. The dynamic language of art expresses a basic symbiosis between the academy and the artist whose *oeuvre* reflects a marriage of mind and heart to a silence. The celebration of this wedding may occur at distant times and places, just as it may be fashioned in close proximity to the fortunate one who is groomed in the forms of the least corrupt of institutions. Only the most pure arrive at the light of day that allows them to bear witness to creators who have surpassed those oft static, lifeless forms.

The artist resembles the trickster who reminds those participating in the unfolding ritual of a show of culture that he is not the form itself even though he masters it. He does not stick to the image he portrays any more than he necessarily sticks to the use of imagination over experience, of theory or other types of practice. He resembles a great chef who presents his finest meal in order that a knowledgeable patron may transform the culinary experience of eating to a substantial way of life. This contrast enhanced rather agreeably the sad, wasteful fact of merely living to eat; the one who wears a tall white hat transfixes, in no less than the elevating power of food, the substrate served up, for having sublimated the imaginative mind or spirit of a consumer, following to the kitchen that of most skillful farm or seafaring producers. The artist macerates in a humor all his or her own as though an individual were pickling without becoming overly hardened inside the heart and hearth of the unknown. Art quietly beckons artists to act as preserving agents for ancient mystery.

Reinhardt's own mental itinerary passed, at some point, through a period where he found himself coalescing in excess of Beethoven. Ariana had experienced a similar lingering about her great friend from the École, a proximity that acted to fasten her identity to another, rather than liberate her. For some, too acutely under the influence of others, it may take untold, not to say umpteen years to uncover the trick to personal freedom and independence of thought.

If Marc, for his part, like Cassandre for hers, was ever to err, he wished for it to be on the side of art, not on that of its conceptualization. Together they found more satisfactory what was moving as opposed to that which fixes, without end, one's appreciation of the world. What was to be considered beautiful and thus, literally moving with the stars, transported them further than that which appears sitting still. Those rays of light deep within the most night-filled reaches, that glowing fold of an involute universe, illuminate the nature of a matter's eternally attractive, stabilizing gravity. This is, at once captured and liberated by any composition worthy of high standing in the eyes, more precisely, in the expanding and contracting pupils, of an admirer. Paradoxically then, the professor reserved his highest marks for the *amateur*, the artist, and the practitioner of art in all its glory even though his own personal and professional sense of theory proved itself, time and again, understated albeit, in no way, deprived. Art complements and supplements reality like an *author* literally and figuratively, as the etymology of the word indicates, *augments* life.

"I feel pressure all around my body, basically pressing everywhere within me. The idea of some force exerting itself on the surface of things, foreign to me at this point, would only double the physics I feel acting on me.

"I sense little external tension to be a part of some creation which is more than flesh and bones, blood, and humor. No moral power, no incapacity for change, is acting on my mind or rudimentary will. And yet I seize on the meaning of ethics as a place wherein one may be born, emerging from these more physical confines. I see my development less from the outside than from the point of view of each molecule coalescing with even subatomic particles to constitute a whole.

"In the first instance, I alone preside over my development, leaving the power of the editor to Mother's body. Her various miraculous systems know how to rearrange any errant body language when it comes to me. Her body just says the word and mine falls in line.

"This can take place even while she or I sleep. Some motions are, like in a wider context, 'tabled,' others are 'shelved,' bound to remain as if lingering in their latent state.

"Even here, without anyone's concerted attention or verbal input, life goes on, increasing or decreasing, softening or hardening, rising or falling, becoming more spirited or not, from hot to cold, sitting still or moving on, and so on."

Although Ariana still felt herself too young and inexperienced in the fullness of life to compose a work of prose, she did find herself fascinated with the act of writing in accordance with principles of prosody. None of the poetry she manufactured, in line with metrics and rhyme schemes steeped in disparate sounds and often scribbled *en cachette*, as if in hiding, contained any overt narrative voice guiding it. She avoided medieval forms such as the *triolet* and villanelle. Even ballads were as conspicuously absent from her hand as *allemandes*, *courantes*, *bourrées*, *pavanes*, *quadrilles*, or *gavottes* were from her feet, her measured dance, so to speak. Her form of predilection was the Ronsardian sonnet following that of the humanist Petrarch. The *canzone* form's alexandrine meter appealed to her most in as much as its cadence appeared as symmetrical, taken *in toto*, as French classicism was to ancient Greek forms of the same genre. She particularly appreciated the apostrophic form since she felt inspired by individuals whom she could address through the various aspects of such a "calling."

After having shared a bit with Marc, his response to her efforts referred discreetly, albeit decisively, to Rilke's writings in French, chiefly those included in a collection titled "Vergers," "Orchards." They painted things in words, depicting some of the fruits of his faithful study in a foreign language the poet adored. He also mused over the recollection of his youth when his pedigree aligned itself, taking shape with readings of Byron and Shelly, Mickiewicz, Krasinski, and Slowacki, those latter creators figuring among the great Polish romantics who sought refuge as much in their writing as they did in France herself.

The professor added Reinhardt was a virtuoso pianist who spoke the language of the violin most singably. Moreover, many notable musicians approached the "musical if literary game" from other perspectives: the thirteenth-century King Alfonso X's *El Sabio* of Spain; the amateur Holborne, a man of many legal talents; and the flutist monarch or cellist King Friedrich Wilhelm II of Prussia, come to mind long before the chemist Borodin. The name of the game for these creators, as for Ariana and other artists, is an informed open-mindedness, an accomplished availability, a sense of intimacy with others' way of speaking and writing. A reader may make this clear and present when he or she enters the voice or voices or a writer.

The professor concluded that Ariana's work carried with it something of a curious translation, an affect or more specifically an effect, whose cause reminded Marc of what he called the left page. For the great reader, dating from youth, this reference to the *gauche*, the left side of a volume, recalled the copy opposite the original of the many bilingual editions he read from the publisher Aubier.

Ariana fully expected the most severe of criticism from her master and found herself happily surprised with Marc's form of celebrated realism. True, she also perceived his backhanded praise and took it for little more than what it was and intended itself to be. Marc was clearly attempting to evoke, in relation to her, a poet who believed one must not write unless armed with an overwhelming sense of the craftsman's imperative to gently lay down one's thoughts, surrendering, to none other than the virgin page, all to the care of one's inspiration, indeed, inspiring words, music, or silence.

Given that Ariana saw the de Beaurecueils as a trio, she found herself composing another small piece for Cassandre and Marcel, this time in her native tongue, which she translated from the Polish in order that they might seize more than just sound. Since she felt unsure about the use of forms other than what was typically classical, she did not believe the decision to call her tiny creation "Poetry" should rest with her. For this type of account or some such accountability, she always preferred to defer to the responsive and responsible professor and the family of thoughts forming around him, much like the train of fluid beauty, which had unveiled flowing form around Cassandre's head on the day of their wedding. To be sure, she had already fully integrated her rabbi's dictum: "I am never the best judge of myself." Thus, she titled her poem as she viewed it, calling it, the very art form and medium, in other words, into question:

"Poetry"

I harbor, in my sails, the waters' edge
I unite the winds' absence from the craft.
Anchored round others, cherished fore and aft,
I'm the shorelines' presence nearby a hedge.

I harbor, in my sands, a secret's tale
That has no end, nor the means to an end.
In reality, as sand, the time I send
Preludes our veiled departure as a vale.

I harbor, in my salts, the vain preserve
Beauty has left, leaving with some reserve
A refreshing grain, inclined here to serve
And bring to life slips' fixed, yet moving curve.

I harbor, in my seas, many like me:
Darkness heightens light, algae our delight;
For vast waves wash us, as stars watch thus bright . . .
Water, bathing me twice outside the home.

I harbor, in my sages, the siren's call,
Where singing lures man beneath the rocks . . .
The rest, his air, arresting at the docks,
This ribcage lunging—once, more, and for all.

Cassandre felt touched by the honor of Ariana's offering, so much so the charmed interpreter of "Poetry," becoming more portly with the ebb and flow of pregnancy, made it a point to bring up Beethoven's op. 1—a piano trio fraught with invention and implications for creative energies, an initial glimpse of tremulous light radiating from a powerful accord of chords. This figured as her way to elevate the young Polish woman's veil-eyed sense of art to a kind of synesthetic sensation Cassandre experienced in reading it. She perceived its contours along the lines of a singing modesty, this soft-spoken ambition as magnificent as it is manageable. It appears as though all particularly engrossed, bemused poets of the real accept exquisite shackles when their line of thought and music carry forth the inflection of a constant, to be clear, a steadying triumph of sacrifice. Name, for example, any poet of consequence and you will doubtlessly find he or she has reformed or sequenced reality in a good and timely way, never wide of the mark as inexperienced artists could be. There is nothing like the greatness, the unique grandeur folded into one who yields to truth and beauty as elaborately as form and content alone marry before the absolutes revealed in their union. To extend this to its logical conclusion, one may venture to say nothingness, unlike nothing, is meant to be molded afresh, with sweeping strokes—divulging slashes and disclosing gashes—in space-time.

In reading her verse, the pregnant woman could not but harbor an odd sense of various forms of fledgling art, art announcing, even in its charming "maladroitness," something less awkward and clearly more encouraging to come. Like a lighthouse signaling the peaceful haven and backdrop of a marina to any craft tossing, turning, and bobbing about in an engulfing maelstrom, a tempest only accentuates a human's floundering search for a place at once rational and sensitive, let alone agreeable. After all, Cassandre and Marc viewed Ariana's writing equally. On the one hand, from a certain perspective, they uncovered therein elements of a voice which appeared wrapped in words, like the song of a young bird, wreathed in downy feathers designed to elevate the creature's flight in the air. On the other hand, they were not unaware of the inexperienced poet's shortcomings. They pardoned Ariana, with the grace of the most indulgent clemency, with respect to her poetic license. In truth, she presented herself as having every intention of composing words for readers, not anyone else, movie and theatergoers or others included. Hers was a natural, unforced gift that showed no sign of specious, scurrilous, or insidious manipulation.

Nothing, nonetheless, kept the young poet from imagining Cassandre's pregnancy as a film, something like a home movie. This auxiliary form of art and extension of her own would represent one in which the actress herself would carry a real child to term. She could as easily envision the same story acted in the theater, one in which the value of action were as preeminent as silence. This tale would reflect a nearly wordless, eminently musical, play. It would turn out to be, paradoxically, an articulate and elaborate, if deliberate, play on words as much as a play between people's and peoples' words, taken together, all right, with their inheritance, will, and deeds. Visual strategies and storytelling methods would be employed as hobbies happily deployed to pass the time. Over the course of a cycle bearing the sign of absent artifice, a creation, in large measure man-made, would reproduce the essence, if not the order of a physical and mental universe, without making use of any special effects. Life here then would willingly transpire, not unlike what they had hoped would occur with death's regrettable arrival due categorically to natural causes.

Ariana's interest appeared to the de Beaurecueils as genuine as an original Rembrandt, one scrutinizing one's own gaze in the style of a nearly impersonal self-portrait. The artist's regard for the world took hold, beginning with the perspective of a person keenly interested in both herself or himself and how people best live together. Not missing from the poetic equation of this unity surrounding both the subject and object, taken together with the objective, was the intensely romantic poetry of their living dreams, sanity, and sanctity as humans.

In the end, through her understanding of things, people, and words in French, Ariana sought universal truth, truths everywhere, self-evident goodness and beauty. In point of fact, she was fortunate, like none other, to have landed in the Vauban family and parachuted into Marc's professional domain since it was here that a vantage point was born, a novel perspective from which she could see that no universal can be perceived without some local color at its foundation.

And little seemed at once more quaint and potent than the world seen from this verdant, vine, and orchard-laden valley surrounding Eus-sous-Soleil. Here lay an ensemble whose silence could be best heard, both day and night, with a view of the university in the distance. It is entirely comprehensible why Ariana had returned here for this extended visit following her year abroad in these lovely, lively parts.

So squarely did the passages of fiction have a place at this superb mountain base, both teacher and pupil, not without the librarian and the works she sheltered, obtained, indeed attained, a majestic sense of *grandeur* through all that is miniscule. Those who lie in waiting behind the scenes perceived the major through the minor, the all-encompassing through the seemingly incidental or uncertain. Valued here was something as common as age itself. The elderly inhabiting this magical world of old, one another within reach of youth and intimacy, were prized and privileged by this very skilled brush with a certain Vuillard and more sketchy if filled with the more brightly doubtful Bonnard. Not only were individuals' years primed, so too their sense of space-time appeared multiplied, extending in all directions, out and into both the present, coming day, and what is more, to a becoming past.

This is how Ariana had made sense of the story Mr. Vauban once told her about the time in which he and his wife were attending a concert for solo cello by Pablo Casals. Together with their firstborn, Pierre, who was five years old at the time, they heard the master instrumentalist play in the eleventh-century abbey of *Saint Michel-de-Cuxa* such that the heavenly airs appeared to eclipse even a violinistic Feuermann rendition of the same masterpiece. There, all was far removed from any of the noise one associates with life outside a cloister, this covered walk, or place devoted to religious seclusion, whose columns and capitals issue the currency of an authentic contemplation.

Like the narrator who believed himself in exile for a prolonged period from the banal quotidian, thanks to a type of asylum situated midst the heights of the day's exalting event, she found herself at home here—in chapter and verse. It was like living in a wondrous volume, one filled, beyond a doubt, with melodious enchantment. It was not dissimilar to coming alive in a fabulous book whose organizing principle was not so heavenly, however, as to disconcert the earth and its underworld of whose rulers one should never lose sight in order that just measures be posed and composed as (well as) possible.

Wordless music supplies the language-bound human with rest from linguistic clutter, verbal noise, shifting meaning and mental straining where one attempts to understand different senses. We are able to engage with the world once suspended. As evidenced especially in the young and elderly alike, music resonates with memory to create a kind of tremolo of happiness, a baseline giddiness over which all the rest of life's vicissitudes may flow and play. A person in tune with himself or herself—like signature melodies of great composers or musicians—may be moved, to be sure, removed even, by a dreamlike animation. All may freely follow a soulful line to its more or less meaningless end.

Not only due to the fact that Mme Vauban was a physician, specializing in cellulite, but also given her keen interest in the true liberty provided to one who leans toward a fictional world, and this not just in the confines of the fictional work, did she too wish to facilitate Ariana's experience in both France and French. The mother of Pierre and another newborn, also named Marc, discovered little by little what she saw as a kind of play in Ariana's words. The movement within her lexicon and syntax left the inquisitive Mme Vauban with a sense of some colorful theater where words stretched well beyond their significance to reach a realm otherwise untouched by any other medium, even music, to speak frankly.

She thought this even though she too loved harmonious compositions, especially by—and by especially—French musicians, whose fluent tunes served as ramparts for a soul in the face or facade of a reality all too solidified by material banality. At the confluence where one of her little sonnets meets a complicated but exactly, if slightly haphazardly, wrought civilization, something elaborated an urbane sophistication of the youth's delicacy, cuing in Mme Vauban's heart a fond memory of both Ravel's and Dvořák's instrumental duet diminutively titled *Sonatine*. The piano's majestic effusion of simplicity was then followed by a kind of operant response to the environment of the first of these sonnets and its echo—Debussy's *Suite Bergamesque*, the highlight of which is, of course, the ever-impressive center, less of gravity than artful levity around *La belle époque—Clair de lune*. The Frenchwoman recalled with hesitating tenderness the love she first felt in hearing his *Quatre chansons pour la jeunesse* (Four Songs for Youth). Furthermore, thought this young mother, it is not out of hand and arm's reach to conceive of the same composer writing his "Children's Corner" or, for that matter, Bizet corralling his *Jeux d'enfants* (Children's Games), for the playful fun of young and old alike. Ariana could only liken these works to a piece Marc had played for her, among others—Reinhardt's late "Romance"—one more lovely work for solo piano germane to the nostalgic idioms of this language-learning guest from beyond the border. Truly simple art may compound our desire for unencumbered ease, natural artifice, intricate nudity, or lucidity through and through.

The private practitioner's manner of reading joined Ariana's in withdrawing from the academic's world of "publish or perish." Here the reader was drawn into the player's parish, one void of more common forms of any praying or preying to speak of. She felt drawn in by an almost childish type of playful illusion, a perception of reality not entirely erroneous however, an attractive apparition no less present in the community of the musician's congregation than in the supreme aggregation to which his offerings referred by either divine combination or genetic recombination.

Here, in heeding the intelligent perspective of a story recounting the muses' august presence, Ariana would freely entertain herself at length and continue apace. In scanning the sounds—together with the rhythms and harmonies—of a sonnet whose beat is marked by time, as well as timelessness, she showed herself to be infused with the art of listening.

The innovative novice was not without others present in the *esprit* of her homage to *belles lettres*, attentive as she showed herself to be to the constituent elements of language. Like as many notes in music might prove to be, in the face of a patient life, that interval, between birth and death, she was finding herself here and there wherein one awaits some sense of unity by virtue of the inward most ear or chambers of one's thoughts. She could attempt to fathom, for example, to what extent one's future is affected in view of humanity's various communities by the constant gaze of others. Even seemingly innocent people passing by cast a look that layers tacit, even taciturn, reflections in such a way as to create the sedimentary personality of someone who is influenced by what otherwise implies an absent regard for any inner life deposited at the core. By this, she persuaded herself the vast majority of people seem to become who they are based on the vain reflection they receive, time after time, from another's gaze, like the painter's watercolors or oils layering beauty on a canvas, however meticulously and arranged. This sounded true, to her mind, this sad reality she opposed in the more fertile reflection deriving itself here, less from a glare, more from the glow of an inner world principally dominated by music, if by only purified silence.

Ariana was further inspired by Frédérique's boyfriend, François Viognier, even when his intellect or emotions stimulated her through the very banal, thanks to the *bon mot*. A strapping young beau with a noticeable birthmark on his ear, François once instructed her, for example, over dinner in the canteen of the École by referring to the metro as he expressed the following with a singsong voice, finishing his observation on the note of a "good," at once ambiguous and unequivocal in French: "When the underground corresponds to the world above ground, when the outer world is seen from within, that's good (*bon*)!" This admittedly obscure phrase left open the possibility that Frédérique's beloved could have opted for either the word *bien*, as readily as *bon*, in his choice of the French *good*. In tall and stalwart truth, the latter was as much a durable affirmation of any number of essentially positive aspects of life, whether they be aesthetic, ethical, or other, as in itself an entrée, in the full sense of the word, to another, nourishing world. It serves, or is served up, like as many bonbons stimulating the life of young and elderly alike. It could pass, moreover, as an apt metaphor for the entire repast of those cherished, dear, even sacred *cènes*, (suppers) last or other. What's more, it could equally cover as many communions representing various stages of the most memorable scenes beyond good, not to mention its inverse. In reality, all this was contained in that quasi-note or bill of sorts, that is the *bon*.

All this was comprised in that form of a *bon* acting as a veritable *billet*. For it signified an implicit and explicit reservation when referring to any good, bad, or evil, in the end, that discreet overture in fact as in fiction, which opens onto an obscure universe with countless fruits of infinitely diverse worlds. This is where every trace of all ages could be savored not only by great minds alone, rather by all members of the community alike. Yes, here took pleasure not solely the mouths of those normal consumers exchanging discourse pregnant with both meaning and significance. Here so too reveled in delicious "commodities of conversation" their guests, recipients of gratuitous hospitality often familiar with a "precious" world. They too were human "elements," supplying ne another with savant conversation as they found themselves cashing in on the subtle verbal currency animating the otherwise bland, soft-spoken, indeed understated, literary and scientific school's dining hall. Here, each individual's story took precedence over any other, often egoistically, as though each believed, without a doubt, in the immediate virtue of Gide's literary imperative: *Jette mon livre* (Throw away my book)!

It would therefore not be by chance were the *good* student to come to the conclusion that Desforges's painting, like *good* literature in other words, indeed filters life, still, for the eye. The good and superlative work of art accomplishes this, not without rendering its rich abundance, even if depicting the austere paucity of poverty among others, even the eventual friendship thrown to the wind wherein the heart winds up broken under the sway of a twisterlike blast of air whose blow levels the most fragile and sturdiest of foundations indifferently.

While various forms, wholly dependent upon the eye, could not necessarily hear the productive and reproductive beauty in which someone like Marcel was currently bathing naked, covered by skin alone, great art cultivates an imagination's independence. True, "the eye hears," just as poetry proclaims. This presumes however the very same visionary or visual organ does not settle for the lesson of anyone who filters those spirited lees, which art in general and music in particular, precipitate in an auditor's blood. By virtue of what inner grace one witnesses coursing through, be it the symbolic sacraments of temples and churches or be it found in the heartening pulse of a sustaining muse, an attentive observer encounters life transformed.

Thus, ever as diplomatic as the skillful maker of light, verbal art, Ariana's response to Claudel's song was a percussive maxim she inscribed on the back of a voluminous postcard portraying Man Ray's "Woman with the F-hole." Here, on the image of this violin, nearly cello-shaped "dossier," she sent to Frédérique and François a couple of words designed to celebrate ever so meagerly what they had painstakingly attempted to show her from time immemorial. This dedication, to the memory of a simple vision, symbolized what she now knew as a more mature woman, a realization she had finally seized on her own, namely, "The ear sees." It seemed to echo, in her mind, the Hebrew scripture, stating ever so ominously, though promisingly if not posthumously, "The Lord sees."

The sensitive aperture screens, she posited, that which is sound from what is not, not too unlike a voice box, that is. It thereby effectively defines the intensity of an opening, be it an eye's or an ear's, whose focal point is the foyer of the soul.

It is here where language and literature, together with their sublimation in music and art, more generally speaking, prosper vigorously. It is at this point that one is able to improve one's lot steadily with each passing creative pulse and impulse. Nowhere else is one able to felicitously witness an invention that peaks, in the same prolonged manner, with the arrival of a coda. This is where one hears a crescendo reaching the heights of a superb summit, *ritardando*. Yes, here one arrives at a culmination which never leaves a happy, productive few without the improbable air they find essential to sustain the love of their life. Here the enigmatic secret of the violin, its soul and mind, felt deeply within the heart, reveals itself to a chosen people, to a selective decoder of love. Here indeed, a response to stimuli may come to outgrow isolated reproductive acts. It is as if this would take shape to accentuate the overarching importance that animate matters bring to bear on he or she who lives—via expressly suggestive means—to any significant end.

"I will soon be engulfed by my own op. 1. The solemn pang of childbirth will soon make itself heard and felt by mother and me, evermore entangled as one, however independent of one another. My crying out will echo her crying inside and out. This duo of a natural 'violence,' this self-sacrifice will mark my definitive entrée into the bloody world.

"Romantic lamentations, molded in scores of poems, tableaux, and musical scores, simply prolong this fundamental cry my entire being is currently occupied with forming before it bursts out to announce my arrival into 'indivi-duality.' If pregnancy is an indivisible duality, life will soon be organized around the uniquely human experience of a being who seeks to recapture, through memory and action, some form of this most fundamentally dynamic duo present at the beginning. I will come to imitate my parents' couple, which has happily reconstituted a distinct dichotomy, together with individuality. Or I will pass my days searching for the long-lost dualism I am experiencing for another brief moment, however slow the movement, here. I will hopefully be able to administer both parts, in equal proportion, to a full life. I am inclined to think I will discover a stable couple, at the same time as a mind, in seeking a basis for living inside these creative parts. Construing a viable duality may preclude excavating, in some parts, the fullest depths of individuality.

"The obstacle of these walls, this divide will soon open, leaving me with endless choices, boundless directions in which to turn into myself. This inner world will soon come to a close, thereby announcing a new life. I hope to not lose sight of the relationships that matter most. It is those twofold latitudes resembling the ones inscribed in my parents' love, their coupling symbolized by a persuasive pair and relationship, which I will endeavor to locate, reach, and remember. If I am to be a creative individual, it will be incumbent upon me to learn how to accompany myself in a unique dialogue I carry on with both myself and any other who wishes to interrogate the most basic, and the most overflowing, of human relationships.

"Once outside, my being alone will—naturally and culturally—encounter other forms of solitude. I will live among others who share a mix of social relations combined with moments free of ties other than those we entertain with ourselves. I wonder what I will prefer, extroversion, introversion, or a healthy, balanced dose of both. If I truly cherish the romantic, bound nature of my current undertaking, I will probably side with souls long departed, individuals who called out to a past in order to give meaning to the present and, thereby, future. I might find warming solace and elucidation of relationships of all kinds in volumes of truth, goodness, and beauty handed down over space-time. Any exploration undertaken relative to myself and others, coupled with discoveries I make there, determine when I will turn in and how I will turn out.

"The mind's eye suggests. It looks as though I will soon see, indeed, listen especially far and wide, for myself!"

Andante Moderato e con Sentimento (Quasi-Marcia)

The small medieval town of Gastières, a few kilometers southwest of Eus, at the base of Les Pyrénées, had long been among Marc's preferred destinations when he set out touring the countryside in his pearl white *Citroën*. While his routes often varied according to the weather, to what was playing on the radio and his humor or mood, he always enjoyed passing through the main square of Gastières, especially in summer as if the heat, represented there, as in so many French villages, inflamed a quiet, almost pastel passion for naked emotion. He loved simply stopping there for a cigarette and, at times, an *anise* or espresso. Variably, these common pleasures of a material nature made him sympathize with the dilemma of a man torn between the duties of a spirit versus the cravings of the body as defined by the part of *Tannhäuser* known as the *Festmarsch*. This numinous choice elevated silence without minimizing any absence of sound, as if Marc were perceiving it as tense light, smell, touch, or taste.

Le Périgourdin, the amateur synesthete's favorite brasserie, faced the eleventh-century church that was surrounded with the same overgrown plane trees, which lined all four paths leading to the center of town. Rose marble from the mountains had been quarried decades before; it functioned as an elegant, petrified vernacular, paving the walkways of the entire village. Something as much Italian as Catalan enlivened the activity and architecture of Gastières. The brightest, highest order of painters, such as Odilon de Saussure, Marie-Thérèse Brunet, and Christophe Lavallière, had not only rendered the town famous during exhibits of their work nearby the *Jeu de Paume* in Paris at the turn of the century but had contributed to alluring a considerable number of writers. Those in perpetual search of wonderful words to match the wonders of sound images in the image of boundless art free of any territoriality reacted, in turn, to the artists' initiation to life, indeed, this invitation to live here by formulating a committed wish to be near this vibrant community of waywardly creative kith and kin. Many had already discovered how friendly this region, not ever-present without giving the observer a good taste of the *terroir*, a tang of the soil that could be appreciated, invested with one's future even, by any sensitive and sensible type of human being. All these people selectively bred and championed a form of art soaking in a fluid part of nature where culture extracted a whole sense of taste from both the *terroir*, the naked land contrasted with all that is soiled, and simultaneously artists' vintage reflections on time. Without a doubt, Claesz or Heda did for the simplicity, calculated rigor, savant effects of perspective, variable lighting and use of diagonals in Dutch interiors of the golden age, precisely what these painters found themselves bringing to life, for the enlivened terrain outside their home. What beauty they were portraying—perfectly, flawlessly, in unassuming fashion, and filled with a rich palette of values—figured, where and when all was said and done, everywhere *inside* their homeland.

Breathing in and out here was like partaking in the voluptuous intimacy of Reinhardt's F minor Piano Quintet. Where and when Marc entered this area, his whole being was arrested by an overwhelming subject. A characteristic theme, pure variations of a truly ambitious style, a limpid voice, and a brilliantly schooled tone all ravished his every sense in such a way as to leave him with no other inclination than to further investigate its original essence at the source. He sensed himself inhaling the exquisite fragrance of a musical windfall blown down from the ages, like the delectably odorous fruit Schumann had cultivated somewhat earlier, with an uncanny savoir faire, in ripening his own quintet. That masterpiece of sudden and unexpected great good fortune would also copiously satiate, once laid down by the hand of the maestro, the appetite of romantic gourmets everywhere, anytime. Or perhaps the verve and vigor exemplified in both these flourishing artworks should bear a more satisfying, visceral description. One could say that neither really sates, or gratifies to excess, the attentive listener; for they have left the attuned ear to hunger and thirst even more, without wanting to sit down to eat or drink anywhere but at the plinth of a spirit watching over poets, artists, and musicians.

From very few spots on earth did the capital, taken with its intellectual and economic or political activities, appear as clearly as from the perspective of Gastières. It was due to a pleasantly altered state of being one experienced, upon entering the main square in town, Cassandre delighted, particularly during her pregnancy, in sharing Marc's experience of visiting this enclave of *bons vivants*. From this point on, she could imagine life via the proxy of an absence in both space and time. A heartbeat, let alone a second, reminded her of how we may partake in a living tableau as though art here expands and contracts rhythmically, throbs, quivers, in short, pulsates within vigorous movements at the mouth where the town's flowing backdrop, if not nature herself, runs on—what's more, runs over—the soul of culture.

A bare minimum of both words and actions did not diminish a maximum of denuded civility among the inhabitants and passersby of Gastières. Although life had moved along through the centuries, the pillars of antiquity, these columns put together through the benevolent graces of intricately arranged good sense, were founded here upon the ephemeral itself. They were fashioned with seemingly effortless refinement, in light of constant symmetry. They amassed and reflected an organizing principle that hardly appeared too antiquated in effect. They garnered a belief in the value of all that is free, in all that a beautiful nature tenders to those living within, at once, its and their own means. Yes, these shafts and drafts of a noble substance mixed with local airs represent one magnificent version of how the foundation of the Old World could be found transliterated, above ground, in the calm eloquence of this long-lost setting, a transformation of sorts acting in unison within those who found themselves living here.

On this day, Marc's thoughts turned to the notion of faith. As he exited his auto just opposite St. Anne's Church, he felt pulled in by the question of humans' sense of value, loyalty, and trustworthiness in one another, ideas or things. The Sun King's portraitist, Rigaud, was faithful, in the largest measure possible, to his monarch, that worldly ruler serving as the standard by which all people and gods were measured in France's golden age. Man has unabashedly transferred his sacred belief, that which does not derive from logical proof or physical evidence, to a profane world. Some loss, moreover some gain, occurred in this transfer. One could hardly express the self more beautifully, more insightfully on the subject than Mozart in *Così Fan Tutte*.

Marc had often observed the inhabitants of Gastières as people vigorously filled with a mental acceptance or conviction in the truth of one another, a belief itself filled with integrity and purity no less essential than one could say of the finest fragrances of Guerlain, Givenchy, or Chanel, infused as they are with something wholly tempting. Nothing anemic or mutilated, nothing overly cynical or dubious animated their common presence.

No doubt, a struggle to survive had always been a part of life here. Yet those present will have combated the odds of bad fortune with a good outlook, a good sense of themselves, whence they may have emerged and wherefrom others were coming. Different people live here, individuals who never conceived of themselves as strangers since a foreign element seemed innate to them.

Action, for Marc, again and again, prolonged the dream of literature, through and through. And in this region of France, life was long on movement or a series of changes in position, also short, incidentally, on insincere faith.

If those around him this day erred, it was perhaps more in the mind rather than the spirit; for although conditions did not appear rich, they were everywhere fuller, more meaningful, more rewarding, all balanced by a full-scale humanity. Even though the situation of the average inhabitant might best be described as living day-to-day, on a past long passed, people appeared to glide above existence here to ease themselves into a way of thought, an utopian perspective of their life, which took themselves, at once both one and one another, as the *raison d'être* for their existence.

The individual had a sacred place here, though not at the expense of the sum of individuals. The cooperative just outside of town struck Marc as the symbol of this common cause at the root of things divine. He believed, after close inspection and introspection, leading a life as an individual carried with it the danger of baggage that others might consider filled with self-indulgence, error, injustice, litter, and noise. Since the premise of one's journey must be measured from the outset, in a life that never loses track of another's presence, even *in absentia*, the import of considering others, of moving with them in stellar harmony, never seemed as great as in Gastières.

Although Marc had made it to the table of *Le Périgourdin* today, he did not see himself without Cassandre and Marcel. Even when the *garçon* appeared to take his request, Marc changed his custom in favor of an *Américano* since he, all of a sudden, remembered the bibulous trip to Montepulciano he and Cassandre undertook when they had first declared to one another their intention to stay together *for life*. Something about the *Cinzano* and orange juice refreshed not only his palate but also, most certainly, his recollection of the vows he had made as a young lover. These heartfelt words, returned in unequalled proportion by Cassandre, appeared all the more pronounced where love was as much in the air as the pungent smell of tightly layered onions and garlic, cooking in extra-virgin Tuscan olive oil, filling the azure heavens with eminently earthly delights that distant day. Together, the concentric nature of the memories, the genial ambiance and the delicate sensations reminded him of the Hebrew *Kol Nidre* (All our vows). Ariana had explained once—accompanied by the record of a little known yet expert Hungarian cellist playing the melody for this moment of atonement—this amounts to the earnest promise, the solemn, binding pledge made by and to oneself before eternity, at the time of Yom Kippur.

Marc slowly sipped his refreshment, drinking "to life!" His cogitation surrounded that lovely expression, which had remained foreign to him and Cassandre before Ariana's arrival in their parts—*L'Cha'yim!*

He felt persuaded, beyond a doubt, every person's or people's approach *to life* would do well to originate in a time whence *adagios* are not only born—with half-lit ease—but indeed, whence these slow, deliberative, and natural movements creatively mother any existence. Marc sensed that a great *adagio* acted like the father he never had to both his inner and outer poetic life, providing a framework for either understanding or mere listening to the world. *Adagios* bring about everlasting bonds among humans, at once within themselves and midst others or nature herself, even where society increasingly fails to integrate ancient and classical rhythms. They can gently round the edge of a society driven by the latest technology more than ethical conduct of any kind, as if *adagios* were velvet slippers in whose footsteps individuals could follow, even if hard-pressed to make more of money than art in their lifetime.

The soul emerges, unlike the body, from a birth that takes time—like music coming out of the dark—to unfold with its form of luminosity and expansion. It may go on, increasingly constrained by the grips of the world. The world might even smell differently if *adagios* delineated our space like pheromones around the territory of untamed creatures naturally securing their land.

Where Ariana may have found meditation intensified in a temple, Marc found an unadulterated *adagio*, pure and well written, of course, provides all the room necessary for what was akin to religious states, namely, pious contemplation and self-improvement.

One did not have to profess one's love to gain Marc's abiding favor. One simply needed be genuine and honest to acquire this man's friendship. Once fidelity no longer figured as a question but rather as a kind of constantly declined response of every action and verb or word, given or withheld, Marc's position, vis-à-vis his friends, resembled that of a parent forever beholden to a child.

It is no surprise that the French manner of devotion to children and childhood is balanced through a culturally acquired taste, without this form of devoutness crossing the bounds of a dogma that assumes the guise of a *nouvelle* religion. Moreover, the French uncover more truth in the novel or short story than in the news, which is to say, in anything new, strictly speaking. The corollary of this occurs when what is most recent takes the form of phenomena as viewed by someone, no doubt a poet, who likes "to plunge into the new!"

The novel itself could be termed not just as an aggregate of united words, lexical units thematically and structurally tied in a manner one can read in a day but also as many unified words one needs the entire day to read.

Little in the news, increasingly so prevalent in the New World, lends itself to nature's rhythms. The novel lends itself more than the nouvelle or novella, the short or journalistic story, to the *adagios* disappearing from a globe swiftly turning on itself to the beat of faster, profligate tempi. *Adagios* create a natural framework for the novel. They eternize pure emotion rather than acting to ingratiate a self-righteous individual. They safeguard enduring truths, making possible the direct storage and stocking of beauty and goodness. They conceal nothing, opening any spirit or soul to the world beyond itself. They represent an individual artist's veracious thinking through a feeling to the proper end in order for one and all to fully attend to art's emotional revelation. With and within them, the local attains the universal as their poetry turns from isolation to the epic from the singular to a chorus of harmonized voices living and breathing in unison.

Adagios, beginning with the classics and extending through Beethoven or his spiritual grandson, Reinhardt, balance competing forces by facilitating the full expression of natural phenomena. Increasingly, outside their bounds, frenetic phrasings multiply. Even minor composers, filled with an abiding sense of *adagios*, offer modernity enriched, nuclear, mineralized perspectives. Noble tears may soon dry up, left for the lone beast of burden pulling truth's funeral cortège into the distance.

Without *adagios*, darkness holds out too little promise to light the horizon of our sighing, longing hearts.

The sense and meaning of a human life's journey may be destined to vanish into thin air, *smorzando* from the point that the *plat du jour* at places like *Le Périgourdin* is no longer *dégusté* as prescribed by a lifetime dedicated to *adagio*. The Old World is best relished with the taste of a savory savoir faire. From the seventeenth-century perspective of good taste, those who view time as money profane the true savior of both stories and histories—that is, time itself.

One must take the utmost care when embarking on a mission, day after day, "to save time." There is no shortcut to preserving just time. So too does a distinction impose itself between "saving money" without spending any and, on the contrary, spending under the illusion that a sale centrally carries with it the overriding dimension of savings.

The individual who consumes meals *à l'ancienne*, most assuredly, *à la française*, need not demand that modernity supply much in the way of art to the artistry of the past. New World artifice has no place in either the French kitchen, or *haute cuisine*, by virtue of the fact that good cooking naturally turns out to be *consistent* with both the past and the makings of a good time.

Marc knew the French for *farm* is ferme, a word designating at once a hardened or otherwise simply "hard resistance" to phenomena passing in one's presence and a place of *jouissance*, a site of useful enjoyment granted to the rightful owner of the land. Notions surrounding the word *firme* (a company, not firm), point to another matter. In one, the good ingredients of an industrious nature can be raised, elevated even; whereas, in the other, industrial culture can accelerate, beyond belief, the distance it keeps over naturally occurring things.

Increasingly, incrementally, those who appear incredulous are thus, properly speaking, incredible. Their mental life is bereft of faith, the premise of their existence having shifted away from the cycles governing true natures and nature simply put. The tempi of their lives far and away exceed those of any *adagio*, any natural-life rhythm. Their posturing situates their likes squarely in the physical realm like prisoners confined to hard labor. It is there where all the hills and valleys of faith virtually disappear from the map. Things, goods, and services thus dominate their lives, given that faith's dominion remains elsewhere. True and truthful credence lie in the more sacred, yonder realm, where a softer and gentler form of labor exists, that is where the poet locates "true life." Those living beyond the slower movements of the universe entrust the foundations of their lives to the God of the almighty dollar or, in a word, none other than God. And if speed is said to be "of the essence" for them, it is only because all is quintessentially derived from nature's essences, including any passage of, or about, everlasting space-time.

Marc saw the country as pristinely as ever from Gastières. He knew how to teach Marcel that money was and perhaps *is* still, to some degree, if anything, but a mere means to an end. And so he found himself conjuring up a variety of boundaries, limits, or conclusions at this time. To begin, he liked the idea of travel, an act he often associated with the journey described in *Le Soulier de Satin*. To voyage is, as he understood it, an intransitive verb, an infinitely open end onto itself in other words. What's more, the means of peripatetic ways, first made famous by the teaching of Aristotle, inched along gracefully in Marc's displacements, whether accompanied or not. In books he found himself taking trips he otherwise could not undertake, peregrinations of the imagination to faraway places or to distant ideas, as well as to those in the past and, in some rare instances, to the anticipated or unexpected future.

Reading and writing were no less boundless, no more limited, than both words and acts in Marc's eyes. Together, these so-called skills prolonged human dreams. Like Mr. Pinlou, he treasured the accumulation of literary references. Through this ebb and flow of allusions, enriching his inner life as he passed from the work of Claudel and his visionary Rodrigue, for example, to *Le Cid* by Corneille or that in Massenet's musical version, he found himself exhilarated. He was, in a profound sense, left to himself, though not without that fanciful feeling of flight he felt afoot in the ambassador's use of perspective, which serves to illuminate the action.

"What wealth should a man amass?" Marc asked himself. He speculated than an individual should collect that which grants him the greatest sense of himself, independent of any external force. He nevertheless believed that said independence should not be so great as to permit one to abdicate a sense of faith and interdependence with respect to others.

This interrogation of himself led Marc to recall Pascal's words pertaining to just how difficult it is for a man to sit quietly, listening to music in a room, attached to as little as possible but harmonious sound and nothing more. With this in mind, he imagined Marcel's birth as one in a constant state of becoming, a natural growth whose mature form would amount to a man of letters no less than a slow accretion adds to the land by a steady, if fluent, deposition of waterborne sediment. Such was the expectant father's most fervent hope at least. Stated differently, Marcel might become a man for whom life's great journey would never have taken place without the richest memory of an absence. Life might unfold, in truth, for him, in such a fashion as to never rear up without the memory of a marvelous, priceless death.

Marc would try to teach his son self-sacrifice, such that each time he would allot money to the youngster, his worldly guide would encourage the boy to think about how to spend not only his time but also to expend on others and, of course, to save. The father would allow his son to perceive just how money is the alloy of reality, a material that lowers its value or purity. This view was the lesson of not just 1 Corinthians 13, but indeed the whole of Christ's mission on earth. Charity was not so much "giving back," as giving in advance of one's own wealth, as if the spirit of religion had already anticipated every move of the flesh, in binding it back, in advance, to some *raison-d'être*.

Even if later French socialism could not always get it right on a grand scale, an individual could still practice the art of withholding and giving within the context of a nation whose presupposition and founding principles included a place for the community of others at the root of one's own existence and prosperity. To die to oneself, in a way, acted to enliven the soul and thus nourish one's physical person, from that point where one would make a living by serving others in some capacity, artistic or other. Understanding this generous end imparts courage, an illusion of motion and a decisive resolution to the human spirit. It invited Marc to view Cassandre's womb at times these days as a most gracious tomb.

This consciousness of death either partner feels in love distinguishes the human animal from other forms of both beasts and plants. It extends to making us akin to the absence of all names, truly insignificant, perhaps not unlike a woman perceived by her young child without recognition of either her person or name other than vaguely that of *mother*. Whence came, perhaps, the self-effacing, generous nature of a language—French—which once served as the most universal, diplomatic tongue spoken on earth, no doubt due less to commercial idioms than to the very art turned out in its phrases, formulas, and encomiums of truth in all its splendid forms.

Marc held out the hope that Marcel would inherit a sense of grandeur about French obsolescence and ways of expressing oneself fallen into desuetude. Modernity, as he saw it, had only forced classicism into abeyance, into disuse, in large measure, not into profound obscurity whence it might never return. Entire theaters remained animated by the likes and dislikes of Molière, Lully, Glück, or Rameau. Memorable verse related to du Bellay's persisted—in terms as near and dear as those in the distance—in reminding children of the possibility of perfection in French. Whole schools endured around the same lights that caused François Premier to found the College de France, allowing anyone attending lectures there to open themselves up to the rapt incantation of an antiqued present. Grandiose novels lying on the shelves of libraries across the land and seas, lying there for people most often delaying their reading, recounted the intrigues and resolve of endearing heroes and heroines.

The inefficient, antiquated, and useless kinship with a certain space-time, the potentially artful, said differently, still had a seminal place in Gastières in particular as they did in France in general. As in the life of this village, so too could books be found where the long, languorous expression of a *slow way of life or love both depict and sustain people* modestly thriving in a common present. And this could be authenticated, not without an acute, sharp, even flat, or grave sense of their uncommon past.

Marc prognosticated rarely. A grand romancer of the present, he squarely believed that one could never truly predict the future with certitude. In composing his thoughts, of only one fact could he be sure when pondering the future, and that was the one reminding him of his eventual decomposition. Life, whether bloodshot, rosy, or other, as it is written, not without copious irony, in *The Little Prince*, is *de la mort* (about dying).

It was the beginning of June 1958, a time when President Coty's Fourth Republic found itself yielding its political life to a more robust presidency and new constitution under the direction of General de Gaulle. Marc first heard about the formation of a new project for regime change, one with radioactive potential, from the *Marconi* radio in *Le Périgourdin*. Like most in his day, he listened actively to the radio since it could cast broad, enlightening definition in forms of the times and space, if nowhere else, between words—had by not just men.

While he mostly gathered news from the airwaves, he supplemented his awareness of current events through sporadic readings of various newspapers and journals, including *Les Temps modernes*. He believed little in the power of television as a common good. He viewed this onset of technology as an indiscretion, an intrusion of a society that would eventually penetrate far too invasively into the personal lives of citizens everywhere, usurping their fundamental right to privacy and the soapbox mediocrity of stump speeches. What's more, television cast people everywhere into a role of the constantly observed. It perniciously served to disrobe their "naked," spontaneous presence by making over the world into a stage filled with actors, "one" more foreign than any "other" to *adagios*. National borders were being redefined according to the outline of what was being projected on the tube.

As a sign of this, Marc foresaw, more and more people, young and old, would wear dark glasses. Glasses used for reading or distance would increasingly become a part of fashion. One would define the self by casting a gaze or a glance on every occasion.

Television, as Marc understood it early on, telescoped a brand of bumptious scopophilia. To this catoptrical day, it highlights a form of pseudoillumination that acts to distort a simple being, inflating the importance of public life, overemphasizing the responsibility of political leaders in relation to the individual, generalizing celerity and creating collectivist mentalities by uniting homes through a single electronic medium based on a steady, speedy flow of often senseless, vapid, mirrored images. Sure, some good could come of this relatively new application of science for swift commercial purposes; but it would be difficult to maintain and enhance the good, given the quickened nature of a medium designed to profit a pushy few by entertaining the masses.

In France, it would require huge investment by the state in order to ensure that culture's balanced composition might endure beyond any more imbalanced "decomposition." At a time when the future president of the Fifth Republic was calling for a "Europe of States," the role of the French government in television programming loomed both back and center stage. Already good French and foreign cinema acted as a mainstay for the entire country. Concerts, adventure series, witty mysteries, and soccer games filled the few channels in the nightly airings of the society.

Modern democracy was increasingly governed by cacophonous "players" who were eclipsing "stars" from the silver screen, as political actors gradually assumed roles defined, for most people, designed for the masses, through phantom appearances in the home. Television viewership was on the rise. This would lead the ostensibly shrewd leaders, according to Marc's interpretation of the box, out of which few would thus rigorously force themselves to think, to immoderate views. Systematic interpretations, prospects, coverage, and popular observations came about, increasingly based all too clearly on appearances, never with the deliberate nature of say a cadastre or sailboat surveying the horizon as it inches further toward its end point.

This moreover explained, in Marc's eyes, why a poet and art historian Ariana often heard lecturing at the College de France, an insightful though not cunning, if decidedly antiquated man named Michel Beaulieu, once translated Hamlet's modernist essence by the phase: "to appear or not to appear, that is the question."

This imbalance of a reflective culture and a thoughtful people, captured within the home, above all, acted, first to mythologize certain public figures like

Le Général, then to provide a new opiate for any given populace. The individual went on, blanketed by words, in appearance either frankly calumnious or more comforting since less unsightly. To characterize them in a different way, these would-be larger-than-life figures appeared more visually imposing. What appeared to matter was the posturing of democratic leaders. What would come to have import was an act once referred to in Latin as a position of the body—an attitude—in relation to another, perhaps collective body.

Positioning for cameras was in its infant days of tipping every point made according to the scales of any semblance of statesmanship, corrupting the diminishing number and quality of disinterested advocates representing the public good, all originating in more private, quietly accomplished, well-carried-out goods. Well-written texts would rule less and less the center of democratic discourse, lining the margins of good thought like a campestral reminder of the city's open-ended culture. If by nothing else than rising prices which art often bereaves, integrity of promise and opportunity would be relegated to the outskirts or suburbs like fiction itself in a world dominated by the current seriousness of affairs, big and small. Personal interests would soon yield to a vague notion of "national interests" as identities of people and peoples would be molded in none other than the same image of an idealized state.

Marc understood the corrosive nature of television on beautiful texts as an insidious influence removing the ear from the heart of the hearth and, in turn, the camouflaged earth. Words would be written with images in mind more than accompanied by enduring wisdom and the candescent art of letters, like as many animals so often invoked in first introducing children to the alphabet. This growing tendency would only increase his appreciation of oral histories and storytelling of civilizations where memory developed along mellifluous lines captured by the mind as if the esprit were a radio receiver.

All these ambient and time-generated factors would contribute to define the bad luck and limit of the academy's hero. That line beyond which he could not, would not, or may not proceed would ultimately restrict his movement. Somewhere, somehow, he was bound to be circumscribed, even if lucidly, not because he had acted badly, even if inconsequentially, in systematically opting out of life in the fast lane or other, *au contraire*.

Those good people trained to seize upon intricate sound patterns have the capacity to both store information and resist most anything that could damage the delicate balance of a mind trained to listen and hear well. The professor did unfailingly tune his ear to a kind of periphrastic, if not uniquely autistic, reality. In this way, both meaning and significance carried the auxiliary effect of being heightened or more pronounced even though silently at times, in the word of others, in any verbal sign moreover, taken together with the world at large. So too would Marc's sense of life on earth revolve, and continue to evolve, around his driving about the countryside, augmenting his life experience, most often with the *Telefunken* transistor radio playing.

It was just after finishing his reinvigorating *Américano* and saying good-bye to Yves, the burly owner of *Le Périgourdin*, that Marc found himself listening to Reinhardt's *Ein deutsches Requiem* behind the wheel as he set out to return home. Since the sky was unusually overcast, he would have preferred the brilliant composer's First Symphony, also commensurate with a gray backdrop in the heavens. More than anything, he appreciated the delicate and serious themes elaborated through long-suffering by a crafty composer who nearly idolized and most assuredly adored Beethoven. It was in this greatest-of-all First Symphonies Marc conceived of the marriage between poetry and music, one where form and content were the instrumental bridesmaids to composition and orchestration. He preferred Bruno Walter as best man if any earthly ceremony were necessary to properly celebrate the elaborate complexity and articulate simplicity marking this very well-paced, exceedingly well-placed work and pleasure. The exemplary German best sensed how the melodies come and go together—with the full panoply of variations in sound—like a regal bed with a most supportive frame.

The Frenchman *par excellence*, for his part, also felt this way about a crowning symphony just now due to the fact he did not like to devote less than his full attention to the words and musical works of the Requiem. The literal and figurative poetry of the libretto added a dimension that required ever-heightened attention. He focused his distracted gaze on a verse drawn from Ecclesiastes: "Behold with your eyes, how that I laboured but a little, and found for myself much rest." Thoughts of his wife mingled with "The Damnation of Faust" according to Berlioz: "Without great pain, there is no great pleasure." He even looked beyond the present landscape, filled at present with the gravity of a most earnest and sobering musician. A thought germinated within him of how he would have much preferred Reinhardt's Second Symphony on a variable sunny day, followed by his last orchestral work—a concerto for violin and cello—since he felt filled with sprouting, long-lasting, good feelings about Cassandre, Marcel, and the full measure of their combined avoirdupois.

And though he was looking beyond the visible to the invisible, ever prone to "listen" to what his vision had been recording, he remained the talented chauffeur to his dreams, which he indeed was, looking out all the while as he winded distractedly through the countryside along the asphalt highway. He imagined his wife back home, outside. This music lover associated the warming peacefulness of such a pretty picture with the whisper of a lush work, "In a Summer Garden," Delius had written for his own lifelong companion. Marc was aware that like her, the English composer more than inwardly enjoyed the summoning, quietly interpellating French countryside, without belaboring the point.

Marc continued discreetly along his route, noticing how well the lime trees accentuated the elegance of newly groomed vineyards. Passing on, he came upon the front of a small and stately chateau, which appeared as if had been displaced from *La Dordogne* where, it is said, God's sack burst, scattering castles everywhere, including one of the least appreciated in the region, the original of a copy known as the White House.

His thoughts included a stretch whereby he came to grasp a complex philosophical framework for a unified theory of quantum gravity. He observed how absolutes and relatives had combined to box him in with virtually everything and everyone else in space-time.

At this point, he arrived at a bend in the road where poplar trees waved in the wind, and it was difficult to see around the curve. Suddenly, from head on, another vehicle collided with his. The spontaneous combustion of the fuel reservoir consumed him, charring his entire body like the fire-filled spectacle ending "The Twilight of the Gods." The pain he felt from the impact and flames was surely as shocking as it was searing. Marc must have perished almost instantly, however. His immediate suffering surely was reduced to a bare minimum. This would prove oddly dissimilar to that which the adorable, loving wife he left behind would soon feel.

It was not long before the gendarmes were pulling the woman who hit him from her car. It would be left to the rescue workers to extract Marc's expended remains from the wreckage. The gendarmes had the more gruesome task of informing Cassandre. None looked forward to this grisly moment. Nevertheless, the young commander in charge of the area near Espardenya-sur-Tet took it fully to heart. To the home of the deceased, without hesitation, or any pause of which one could speak to collect his words, he went personally. Accompanied by two other officers from his unit, he obligingly offered the most civil of condolences to Marc's wife after having informed her of what would be the utmost regrettable event of her life. She might react very differently in the near and long term. What she would do with herself frightened her, try as she might to fill the black hole of unfortunate circumstances now emptying her life of meaning. She would have to weigh fully the effect this would have on her relationship with Marcel, now and forever.

Like anyone overcome by death, she began, rather unduly, to embellish the man and his befallen memory, in his absence, as the philosopher suggests any would when he foddered the raw material of creation's eternal cycle turning around the more unfortunate axis of destruction: "The dead are the prey of the living." This form of axiomatic truth takes shape from the same school of any but automatic thought Romain Rolland develops in reminding us with what transformation we are endued by death: "The soul's laceration is the spirit's intoxication."

Cassandre received the uniformed men, first at the door, then inside, with surprise intensified by utter shock. Their civility did not lessen the most bluntly sorrowful heartache of the man's most awful news, nor did the invariable gentlemen's unseemly presence in her living room alleviate her acute, shrill misery. Death stupefies the tender heart and renders it hard to believe the object of one's stupor is no more, no less than nothingness itself.

By virtue of a bond she felt with all her fellow citizens, however, Cassandre could make a kind of abstraction of the messengers and concentrate on the totality of their message: Marc *was* no longer. Marcel's father was gone, never to return—he was dead!

No more life breathed from his chest, no more blood flowed from his heart than that of a skinned animal in a most somber *nature morte*. How may hope's flame continue to burn when all that is left to a love remains but the faint embers of the beloved? Why should even birds have a happier fate, chirping and flitting, weaving meaninglessness with the twittering incidence of song to the *bitter* end?

Cassandre's first thought was one of stunned disbelief. Her initial move was to turn off an unknown *opera seria* by Paisiello titled *The Bride of the Shepherd* to which she had been listening while awaiting Marc's reappearance. This most grave of peripetias thrust itself upon her like a devastating earthquake, not dissimilar to situations changing abruptly in any character inflected by literary works, more generally speaking. It would radically change every course of events in her life. Something like a congenital hole had perforated and undermined the core of her wholehearted prosperity. The various rhythms and colorful instrumentation, which had begun to accompany her heart's sense of melodic invention just moments earlier, transformed all at once any romantic impression she was feeling into the horror of a diabolical metamorphosis. Crestfallen, she wanted to be alone though she did not wish to appear inhospitable in front of the most respectful civil servants.

"May we do anything for you, Madame?" inquired the commander.

Cassandre was at a total loss, especially for words. A fatal accident had knocked at the parlous door of vital essences. How was she to respond? It felt to her as though all the humors coursing through her veins had forever assumed some fatally accrued viscosity. She took a bare minimum of solace in knowing that, at the very least, Marc had not perished due to intentional violence or the willingness of another to do harm onto him. Remained intact his reverence for life.

Cassandre could sense the warmth of the officers, and yet the chilling effect of their report froze her every action. Her heart felt as though it were seizing up in grief. Her spirit was crushed, even if the gendarmes could only intuit what deep down the overall effect of such a blow could be, leveling all hope of sharing some unattainable happiness midst all the confusion.

Her thoughts turned to Marc, to what life would have meant to him in the near future and in the many years that they had planned together. The silence was heavy, though not burdensome, since all those present shared in a profound empathy for the fragility of life.

Cassandre spent several consternated minutes pondering the unseemliness of this tragedy, bowing her head in silence. From a moment in life when she enjoyed the rapture of childbearing with a man who hovered above the physical world as a swan sliding across the waters of a scenic lake from a moment of essential simplicity, she now found herself passing into a world whose monuments would forevermore bear the mark of death and dying. She had made choices, thanks to the genuine-sounding board for an authentic voice she and Marc experienced in one another. And now it appeared that her words had been emptied of a significant quasi-certitude.

It seemed as if an accident had voided any essential meaning of life. She had chanced a dream by wishing to share a new life with Marc. Once again revealed at this unexpected juncture, what would prove most uncertain, most precarious—life itself, coupled with its negation—had struck down that part of her, which provided any real sense of fullness. Here she was, replete with the promise of burgeoning life, and yet cut off from its pleasure by unspeakable emptiness.

At the same time, Cassandre already sensed a troubled joy at the thought of carrying to term something of what would become known, a couple of years hence, as Marc's DNA and this quasi-soluble biological alphabet of sorts combined with hers. If she could indeed hold her own, she nevertheless wished to remain this side—where and when emotional dependency rings true—of categorical, free, and clear independence as others were increasingly seeking it. Through all the turmoil, she somehow knew that a small parcel of great good fortune remained inside her, a bit of luck to countervail what chance had robbed from her this day of unspeakable *gravitas*. She seemed to quickly grasp, with a kind of reason stronger than words—like a measure of music characterized by *rubato*, where speeding up alternated with slowing down, only to profoundly alter the experience coming alive in art—to realize then that she had already made a choice to have Marcel as had her husband so freely elected too. The effect of this natural selection remained omnipresent, insofar as she would soon be running around with her child in the world, like a partner in a lively *passe-pied*. She committed herself, then and there, to carry the child and thus the dream, to term, both *for good* and *for life*.

Cassandre already felt as though she were another person. One-half of her couple had vanished in a split second. She was torn between living and dying. This tear dismembered her dream through Marc's dying, her own emotional decomposition, and the grander thought of life's disuniting terminus. She found herself suddenly all too aware that she would see more than a single tear flowing from the source of a life now separated, save in memory, from her. She knew it would be incumbent upon her to live on with the unprecedented pain inflicted on her by divided fate. Marcel was due in barely three months' time.

She felt like talking with her brother, the family doctor. After having called to inform him of what had transpired, she heard him promise to come over without delay.

The shutters were closed. No music was playing. Cassandre lay crying on her bed, comforted too little by a bitter absence, a cruel ending just when life seemed to be taking form with a new, sweet beginning. How wise Marc appeared to her to recall the womb as a cocoon!

An acute realization of suffering's value instilled within the mourner a sense that we only truly learn to live when life has been altered or, in some way, lifted from us. What habit and commonplace routine take for granted, suffering repositions, recasting with its unique and piercing lessons, all that which appears as if it must henceforth be just so. Fatality has the virtue of ushering in the ruinous outcome of an inevitable event that serves to accentuate the fortune remunerating our very breath. Scarcely could even Reinhardt's *Gesang der Parzen*, (Song of the Fates) support her misery at this point.

We are able to gain wisdom in two ways: The first is through learning without pain and the second by virtue of sustained loss, distress, injury, harm, or punishment. Of these, the unpleasant experience causes us to treasure most deeply life's lessons. The most profound meanings associated with being alive, arising out of the disorder and serendipity of catastrophe or disturbance, take shape, as if molded or etched once and for all, most saliently out of suffering. *Surely,* thought Cassandre, *even the corrosive Mr. Homais adjusts his depraved sales pitch according to the volume of pain he feels in what he represents as his bottom line, namely, financial terms.* She, on the other hand, reserved the ultimate expression of things from the perspective of other domains, whether generally artistic, poetic, philosophic, sociologic, spiritual, simply amicable, or fraternal.

Mme de Beaurecueil's brother, Michel, let himself in and approached her bedside in tears. "Oh, Cassandre dear, I am so sorry," he lamented *sotto voce.*

In the presence of this most familiar human warmth, there was little to say.

Cassandre's mind was lucid, her esprit indomitable like a chatelaine in control of all her worldly possessions. She knew all the time she and Marc lived as if to develop a sense of shared solitude, one that had now come full circle. Here she was, in the presence of her brother and the son she bore inside, positively alone.

Nowhere with Michel did Cassandre feel self-conscious. From time to time, she would let out a plangent sound of pain piercing her most profound being, as if she were already in the throes of giving birth.

Her sadness reminded her, strangely, of something Japanese. Something completely foreign surfaced; something foreign to anything else she had ever heretofore experienced, something conducted or directed by entirely other domestic concerns, something outside the scope and range of her essential nature and culture.

It was as though Marc had introduced her to a universe so delicately interwoven, with a texture and tints derived from worlds of passions' colors and a tone's artistic provenance or provinces. He had presented her with a world where every hue defined some form of love and appreciation of life, only to make it all the more biting, *mordant*, all the more fist-clinching, all the more acrid by the unforeseen misfortune of this imposing, pervasive scale, this balance where now hung, in abeyance, injustice in its most brutal state.

Fortunately, Cassandre lived in a land where moods held sway. They could reveal themselves freely, expressing without any constraint, the full range of their swing; death was here as old as the reaper of time; and mourning could, in most instances, willingly or not, last and outlast even a lifetime. For the meantime, at least, she felt no other mood than one of the most utterly despondent, overpowering sentiments replete with grief. She was not vanquished for as much, however.

One does not set out to replace one's love in the case of loss, of one such eminent "disappearance" in France. With friendship and love come obligations, indeed ethical links, "ligations," which exceed the moral realm by virtue of essences communicating inextricably among complimentary worldviews and beings. No accident can disentangle, untwine or disenfranchise one loving being from another. Though a stranger had lifted life from Marc's pulsating breath, this did not take away, in any uncertain sense, the figment of Cassandre's literary inspiration.

If a foreigner had become an "other" creature, a future child concurrently provided her with a sense of herself going beyond a simple being; this other reminded her of that remaining one she would be for Marcel. This latter being would be one, of perhaps several, who together unite in the gifted and talented, giving rise to a conception of oneself, in tandem with the world, thanks to an alternative presence at the core of visionary humans.

Marcel remained within his mother—untouched—as both a physical and figurative reminder that one may appear alone at times, but that this appearance is always a choice given others exist. Within the notions one bears to the world, as surely as in one's acts and deeds, alternatives are even more plentiful than elected officials who always seem to exist in great quantity and ample, demanding even, supply.

In babying a most highly tender conception, Marc had given everything, in other words, including the spawning of the notion of a certain fatherhood whose core would be inhabited by, at the very least, the metaphor of a foreigner. Here lay a kind of scribbling phantom, a death-defying presence, where not death itself, so that the boy would grow up "unself-conscious." His creative need would define his unknown self, one he would discover like Columbus a new continent, space travelers a distant planet, historians a new time, and divers the deepest parts of the seas. He was to be both raised and elevated as aware of others as he would be of himself like a violin incorporating the ancestral sound and tone, the volume and proportion, of the *rebec*, *vielle*, *viol da braccio*, or, at the limit, *viol d'amore*.

Marc's untimely eclipse mirrored the less-than-brilliant daily effacement he had hoped would occur in Marcel from his very first day in this partially and impartially evolving world. To be at one with oneself, it is imperative to live ethically and, what's more, aesthetically or poetically. For only by apprehending the other—and all the others within or without us—can we come to live fully with ourselves. In this way alone may we come to what Montaigne termed *vivre à propos* (to live timely).

The new role Cassandre was forced to play in relation to Marcel would lead her shortly to an increased dependency on Michel and Isabelle. She could not rely on her own aging mother at this point. She would not arrogate to Michel duties that were not rightfully his, *devoirs* that Marc was readying himself to assume by assigning himself full responsibility in fathering his own self-effacement in the face of his son. It was as though she were trying to sift through the confusion to filter any new verbal messages arising out of the disappearance of her beloved. These messages, confounded by death's silence, seemed to be molded in order to embrace the richness of what material lingered in the elements, like as many songs without words that promulgated the intimate decrees contained in a few lines of music itself.

By the force of events, Marc had unsanctimoniously rendered his soul. Cassandre's tacit wish included the perspective of a modern-day Bossuet, one who could artfully resurrect a spirit of orison, pronouncing a funeral oration of simple yet grand scope over Marc's dead body. His body of work, setting records for sensible gentility and taken along the lines of a potent, synthetic mind was simply too important, too significant to go unnoticed without a summation over time in the near term or far. At the same time, much of Marc's contribution to the world paid homage to realms that would prove so pointed, so specific, so learned that it surpassed, by far and away, any biographic or bibliographic résumé.

Marc's very affection for Gastières demonstrated the place for what is particular, what is beyond any universal truths, without any trace of solipsism. He sculpted a kind of pedestal for an individual in light of the collective, like a poet who shapes beauteous ideas, marching to various beats—bearing in mind, all the while, blooming metrics typical of Calliope, Erato, or Thalia. He placed here that which lies outside all categories as if it lodged itself in another world, like the object of a nominal sentence whose import lies not in the action to which it bears witness but in something rather transitory. It appeared as some object, or objective, whose specificity is not given over to description without a random sense of the ephemeral, whose particularity is taken with what only presents itself in very rare instances.

Michel reassured Cassandre that he would speak with Mr. Pinlou and the president of the university, in due time and in the appropriate place, in order to find the most suitable caretakers, the least cliché, for that memory touching his professional person. This latter-day humanist was the one responsible for sending numerous literate shivers down the spine of people who felt he could remodel the world as if guided by the musical sensation of a beautiful story recounted in braille. Meanwhile, Marc's brother-in-law himself would take care of all the personal and mortuary arrangements. And Isabelle, with whom Cassandre had shared memories, travels, and friends since the age of three, would tend to the grieving woman's everyday emotional needs, if satisfy any she could; the eternal feminine would be forever altered when it came to experiencing a wife's profound enjoyment of living with an irreplaceable man.

These sensitive caretakers only served to reinforce Mme de Beaurecueil's sense of gratitude. Not exclusively insofar as life had bestowed to yet more of the living the genes of excelling but also in that love had surrounded her at every bereaving, dirgeful moment, Cassandre continued on valiantly. These hard times were transformed by a tender softening of the soul.

Cassandre asked Mr. Pinlou to contact Mr. Vauban in order that Ariana might learn of the tragedy that had befallen her most loved and admired teacher. It was natural for Cassandre to think of how Marc's disappearance and demise would affect others. She was already acting as a mother to the young foreigner, for both her husband and carefully chosen words had instructed her how to embroider feelings with a blanket of comfort designed to cover others' needs.

And Ariana, in turn, shared the same impulse of thinking toward those individuals closest to her professor and friend. She felt an immediate sense of horror in thinking of Cassandre carrying Marcel without the exemplary Renaissance man, the eminently able human being she knew, by her side.

She quickly realized however that if there was a woman who would have learned the lessons of the student's master, the truth derived from solitude, the beauty in looking for what is good in all things, the essential value of music that leads one to conducting a good life, she was doubtlessly Cassandre. If ever a heroine of the poetic life had come to pass, it was this man's, this boy's, this young woman's woman.

Ariana's first instinct, in thinking about how to convey her condolences, took the form of a massive *mémoire*; for it was in remembering *per se* that Marc ushered, chauffeured even, the future into being. Remembering through both memory and memories should rightfully be present in order that Marcel's own mindfulness could beget the signs of both memory (*la mémoire*) and any memoir (*le mémoire*) pertaining to life's eternal terms. Therein, she felt that she could recount events in her life, notable incidents whose central thrust had been formed and enhanced by Marc's enduring gifts. Before and after all, his talented offerings served everyone equally well, so long as individuals and collectives acted in a manner consistent with his musical messages and noteworthy passages, all aligned in good, informed acts supplementally furthering the potent presence of his interminable absence.

She sought to convey how he had anticipated this most severe, most austere absence, by simply initiating her to the correspondence of Mme de Sévigné and Mme de Grignan, the epistolary marquise's daughter. The young woman somehow managed to extract some highlighted strength from a feeling of weakness in reformulating to herself what her high-minded master had imparted to her, namely, humans are born free and alone long before any brow is beaten, whether high or low.

We are everywhere surrounded by life's little and sizeable disturbances, where and when we are not intertwined more rudimentarily and summarily by obliging relations of all kinds. Relationships, the glue that holds lives together, are thus best engaged with a memory of absence, a recollection of self-effacement, a realization of death, clearly in mind. Paradoxically then, it can be truly useful to conceive of the womb as a vault or chamber serving as a repository—for the dead, both past and future—from time to time.

Ariana imagined Marcel's early years and the time during which he would grow with this gaping lacuna of a missing father. This gap or cavity, already present deep within an obscure depression, struck her as ripe for the teachings of that other great absence or *agape*.

She then set out to modify and limit the amplitude of her immediate ambition by focusing on Cassandre's personal sense of loss. So it came to pass that she carved out the will to write a small note, choosing to reserve her other intention for a later date:

Dear Mme de Beaurecueil,

Monsieur de Beaurecueil's death could not have come at a more inauspicious, premature time. It is with deep regret and unequaled sadness that I have learned of your most tragic loss, indeed, as I find myself crying profusely in writing you. Destiny has taken from you a perfection of nature, a summation of culture, an exemplar among men and women here, if not everywhere worldwide.

Please permit me to remind you that your husband was the subtlest master I have known. He commanded decency, integrity, humility, honesty, art, formulas, and supple understanding where a human's humors flare. He indeed tamed a being's infinitely uncultivated or unkempt nature and fragility. He went well beyond women as society's irony, to a form of honest rhetoric, unnamable by and in itself, where and when society alone is unable to domesticate anything or anyone, especially beasts led by a man-head whose fawning body follows all the lines of sheep, half-asleep.

Marc himself was one of a kind who has now very nearly passed from the wilds of earth's daily existence like, unfortunately, a dated fashion. Would that generations of *Câgneux* and pupils beyond *Terminale* or the *Baccalauréat*, the "elevating" type preparing for a life of notes and letters, might read and study his work; would that they might tap into at least part of the wondrous remains of beauty's eternal life span!

Yes, would that readers throughout the world might find themselves taken with the enchanted art of memory he sought to cultivate, ever so quietly, so surely, so estimably, in each of us. Would that all who come *to life* might glean, in the end, the lessons one is able to harvest beyond the grave from the likes of Rousseau, Chateaubriand, and the very creator who has joined their ranks, leaving you with the lifeblood of a child you bear everywhere inside.

May you soon find peace restored in the littlest of things, in the smallest of words, and in acts of the tiniest of creatures where, apart from the memory of your most beloved of course, next to a bright new life, all else pales. May you find the courage to honor your own animated vitality as we honor Marc's, together with that of his near namesake who presently thrives inside of you. And may you call on those around you to bear a part of this unexpected weight, this burdensome handicap of sorts, as light soon comes to these darkest days.

At your every disposition, I remain now and forever,
affectionately yours,
Ariana Kaplanski

Cassandre received Ariana's missive with great emotion. Mme de Beaurecueil recognized the touching quality of youth's overriding sincerity. She remarked the genuine will on the part of the young woman to comfort her master's wife, not to speak of her pronounced wish to place Marc in a constellation where but a few shine beyond all disasters.

It is here a dying celestial body lights up the firmament for one and all, once and for all. Cassandre felt this all the more keenly when she found herself suddenly reminded of Mr. Bonnefoy's insight pertaining to young readers. Her teacher highlighted how youthful minds read into the magic of words and texts, only to wish, upon closing the work at hand, to go out into the world and live it. Just as the supernatural charms, spells, and rituals of great authors portrayed their characters questing after something holy or sacred, something mystical and mysterious, something solely attainable through adventure and hardship, the professor's surviving partner participated in this form of elevated naïveté and enthusiasm, thanks to Ariana, not to speak more summarily, by virtue of books. Cassandre was moved to want to embody the person and personage described by this fabulous example of youth in her noteworthy letter. The ageless wisdom and good grace of this foreigner served as powerful reminders to Mr. Bonnefoy's former student that she herself would be more than the one to simply outlive another rather an individual who has taken her lessons to heart, a lively learner of and *for life*, together with all it(s) forms.

Reading Ariana's wistful condolences, moreover, prompted Cassandre to want to hear for a long time the slow movement of a Boccherini Symphony. Something of a light melancholy, a transporting nostalgia, coursed through this part of the great symphonist's, no less finely than the least coarse of the poet's work. This feeling echoed the more gently walking rhythms of a *tactus*, or heartbeat, in the andantes of Bach's youngest son, Abel, Benda, Scheibe, and the string quintets of "The Eternal City's" Ambassador to Spain. She went to Marc's collection of records and found what she was seeking. As she glanced above the old-fashioned platters of sound, she perceived a volume of Shakespeare's Sonnets, opening them thrice:

For where is she so fair whose uneared womb
Disdains the tillage of thy husbandry?
Or who is he so fond will be the tomb
Of his self-love, to stop posterity?

In searching then, her mood shifted a bit, moved by posterity's absolutes and relatives. She was inspired, *presto*, by a feeling of good fortune for having been bequeathed such a formidable, indeed, magnificent aural legacy. The records themselves, musical *mémoires* of sorts, furnished some solace following the student's letter and poetic note.

It was still to Italy that her mind remained turned, still to the home of Italian maple trees and Stradivari. This caused her to long for one of the first works she had ever heard with Marc in the cathedral of St. Antonio of Padova. Together, they experienced, like nothing else, a marvelously finished piece crafted by the great violin virtuoso, Giuseppe Tartini. One of his violin concerti's subtle *largo andante*, its languishing suppleness and poetic longing, reminded her of the entire architecture of youthful time that founded her relations with Marc. It referred to the "Devil's Trill," the work of a figure divinely envisioned by a baroque obsessed with angels, their opposite, and just how these curators or custodians of time can be found everywhere angling, playing, in short, with human life.

Cassandre thought of how this composer was trained in a monastery that she and Marc had visited in Assisi. How his learning and craft, like her beloved's curatorial lessons, would be at the service of great individuals and families! How he showed so eloquently, so astutely his familiarity with ancient Greece! How, once returned from travels, he would found a reputation in both his native land and all of Europe! And how the Europe of his day appreciated his depth and range in extending the breadth and technically attuned breath of slow movements!

Yes, how the proportions of sound and sense, laid bare by the maestro in his *De Principi dell'harmonia musicale*, gave her a profound insight, a sensational view that Ariana's poetic prose and verse grasped in especially large measure. It was herein, she felt, a language exists with a lexicon hermetically resistant to translation. Here an *adagio* could breathe as soundly and roundly as a child *en plein air*. For Marc's most avid reader, this offered some perspective concerning a taste for an idiom composed of sublime notes (even more than the one making up the alpha and omega of letters).

The memory stemming from music is more inviolable than a *coffre-fort*.

The rich excesses of the baroque had vaulted Cassandre's love for Marc, eternally inscribing it in every other artistic movement. She could date it from before the Gothic all the way to Abstract Expressionism. Her mind had been made into a harmonious strongbox, enlivened with each beat of her heart and every inhalation, each inspiration really, of her lungs. By occasionally meditating about this inspired memory, Cassandre transformed a moving reality into one to which she would soon come to live more out loud, and this, despite her penchant for the calm of resting or arresting, quiet times.

With Marcel marking time inside her, the body she inhabited lent her an impression every bit as densely rigid as the one cast in the black marble that sealed Marc's coffin near his own mother's grave at Angeles-sur-mer. Marc's tomb resembled St-Dieu's, save the family names written on the sides of the latter's grave within the confines of *Père-Lachaise*. Its simplicity laid bare a stark contrast with the ornate monuments surrounding it. This appeared as if, on the one hand, a man of profound eloquence had nothing more to say and, on the other, the traces of others persisted beyond their years in the shrines of those who had posted yet more verbose signs of the very same impoverished taste governing their lives, no different the ones from the tyrannical others. For one and all were now forever enshrined in an ultimate resting place. It is a question here of what amounts to a representation of their final judgment, if only their sense of rapture, in the familiar name of love.

Just a short time before her due date, Cassandre called Ariana in order to invite her shopping in search of a Moses basket for the baby. Ariana felt honored to accompany Marcel's present-minded, future-leaning, past-loving mother-to-be.

The young Jewish woman let Mme de Beaurecueil know over the telephone line that Moses could have been born of the Egyptian word *mes*, meaning "child," abandoned or other. A small thought like that buoyed Cassandre at this time, as if to suggest to her nothing should, or would, separate her from the dream she and Marc had set out for their creation. She would no more desert Marc's memory than she would leave the child to float away, in the constant and inconstant flow of life in which all, even the inert, bathes.

Cassandre wanted to find a straw basket *à l'ancienne*. She went to the main square in Eus, high atop the hill, across from the church, where a boutique called *Coucou* was said to carry old-fashioned items for the time of a newborn's first cooing. There she found a wicker basket that corresponded perfectly to the one she had in mind for having encountered a similar one *Rue des Bons-Enfants* when her romance with Marc first flared with the incipient stages of bridled dreams. She also picked up a navy blue stroller that appeared like something of a classic French carriage, with its four oversize wheels and deep arch of the bed, where the child would find a comfortable shelter from fatigue while the mother would labor yet again in the infant's transport. There buoyed, as if half anchored and half floating on waves of air propagated from point to point in movements up and down, back and forth, making of the hideaway something of an ancient mariner, oscillating between a wake and a sleep on the high seas.

To line both of these purchases, she hunted round for a small blanket, which would not mismatch the one Isabelle had given her and which she had planned to use in covering Marcel. The shopkeeper pointed her in the direction of just what it was she sought. Ariana agreed that everything looked just right; and soon they were off, returning home for high tea.

Cassandre had already picked up some *petits fours* and lemon tarts after leaving for others, in a passing thought, some *éclairs*, at the patisserie named *La Douceur*; so all that remained was brewing some herbal infusion. The sun beat down heartily this August day.

Thus, Cassandre feeling especially warm, the two ladies sat, talking inside the salon. They mostly discussed Eastern Europe where Ariana had experienced her childhood, family, and early schooling. The tone reflected a nearly all-encompassing serenity. It seemed as if Cassandre had not only acquiesced to Marc's disappearance to the extent that she could at this early stage, but it was no less equally evident that she had accepted Marcel's imminent appearance. She was evolving, though not too quickly; and Ariana followed her remarkably closely.

The student shadowed each thought of the teacher's wife, just as if she herself were the child and future learner within the mature woman. Ariana reminded her, by the deeds of her mere presence and by the sparse words fortifying a calming silence, that the child would soon come to know the world to a significant degree, for a change, outside the body of his mother.

Just before Ariana left, Cassandre showed her Marcel's bedroom. Its wallpaper was a light marine baby blue with a slightly violet trim around the wainscoting. A small crib made of faint maple that had been used for Cassandre in her infancy bordered a chest of drawers. The commode too was made of the same wood, though a hint of a tint darker. A small rocking chair, handed down from Marc's great-aunt Régine, embroidered the corner nearest the window with its motif *à la Fragonard*. A small walnut table, made near Cremona in the earliest days of the eighteenth century, awaited the infant's changing needs. Relatively ornate reproductions of baroque images depicting cherubs and children at play painted by Cortone and Vouet mythologized youth on the western and eastern walls, respectively. The remaining southern and northern walls offered, in turn, an abstemious contrast, moderately adorning the eye—one with a modestly framed poster of an aristocratic family portrait commissioned from Sargent, the other with an original gouache of a florally painted porcelain vase, visibly in the style of a *Limoges* piece. This open vessel held the interest of anyone familiar with the earthenware displayed with tasteful ornamentation and tact overflowing in a colorful bouquet by the dean of American muralists, La Farge. Bringing up the rear, a small collection of children's books, none of which attested to any new purchase, save one recently issued, comic volume by a student of the École Normale about *An Elephant's Memory of the Retirement Home*, juxtaposed the infant's morning, noontime, and nightly resting place. The de Beaurecueils had preserved numerous tomes from their own youth, mostly fables and animal stories or parables that set just beside the rocker on shelves Marc had made for the occasion of retaining illustrious morals and other delightful diversions.

Just before Ariana abandoned the tranquil pleasure of her visit, Cassandre turned to her own bookshelf beside the bed. She wanted to read, for the flowering poet, a telling poem. She had once upon a time discovered it, inscribed on a stonewall lining the beach just beneath the fortified *Cathare* tower at Collioure. Like the Cathares' own existence, it appeared to advocate a type of absolute purity of mores and morals.

This poem was written by a little-known local author who seemed to compose the increasing and diminishing tides of a lovely language, like the most wholesome of muses, "Midst the Waves." Cassandre's term seemed already prophesized her virtual marriage to more life than a single man could bear, announced here in the work titled *La Poésie*:

> Je ressemble à l'onde dont j'épouse la forme
> Sous l'étreinte amoureuse d'affluents énormes . . .
>
> *[I resemble the wave whose form I marry / Beneath the loving embrace of enormous tributaries . . .]*

Ariana remained speechless, moved once again to tears by Cassandre's reading of *La Poésie*, "Poetry." These columns of verse surely stood on their own merits, reminding the less experienced poet of a formal reality traced by Chausson's *Poème pour violon et orchestre* (Poem for Violin and Orchestra), and Baudelaire when he wrote *Corréspondances*:

> La Nature est un temple où de vivants piliers
> Laissent parfois sortir de confuses paroles . . .
>
> [All Nature is a pillared temple where, / At times, live columns mutter words unclear . . .]

And yet this recollection nevertheless served to prop up a sense of classical symmetry with her own work, granted, in its infancy, as anyone could see.

Little was left to do or say, so Ariana bade farewell to this version of humble bravura, together with its most sensitive reader and listener *par excellence*.

Cassandre was nearing the end of her journey, her *journée*, her journeyman's apprenticeship in pregnancy. She yearned to bear witness to what followed in her couple's creative wake and to apply herself to her new charge. The trail she and Marc had embarked upon had taught her how to live aboard poetry's craft. She now knew how to survive as a mythical creature beyond any one man's shipwreck.

The traces of the tale she had effectively begun composing with her husband were no less plentiful today in his absence. Most of these signs, representing an endearing passage, lingered and thrived in thoughtful expressions of beauty, truth, music, and love. They could be read in the air, whether by listening to nature or intently lending, indeed, "giving" an ear to the culture set out by a great composer. She heeded Reinhardt's use of Saint Matthew, where the poetic librettist proffers: "They that sow in tears shall reap in joy." As if to head off a tear when she thought of the absence of Marc's mind and body, she thought of her enjoyment with respect to dances of Beethoven, Mozart, Reinhardt, and Dvořák, even suites of Bach and all those who followed him. She was comforted, as if cradled in her own right by her own realization, by the idea that while movement was indeed the *sine qua non* of art while dance was the initial form of art, great writers of music composed masterpieces with or without a partner in reality. She felt as though she could therefore go on, especially given that these composers' greatest works were not expressly written as dance tunes—music, that is—which is to be lived out with another in more than mind, indeed, with an equally adventurous, cooperating hand. Perhaps, to twist a phrase of Joyce, reproduction is the beginning of death's *Danse Macabre*, as if, in any event, things could readily turn into a *Marcia Funèbre*. Perhaps, she conjectured in reverse, dance does not retain the ultimate say. Perhaps it is the rest, which includes living well within and by oneself, within one's means, that matters least stridently in the end.

In the body of her memories, in the delicately etched quarters her mind occupied, one could read the result of an essential equation whose sum amounted to the elements derived from the principle lines of a quasi-mathematical matrix. The input of one, plus that of another, equals more than the original two. One, indeed, sprang up, one, this cardinal number in which the recollection of a couple remains forever present and productive.

A fetus, not unlike silence, not unlike science no less, must be maintained in the matrix of poetry and imagination, in the clutches of the composer's watchful eye. The artist's guiding hand and nest allow order and patterns to loom up for the developing child, like the young poet or word dancer to explore and discover. Herein lies what is most truly worth remembering. A womb of silence rocks different, lumbering, less heavy, slow movements first, then sound.

In this way, anything meaningful must retain these essentially meaningless dimensions upon which all the rest—any great work of art included if it is to be grounded in truth—is found. Ultimately, if a work is to have an unequivocal base laid and established, it is indispensable that the artistry never lose sight of its amorphous groping origins. The writing of great literature is a nascent, solitary act resembling the act of reading. The discovery we make of ourselves creates an *ars nova* when expressed in the *sforzando* tone and life-sustaining chords of a Reinhardt, following the imperator Beethoven. It is no less the act of reaping what has been sewn meticulously by others who have, at once, preceded and enriched our existence, indeed, our *lives*.

A fortnight from her due date, Cassandre was perusing what could now be called the de Beaurecueil record collection, complete with early electric and acoustic recordings from around the turn of the century, when she decided to switch on Marc's last purchase—the *Grundig* hi-fi—in its place and time. Her diamond stylus read and thus played a recent performance of *Die Meistersinger von Nurnburg*, with Fritz Reiner at the helm of the Chicago Symphony Orchestra.

The serious intensity of the players, together with the contrapuntal style of the composer, reminded her *con fuoco e brio*, the artist nearly signs a pact with those creatures exposed to the art at play. Monteverdi, *Il Divino* (The Divine One), exhibited in his first madrigals a new audacious sense of melody, polyphony, and chromatics that arose out of his experience with the church parishes and audiences of his day. Following his master, Sammartini, whose modernization of the symphony and musical theatrics influenced the young Mozart, Glück wished to create a "language of the heart," where music would find a touching energy and new passion according to the ear of a public trained on Italian opera. Carl Maria von Weber sent romanticism's first shivers up and down the classical spine, following his teacher, Michaël Haydn. When all is said and done, musical drama, a term Wagner preferred to designate his last works, arises out of the collaboration between the individual artist and the public. This arises not unlike what germinates in the nucleus of any expression developed by the writer with a mind out for potential readers or contributors to the esprit of *salons*, or what would become known as book clubs, everywhere, yes, not too dissimilar to the complicit relations shared by women or men and the object of their love.

Marc's absence was all the more dramatically resonant that he had combined both musical and poetic dimensions with the human experience. Together with all the material goods accumulated in a modest lifetime, he left behind the immeasurable good of great words and deeds. This made anyone in his midst infinitely more cognizant of what it means to be *alive*. The exhilaration he brought to his course of study, viewed from the outside, resembled Reiner's compact in a word. Theirs was a dense covenant with the players and public at large. Their most intimate contract appeared, in truth, as Reinhardt's own with those who subscribed to his sound.

Through symbols and a language of notes, humans can master themselves to the extent they address humanity's quintessence. For some, this account of humans confronting their destiny can be elaborated through writing, as attest traces of thought on the subject from Greek literature to *A Sentimental Education* and beyond. Mr. Pinlou remained, among others, to bear witness to this fact. For others like Desforges, wordless, "noteless," "letterless" art, not exactly manqué, *au contraire*, can both denote and connote the human experience. To the extent an artist assigns humankind a place in the universe through a myriad of gazes, takes, colors, and perspectives, he or she becomes that very individual who constitutes an independence around the greater outside world reflected in Art.

Adagios, similar to *andantes* moreover, simply serve to enhance this type of human, even adding little more than a fraction of abstraction to the attraction of a humanist's artistic view! They exhibit all the makings, all the markings of a global interconnectedness by plumbing the most tenuous depths. They generate the connective tissue that makes the whole universe appear as one vast form of interdependent life. They gently caution the human system to attune the whole of the organism with all systems, at once worldwide and beyond. *Adagios* allow us to affirm we are most alive when we are self-organizing, self-maintaining, and self-renewing. Self-transcendence evolves from this basic premise of the self-reflective soul calling upon life to redouble itself like water continually remaking the shape, tone, and consistency of the sands. *Adagios* make every moment and every place wherein they are writ large or heard a shore upon which to embark with the renewed energy of a discovery or simply pure feeling. Waiting for us at the end of our conquests governed by *adagios* are creation and creativity, born concurrently with us when we find and surpass ourselves, not just marking the loam of time.

The artist is, in the end, like the child, nourished by the collective representation of culture and civilization. He who lives by the natural stateliness of these slow movements presents the foremost chance of remembering what is worthy of being borne by other humans in the future. We need but think of precious little else in hearing a Mozart quartet—say, any of those witty six, packaged as a present for all of us, and dedicated to the most admired musician of the day, the greater Haydn—for the first space-time.

In any event, it is perhaps opera, at least as much as outer space reflected in scientific literature, in which the public person, like youth, both experiences "the works" of the world and takes in the consummate art form. The eye, ear, and tongue unite in the operatic, often exotic and irrational, light.

The stage of a theater in the Italian style is like a womb. It is adorned by a velveteen curtain (an opaque window of sorts), an otherwise soft material acting as a membrane. This constricting barrier, what is the proper domain of curtains, connects regions, structures, or organs that sustain life. What lives is what appears here assembled or recollected by the presence of actors. It sets the scene, no less, for a remembering and a gathering of individuals' memory, collective or other. The more a solution to dramatic problems is present, the more porous is that which goes on, covered by the workings of the auditorium's pliable layers of memory. Some tragedies are however, beyond a doubt, without resolution. A certain number are dry, devoid of life, as if nearly standing still, gravitating, according to different laws of mechanics, like the very earth and umber terrain covered in *Roussillon* by Marc that heart-wrenching day.

Cassandre looked around the home as she listened distractedly to the music. She keenly sensed Marc's influence, detailing the flow of his memory on everything around her. The burgundy velvet sofa echoed the endless days and nights she and he had listened to great art, watched uplifting cinema, read cover to cover the pages of eternity side by side, received guests who brought with them boundless enchantment. She would transport, come what may, all this remembrance with her—together with her perpetually adored offspring—into the future.

The painting of a sailboat, perhaps unremarkable to others, though reminiscent of an embarkation depicted by Watteau or Claude, caused her thoughts to come about. She recalled the tack all the vessels contained within Marc's body of work had set out against the tyranny of the dollar, against the venality of excessive hubris put to use crippling entire peoples, against base villainy looming out of unjust independence anywhere. The Americas have been born from the great European sailors, only to partially ignore the fate of civilizations obsessed with the numerical, financial worth of gold. Mr. Smith and the Earth Development Bank could bear far and wide the lessons of systemic interdependence Marc offered him and his employees—what's more—free of charge. Harvey would escort some salient lessons in particular back home. *Hopefully,* thought the master, *this would cause their smart, ecologically, and personally interconnected focus on life to proliferate.* And yet excessive capitalist competition in general and its fanatic proponents like Mr. Homais in particular could last, even with the law of one form of democracy on their side—where an ocean of uncharted waters may flood good works like an insidious imagination—so long as poisonous pride rules the till and pirates the tiller. One could craft a work, or at a minimum christen, a vessel with the quizzical title the Phantom of Democracy or a Bastardized Republic!

What the music of Wagner brought to Cassandre this day was a revelation that her home too was like the womb of the theater. Unlike the Wagnerian mime and plastic poetry, largely speaking however, she was acting still in the best interest of life, without competition from death. She was guided less by the baton of an eclecticism, a nihilism mixed with Christianity, for example, than by the conduct of a system of ideas, which blended earthly pleasures with a blissful detachment.

Cassandre mixed *terre-à-terre* happiness with a basic renunciation. She felt that what Marc offered was, in itself, a sense of giving up without capitulating, a sense of disowning if anything. This renouncement carried with it a message inside. In itself, it was not unlike a beautiful book, an angelic tale, or, in somewhat equally real terms, a gravid woman. For in the silence of her home at this point, she heard and saw everything less in the mono of some coveted number one than in newfangled stereo by virtue of a heavy absence underlying everything present here. She mused at what new blood Saint-Saëns's Organ Symphony provided to merchants who wished to showcase stereo's first echoes around her time.

The various strata of agreeable memories that surfaced in the guise of things around the house acted as polyphonic reminders of the pleasing harmony in the name of which her home had been built. Even the landscape first struck her as a topological inscription of an inner world if not of the mind's eye and ear. A tree referred her to the idea of a tree, just as, inside both the home and theater, the wood planks delivered the metonymic message of a book. For even a bound volume derives meaning from a particular tree or the woods, globally speaking. It is to be read carefully, to summarize, with the poetry of its leaves and one's own renunciations in mind. One must be, in reading properly, at once attached to the story and sufficiently detached from it to view either a subtext or "supertext" where and when figurative speech there may be, meaning everywhere, like a text which acts as a pretext for ubiquitous life, if anything at all.

Each object in our midst serves to instrument the imagination as if the home were the foyer for a giant symphony of rhythms. Things here had been gathered in a concerted fashion, not so much as *souvenirs*, as memories to sustain the future. They represented collections of past activities, metrically flowing within a space-time, indeed, animating the very absence around which a mental and metaphysical life found itself forward—looking from the outset. Through a memory of things, no less than through a recollection of passing events, new life was being created here, like as many *adagios* for the heart and soul, all the time.

The gusto or good taste with which these artifacts were originally assembled still bore witness by the zest of as many percussive recollections, in sum, to a life of the mind *coming together*. In a regulated pattern of the accentuated and unaccented experiences of a lifetime, *beneath the surface*, purely physical matters coalesced. Even with respect to matters relating color or chromaticity, indeed, light's wavelength and purity within the material world—here too no less—things appeared to Cassandre as black and white, where not properly in between a stark contrast.

Everything, objects or subjects in her life, ultimately found a place and beat here. Both time and timelessness bespoke an overarching harmony. Rationality was seasoned, in the final analysis, in and around her kitchen with aplomb. Time as well found the delicious coating of a sound rime here. Would that Marcel might early enough come to know what Ariana, the Pinlous, and others could always discern in her presence—to sit at Cassandre's table, not dissimilar to participating in the setting of her living room and, accordingly, home viewed more broadly, was to take a seat whose basic property lodged the legacy of a predilection. This "before taste" satisfied literally everyone present, satiating the benevolent with a thoughtful gaze on absence. All sensed a specific remembrance of what had come together to make, form, and compose the period of time perceptible between the past and future, the all-too-human, ever-unfolding, accident-prone, and imperfect now.

Cassandre thus acted as a harbinger for beauty in the truest sense of the word, naturally ingratiating, often with no other purpose than to gratify, guests and would-be hosts alike. She strolled leisurely into the future. Here, the only certainty that appeared to her more profoundly ignored, unknown, or misunderstood than the delights of the radio or record player to her esprit, to the past pleasure of Marc and the patrons of *Le Périgourdin* too, as well as to the world at large, was knowing to what extent the greater world might see itself, indeed, dead set on driving meaninglessness home at every turn. To recapitulate, in some small measure with which to begin, the whole of humanity might feel some misgiving in attesting to the mistaken fact—and forsaken pact with—things are moving, just as Marc was one mortal day, that is to say, ironically, in and under a direction the creative mind appears solely left to characterize as "one," which is not right.

Vivace appassionato e grazioso

Nearly nine months had elapsed since one lunar cycle before January 11, which points to the first awareness of the day and night Marcel was conceived. It was now September 1, a single day shy of the eleven days from Marcel's due date of the eleventh. These numeric coincidences made Cassandre, something of a solid eleven-stone woman, think of Marc's *aggrégation*, the examination session during which French students demonstrate the condensed summation of their knowledge on a subject—first in writing, then orally—before a jury of university professors. Marc's score carried with it the eleventh place, one above the duodecimal contestant. This figurative fact, interpreted in Cassandre's sporting mind, made him twice the *cacique*, more than once, in other words, the number one *élève* or student. It was as if he were a member of the French elevens, the first eleven, the first squad of the soccer team, the Blues. Knowing his rightfully premier place among the country's intelligentsia made her all the more aware of the World War I armistice, signed in the eleventh hour on the eleventh day of the eleventh month. Knowing how space-time rolled this eleven exerted a similar serendipitous force of attraction on her inner life as if she were a musicologist remembering that Händel's *Water Music* debuted January 7, 1717.

Countless people derive meaning from merely toying with numerological coincidences. Fifty-four and forty-five might amuse them in tandem since each adds up to nine and taken together the sum is ninety-nine, itself two nines in tandem. Even nine and nine equals eighteen, which, adding the two constituent numbers together, yields nine once again. Life is ushered in here by the play in the numbers, just as youthful lovers of language feel stimulated by a vacillating oscillation between the bright and dazzling brilliance of another's body or thoughts. The child in us loves any good play on words, words shimmering tremulously like sunshine on the glimmering sea.

Cassandre let loose her light-headed mind while her thick-blooded body felt ever more anchored to the life of childhood and playfulness. She knew that, for instance, the difference between first and eleventh could as easily appear as *trompe l'oeil* as, simply put, false. At times, the lower placed student could merely have fallen on a deaf ear for his or her interpretation. In Marc's case, the committee solicited an *explication de texte* of "The Crow and the Fox" ["Maître Corbeau, sur un arbre perché . . ." ("Mister Crow perched on a branch in a tree . . .")], insofar as "the verse exposes a poetic master of fabulous musicality."

Marc was no more a dupe of the members of the academy than he was a sycophant to anyone of influence. Since he did not easily yield to the professional doctors of the university, he, in no way, falsely flattered them as a fox might when searching to fill its mouth with food. It is thus possible individual *maîtres*, present for his brilliant, intimidating, "nuanced" exposé, might have confused slightly gradated variations of musicality for the raw grades of politics. This came as no surprise to him since, even while young, Marc always knew not just his limits but no less equally the inherent boundaries of others. He burnished perfection. He comforted those near him by an easement glossing their right of way with the real property of excellence. The eternal student could easily deduce, beginning early on, many of those who had mastered a body of knowledge, through understanding and wisdom, were not any different from those who thereby believed they knew everything. In lieu of seizing all that is true, as perceived through what they do not apprehend, know-it-alls frequently profess, when they do not halt at assuming, that brilliance comes from bright light alone.

This experience had been one of the more significant times, in aggregate, which confirmed for Marc that *following actually betters leading*. Given he figured as a professor of letters, this maxim constituted the preponderance of Mr. de Beaurecueil's *modus operandi*. He felt convinced the teacher should move carefully behind, underneath, and in the same direction as the student. He envisioned a memory that guided the future, one that foreshadowed any remembrance taken forward. This position of a follower informed by the past diametrically opposes that of the overtly advertised *numero uno*, who generally makes known the fact he is best in order to seduce, or force, others to come to him or, more globally, to bend or bow to his country.

The good reader also trails the writer—even if at a considerable distance or in due time—just as this latter does well to follow his own writing dozens of times, subtracting and adding here or there, before publishing the finished product. The great musician makes a piece his or her own by concertizing numerous times before etching the sound—for good—in the form of a recording or during a performance in the mind of a listener.

Like a grand instrumentalist, it was Marc's personal and professional posture combined that elevated students, friends, and family. He lightened things, at times in obscure ways and manners. As if armed with his ability to penetrate darker, more somber recesses, Cassandre now felt the fullest weight of raising Marcel in such a way that made all that was heavy light.

The eleventh hour of her pregnancy treated her to countless happy pleasures born from some of her sweetest and most erudite memories. She waited patiently for the day a "final" hour would usher in the one to whom she would turn the totality of her affective, indeed effectively sensible and sensitive, *life*.

On this first day of a month—which hinged on the turning point for the seasons' leaves, for it is naturally called the fall in brief—Cassandre paused one more moment to consider yet other aspects of the cardinal and mythical "number one." She thought of the leading empire at the time of the first days of the Roman calendar. She thought of how the Caesars' government may have fallen but how, in a less secular realm, Christianity continued to burgeon. She realized the spirit makes room or a place for both forms and content, like the church or temple itself makes a good old place, a piazza, or square.

This occurs to bring about structural unity in such a way that no rule of profane regulations is able to accomplish. Unity cannot be governed or created from the outside; it begins from the sanctum of inner chambers, *cameras*, where listening, no less than praying, takes precedence, by far and away, over speaking. Indeed, to pray, recalled Cassandre, means to measure the distance between what anyone praying *is* and that for which he or she is praying, that in the name of which or whom one finds oneself praying. Prayer defined space-time the hours prior to the period where and when Tuscan perspective was bound and born to reshape the art world of the Renaissance. Thus, true unity may be found intrinsically within an individual, no less than it is carried on in the coupling of instruments, following concerti that began a musical transformation in the period leading to the Enlightenment.

The ethical or moral realm of the *good* becomes obscured when an attempt to *better* that self-same good is brought, like as many suits *reasoning* before a court, by those seeking to define themselves, irrespective of a price, as the *best*. Ill effects from one-upmanship inflict pains on the national psyche of a people who inscribe, in their everyday code of conduct, the status of one who is not selfless, but rather competing against others primarily in order to develop an identity wholly dependent on being or putting oneself first.

A good hostess, Cassandre repeated to herself as she sat in Marcel's room, just off to the side of aunt Régine's rocker, comes second in the equation of the company. *A good democracy,* she thought, *effaces itself to unite individuals within and without themselves.* The host or country entertaining those who seek wholesome refuge strategically and generously places the other, the invited guest above all else. It is indigenous to the Latin notion of the host to conceive of oneself as the one, the individual being invited, in order to fully envision any second point of view more than an other—say, one's own at the outset—before entering any foreign space-time. All countries worldwide would do well and good to recognize the sprawling generosity expressed—beyond the frontier of a felicitous name, one united to various states of folks there—by the foreign author of the American Quartet. Such is the kind of records to set in surpassing prior generations. Such is the height of a feat to scale. Just as Rome, Florence and Philadelphia had done astounding the world, collected humans of certain epochs set themselves apart, less by breaking records than by etching more potent, balanced measures into the myriad memorials spiraling around the cycles of space-time.

Hillel could have prospered, Mme de Beaurecueil thought to herself according to the lesson Ariana had offered as a learned poet of "The Eternal City." On the other hand, it struck Cassandre as unlikely that the same Hillel would ever have come, *in absentia*, to occupy the principal, strongly held bastion of a country that is far too self-conscious.

The life of the mind and spirit, like metaphysics more specifically, matters little, *in situ*, where a land conceives of itself as the world's biggest marketplace. To define this space on earth, one need only look to the relationship Yves' Bistro has to *Ste.-Anne's* Church in Gastières. The place, the space, the capacity for squarely sustaining life, arises from a reasonable sense of time and tempi. A conquest of both the globe and universe does not condition what is conceived by a person and all who find themselves at one at peace in Gastières.

No overtly bellicose action, be it in film or the fiction of "consensus reality," drives the state of mind of inhabitants here. Behind the wheel of good fortune sit individuals whose dreams have chauffeured revolutions to reality, people who collect themselves in time, in order to share places with the more or less naturally occurring revolutions cycling throughout the planet and beyond.

Even if they exist, driving rhythms of life rarely surface here. The conduct of the people intimately associates itself with the feedback of the conductor's direction. People do not use their understanding of the alphabet only to go from *a* to *b* and on to *c*. They too may seek their equivalent of As in school yet not without cultivating at least a sense which vectors their travel from one letter to the next, like as many purposes added up to amount to the most noble of purposes, every step of the delightfully truthful way, so to speak.

Their destination equals their destiny at every moment of the way. Indeed, they can sit for hours with their fate, almost as if their point of arrival no longer matters so long as the progression, the advance of their course, assumes a form that attracts their train of thought, like a picture book luring the eyes of a young reader. Elaborate idleness may heighten the lulls, as well as the busy periods, of their schedules, some of which may meter a business day and some not. The variance of key, mood, and tempo in Reinhardt's sonatas for violin and piano would coevolve with all living matter, modulating existence here, and bringing good thoughts—together with inviolate intimacy, refashioning a permanent tradition of the form—*to life*. Both of his sextets would improve a sense of meaning and purpose, setting a tone for even how the sun is seen to rise, shine, and set. The last great romantic incarnated as much, following the Mozart and Beethoven quartets, for example, in his own work of four conversing implements of music, together with a piano quintet filled with movement and these two vigorous masterpieces for six stringed instruments.

Sophisticated ruses of those living here find themselves playing with space-time. They might mark it off and, at once, "push it back," in a word. A certain nature herself might break through here, as if to peep out and gaze upon cultures of various kinds all around, in a divine silence she alone might have perfected. Talmudic rabbis, Ariana might have suggested, gathered no less from nature's bounty. And it could be said, quite literally, rabbis have rarely shown themselves to be, from the beginning of the Hebrew calendar at least, godforsaken.

Nature alone is in a sovereign state. It is in natural states, in natural stages of life that enduring traditions of many kinds have found true edification. For industriousness that fundamentally disrespects this ethical posture vis-à-vis nature, there is no looking back. Without remembering an ancient mode and mood of time, there is no collective memory other than one leading to a collective solitude.

Nature could be made to show herself, in other words, where a will to preserve truth, worthy goods, meaningful unity and beauty, does not demur. This could take place, whether in a realm not unlike the one filled with an infinite number of advertising, self-promoting images Marc had hoped students and citizens at large might learn "to repulse" or in the one with which humanity may choose to entertain itself. Humanity can do better by itself without causing too much harm or fraud to its neighbors, read no less in the zones of yonder unknowns. If this form of truth appears here and there, now and again, it appears to remind us not to forget the even less conscious climes unearthed by unsung dreams alone, dreams of a realm free of any bonds binding back a conscience that hitches itself to the stellar art of science and science of art.

Knowledge, *la connaissance*, breathes new life into existence to the extent that it is born from the seed of an *honnête homme*, what one could call a type of conaissance in combination with the egg of a woman who *re-cognizes* the value, the place of pure conception in the sexual act. If eroticism was once bound to heroism in the Middle Ages, it arose out of a deep association of the physical with the metaphysical, like fresh fruits with their ambrosial juices. In a society where the concrete metaphor governs the natural path to knowledge, love transforms itself into an abstraction, a state divorced from all other states, the physical first and foremost. Paving the way for knowledge, which is neither misused nor abused, means "coming together" in a common understanding. Full knowledge means what it signifies, namely, "being born at the same time," as the facts of life themselves.

Increasingly, in French society, people are becoming used to participating in *the act* of love without knowledge of the other sufficient for it to be true. This amounts to an act that falsifies the relationship from its inception, no less than the act of indifferently transacting in *actions* (stocks) at the Bourse de Paris in order to gain some competitive advantage over another in *la société* (both "society" and "company").

More and more, love appears as if counterfeit. An accelerating number of people find themselves in the company of a kind of professional success while they look to a private life that bankrupts the foundation of any belief system (*système de* crédit, *système de* croyance) in which to develop any real trust and détente or entente with the other. Upon first inspection, it might soar up to one's conscience that the separation of church and state, first germinating in late nineteenth-century France, brought with it a good life for those who sided with the state. And yet one must remark how many nation-states have come and gone in the time since the church (and the temple before that) found its foothold in the hearts and minds, the universal esprit of the faithful. An *adagio* bears, with its trustworthy measure of space-time, all that which covers and recovers this.

It seems safe to say that understanding the state or states, might forever vouchsafe borders on matters related to the "busyness" of businessmen and women. What one could term the *static* corporation, a society built on the market principles of business, remains in place, trying, litigiously or not, to grow at the expense of nature's dynamics.

Cassandre, like the Vaubans, attempted to avoid the push of marketers to consume more than one needs. It is no surprise certain states appear to sanction, indirectly at least, physical, if not spiritual and metaphysical, obesity otherwise known as the very fundamentalism they proffer and typecast as invidious.

The extremities of the world no longer touch the main body of humanity. Such human error does not become a mistake or contretemps unless, through the power of language's arch-tectonics, it is let remain standing, uncorrected. One way to reduce, to deflate the body of humanity's collected works, inflated *in extremis* in many parts, might be "to build down" everything. Skyscrapers are, like the modern-day Tower of Babel, or the great pyramids, a not-so-incidental symbol of something that has imbalanced exaltation of the human spirit and traded it, together with the world, for a persistent quest to strive to strike, not a balance with human nature but rather a target out of this world. While they may take shape in a universal yearning to "attain the highest heights," oversized edifices cast too long a shadow over a multitude of vernaculars that define all people. Uniquely, memorable music best comes close to speaking equally in the name of the whole world—that is, for all of us.

Those people(s) seeking to create the biggest "whatever," wage no less than inherent war against peace itself. The populace of any given state does not necessarily want so-called leaders, politicians whose ceaseless mode of action is fighting for this or that at all cost.

The real passion in life, according to Cassandre, real grace, is born of a type of lowercase knowledge that lives, like a fetus floating without the need of any other form of life preserver, inside its mother, within her equilibrated means. This means that following cognoscente more than businessmen, marketers, and advertisers, would-be politicos in sum, might just more fully restore men and women to themselves. We could be redeemed by no less than us ourselves. Yes, this might just render unto humanity what is simply human and humane, at long last.

Marc had understood the follies of the marketplace and free marketeers. So did Cassandre. Neither one nor the other marked up reality with marked untruths. Each marshaled facts and fiction without losing sight of human nature. Both prolonged worthy ethical systems of belief. Their sense of wonderment extended to all of nature's veritable, verifiable (*fiable*) realm. Their analyses and reasons included a sense of any number of extremes, shielding them all the more from error and extravagance.

Their creation would be destined to look onto a world where all was not exactly reasonable. For example, Marcel would not be free from comprehending, they thought, nothing is truly, literally priceless, even freedom itself; not even love is born(e) without a cost. In full knowledge of this, in understanding both the very nature and culture of understanding, he could take wise solace and have informed faith.

In understanding this compensatory reality, the child might come to know a very simple truth, indeed one that could be described as a sure thing taking hold in the most quintessential of creations. Nature is the most glorious creditor! It is in her magnificence one should place one's trust, there where one should inseminate hope and beliefs in general. In her, the good times of *adagios*, *lentos*, *andantes*, even drawn-out *allegrettos*, or slow movements, generally speaking, take hold, thrive, and herald a form of dependence on trustworthy means, independent of all other ends.

If one "runs the numbers" of the people beneath the sun, those of us coupled with the species in the shadows, there empties out a kind of Bernoulli's principle, which defines the full conservation of natural energies. If life can be systematized, if one can be made to be systematic, this suggests a closure, thanks to which everyone communicates. The result is not only that someone's gain is another person's loss and vice versa. It is that we are all able to gain by understanding loss.

Loss amounts to more than just a statistical reality. By seizing upon a losing experience, we can more fully embrace what it means to seek winning alone. There is a taxing trade-off for people who believe in competition at all cost. This overriding notion can be the source of great construction or rather destruction, primarily and ultimately.

A piece defines a whole, puzzled together or by itself. An odd bit of humanity reveals itself in even the most even-tempered among us. Marc was convinced his associate in the world banking community understood precisely what legacy is freighted to modernity by these basic principles of life on the planet.

As Cassandre understood Mr. Smith's native English, she was struck, more generally, by the excessive envy of game players whose goal appeared, at all costs, "to score." Given that this carried over from athletes on the field or enthusiasts spectating outside or inside the home, to the bedroom, scoring defined the purpose where, at some almost-divine point, the fulcrum of one's vital fluids turns into elation and a mode of ecstasy.

Scoring may be central to understanding the "bang" at the core of our universal origins. A country whose main gaming activities center around scoring perpetually may not handily excel beyond the others at the most popular sport worldwide—soccer—where a zero-sum game can variously be considered the *best*. One cannot fake or inflate what individualist countries invoke with their obsession over *team spirit*, as if they were trying to have it both ways; for in what the rest of the world refers to as *football*, the sprit of the ensemble appears to originate in matters of a different composition or constitution. Something about taking the act of walking (*marchant*) to its extreme in roundly running hither and thither with the same feet, not planted like fields of grass on the ground, together with the simplest of presences embodied in a few lines, a goal or two, nothing but a ball, child's play, and a clock that continues to run without artificial time-outs, make this game of denial, a sport for innumerable arenas of simplicity, honesty, nudity, dancelike movements, and poverty. Soccer may always be a sport, less for the first among us, but rather, quite eminently, more for the last.

Cassandre knew that Ariana would be returning to Poland shortly after Marcel was due. So Mme de Beaurecueil phoned up to see if Ariana could pass by for a simple chat. The younger woman agreed without hesitation that the next day she would join Cassandre for a brief time, whereupon they might find a place for some conversation. For the moment then, Marcel's mother played a recording of the Chorus of Santa Cecilia singing Fauré's *Requiem*. Marc had always found that in as much as M. Ravel often seduced the listener, it was actually Fauré who ravished, properly speaking, both the ear and entire body. Something of a misnomer was very nearly embodied in the former's name.

In no time, though not without its proper place in their shared memories and reveries, the day was done. Cassandre slept soundly, awoke, and broke her fast. Before she could sit down to call her ever-available sister and brother, she heard the doorbell ring. There then, at the threshold of pain's gateway to sensational discoveries rarely as pleasant and inviting as the pangs of childbirth, she greeted Ariana with tender affection and a couple of ambidextrous kisses on either cheek. The two ladies sat for a while, speaking about the eager Polish woman's impending rediscovery of her homeland. They also broached the more pressing subject of the delivery.

What's more, Ariana harbored an unrelenting wish, come what may, to go to Angeles-sur-mer to pay her last respects to a master who remained, to her way of thinking, far more than a late man tucked away in his grave. Cassandre appreciated this touching gesture; and so they were off as early as Ariana's desire was expressed even though something had come over Marc's student, whose competing desire made her long to hear, whether here and now, or graveside, Kathleen Ferrier singing notes and words written by Richard Strauss in "Four Last Songs."

Ariana believed she had heard Marion Anderson sing these colorful tunes but never in the context that so affected her soul; so Mlle Ferrier's interpretation overwhelmed her to the point of tears. She would later write, she felt, a poem titled "Lacrymosa" in honor of this prodigious, almost superhuman voice. For now, however, she contented herself with thoughts of her teacher's courageously mourning wife.

She mused how her hostess seemed to resemble the Virgin Mary in many ways, so closely had she followed the dreams of Marcel's parents in their wish to be a kind of secular holy family. There was an essential distinction to be made, however; Mme de Beaurecueil's piety did not devote itself to God as much as other humans. It in no way was naive or unfaithful either.

While Cassandre let Ariana know the former might reserve her judgment of other humans, she was always capable of assessing their actions and behavior. This provided the basis for facilitating the creation of art, and this, on the part of others coming into contact with one such harmonious, most inviting home.

As they drove together, a "Magnificat" of Bellini, playing on the radio, animated things as that of Bach had long before. Both Cassandre and Ariana witnessed a weak spot, deep within themselves, for Italian sacred music. The lyricism and melodies of this piece brought home a sense of noble death's truest grandeur. It made the young Polish student imagine just where the heart and spirit, the heritage of Chopin's *etudes* lie.

Fortunately, it was still early enough in the day for the heat to be tolerable with regard to Cassandre's system. Soon they arrived at the small cemetery, just removed from the point where the town's habitations announced the more barren country. Cassandre took in hand a small pail and some water, together with a horsehair brush that reminded Ariana of the violin's strings. She gently kneeled down and cleansed the grave, stroking interred love, strumming her vibrating dreams, and dusting off the years like some ethereal maid of time. She purified, as was her ritual, the entire surface on the top and sides. While her time spent on the singularly dated life enshrined within this name-bound block was nominal, its counterweight remained substantially alive.

A slight imperfection of the marble, a dark spot, caught Ariana's eye. Cassandre interjected that Robert Pinlou was fascinated by the same small mark. Visible to the eye, at least, there was no scuff or scratch on the tomb however, no sign as yet of any wear from its fading place among the elements of time. Like the very tissue of Marc's spirit, no less than Reinhardt's, this ineffable sign of an unknown universe that would likely forever remain known only to itself—closed like a world giving on to none other than the unfathomable, unintelligible, and unbound—appeared indestructible. It was as though, in the context of a nearly perfect slab of polished marble, the tiny dark dot marked off the passage of a human presence, the time of a heartfelt creation that was not quite finished, a work not exactly perfected. This link joined her to a series of chain reactions, to the interconnected realizations that, in some vague fashion, lying there wrapped in the darkness was precisely what may never be ascertained or identified, whether as part of anyone's identity or any principle of certainty about anything or, for that matter, any word. This small part of a physical and metaphysical arrangement, a series of notes taking afterlife—notes followed by letters, whose ineptitude appears forever condemned in advance, letters whose inanity appeared as our common insanity that would quite possibly remain forever an open question—appeared to give onto an unobstructed passage exposing the observer (passing here as the unstoppable observant), to the greatest possible beyond, well beyond the improbable.

A surfeit of emotion overcame Ariana, making her cry once again, though not in Cassandre's arms, rather, alone. Marc's wife had discreetly removed herself to both leave the student by herself with her metamorphic reckoning and, now around the corner, to visit her father's grave that lay around the back of the de Beaurecueils' family site. She had the evanescent silence of Mahler's *Kindertotenlieder* in mind as she thought of her defunct husband's shortened life.

Ariana marveled at the setting, finding that she lacked imagination enough to conceive of such simplicity and grace, a sign of such humane science and wisdom; for she would have much preferred to see Marc's grave among the kings and queens of the country's first cathedral at Saint-Denis! Even though her eyes flickered like a taper, she did not however notice the place next to Marc's tomb where, at some point in time, Cassandre would cease in her living movements, where this great Dame de France would come to terms with nothing less than *life*.

If the young writer's thoughts revolved around death in its cold metaphysical manifestations, Cassandre, not unmindful of an irreconcilable absence, bore all the signs of a woman immersed in the physical world. If Ariana felt that we are all on earth as foreigners and wayfarers, as interbreeders increasingly involved in miscegenation but also as intrabreeders evolving in relation to ourselves, Cassandre believed herself most "stranger to herself" at this point. Extending herself physically as far as one may go, she felt herself at odds, in a sense, with her singular nature as if she were carrying the counterweight to simplicity.

Mme de Beaurecueil longed for Marcel's arrival so that at least her body could be restored to a state of normalcy outside of pregnancy. Nine months struck her as just the amount of time commensurate with fostering the preborn child and nurturing a sense of motherhood before actually embarking on its exercise.

She could certainly follow Ariana's ambling thoughts which read into the pockmark on her master's grave a vision of the deepest and most obscure pits, these dappled spaces created *for life*, which often passes without a final unction or poeticized honor.

She could further enlarge her scope in listening to Ariana's reflection on what the younger woman called a heavenly body. As the wife and maiden looked one last time upon Lord Marc's final throne, Ariana then undertook to recite two separate parts of the Bible, preying on a few happier metaphors prying open poetry, in his quasi-invisible honor:

> Je louerai l'Eternel de tout mon Coeur,
> Je raconterai toutes tes merveilles.
> Je ferai de toi le sujet de ma joie et de
> Mon allégresse.
> Je chanterai ton nom, Dieu Très-Haut!

[I will give thanks to the Lord
With all my heart;
I will tell of all Thy wonders.
I will be glad and exult in Thee;
I will sing praise to Thy name,
O most High.] (Psalm 9)

L'Eternel est dans son saint temple,
L'Eternel a son trône dans les cieux;
Ses yeux regardent
Ses paupières sondent les fils de l'homme

[The Lord is in His holy temple,
The Lord's throne is in heaven;
His eyes behold, His eyelids
Test the sons of men.] (Psalm 11)

And all the while, Cassandre's entire organism bulged with a form of high visibility just now full of impatience eagerly anticipating her little Marcellino's or Marius' first appearance and her minute, taste-filled *calzone*, her would-be worldly earthling's unearthing to the light of day. She realized that "life goes on" as the cliché of popular wisdom would have it. Fortunately, we are left with more than a single composer standing in this friendly countdown thrusting us gently without stinging into orbit around resplendent musical solitaire—the *Farewell* symphony—or that German romantic sonata encapsulating rhythmic vitality in the border-crossing title, *Les Adieux*.

Even if it might appear Marc's magnetic motion had ceased to exist, when faced with eternity's final decomposition (the bedrock from which one could conceivably, reasonably or other, extrapolate some form of reincarnation), one could find a compelling argument, emotion aside, for a theory explaining life and death as one. After all, they form a single being in some sense in the same continuum of movements, whether measured or not. Cassandre's *slow movement*, after all, signaled to her the significance of viewing the world *with* various rhythms. What she would forevermore produce would have come from what she and her love would have reproduced. Fecundity fertilizes further productivity in time. Without these slower movements that constrict nothing less than haste itself, she would never have been so quick to appreciate the fullness of the year's cycles, the wealth of serenity's plenitude or the natural mobiles of age and the ages.

Wisdom, like maturity, more generally speaking, necessarily passes through a phase whose tempo is like the *adagio* of a *pas de deux*. The greater the *largo*, the more one discovers the splendid *largesse* in the manners of adages—whose proverbial style puts the truth of some maxim at ease and *adagios*, which embody ease, if not comfort itself.

Cassandre felt, at this point, she was, not without the spirit of her partner or masculine counterpart, lifting, balancing and letting Marcel freely turn inside the embracing envelope of her body. Never had her movements been so slow; her speed of physical articulation had never been so low.

This is undeniably where and when Cassandre nonetheless drew on the highs of happiness. This is where she dipped into the riches of a world whose triumph contoured her *allegros*, shaping the sound and sense of her every phrase. This is where she enjoyed believing, not in love at first sight, but rather in what she fancied conceiving of as a kind of "love at last sight" since hers was an intense endearment, an adoring affection, a devoted sense of mercy and grace, which have everything to do with what the ear sees and retains.

Cassandre navigated the wheel of her fortune like Reinhardt himself—boldly, resolutely, cum fortitude, tenaciously, poetically, and, to finish, humbly. She guided here nascent dreams whose prolongation extended the imminence of a child to the full realization of his or her potential.

These were the points of trancelike bemusement, the extremely pleasant lines of thought, she shared with Marc, in a reality which was about to come, in large measure, at least, true. This is ultimately where the lords of abnegation deign to deny themselves yet further, in order for life's most positive turns to transpire, evolve, inspire, revolve, and return to those born gods, rendering a form of justice supported by the blood, sweat, and tears of most eminently human dues.

Music is written in the sublime book of the universe, which reaches out without end as a tried and true parent to our listening gaze. To understand the book, one must be conversant in philosophy as well as in the symbols of a language whose alphabet unites science, and the conscience, in a world of letters. An elite knowledge is born at this often disjointed juncture of reason and faith; whether it should be given absolute priority over politics is a real question. Society often moves forward debased, in fact, based on the *ad hoc* criteria of salesmen adding their two bits to a falsification of truth and subtruths or any subset thereof, including their corollaries steeped in bad science, uninformed philosophy, rampant ambition, ideological prejudice, economic stubbornness, or unenlightened politicians saddled with power.

Short of finding the various characters of music's language intelligible, one could linger all the while in a dark maze, just as if one were predisposed to circumnavigate, midst the signals of a labyrinthine universe, without ever having been initiated to its most vital idioms. One can only discover the full, deep beauty and unity of the physical world by passing through the language of the metaphysical; for this is where any personage involved in basic physics exercises a dream of increasing the understanding of his or her own character. This is where a semifictionalized novel may be imaginatively invented to serve the attentive listener and reader with a taste for simple sophistication.

To conclude, one must recognize whence viable music came in the beginning; a tune surges forth from infinitesimal movements, vibrations *rinforzando* in the air. In the course of a pregnancy, these movements may naturally pass from a *piano* to a *forte* through a *crescendo*, just as they may have acted in reverse, *diminuendo*, at the outset and onset of time, *viva voce* or other. Cassandre understood—now that she found herself most distended, and nearly at her most static, with Marcello's first movement toward the world outside (a virgin bundle of viviparous vivacity vivifying any related substance or person, to come any day now)—that enveloped in, yes, behind every great life, like backstage from the theater of any worthwhile autobiography, soars up a part constant, part evolving form of ever-revolutionary science. This future conscience may well be physical, social, literary, or other. It turns out to be the contour of self-consciousness, one aware of who is doing the measuring. It is truly a cognizance that has hitched its train of thought and taken it with the sum of all measures to a star or, with respect to less-fixed, more rapidly moving celestial bodies to a planet not unlike this self-proclaimed, self-designated, self-honored, and otherwise dishonored earth. We would surely come to know this place in time, indeed, this time in place, one and the other moving through any part of space, where we all to cleanse ourselves of our dirty little secrets. First as individual people, then as peoples recollecting which of our purest forms beg further purification, we could collect ourselves in harvesting both the quality and condition of relative freedom of movements. All of us could be led to follow the well-bred, full-strength lead of good style, absent-defiling faults, sinful guilt, inarticulate chastity, vulgar posturing, even empirical reasons.

Dynamism, indeed, the motion of this, read any kind, understood with or without emotion, forms and informs the fundaments of natural philosophy. Any literary, if not musical, truth flows from here. Unity follows, like a *vivandière* her French troops to whom she provides sustenance in the form of viands and liquor. As Aristotle said, to be ignorant of matter's constant flux is to be ignorant of nature herself, like ants monotonously maneuvering in the Sahara, unaware on the whole of the hustle and bustle, in and around New Amsterdam.

It was Marcel's corporeal hostess whose sentiment afforded the mother-to-be a belief that *Gaia* had always been pregnant with an understanding of herself in this domain. This credence encompassing all of nature's myths chaperoned her pregnancy with a lived-in feel.

Cassandre knew her place in the *Via Lactea*, the Milky Way. She felt a surcharge of feelings when she imagined breast-feeding her newborn in the coming space-time frame.

This sensation stimulated her to recall a series of *Madonna and Child* paintings, particularly those comprising the study of Byzantine and Italian, principally Sienese, masters with whom she had grown familiar in her youth. It caused her to realize that what is most often moving on earth is vivid emotion itself, making us redden like children whose blushing recalls the rouge effects of terra-sienna. What marks this planet from the others, taken together with the less "wandering stars" as far as we know, remains the presence of human life, among others.

And what typifies humanity is not just its recognition of great swings of humors, moods, and emotions but also an acknowledgement of the elaborate and rich documentation, which describes them in either a perfumed world or its opposite.

Being a *documentaliste,* a librarian of rare materials, Cassandre's professional person acted consistently to preserve what her private person knew all too well. When she would sit, as she did in her final days of pregnancy, reading *La comédie humaine* (The Human Comedy) by Balzac, she did so fully aware of all the dimensions, both literal and literary, of life's great stages. She understood, going beyond the life of certain protagonists in this magnanimous work, she would be obliged to continue making an honest living, in order to furnish the main characters to come into her home with all the necessary commodities of comfort and happiness. The various volumes of this collection of stories passed down by Society's Secretary made her ever more thankful, *reconnaissante*, to be alive. She knew that ultimately all the formulas in the world, whether literary or scientific, amounted to less than the near perfect vibrations she was still, in a sense, hosting within her.

Here did the unmuffled mark of literature and philosophy adorn her as she adorned, in adoring the future as well as past man, the mandate of science's entire body, and the works, the *opera*, surrounding a distinguished worldview. Here alone, coupled with a burgeoning second life, did she find the makings of not just a spectral philosophy, but quite plentifully, a truly organic music indeed. It appeared to the ear like a distant echo of Reinhardt's "German Lullabies." It was a welling up from any abyss where sorrow blends simultaneous with joy, bar upon bar, note upon note, accent upon accent, inflection upon inflection. This appeared just as true as its comeliness seemed to strike the eye's regard for its contents as a distant reflection of a piece, a morsel of Marc's thoroughly complimentary grace.

A revolution was about to take place in Cassandre's life, a bit of bloody, bittersweet violence that would change the worldview of those involved, those evolving at once together and apart. She would soon pass from being a sentient being, implicated in a couple of beings, to the king-size "queendom" of motherhood, where the creator and the created would each be alone, with stately solitude, to some highly variable degree. She secretly hoped that any presumption she may have entertained in her life to this point would never have come to surpass the object of her delivery.

Once this earth-shattering event would occur, her body would once again regain its prior form. She would assume all the other realms of normalcy of daily life, at least, with the lone exception that a boy would have replaced, in a sense, the man, indeed, a man of singular unity, in her existence.

While she believed Marc's remains now figured among quintessences as if they occupied the most essential of airs, his presence could no longer be counted as essential, properly speaking. She had to rely, to count on herself in nurturing their common, if rare, reverie, what was presently coming, in part at least, true to all and sundry.

She had no doubt that, just as Mr. Bonnefoy had taught her about good French compositions, there exists in life a "before, middle, and after." At this point, her midsection could best be described as "on the verge" of the hereafter. Just what would yield this most eventful extension of her dreams into the space-time was about to become self-evident. She could hardly anticipate the living lessons derived from her ritualized conception of and *for a new world* as Wagner had made inexorably clear in the legion of notes inscribed in steadied, centered space-time as the *American Centennial March*.

Cassandre now found herself on the eve of her due date. Her sister was present, having planned on staying, what in English is couched in terms of spending the night with her. The midwife, an upright, corpulent, motherly Nicole Parmentier, was on alert for having seen her the day before. All Cassandre felt like doing was to listen and attend to music, cautiously gauging a *ritardando*, which allowed her at once to long for a past with Marc and that which she clearly distinguished from the other subject of her yearning—a future with Marcel. While she lay on the bed, she asked that her sister put the rock solid stylus to the shellac impressed with a succession of pieces.

First Cassandre heard Schubert's Unfinished Symphony. The now-emotional listener sought to sustain a tone of newfound serenity, a brave fermata that would transport her last moments of rest beyond their nominal value of tranquility. She found herself delightfully prolonging her prelabor hours like the precocious symphonist extending his work and that of the likes of Salieri with whom he studied, in a perpetual labor, one with no end in sight or sound. She had the impression this poet of nature who had completed so many other gems with unending melodies like The Great C-Major Symphony or the string quintet titled *The Trout* must have also taken pleasure from an effort which never saw a final anointed hour. She inevitably likened this unavoidable dimension of success to her most private sacrifices. It was as though the great luminary of the invisible knew the pains of childbearing; for he had already experienced a sense of unfulfilled accomplishment with his *Rosamunde* Overture, this incidental music nearly aborted by the public of a romantic ahead of his time, due to the fact it accompanied an unpopular play in the theater. This made Cassandre empathize with how much a tragic flaw loomed at the core of every piece of artistic creation, just as in humanity by and large. It caused her to recall even those youthful, playful pieces Marc so loved of Schubert—his *Arpeggioni* Sonata and Moments *musicaux* for solo piano—carried with them a backdrop of long-suffering, which more than makes do, devising art in and out of isolating solitude. She calmly marveled at how the perfection of one being, like those creations of fictional works, may act as jubilant genes for the vibrant growth of future people.

Cassandre wished to follow this selection with a flurry of other works from the period just before the heart of romanticism. She asked to hear two of the late Mozart piano concerti, nos. 21 and 23, to exact her fullest transport of a unique dream, following the eleventh played by Arthur Rubenstein, whose performance suggested a capacious insight to the thriving Austrian capital of music, making the listener believe it was either Beethoven or Mozart himself at the keyboard. She imagined this player, whose name begins where his person fears nothing in the end—with art—sitting in the most satisfied setting, behind the piano. Her preference for the two former concerti—arising out of a sacred brush with this wooden wonder, this dentured pluckiness wherein artists box a potpourri of noble emotions and desirable gifts—was modulated by performances of the Royal *Concertgebouw* Orchestra of Amsterdam and the *Gewandhaus* Orchestra of Leipzig, respectively. Both showcased pianists of whom she had heard but indistinct echoes, the second for having been a member of the same tribe as Mendelssohn-Bartholdy. She sensed a remarkable marriage of the piano with the orchestra, reminding her of Piano Concerto No. 27, Mozart's last of this most evenhanded, though blistering, genre he had fashioned for a variegated eternity. With each well-born and thoroughly bred bang on the keyboard, the listener felt horrified remorse and a sharp repeated pang traversing the rue one experiences in realizing that war and an economic slump in Mozart's capital terminated the sovereignty and power of poetry's latest, remonstrant appeal to the symphonic sublime.

Cassandre turned her attention away from quiet admonition and calm reproof of mean-spirited violence to a pirouetting version of this ultimate concerto played by an anonymous pianist with the Vienna Philharmonic. The playing seemed as delicate and balanced, as pristinely unclouded and perfect, as pointed and clean-cut, as any she had ever experienced, especially in the authoritative arpeggios and penetrating harplike runs. Since the player chose to remain nameless at this occasion, depth appeared even more profound in this palpitating piece since absolutely free and clear of unwanted, arcane aggression, as if the person at the keyboard resembled those countless faithful contributors to the great cathedrals of Europe whose spiritual focus guided the most manual of labors. This served to remind her of parents everywhere who take pains to hunt and gather names for their would-be children, all with varying degrees of flawless meaning and significance attached.

The rapid succession of pieces and notes did not prevent her from thinking that the future child, on the verge of appearing, was still, in fact as in nominalist terms, nameless and yet acting, in some ways, similar to the great soloist with respect to Cassandre's body. For her organism, the main and central part of her life was orchestrating his welfare, indeed, the highs and lows of his preexistence. She found herself astounded at the length of the concerto, together with Mozart's own cadenzas, given that it had all come out of the melody in a simple song the composer had crafted just prior to elaborating the more complex and stunning work for piano and orchestra. A thought of the origins of the word *orchestra*, signifying the very stage on which the musicians or actors play, caused her to appreciate even absence as if it were staged everywhere in her life at present. She told herself the ample piece, the majestic concerto, assumed the dimensions of a chamber work insofar as the woodwinds dialogue with the strings that in turn seem to converse with the piano. Cassandre was reminded of a thought she was beginning to formulate which confirmed this sensation of intimacy, interiority, and the world beyond names; when she was younger, symphonic works occupied the rose-colored corolla of her ear while aging afforded her an inward-turning life of abundant measure more consistent with the fused inner envelope of chamber music.

This embosoming reflection—about a kind of intellectual cleansing washing over the heart of prodigal music—led her, part and parcel, to long for the purifying slow movement of Beethoven's Emperor Concerto, his last of the same genre. Ariana had once confided in her, upon returning from the graveside, and just before saying good-bye, were she to die young, like the maestro of metaphor who ruled her sense of music and life, she would want this movement played at her funeral. In exchange for her embowering, surrounding confidence, Cassandre explained how this particular concerto got its name, bordering on the very stirring brinksmanship to which it declared the muse titled. Thus, Ariana was made to recall that the French occupied Vienna at the time of this partially sheltered creation (as if the most tender spot on earth were overshadowed by Mars's truculent eclipse of Venus). The piece was baptized by the spontaneous ejaculation, the emphatic utterance and the thoroughly captivated *corps* of a soldier who, upon hearing this great work for the first time, put an apostrophe at the end of a sensation: "It's the Emperor!" None other than the absent figure of *amour propre*, Napoleon, was thus invoked to give new life to the already new creation. With the absent father and bard in mind, Cassandre called on another sonnet out loud to interpret both the unifying anecdote and music bookmarked for generations:

> Mark how one string, sweet husband to another,
> Strikes each in each by mutual ordering;
> Resembling sire and child and happy mother,
> Who, all in one, one pleasing note do sing.

The intimacy of this form of confidence acted as notes that add body to the dissemination of a dream. They cued Cassandre to request there then, one of the last works of chamber music made by the most highly inventive progenitor of the quartet, Haydn. Franz Josef's own late "Emperor" played in a rare *belle epoque* recording by the Fin-de-siècle Quartet in honor of that other ruler whose name was well-known to both this "other" great composer and his adoring public.

Just as she had so often felt in Marc's incrementally gratifying presence, Cassandre believed the artist approached as close as any of the species the essence of the supreme lord and measure for all measures, the self-designated absolute One and Master, the omnipotent author of the world, if not the most divine creator of the universe. Like Marc, the artist made up or is made up of a *corpus mysticum*, a being who lives on in evolved fraternity, intellectual liberty, balanced equality, and a *dolce cantando*. On a whim, Cassandre told herself that, in this sense, Marcel would be raised as a type of Dauphin to a self who thrones over petty demimonde and grand society alike, society over which nature reigns supreme. He might well become a soloist himself, following life's *grand reveille*!

After all would be said, or played, and done, it would have been themes in nature herself which would have surfaced in such a fashion as to unite and transfix all these wondrous works and presage a good future. Even the phrasing of the interpreters, as the musicians themselves "uttering" the language of the soul's universe, the idiom of coherent thought and the mirror of dreams, yes, all this would have transubstantiated and transcended time by virtue of the composers' first decoding nature's muse.

By this time, the laboring mother-to-be felt unusually fatigued, astir with extreme emotion; nevertheless, she wanted to conclude the prolonged prelude to Marcel's birth with another work the short-lived and precocious composer did not himself complete—Mozart's Requiem, ending with his last movement—*Lacrymosa*. Even birth does not reach the end, she felt, any more than it brings life to a head.

Death alone reserves the ultimate privilege of the living.

As she listened to the author of a music which seemed to attest to his faith through and through—in a piece that appeared like a pale reflection of yonder light—she could not help but think of the many suites and German Dances. He and others following his musical beat, like his most gifted student, Johann Nepomuk Hummel, had left the carpalistics-loving world these prescribed steps and improvised gestures to enjoy while frolicking with rhythm. All of the fleet-fingered Mozartian passion nested and nestled in pure—as only pure may be—musicality. It made up the constituent parts of calm and tranquility's composure. They caused the listener, attentive to the connotation of a certain ball contained in the detonation of a "dance," to realize that, similarly, a "walk" was an event of spiritual and more sensitive proportions than, say, the act of jogging or globe-trotting. Here, there, and everywhere, this music would be heard, the most rapid of minds knew how vital it was for men, women, and daring children to slow down to a pace where couples could remain together, hand in hand, arm in arm, heart in mind. All of the grandest child's confidence in humanity lay in the melodious momentum of a wide-ranging art at the confluence of foreign lands, territories as diverse as France, Italy, Germany, and Austria, indeed venues that have charted the crossroads of the heavens' modern-day zip codes.

Reason joined happiness rooted in a kind of extraworldliness and almost casual brilliance, worthy of undying veneration, which never moved beyond magic mixed with a sense of possibility. No human motion or emotion went uncovered by this poet of the day and night, this music maker of hope and doubt, this creator of works and plays of all kinds.

Death alone marks the term of the drama that occurs between the two poles of the great artist's creation. Death alone adds or subtracts color from a type of nostalgia for which his youth-bound presence cast itself, like no other precious material, in the limelight of the musical stage.

Cassandre suddenly felt the full impact of a realization; like the night Marc had orchestrated their dinner party with a baroque theme, the common thread uniting all her days wove music through everything and every word. She felt as though leading a life like the one he would have followed with emotion and science in balanced rapport, without the code of musical fiction's *gravitas* and poetic *veritas* by which to live beyond the confines of a book, was akin to reading a novel or ingesting morsels of music with excessive abandon and without deplorable end. One does not need to make an orphan of oneself in need, as we all are, of proper guidebooks and rightfully reassuring guideposts in our lives. Art alone must never be—no more than it should ever call itself—sorry and ill or poorly shepherded. Art's gift to the world frees us from any need of forgiveness for the rendition of truth we perceive and esteem as most beautiful or redeemable. As she scooted a wee bit to reposition herself, Cassandre thought of her contemporary, Karl Amadeus Hartmann, founder of *Musica Viva* in the city of monks, Munich; "If perhaps Marcel were given the least violent of middle names, videlicet godly love could live on forever—front and center—within him, in the vein of Mozart's art."

Mme de Beaurecueil was clearly concerned about the risk of infection that had caused many a childbirth to leave the mother dead from *purperil sepsis;* for hers was a home anything but sterile. Nevertheless, neither she nor the womanly Nicole had taken any unusual measures to prepare for the big day.

It was around midnight, during the beginning of the eleventh day of September, Cassandre awoke with moderately strong contractions. Her sister had never dozed off as Cassandre did at the universal language's end; and so she called Nicole, Isabelle, and Michel immediately.

Within less than an hour, the petite midwife was present, coaching Cassandre in her breathing. Cassandre felt herself like an entire symphony under the direction of Nicole's steady tutelage and forelocks of auburn hair. The deft-handedness, yes, the deftness of the young yet experienced and very competent expert in delivery of "one of the ultimate goods," countered any of the birthing woman's fears. Perhaps chief among Cassandre's preoccupations was the idea, hardly physical in nature, that she would not be able to bear forthrightly all the lessons of St.-Dieu's meteoric *oeuvre* in the future. Her child would amount to the metaphysical summation of an integrated remembrance, a powerful force of thorough memory, which could act, at any given moment, to attain human heights no less lofty than the imposing elevation of Rilke's *Duino Elegies.* As would be true of anyone, whatever his or her mother tongue, the very female, in bearing offspring, would prove to be the first line of response for the child.

In the near term, however, Nicole was having her full say about any and all matters related to Marcel. Her vigorous appeals to push the child out of her womb followed several prolonged moments of quasi-relaxation. From a small floral pot of water, the midwife occasionally took a cloth and dampened Cassandre's perspiring visage.

Mme de Beaurecrueil countenanced composure mixed with inexpressible eagerness, self-control laced with anticipation. The mild-mannered midwife murmured gentle directives. By early morning, Cassandre's contractions grew in intensity and, naturally, accelerated in pace. Her whole body began to writhe less and less slowly.

The baby was near! The birth of a new life was most assuredly in the homestretch, the prolonged, continuous period of time that would produce and henceforth be responsible for its own special marks! With this, Cassandre reflected, came a sense that Marcel's literary antecedents had sacrificed themselves in order for a future to be born, one fulfilled, pervaded even, by an intricately woven accumulation of the past. Soon enough, some real weight would come to measure the import of Marcel's name. Knowledge of the world would follow, just like the child's constitution or composition. To assist her choice in this most revealing matter, she would consult her memory of the articulate and intrepid spirit expressed in Beethoven's *Nameday Overture*, a work whose echo may be found in the musical conquistador's "Victory March." Like all of this nominal mortal's razzle-dazzle introductions to his poetic music and generalized readiness to undertake a life as fully sensational as possible, this particular overture was quite literally an ear-opener.

At the close of a luxuriant reverie this small musical jewel engendered, a dream about no less than the name itself of a work, itself indicative of a man who overtly distinguished himself from others, Cassandre spontaneously asked her sister, wearing *crêpe de Chine*, to both play an adult piece even closer to home—*Daphnis et Chloé* by Ravel—and invite Ariana, together with the Pinlous, to attend the whole world's population's latest, most proximate birth. And just like that, *presto*, the final push occurred. Flowing and flowering from her midsection, like sensible and sensitive time discharged from the hands' unfolding movement on the notched surface of a finely tuned watch, the distinctively fecund fragrance of motherhood filled the air, marking the transcendent imminence of a new human pair. It was the tangy, hemoglobin-filled, singularly gushing smell of coherence, vermilion connection, ironclad bonds, ferrous faith, unfiltered trust, unedited hope, and readied intimacy. As much as Cassandre's full attention bore down on delivering her creation to the world, she recalled in this most tense of moments the words of the great French composer of this single-act ballet: "My intention in writing [this], was to compose a vast musical fresco, less concerned with archaism than with faithfulness to the Greece of my dreams, which willingly marries into the one imagined and depicted by French artists of the 18th century."

At sometime past what the Renaissance knew as the seventh hour—and just as a recurrent thought returned to Cassandre like *le dernier cri* twitters, titters, and flutters at the onset of fashion ever à-la-mode, reminding her Marcel would be a credible child, offspring, and man of his times, an objective Renaissance boy knowing all about those periods preceding him and his—the woman who had forecast tempered joy and happiness for her creation agog, heard an insistent knock at the door.

Ariana's arrival, following the literary neighbors', just now prompted her to push and groan one final time, *sostenuto*, as the heaving, perspiring woman responded tremulously and without *faux pas* to the exhortation of the midwife. Lo and behold, just the other side of seething and tearing pain, a beautiful collection of shuddering cells, an ensemble of living miracles, was born forevermore!

And it was a girl, as unforeseen in her halting *genre* as a precious, priceless love! This *sui generis* creature appeared as "humously" novel to those who were humored by a variety of humors as they found themselves expecting Marcel as living in the air would be to humans, those artful bipeds for whom flight comes closer to a fugue than a bird's form of movement. Before anyone present could even hear her first breath, broadly torqued by real-world oxygen, the babe made herself known (*La belle s'est fait connaître*), without warning then and there, by a prodigious, yawning, caterwauling scream, *più mosso*. She squealed, bawling at the high end of the wiggling, wriggling, twisting, and squirming muse's register!

With the long-prepared advent of a mere sound, so stunningly sweet and marbled with blood, Cassandre appeared to have transcended her mind and, at once, solitude. If literature naturally contained some obscurity in the underbelly of its metaphors enfolded like the woman pregnant with a living mystery, now fully upon her was the enveloping light of her life. As *adagios* alternate with more vigorous movements, defining the very rhythm of life, fiction would now yield a part of Cassandre's flushed midsection to the collective reality of our unfolding, unsung heroine. The child's entire organism would encapsulate its individuality from birth, just as, at the other end of the spectrum, a munificent, choral "Ode to Joy," with which Beethoven signs off on all his bountiful symphonies, triumphantly finishes off an inner and outer life of generous listening, with or without hearing, *bien entendu*!

The two were bound to care for each other in both spirit and letters as one partaking in divine serenity in the aerial balance of *adagios* and in the homogenized though unsterilized proportions of a harmony exceeding even music herself. Just how this most tender form of Greek harmony would play out, corralling in their mutually divided souls, remained to be seen and heard.

And with the child's initial sound and Cassandre's accompanying, nearly unsuspecting pleasure—derived from imagined action, speech and thought—as if beyond all movement foreign to nature's own, the mother did not miss a beat in pivoting on the totality of her now seven-pound-six-ounce brunette marvel, *vif et très doux*. She thereby found the rest, indeed the remainder of her early love and pregnancy, as insurance that the prepossessing gamine's equally unexpected name would turn out, manufacturing nothing less than an eternal, at least perpetual tribute to the literary lord and all-knowing father. He too, after all, figured in life as an eminently literary, truly fabricating character. Even as he was growing older, not unlike his wife, though dissimilar to most adults, he remained both giving and receptive to genuine surprise. Like him before her, Cassandre was eminently available, open to change, what amounted to the watchword and hallmark of nearly endless adaptations to life and death.

The father's absence would invariably chart, to some degree, any presence in the life of not just the forbearing mother but also the child. Her girl showed herself to be the pleasing manifestation of Marc's dream, specifically the one that had given birth to the Madonna's "other" child. Her downy complexion rivaled none, save angels' very own, that which they might never withhold from others who wish for and desire adopting such natural color, texture, character, appearance, and constitution of the surface. As they peered out at the world for the first time, her deep, almost-French blue eyes glittered like the celestial sea with the sun hanging, on balance, at its highest point in the heavens. Their orbit recalled, for the one around whom she was gravitating good-naturedly, a sparkling pair of aqua marines set in a field of vision's dreams—that flesh and bones drawn to another like statues anchored as an ensemble in their proper place and time as if wholly a part of the *Uffizi Palace*.

Her extremities curled unlike her upright spine, as if she were still tucked away in a protective pouch. She seemed to descend from the earliest hominoids, armed with chimplike fingers and a rudimentary agility that reminded the evolved female hovering above of splendiferous gorillas, orangutans, gibbons, and siamangs in a royal menagerie. This sense of heredity, mixed with brut irony, revealed her external ears as parts of an age-old whole, ears equalizing, through genetic equilibrium, the mother's larger roundness and the father's measurably more petite conchae. Love's hand-hewn labor had not been lost; her male parts of the genome had not worked themselves out in vain. The embryonic had now come full circle, this advancing, developed side of great death.

Marcel had now metamorphosed into some divine surprise like the gods of Marc's vision, views, and reveries—in concert with great authors, as well as *maîtres à penser*—whose precepts and, far rarer, concepts guide insightful people, guaranteeing their overarching love and passion, to this day. This change mattered as all that which primes over the most sacred book, like a tour de force of nature; for without the regency of a feminine presence, even youth or youthfulness would not flesh out and maneuver around the dearest word.

Cassandre was filled with a defining sensation as the new-coming one Ariana's rabbi described in reminding her: "A whole heart is first a broken heart." The slight fever she had contracted before birth—warmed by queasy, if dizzy anticipation and the earth-shattering prospect of a most liberating new lease on life, an unqualified, gratuitous release, yes, her life—was taking a turn for the better. Most everything, with everyone by her side, was coming together now, like the pieces of the shattered commandments scattered around Moses's toiling feet at the base of Mount Sinai; her faith in life was assuming a distinctly human hand at this point. Following the scattering of Babel and man's fall before the tree of knowledge, all the languages of the world seemed to coalesce and coagulate here, in this soft, semisolid, unified matter already nibbling on humanity's fact and fiction. The value of a voice's initial manifestation is incalculable where and when heard in view of all the negotiations, interpretations, and commentaries upon which it embarks at any given point.

Unnamed, anomalous, vulnerable, direct, and scarcely veiled life seemed as synonymous with Frenchified beauty and *adagios* as security with a dainty baby held in her mother's arms. This form of dark energy moved forward as if the same antigravity binding the universe were holding her together and in place. Motherhood appears to be the archetype of definitive beauty clinging to time since its forms, at once illusory and tactile, secure all our senses in a perpetual rediscovery of who we are since day one. Beauty is thoroughly like truth, goodness, and the unity brought about by *adagios*'s pure passion to and at the core, not only skin-deep.

Unflagging mothers spanning the globe, no less than never out-of-date beauty allay fear and doubt, anxiety and insecurities, dejection and rejection; they are the first in line to furnish hope, charity, faith, and, the greatest of all, love. They are the first connection of all the connections linking us to the universe. They are able to create the illusion of making space-time and sentiment stand still, as if we have access to a unique place, which is timeless, a never-named planet unmarred by ages, eons, epoques, and notions of eternity. They appear as mythical mummies come *to life*. Mothers are the somewhat hypnotizing guarantors of well-fastened mental and physical stability, strong vision, self-assured certitudes or doubts indigenous to the spirit and letter of high art as well as a thing of beauty. They mortise reality without vain debate, securing a child as if with tenons and tetons, to the likelihood and livelihood of a recognizable if only provisionary future. With their naked splendor, mothers fashion our most authentic pledge *to life*, indeed, to love through and through.

Cassandre's voice seemed to massage the young soul like a vibrato playing minute, sustained and rapid variations on the strings of a marionette. It is in a mother's murmuring, in her vocal organs, and giggling consolation that cascading chords may be heard in relief, salving any hurt or discomfiture we may feel. Cleansing bars of soulful sound erase any pain for most of us, wiping away our fear of the unknown, among other. Like music, our physical creator lathers our body with a metaphysical froth that makes anything in the material world tolerable like scuds of blood healing all wounds. Enchanting glissades of words filigree our most intricate realities, enriching us with detailed meaning and delicacies as we slide into the golden future. Like a goddess or artist never content with her or his creation, mothers may find some repose in the nostalgic lassitude of an *adagio*, but their conscience evolves into a never-ending exile from the simple rest they knew before conceiving.

Sensitivity founds the music a child hears in a mother's discursive song. She is the positive or negative origin of our own sensitivity, like it or not. She is the child's first superordinary teacher as a result, not unlike every great musician who apprentices with a master before assuming an original style that may be easily associated with his or her name. In a most profound sense, the child has nothing in common with herself; and thus, she grows from the outset, learning another's way of speaking, moving, and feeling. We are thus able to explain that Cassandre's baby would most likely—yes, most assuredly—come to learn French in lieu of some other language.

Muted by a sense—to be sure, a day—of awe, Mme de Beaurecueil lit a candle, bowed her head, and counted her invisible lucky stars, thinking delicately, *A people reading and studying—just as individuals, both males and females, listening to the world and beyond—may be the subject of ignorant speculation and scorn.* Given people fear the unknown (like the unborn!), beginning with the moment the thoughtless remain unknowing, unmindfully attending, in other words, to their lives without knowledge and wisdom. All too sure of themselves, how many demonic despots, supernumerary fools and all too well-placed knaves have cremated virtue high and low, plainly trying to butt the wit and judgment her almost-trotting, often meandering conception of *adagios*, in combination with livelier movements on either side, would bear down on—lifting up—her child! True, she believed, study increases wisdom as wisdom fortifies life. Further, life reproduces study as nature's cycles augment eternity, spiraling multiples of space and the multitudes for the rest of time. Those opposed to these natural, elemental, or fundamental movements of sensitivity, sensibility, education, knowledge, awareness, being informed, teaching, learning, literacy, and letters do not want a truly artful, good, civilized, unifying product imbued with the culture of *adagios*; they want it Monday!

No longer alone, the newest of mothers felt as keenly as a keel feels the water parting along its prow, the oldest of words, which close *Ein deutsches requiem*: "Blessed are the dead which die in the Lord from henceforth: Yea, saith the Spirit, that they may rest from their labours, and their works do follow them."

As it is written by a too-little read student of École Normale, "In dreams is often divination; one sees better with the eyelids closed." Drawing the curtain on one's eyes quietly loosens and tightens thought at the same space-time. People are thus free and freer to establish new patterns of recognizing themselves in the world. Anyone may come along to reestablish old ones along new lines of reasoning, emotion, and feelings guided by imaginative and creative forces. Cassandre's pregnancy seemed enveloped by this form of educated guesswork and visionary play. The surviving dreamer would live on, cultivating the obscure voice of the gut and the enlightened will in order to leave the world a better place for all its inhabitants.

Thus, Cassandre found herself in afterbirth, fluxing like the purged animal or tractable child, both physically and artistically, with respect to choosing a name. Convivial art was at hand in a doelike, wide-eyed, skin-so-soft mass and incarnadine mess nature knows best. And it begged an attentive appellation, some substantial *etiquette*, which would beget even more than a good life. It would configure, *a priori* and *a fortiori*, the most delicate of human endeavors—all relationships—as Marc's name before and after death represented to her and those who knew him the art of living for a metaphysical realist. The latest name would come to mime, supplement, reconfigure, or change nature's works through mirthful reading and study of that which could, in some small fashion, suggest to the engaged subject, no less than music.

The incipient mother found herself—like a smile fully suspended and expended—at a conjunction where life beckoned, thanks to the appeal of an unsuspecting creation, a brand-new, timorous, potentially terribly sensitive person attuned to beauty's commissure and thoughtful demesne. She was in fine fettle, and at a jolly conjuncture, where and when the sum of her conception's various movements cohered, hearkening to the abundant sound encased in a name's fixture. Thus tied down like the death and transfiguration of as many copiously outflowing births, creations, and inventions coming within the terrain, there, with stolid patience, laid the fragrant *terroir* of an appealing title such as the one unlimited multitudes have reserved for *La France, La Douce France!* (Sweet France!).

She was now charged to do her best in immortalizing the dearest poetic nature and *beaux rêves* of her matrimonial concretion, once removed and more than twice remembered in the infantine presence of this fresh sanctum of flesh and blood. In such a way, a person ensures that the surprising majesty of a girl could end up to be no less evocative, at all times, than the omniscient one contributing, albeit essentially *in absentia*, together with a now-relieved and adoring Cassandre, to leading the darling, the dearling of a poetic harvest and redeeming life.

At the same time, at this point, Cassandre wished for little more than to embrace the seismic change of the world as she just underwent it. Nakedly, brutally if necessary, without category, steadily booming sonically, she vigorously hoped resonant mother and child could be one and one with consonant nature. Herein, she could act as one able to be humanly wild, spontaneous, and free—here, in these places and at quietly exulted times such as these. She found herself amiably reconnoitering, confronted with seeking to embody—yes, to nurse—the kind truth and beauty, the goodness and unity of a genteel tradition impregnated with the reference, indeed, the usufructuary deference of a name. Certain knowledge would be as if genetically programmed, always latent, present, and ready for expression, framed by the name. Cassandre wanted the father to be couched therein like a potent, dormant dream of all that which the new individual would herself recognize as her own for the rest of her life.

In using and enjoying her voice, the new mamma seemed to massage the young soul like a chivalrous vibrato playing minute, sustained and rapid variations on the strings of a marionette. The little doll bore some simple benefice in the mother's heart and mind as if she were endowed with a spiritualized sinecure by the natural office of childhood. Cassandre entertained a passing thought of royal children by remembering Elgar's *Nursery Suite* and his earlier, op. 1 *Wand of Youth Suite*, with their fairylike, erring, creeping, and scurrying, spry dances designed to portray the nimble life of brisk sprites, pixies, specters, and ghosts. It takes a mind and heart blithely in tune with *adagios* to appreciate the pace of life portrayed therein, not unlike Debussy's *La Plus que lente*. As she felt herself gently, patiently swaying then, with these health-giving thoughts attached to the baby and the English composer's *Dream Children*, a part of Fauré's *Dolly Suite* animated her most tender thoughts as though the munificent woman were now both the youngest heir and firsthand patron of *La Berceuse*. She wept more than slowly.

Like the ever-present, celebrated *marc* of effervescence contained in a Champagne flute for which she not infrequently recalled to herself her predilection, an enchanted flute that was now raised to and from, indeed, *for life*, the child's emerging, ebullient presence on a post-Gaian earth clamored voraciously for a name. With this specific, individualized indication of some qualitative value, any great human being could, from the family of man and the "internation" or introspection of artists, live. Dead perhaps was the man of the house, albeit not dying any time soon, if the matron would have her way; for she would find a way to fuse his memory and métier, without confusion, to that of the very Marcel, among others, of whom he had so constantly conceived. If it is true that one sees most clearly with the heart, one could as fluidly suggest she would once and for all see Marc with her heart and the art of her ear. The child would thus learn, in time, her father's character stood, in a most satisfactory fashion, with literary lords and high-flown or low-keyed masters, indeed, maestros *par excellence*.

As the assembled human beings drank effortlessly and partook in deviled eggs with a chiffon mousse and some enviable *foie gras pâté*, generously spread like nutritive slivers of their tasteful culture on Melba toast and crackers, a suite from Ravel's *Mother Goose* danced languorously with the enlivened background. Good vibrations appeared to furnish the air, hatching and breaking out of the clutches here—reaching beyond their individual grasp for precisely that which was emerging from the remarkable pen and hay of these females finding one another for the first time. Life was embedded here in a home restored—through foresightful design situated at opposite ends of any adventitious blood and tears to a reasonable plan led by the modestly stylized yolk of wholesome reality drafted in a light, airy, and "sweet home." Inside, as outside Cassandre's walls, it was all about the art of living for both the living and the long-lived dead. Everything appeared subordinated to the reigning voice of an inner and now outwardly regal, exploratory life.

In order to honor the nameless of a similar type to that of Ulysses's return in the direction of civilization's bastion cultivated by the ages, Mme de Beaurecueil entertained the idea of calling her unique brood by the sobriquet *personne* (no one). This type of anonymous cognomen carried with it the virtue of implying the *de facto* presence of not one person but all people, diffuse and intermittent, from who knows where. Not too dissimilar to the one she would soon assume, one such name would remind her in perpetuity to never take anything or anyone for granted. Or perhaps, named as such or nonesuch, with the antiname, the person could best approximate an exquisite thing, a work of art or being in itself and nothing more or less.

And thus, Cassandre knew she would engender an entire world (and then some, for good measure), beyond her docile daughter's first, magnanimous, if loyal, nom de plume. The name would always end up swaddling art's newest consort throughout her life as if an invaluable treasure were permanently preserved and safe, thanks to a scrupulous custodian of space-time. Beginning and ending with the virtue of her name, at once immanent and soon-to-be-dubbed or doubled in an eminent transcendence, she herself would carry on with art from this point in life in combination with the attraction of listening rather than merely pushing herself forward.

Therein would be the first truly unifying mark of her mother's education, meaning up-bringing and leading out. Never would Cassandre consciously intrude, thrusting knowledge into her. On the contrary, however, following her principle of leading a good life, she would always try to designate a way for her miracle of creation to lead herself out into the world with that which will have always been there, at the starting point, namely, within her own body, mind, spirit, and soul. The eternal feminine too would lead her outward and upward as if she would follow her mother in the Venusian instinct that yields to nothing less than individuation born from love's sacrifice of the spirit, flesh, and bones. In a word, the improbable and surrounding world would now and forever appear to poetry's freshest nominee—before a host if not a beautiful hostess of eternal truths—as wide-open as possible, a glance at a time.

This woman agleam, already smitten with being a mother and still moved by her Latin tongue, whispered to herself inaudibly that whatever she would designate—for the individual she now held in the bosom of all others—would guide her through all of life's peregrinations and turning leaves. Just as Beatrice had once led the divinely human poet in a *tête-à-tête* with the creator of *Paradise*, anyone may follow the poet's light-footed lead to this day and age. So long as the individual attends to the gentle soughing of the wind, one may distance oneself from the masses at one's utter leisure, according to the meter of a drunken silence whose measure of good, happy times and places, may bypass at any point and in any way, more hellish noise. In so doing, in so acting and in acting so, one may thereby find oneself pleasantly surprised by culture's wonders most fully consistent with nature's own. Thus surpassing, in no uncertain terms, and beyond a reasonable doubt, more raucous bars, one could counter objectionable pressure with ease by raising the bar beyond any rigid staff fastening itself to nothing but barriers in the way of conclusive, all-inclusive, decisive music, vertically inclined, indivisible, unimpeded, and measured music in the most extensive making of the ultimate.

No matter what people might say, and irrespective of how others may disagree, the final word, like the witty remark taken by silence, is given to silence.

This very account amounts to a silence for silence rendering, whereas foreigners less conversant with such unspoken laws of language might be led to believe that another form, another format, another formality, or, better still, a certain informality, best translates the word-for-word renderings of some presumably omniscient muse or presumptuously omnipotent figurehead.

Given the mother had, as is commonly said, "wasted" so much time methodically pondering her offspring, from the spacious depths beyond any renewal of *le printemps*, she and her daughter would share a most highly unique bond. The name would symbolize that specific interconnected relationship to the cathedra of a dream like the finial that seals the heavenly arch of human faith's most resounding, anonymous creation. In the final instance, Cassandre ultimately wanted more than anything to make a grand, equally prophetic, literary name for her child—as early as this newborn would set out to make a name for herself; both would therefore be perpetually lulled to poetry by a type of lifelong cradlesong.

In doing so, she would differ notably from the hero of arts and letters with whom her parents tried unfailingly to come to terms. Think, to cite but one example, how her more feminine life resembles, to some extent, the one Marcel might have undertaken as in his autobiographical enterprise where the author of *Place-Names: The Name*, among others, set out in search of taming the narrator himself. This unexpected difference—in the *genre* foreshadowed by Cassandre's original dream of someone other than a *fille fatale*—could doubtlessly engender a polyvalent rereading and tuning of the vision with which she first embarked upon life's greatest odyssey. This latest unambiguous arrival startled even the mother's sense of beauty *à deux* by making the latter think and believe, by sensitively dictating to her conscience, that intriguing wonderment is related or rendered from the moment and place the former—as one generally—is true to character, basically in unison with nature.

What combination of science and conscience would form (in) the child? Which parts of nature would impregnate her whole name and culture with goodness, beauty, unity, in addition to a fine sense of untruth, a balanced recognition of human fabrication? How would she come to live with illusions, useless ideals, stultifying nationalism, violence, and deadening falsification of all subjects other than poetic art? Would light and laughter (and their interplay) forever animate her heart?

While silence would complete her appreciable majesty, vertiginously spooling through the fabric of her body, mind, spirit, and soul, time—the unfolding of the seasons as deciphered or read in all the density and complexity of their natural code made manifest here—yes, time could and perhaps would tell.

Is there any other natural or cultural entity, any alternatively organic or inorganic form of creation, if not a creature, whose epistemic phylogeny counts divine surprises in the wake of its passage where any individual is born with some measure of critical knowledge?

Yes indeed, time, bound to space like thread to a bobbin—whether reeling tragically or comically, sadly or happily—this first of humanity's unlocated creations, this irreversible succession of events ostensibly passing everywhere through the present, so it might be said, this interval passes between one and one no more alone than an(y) other. It is as if it were here, there and nearly, if not everywhere in the farthest distance, moving still and still moving, separating two points on a continuum that may never show itself as related to that very similarly different time one could call at once, in turning to the point of returning, all words and all things being considered, all-in-all, easily and yet hardly telling enough!

Quickly, immediately, making time as if to make progress, you might say, "You don't say!" If this arbitrary flux of phenomena, events, conditions, rhythms, tempi, reasons, feelings, perceptions, and the like have run their course, you might say that to allow the newborn a rightful place among heydays, we might begin by redefining the course of those who run for office. We might freely choose to nominate solely those who consider walking an essential way of advancing every walk of life, in line with the poet's well-placed, slower-paced feet, covering every meter of ground essential for creating the life of a mind at work, simultaneously creating, if not recreating, the grounds where the little and big ones play together for good measure. In thus exercising the right to have left those in the wrong run on and off with their booty as they push on and pull off a "fast one" in full view of others, this ensemble conducts itself without regard for any such distasteful "quickies." Rather with full respect given to outdoing, outdistancing, outrunning those from whom they walk away, walking off ever so unexpectedly with the prize of lifelong self-awareness and honor, they rate, on more moderate and temperate balance, among the most honorable who, not inexplicably and not without some measure of paradox, remain among the least honored of all space-time.

Their names, foreign to the daily contagion of increasingly widespread fame, just as they may fasten one who learns of them to a quickening inspiration, are even more quickly, ever more globally, disappearing from our collective conscience. As the species they so nobly represent extinguishes the flame of their heartfelt and artful science without an afterthought, which is to say, "Without a worry in the world," the dodo appears more and more hopelessly passé. This poor creature deprived of any possible flight where birds from another world may land, yes, where the more fortunate beasts come down to earth, feet firmly on the ground, well served by their runways and heliports, this extinct member of archived empiricism and impotent imagination lives on though only in absence. Not unlike similar monsters—whose genial wings have been clipped, hopes dashed, and fears came as true as their nightmares—this cousin of the albatross has gone by more than the waist side of a more socially acceptable genius. Gone forever is, so it would appear, the very nature of a creature cultivating originally clumsy ideas, dresses, and addresses, manners of living that formed earthly inhabitants habits and customs, moreover, aging well in the developing style and growing good taste of France's highly decorated golden age. Gone evermore, and this, unlike the raven who remains behind, as if to remind us, yet again, of all that is "nevermore!" Each takes a fleeting imagination for a ride in a good way, just as the masters have lent their shoulders to those who wish to stand higher and understand yet higher and ever lower forms of life. They drift may be caught if one is attuned to how to be off with the ungainly, only to find a more aerated way midst the back roads and seemingly backward byways of what appears increasingly as awkward as a cakewalk, a walk in the park. The great distance these creators of diurnal dreams cover with all the self-control of livestock advancing one step at a time, one foot firmly planted in front, in no way ignores what the other foot is doing, it too, fully behind yet another. Ruminating all the while, even without speaking, chewing on ideas, meditating at length, and salivating at the very thought of finding the simplest of sustenance photosynthesized, thanks to a light that has never ever, knowingly or willingly, forever banished any form of darkness, such wonders of nature, progress along the lines of the must sustainable aggregated culture. Their most admirable sense of beauty, spontaneously respectful of harmonies echoing ever more magnificent contemplative delights all around, holds life in place, thus holding on to and for dear life itself, still surviving, magnified in the littlest and most modest of creative endeavors, here and there, potentially emerging everywhere among us, just in time.

"L'Cha'yim," joyously cried one and all whose presence around the mother's hearth and home blanketed the air—without cunctation—animated by a rejoicing chant about felicitous accomplishments and simple gladness. "To life!" exclaimed one of the suckling girl's first human relations, *gioioso*, as all were merrily reminded by the newborn that this willful devise means true beauty and fantasy really are, at hand, within grasp, not impossibly *out there*. Everything, just as everywhere and everyone, connects us to life and death as profoundly as dreams interweave themselves in sleep, no less restful and restorative than a visionary's unified view of the interdependent world and beyond.

"To liberty, equality, and fraternity too!" proclaimed another surrounded by so much virgin vim and fostering vigor. "To leading a good life by following happiness and shadowing sadness!" curiously added Michel, who wished to solemnly imply *hic et nunc*, wherever a *tear* is born, there may well be a laceration of the soul *de rigueur*, a "tear" in the fabric of a being who has yet to heal. In something like melancholy or discomfort—and the tears we shed due to one or the other—may linger, potentially forever and everywhere in our midst, more than the reminiscence of space-time's ostensibly anchored passage.

In a tear, Professor Pinlou had surprisingly written elsewhere on English poetry—furthering Marc's independently developed thought that the artist who cries actually incites an audience or reader to withhold more tears flowing from the emotive source of art—one could even read "a movement of heedless speed, a rush headlong" on the world. There is a split at the center of this homophone, a division which may be united by an individual who never ignores the suffering indigenous to the tear and discomfort, perhaps even the disease of those tearing or torn. Like Mr. Pinlou, Michel deftly subscribed to common sense of internalizing this regard—the greater the tear, the slower the healing. This was true even if the professor was stretching the proper use of two terms whose etymologies descend from different linguistic ancestors.

Slowness ensures nature's own form of *adagio* may restore a being to all of his or her singularly human potential like a bassinet that reestablishes a baseline of the child's energy. No less true, no less ingenious figures a majestic, prolonged patience—what is the mark of genius—one remembering the integrity of a person, "wholly" real, literary or other, bathing in the culture of a greater people. This may be seen in light of humanity's "hardening" as the elemental sign of both animate and inanimate life—water—dropping from the eye that turns, at once inward and outward, to listen to the "noise," the backdrop of a chaotic, often quasi-silent universe.

In the beginning, as in the end then, the child appeared to feel, in her as yet barely articulate way, a simple *tear* may foreshadow or recall a defining moment. Hence, it could be said, a "tearing"—a cleavage—natural or other, crystallizes a child's earliest world as if this first division, following a couple's multiplication, cries out at the core of a premier, earthly experience. Anybody present at the de Beaurecueil home could therefore make one of the principally literal and actuate points *du jour*. To be sure, beyond the *soigné* idea of a tear, a tear itself emerges on one such scene in need of little explanation or introduction; it acts, or rather serves, in the very least, as in the tiniest among us, as an *opening*, which begets an immediate *recollection* of our entire self. It furthermore bears with its flowing, like a pregnant reminder, a sense of our overarching remainder—cumbrous mortality. What's perhaps more, it thereby naturally makes for a healthy *closure* at the very same time, the opposite of an overture, which instantaneously orients our occidental *esprit de corps*, like a meaningful pilgrimage to and from the noblest of sacrifices—steadfast mother and fatherhood. At times, like in these beneath our unwavering eye, our organ of vision beholds, indeed, perceives, or even "listens" to the world with the utmost, cumulative regard *for life*.

"L'Cha'yim!" cried out everyone in unison, under the influence of Ariana's more or less foreign initiative, returning here for the prosperous relationship occasioned by nature's most felicitous happening, as each present exchanged good wishes and experienced marvelous feelings of uniquely human grandeur, taking in as well as giving out tears of joy—the primordial virtue—before their happy *congé*.

The lactating mother could hear the collective clamor of a youth-bound culture, not bereft of the all-encompassing jubilation around her and this novel, nursing life. Exhausted, nevertheless exhilarated, and true to form, she spontaneously let out the following, eminently leading cry, *dolcissimo*, "Vivent the imaginative pursuits in and at the heart of Marcia Adagia de Beaurecueil!"

In Lieu of a Coda

Were you to perceive any hint, scents or traces of some reasonable form related to reproduction bearing (with) even part of a partial sign relaying imitable Art—bound to be bound back, and so forth—to this point, it is the mark of an endearing present: anywhere an enduring Gift of cognition (like that emerging in and out of say a single book among singularly singing books) finds and founds some selfless recognition—otherwise known as understanding Knowledge—I count myself as one given to give none too generous a good, none too fine a shape to these very grateful thanks delivered with barely enough respect to the dedicated passion of a nearly matchless fire in the theoretically practical belly of the succeeding *beau*ties, namely, François Brunet, Dan Fineman, Jean-Michel Rabaté, Norm Shapiro, Geoff Waite, Arthur Flannigan Saint-Aubin, Annabelle Rea, Henk Schram, Deb Martinson and the entirely tireless Occidental College Writers' Workshop!

Where and with whom else would, could and should *Adagia* have explored, covered and discovered far more than a proper noun's greater, if nonetheless larger place in the midst of self-aggrandizing conditions, situations, circumstances and conversations defining virtually any classical or modern agora, evolving if revolving round the geological time spacing out more (and more!), this very frenzied pacing du jour or that (co)incidentally small (ex)change of words, things and ideas, devolving, if to nothing—if all for neither nought nor anyone—else, to the knotty point of fully living and living fully with(in) a curious race?

In rendering onto those who finish what they will have begat with authenticity and begun cum brio, a more polished rendering of critically poetic Art [born(e) of no unsound note], there comes to mind, involving a greater body of hearts enriched with a fairly hardy sense of poor souls—therefore, to the fore, in a doubly palpable palette of palates—these overrefined words of appreciation I wish to render, yes, tender in view of the genuine likes and the (unlikely) loves of Pierre Bertrand, Jim Michael Montoya, Bill G. Tierney, Lilli Parrott, Christine Renaudin, Janine and Charles Vilar.

Michèle Bertrand's common sense and uncommon presence commune, like none other, with exquisite absence, the world over ("just" maybe everywhere, and yet no more moving than still, yes and no, virtually, if not actually, nowhere at once . . .).

Dorothy Federman married Paul Hartstein (and the inverse in reverse, nonetheless . . .), playing much to the strength of their modesty and humble hearts' content (much to my otherwise inconceivably unrelenting contents!): thank you for placing some sincerely humorous form of distinguished distinction between the class, classifying and highly classified act (of conception) and the so-called "facts of life!" To my sole sister, brothers, cousins, aunts, uncles, nieces and nephews too (to those who have adopted me and I them), I turn again, as a gain, if none too economically, with a few chits nevertheless, even if one like an other (s)pared, even if paired with excessively gushing signs and symbols of accumulating Interest close to my capitalizing heart.

Francesca *Cernia* Slovin has made far more than a ream come true (to form, if true-to-life!), in more ways than one singularly private publication of exaggeratedly poor, if over(t)ly precious words: as O/one with none too unduly magnified a spirit mindful of the thoughtfully heartfelt, ever the otherwise underemphasized seeing and believing soul, she is o/One to echo Echo H/her S/self, (in) virtually any music made in the name and image of say, minors' major K/keys!

Enter—in the physically and metaphysically literary game of arts, letters, sciences and consciences—a catch "caught" in the live-long act of (f)acts and proverbial action! She is one as likely to be as lovely as virtually any "really and truly" lively one, this great score-keeper, that sensational B/beauty, namely, Stephanie Marie! From her smiling countenance, a smooth-sailing glissando of note(s) forms round her lips, bordering there, on a sharp, an acute, and yet somewhat grave sense of tasteful tongues as moving as Gravity, as selfless as any phenomenon, as potentially powerful as a true force of nature disseminating a grain or two by way of games taking routes along with roots interspersed and dispersed here and there with gametes of genuinely generated and regenerated culture! Yes, by feminine virtue of my (mid)wife, a sensational cognizance appears to realize a fully dreamlike consciousness akin to none other, at the very least, in my heart and mind. Herein then, just as there where she flowers like brilliantly sunlit flourishes engrained with the mark of more than a single germ of viciously contagious laughter, she may in effect till the air(s) like the lands I seek to sew, the seedy plots from which I reap some sensational fruits stemming from more than the fluid embodiment of grey matter alone and to which I yield if in(to) something germane to the headwinds of an apparently partial paradox, one (hardly) outliving a very uncertain sense of either sound or unsound ambiguity. Thanks to all she wants and desires to harvest at will, gobbling up the well-acclimated flesh and blood of aerated life to her heart's content, I may hereby add that she is the one who thereby makes out all the ambient buzz of a bumbling bee to be a variation on the theme of honey-combing sound (rounding-out as it does, existence, and this, in timely fashion . . .): by hearing-out masses of sensate B/beings, by seeing any and all through with follow-up and follow-through, processing virtually anything, if not every first and last word, trying—all the while, with a fair share of wiliness intimating some wholly desirable willingness to become an intimate mate—to make sense of the very (in)famously designated "process" (round which she finds herself *processing*—hand over fist—one and all causes, effects and affects with perseverance . . .), therefore heading evermore and ever more to the (s)core of the fore, she is one to be moving—in perpetuity—as those happy—those fortunate, those unlucky enough to be too few—throughout space [. . . relative(s) to the sweetest of plum scents succeeding yet further trail-blazers . . .] . . .

Custom-made to be appreciated by both readers and *auteurs*, Daniel Fineman's gentle vice-grip on language(s) and literature(s) holds out, if onto something larger, broader and deeper than even the rarest of refined and well-defined words. The varieties of objective-subject matters he addresses in so generously succinct and elegantly eloquent a manner hearken—back and therefore, again and again, a gain, to the fore— with decisively incisive concision. His severe, if severing brevity, moves in and out of pointed and yet nonetheless pointless categories, classes, groups and groupings like a needle in a haystack piqued by the piquant! Thanks to the Great and grander part of thoughtful Grandeur's ethics and esthetics, those figuring in timely images, this "author's author" surpasses—among others(')—those whose acts simply make far less musical pronouncements on the score of insightful novelties: insofar as none appears any more subjectively objective than lo, a most highly heartfelt I/idea, (t)his author(ity) of author(ities) paints a well-framed picture of (t)his very authoritative I/ideal!

Yes, in the end, we may seek to recall some sense of the beginning of both our physical and metaphysical O/origins, insofar as we may have come (to be made . . .), to know them, drawing virtually all, in some measure—in part and perhaps endlessly moving parts—out of obscurity, thanks to others('), young and old, and all "in between": as early as the greatly good professor's ground-breaking preface of an I/introduction appears (as a poetic reduction to a critical induction moving energetically to something of a philosophical point, to spot an articulate coordinate round which gravitates an(y) essentially ground-breaking deduction, to a conducive inducement electrifying a particular type of conduction, if not to conducting!)—it is as if it too were made [to be one (and one passing beyond the nearly earth-shattering point of surpassing all surviving in far more sensational phenomena relative to those invoked—by way of repetition, by something of the same symbolic token of enchanted appreciation as the one convoked by virtue of a singularly evocative name . . .) . . .]—orchestrated as it were, as symphonic(ally) as harmoniously, in its very own verily and veritably, if mellifluously fluid image of I/images, one's I/imagination, in sum, seizing upon some indescribable effects (. . . propagating with various strata of past and future, if present in some elements of a full and fulfilling circle engendered by a genre of sedimentation taking time and taking place—layer upon layer—upon some uniquely given affects . . .), perhaps the very causes, if not some of the very variable things put to the wordless test of phenomenally inimitable life per se.

Get Published, Inc!
Thorofare, NJ 08086
07 May, 2010
BA2010129